THE BLEEDING HEART

"A MONUMENTAL ACHIEVEMENT BY ANY STANDARD . . .
Dolores, volatile heroine of Marilyn French's superbly written novel, is not the wife but the Other Woman. Victor, her lover, already has a Mrs. back home in Scarsdale. Their love story is both startlingly rancorous and wholly convincing. As the affair progresses, Victor gets his consciousness raised, but not without anguish . . . French's rage at the plight of women in a male-dominated world is brilliantly argued."
Cosmopolitan

"TOUCHES LOTS OF RAW CONTEMPORARY NERVES.
French makes her point. What happens when nobody wants to be the wife? Are women programmed to think of others first and to squelch the demands of self? Can men nurture, feel, ache?"
Newsweek

"UNLIKE ANY LOVE STORY YOU HAVE EVER READ . . .
a powerful feminist statement in which love, where the two sexes supposedly become one, is viewed distinctly from the woman's angle. This *is* a love story in the fullest sense of the word, but one in which the case for the woman is revealed to her male lover with rare power and eloquence."
John Barkham Reviews

THE BLEEDING HEART

MARILYN FRENCH

BALLANTINE BOOKS • NEW YORK

Library of Congress Catalog Card Number: 79-26346

ISBN 0-345-28896-3

This edition published by arrangement with Summit Books

Manufactured in the United States of America

First International Ballantine Books Edition: June 1980
First Ballantine Books Edition: March 1981

TO JAMIE AND ROB

I

1

WHEN THE dream ended, she awoke. (Rock, sway, a railroad carriage.) She lay absolutely still, almost without breathing, trying to sink back into it. She kept her eyes closed, she clutched it with her mind, the feeling of the dream, the sensuousness of the warm body she had fully inhabited back there in that other place. She tried to grab it as it receded, she followed it, she rolled it around the palate of her imagination, sucking it dry. (Rigid in my seat, back stiff despite the train's motion.) She tightened her eyelids and tried to fall asleep again, although she knew that never worked. Even if you fell back to sleep, even if you dreamed again, it was never the same dream. And she wanted that one, the same one.

(No, a different compartment now, square, like a box. No fixed seats. Man. Sitting there, staring at me. Stares. I can feel his eyes on me. He's standing up, he's coming towards me, why? Passes me, goes behind me, stands there. He's pressing his body against the seat back. His body is breathing behind my head.)

She remembered the pressure. Terrific, the force of silent existence, a body alone is power, standing there behind her he made her feel his presence. He did not touch her.

(Then, suddenly, it was too much. Too much and she had to let go, and did, ah, bent her head back, let her neck flex, leaned her head, ah, against his belly. Warm. Rest. A sigh ripples through her body, the wonder of it, rest. Warmth. Another.)

Trust. That's what it was about, that's why she wanted to have the dream back again. It had left her

1

body flooded with warmth, liquid, soft. She lay in the lumpy bed in pain with yearning: her body wanted to be lain in some arms, against another body.

(Soft and firm his belly was. Accepting my head. Letting me rest there. Then he touches me, gently. He pulls me up, we go together and lie down. We are lying in a hollowed-out tree trunk, or maybe a large cradle. We lie together fully dressed, holding each other. The cradle rocks, very gently, like the swaying of the train. We do not move ourselves, the motion moves us. The air around us moves, it is electric, vibrant, charged. Everything moves and we with it, accepting. No holding firm, no opposition. Rock, rock and sway.)

The dream and the dream feeling receded further and further, leaving her beached, hollowing, drying. Her body was tingling, her genitals ached. Sandy body drying out. Her cheekbones longed for water. She sat up in bed, frowning. Her body was dying of thirst, it was telling her so. She didn't like the thought, didn't want to believe it. Her body was undermining her! How dare it! How could it?

She turned, as always, to analysis, being a twentieth-century woman and so subject to the superstition that what the mind could understand couldn't any longer hurt the heart, that what the tongue could utter was in the hand's control. Was that what this dream was about?: sensuality insinuating itself again after all these years? Insidious, invading her body against her mind's will, after all this time of quiet self-possession. But, no, because there was more. Vaguely, she sensed there was more. She leaned her head back against the hard wooden headboard of the bed, and closed her eyes again.

(Compartment is large, full of people sitting on packing cases. Men on crates sit leaning against the wall looking at nothing. Heads bowed, seeing nothing. In the center, the women with their children, crates dragged up so they can be together, all at angles to each other, but somehow still facing each other.

(Where is the man, my man? In the corner, against the wall, staring at me from his crate. Staring, intense. I look at him. The women are chattering. It is terrible, they say. But did you hear about Anna? And then

2

poor Rosalie! Their voices are easy and rich, they sigh and lament, their voices swoop up and plunge down, they whisper, they laugh. They are telling the stories of their pain. Every woman has many stories: her own, her mother's, her sisters'. They are wearing scuffed shoes and shabby coats over cotton housedresses. Some of them have babushkas on their heads. They hold their babies in their arms, they bounce them gently while they talk. A woman interrupts them. She is pretty, with a round rosy face. She says her pain is worse. The women fall silent, listening to her. She points to the baby on the crate next to me. It is a little girl about eighteen months old, round and rosy and golden, her hair is a mass of tight golden curls. She is happy, she rocks herself on her crate and babbles and sings to herself. She looks around at us with wonder and pleasure. She does not know, I think, that we are tired and hunched and shabby, with scuffed shoes.

(The woman points to the baby and says she is her child. She tells about it in an even sweet voice—the travels they have taken, she and her husband and the child. They have no money left, they have nothing left. They have been to doctors everywhere, all across the world. But finally the last one gave them a conclusive diagnosis: the little girl has cancer. She is dying.

(The women hush. They hug their babies, silent. The lines in their faces are weeping.

(I look at the baby, at the woman. I look over at the man, my man. They are a family. The baby is his. I lower my eyes.)

She raised her eyes.

Oh God. Yes, a boxcar, that's what it was supposed to be, as she had imagined boxcars when as a child she had read about their use in transporting people to death camps. Yes, they too, the people in her dream, were going to some terrible place, some final destination. Every one of them knew it, all of them were sad, but the women were lamenting their lives, not their death. Yes, they were simply journeying to death, as anyone does, warming themselves with each other's company. And across the car, the man, her man, the man she could lean her head against, could trust. Not her man at all.

She did not want to think about it anymore.

She got out of bed and brushed her teeth and dressed and climbed down the three flights of stairs, careful of the dangerously shabby carpet, to the dining room and the greasy eggs, cold toast, and thin coffee that came with the price of the lumpy hotel bed. But now that she didn't want to think about it, it kept returning. That beautiful baby, sick with cancer! And the relief of leaning back, the wonder of comfort in his body. What was happening to her? She'd noticed herself feeling strange things lately—that odd attraction to crippled men some months ago, searching their faces, thinking that crippled men suffered as women suffer, that they must be more human than the rest. Or once in a while letting herself fall into conversation with a man on a plane or a bus: she hadn't done that in years. Or talking almost flirtatiously with José, the waiter from Barcelona who served the greasy eggs. He was grinning at her now, as he poured her coffee, and she knew the smile on her face had more than friendliness in it, it glimmered a bit. He was a beautiful golden-skinned boy, he must be starved in the London greyness.

"You leave today?" He smiled, and she nodded. "You come back soon?"

"Yes. In a month or so," she promised, promising him something, unsure what.

He smiled with satisfaction, knowing he'd been promised something.

She walked back upstairs feeling a little dizzy, seeing things at a distance. Had the eggs been especially greasy today, was it her stomach? An old feeling, terror, feeling as if she were about to fall, something, rose from her stomach, dizzied her head. As if she might suddenly lose her grip on . . . what? and burst out in uncontrollable crying.

Stupid. Just the lousy sleep on that damned bed, the lousy food, that damned dream. She felt as if she were about to disintegrate.

Carefully and competently, so that nothing was disordered, she packed her notes in her briefcase, and her night things into a small canvas bag. She gazed out the window. The whole world was disintegrating, turning grey and liquid and unclear.

4

She put on her raincoat, picked up her bags, and went downstairs and out into the drizzly London morning to catch the train for Oxford.

2

THE DREAM kept coming back, obliterating what was around her. Yes, that was why one wanted it, the dream was true, truer than the drab London street, the swaying Underground train, the grey-brown people holding to poles, or the ones swaying in their seats, letting themselves be moved by the motion of the train. She never did that. She held herself erect and still, counteracting the dominant force. Always.

Okay, the dream was true, but what was its truth? The thing that seemed most vivid was the man standing there and the glorious moment of relief when she let her head incline backwards, let herself lean, and her head met his body and lay there secure and trusting, and she felt him solid and accepting, standing there for her, having waited not just for anyone but for her. That was absurd, of course. Who waits for just one person anymore? Who ever had, outside of books? And the leaning back against a stranger—that was a relinquishment of control she could not even imagine feeling in life. Not ever, not even before.

Before. Before my feelings dried up, my vagina too. No gushes shot up her sides anymore, no thumping heart blinded her vision. After all those years of tumult, all that screwing, all that passionate conviction of love, degrees of love, kinds of love, subtle discrimination among loves. Now the word itself disgusted her. Enough. Never again a man in my life, in my bed. "I don't screw anymore, but I don't cry anymore either," she lied to her close friends. It wasn't a total lie: tears came into her eyes, but they never fell, they dried up on the spot. A dry well, that's what she was.

It wasn't as if she had *decided* to stop screwing, had made a New Year's resolution five years ago that she had since been forcing herself to keep. It just happened.

That affair with Marsh that had left her so bruised that for months afterwards she couldn't draw a breath without feeling a burr in her esophagus, yes, that was it, probably. And the kids had liked it. No more strangers in the house for them to adjust to, resent, work up a whole emotional graph with which she, of course, being responsible, had to monitor. No more drainage of her energies into things that were anyway going to end in barren boredom or some turbulent scene. Passion: it was all just invented, you make up the object, you make up the feeling. You model both on movies and books that show you how you're supposed to act, what you're supposed to feel. You call it life. You say, "Well at least I'm alive," to make the pain more palatable.

Things were so much cleaner and clearer since she stopped. Everything was easier. You didn't have to watch yourself every time you talked to a man, wondering what messages you were sending, what messages he was sending. No messages sent or received here. Clean and clear. This telegraph station is closed for the duration. And even when the kids had gone away and the house was silent and clean, it was still good, like living in the plains, no emotional bogs or mines, no scratchy briar and underbrush in the forest, no animal traps, no mountains that invariably turned out to be mirages after all your effort climbing them. Mounting, heart beating, air grows thin, feet slip. Put your foot down expecting a rise in terrain and it falls with a shock onto level ground. Look back, it's all swamp and potholes.

So when she got the grant from the National Endowment for the Humanities, she could let her apartment, pack her bag, and pick herself up and come to England for a year, a whole year. No one to placate, argue with, cry over, feel guilty towards, about. Yes, that was the killer—guilt.

Berenice's story about the day John Kennedy was killed: she'd planned to have dinner with two Catholic friends. Tearful on phone, they decided to go ahead— better to be together than alone on such a night. But they'd done nothing but lament all through the meal.

"But one thing is a blessing," Anne said. "At least Jackie was with him. You know she hasn't been well,

6

she hasn't been going on trips with him recently. Thank God she was there! Imagine how she'd feel if she hadn't been with him!"

Berenice raised Jewish eyebrows. "If I were she, I'd be sure it was *because* I was with him that it happened."

"Oh," Gail said knowingly, "that's Jewish guilt."

Jewish or Catholic, it was women's guilt, one way *and* another. No way out of it. No way except hers: if you don't get involved, you don't feel guilt. If you do, you do, no matter how you act. Women were supposed to be whatever men needed, were supposed never to fail them, were supposed to be everything for them. It was impossible. Why was it that men didn't have to be the same things?

Well, it was all academic now, she shouldn't need to rationalize what was in any case an accomplished fact, and her life. And a fine life it was too, her time her own, her emotions her own, her space too. Five whole rooms, not big, but enough for one person. No arguments about open or closed windows, who snatches the blankets, TV blare, grilled cheese sandwiches instead of meat loaf. Arguments, of course, wonderful and uproarious, with a set of friends who went quite crackers at the mention of Con Edison or nuclear plants or Joseph Califano or the Bible Belt or strip mining or Phyllis Schlafly or or or. Eccentrics they were, she supposed, her friends, but fun. They had minds that had not been downed, had never given in to the prevailing motion.

On the other hand, maybe they *were* the prevailing motion. Who could tell?

But you couldn't sit until five in the morning talking about sex or religion or love unless your friend came and knew the two of you didn't have to deal in the politenesses imposed by coupledom. Her aloneness was an opening, a chink in a wall. People came and said things they said to no one else. They raged, they lamented, they tore out their intestines over lost love, betrayed friendship, failures. They grieved and raged most about their parents, it was astonishing, fifty-year-old people weeping because father never and mother did and then I tried but it didn't work and I wanted

7

to show them but then they died and now forever it is too late. And she will never forgive he will never know I can never say. Parents. Children.

Her eyes were clouding and she pulled herself up. Paddington.

3

SHE WAS early for her train, and chose an empty smoking compartment. Generally, she permitted herself four slim cigars a day, but whenever she took this trip, allowed herself one extra. She loved to sit back comfortably in an empty compartment, smoking without worrying about bothering anyone else, and gaze out at the London-Oxford run. It was not, as she had long ago expected it to be, an orderly progression from city to country. It was, like all of England, she felt, just things happening. Such a socially ordered country it was that things were simply allowed to happen at random.

Leaving London there would be warehouses and factories, sooty row houses, but each with a garden, and each garden held roses. Then suddenly, canals and the river, trees, horses, cows grazing under huge metal power poles. Sometimes a small barge on a canal, which would always make her lean forward, yearn towards it like a plant towards sun. She wanted to be sitting on the deck as the barge slid along the smooth waters, and try to catch sight of small game in the fields, to name the wild flowers. She wanted to be sitting there plump in a heavy holey sweater, saying to the stocky bargeman, "Would you like a cup of tea, luv?" and watch him turn and smile, showing a few gaps in his uppers, and say, "I would, old girl," the sex between them still alive despite the years, their pillowed bodies, hair grey and wispy in the light wind.

A dream: he drinks; she nags. She stays at home, ostensibly because of the rheumatism, but really because the silence betwen them oppresses her, and she

8

has nothing to do on the wretched boat but make him stupid cups of tea. He listens to the football on a transistor radio, and on his stops he eyes the occasional barmaid or waitress and drinks his pint. At home, he spends his evenings in the pub, arguing scores, players.

Why is it that the miserable always sounds truer than the felicitous?

Because it is, dope.

Yes. After the bargeman there would be open farms, then suddenly, inexplicably, high-rise apartments. Then warehouses. Warehouses? Granaries, perhaps. Then again farms, wonderful old ones with walled courtyards dusty with chickens, old brick walls dusty with roses, like the farms in Normandy and Brittany. Then Reading, full of soot and chimney's, people rushing on and off. Then green farmland threaded by the river and then! Of course it had to be sham, and was, but there it rose in the sunlight, all medieval tracery, spires, and towers: Oxford. It looked older than the buildings really were: it looked like fairyland and it shone in the sun. The first time she'd come, she had entered the town warily, as if it might turn to Disney if she put her glasses on.

She did not light her cigar. She would wait until the train started. Deferred gratification is good for you, she told herself. All the little games you learn to play as you grow older, things designed to make life more pleasant, to stretch the little pleasures out like a thin swatch of flowered fabric stretched out to cover an open wound. Smoking is bad for you, so you smoke less and look forward to it more. Obscene, somehow, life measured out in coffee-spoons. But what else could you do?

Her students, sitting cross-legged on her living-room floor drinking wine, smoking grass, listening to her jazz records as if the music were an ancient foreign mode. Leaning back and scratching a taut belly, or twisting a strand of long straight hair, and asking, asking, "Dolores, tell me. Tell us." The question was always phrased differently, but it was always the same question. Tell me, tell me, how can I live without pain?

I don't know.

You do! You do! I know you do! Look at you! You

have it made! A great pad, two books published, tenure at Emmings, two kids, Europe in the summers, and all those jazz records! How can I get to live like you?

You can be me if you want, she wanted to say. All you have to do is pay for it with lines, as I have. This line along my mouth, now, that was a particularly expensive one. "The only prescriptions I know for life without pain are early death, daily skiing, or smoking dope," she'd grin.

Impossible to tell them much truth. Didn't want to. Why poison life for them before they'd barely begun? Weary, she'd send them home feeling full although not full enough (never full enough), and sigh her way to bed alone and lie there feeling it, the pain that was with her always, so familiar and accustomed a guest that it could be ignored for long stretches. It shuffled around her house in bedroom slippers, and made its own tea.

Dolores the walking robot: push the button and the creature weeps. Her eyes and throat would fill with tears even watching TV photos of famine victims, reading newspaper interviews with parents whose children had been violently snatched to death, being handed, in Brattle Square, a leaflet describing the torture of political prisoners in the Philippines. God knows there was never a dearth of things to cry about. And she, she was like one of Pavlov's dogs, salivating at every gong. Hard to say which was worse—the fact that the horrors of the world aroused in her nothing more forceful than a tear, or that every one of its horrors aroused that same tear. Something indiscriminate about her. Weeping, of course, really for herself, as Homer knew. Something terribly female about that. But men did it too, didn't they? She'd read some survey recently: men in huge numbers watch the soaps. But did they cry? The surveyor hadn't asked that.

She had tears even for success. Sydney had called her the other night all the way from New Hampshire, had paid for it herself. (Of course, you can't call transatlantic collect.) Crying, saying Mommy the way she had when she was a little girl. Devasted by her latest affair: can I come to England and stay with you for a little while? Sydney's latest lover had done so-

10

and-so, what was she to think about that? What was she to think about herself, why did she drown with every hurt, every failure? It must be that she lacked character. Why did life hurt so much? Was there something wrong with her? There must be. Life wasn't supposed to hurt so much. She must be weak, or selfish, or insane.

I took her pain and shaped it, I turned it into an obstacle course, a clear run with victory at its end. I listened, and slowly, as she spoke, I kneaded her words in my hands, giving them form, and since form is finite, an end. I made pain linear by giving it a purpose, like some king in legend, assigning tasks: when these are accomplished, you will be a knight of the Round Table Holy Grail Valhalla Elysian fields. You must live through this to learn and grow.

Sydney felt better with every sentence. I could hear her voice lightening, laughter and confidence seeping back, courage firming. I transformed an insane agony that was agony and insanity because she saw no end into a sane linear process with a knowable goal: when you grow up, you will be an adult. Read, invulnerable. Or calloused. The suffering of x added to knowledge y equals strength, harmony, and wisdom: Z. Oh, my child felt better, stronger: she felt full of heart.

I felt like the mother of lies.

Dolores gazed blankly at the train platform. Well, what was I supposed to do? Tell her, sorry, kid, that's life, might as well get used to it? Twenty-one and just embarking. After such a past. She needs all the lies she can get.

A shadow darkened the window in the compartment door. Dolores turned away towards the outside window, hoping the presence would move on. The door opened, however. She heard it and turned her head slightly and saw out of the corner of her eye a man with a suitcase. She turned away again. Fuck. Maybe her coldness would repel him. It happened sometimes. People could feel what you feel—electricity, sound waves, fields of force? We pick up so much more than we can process with what we arrogantly exalt as intellect—little things, things we know without knowing we know them. She had pulled people towards her

11

when she needed them, pushed them away when she did not: by what invisible wires, what imperceptible magnetism? She exerted it now, sending out cold waves.

But the man came in anyhow. Dense or aggressive, she decided. His back to her, he lifted his suitcase to the overhead rack, removed his raincoat, then sat down holding a newspaper. She glared at him, but he barely glanced at her. He opened his newspaper.

Dolores looked out the window. She felt tremulous, as if she were going to cry. Her whole lovely trip ruined by someone too dense to know he wasn't wanted. It wasn't as if the train were crowded. Now the whole time would be spoiled by a pair of eyes to be avoided; movements and breathing to be blanked out, perfunctory eye-meetings leading to perfunctory and uncomfortable facial expressions—a smile? a leer?

The train started up. She reached in her purse and pulled out her cigar case. She would light up without even asking if he minded. That's all he deserved, the bastard. And if he looked at her full face, damn it, she'd glare at him!

And glancing at him as she prepared to light her cigar, she found he was, the fucker, was looking at her, straight at her. She looked back coldly and puffed the cigar to life. Still, the cigar was half-ruined for her. Since she allowed herself so few, and waited so long for each one, she felt, as she lighted them, a deep sensuous pleasure, a surrender to the welcome aroma, the hot smoke in her mouth and nose, the feel of the fine smooth shape against her lips. But she could not let herself feel this now, with him watching. Her surrender to pleasure would show, and somehow it seemed shameful that someone else should see that. It was too personal, intimate, even. He leaned back and pulled his newspaper up, hiding his eyes. She closed her eyes and leaned back and let herself feel the pleasure of the cigar after all. Apparently he had *some* decency.

Smoking, she gazed out the window. But she barely noticed the landscape as it passed. That was what happened when someone invaded your space: you were too conscious of them to feel fully, see fully, be. You couldn't just *be,* you had to be *something;* sloppy, correct, flirtatious, friendly, proper. Skirt pulled down?

Be careful not to pick your nose or scratch your groin or spread your legs. Not, she had to admit, that she usually did such things in a train compartment even alone, but knowing she couldn't constricted her, made her feel self-conscious. Oh, well: retreat inward. What was I thinking about? My life, solitude, yes. (Why isn't he turning the pages of his newspaper?) Yes, it was a good life, it went on being good and vivid although a certain sameness had set in. But that happened to everyone, together or alone, didn't it? (Why is he so still?) Still, there were things that never palled. A fine fall day in Cambridge, the burnished leaves, the smell of them in the nose, dusty and acrid and sweet, the light on the brick sidewalks; or mornings when she didn't have to teach and had time for breakfast and boiled a two-day-old egg and smeared a fresh sisal rye-bread slice with fresh sweet butter and smelled the freshly ground bourbon Santos coffee slowly dripping through the filter, and drank it with just a dollop of cream. . . . (Even not looking at him, she could sense he was utterly still. It felt as if he was looking at her. Damn him!)

Yes, and friends and dinners and parties and wonderful arguments and coming home late and simply collapsing in bed with a smile pasted on her idiot face. And special moments, like that first morning in Madrid when they could not sleep despite the seven long wakeful hours on the plane and had charged out into the city like horses freed from a corral, she and Sydney and Tony, and had rushed to the Plaza Mayor and stopped and Tony stopped and looked at it (his first time abroad) and she looked at his face and her heart stopped because he was seeing it, really seeing it, and she could see him seeing it. What was he seeing? Ah, but she knew, it was what was there to be seen— a different world, a different century, and that time, the eighteenth century, was still there somehow, hanging, the way they say sound waves linger in the atmosphere forever. The women with their high white wigs and hooped satin skirts, the men in their satin coats and white silk stockings, the carriages and footmen, the rolling bump of the wooden wheels, the maids and beggars, the blood, the flirtations, the foolishness. The lovely formal square, decorous, bowing, brilliant, had also been home to horseshit and straw, urchins skipping past the urine-filled gutters, to a stray cow and its offal. And which was the real, which was the life, if not both? She had watched Tony's face: it was shining. Everything on it was open—the eyes, the mouth, the very pores.

Open: the way Sydney had read her a Yeats poem she had just discovered, her voice sounding as if she had just discovered a new dimension. "How can we know the dancer from the dance?" Sydney had concluded, looking up at Dolores with wonder on her face. "How can we, Mommy?"

Open. And she too, despite the routine of a tenured professor, years and years of freshman English, years and years of trying to find a good way to teach Spenser, years and years of committee meetings, the same questions, the same speeches: despite all that, she too had remained open.

In some ways.

(He *was* looking at her.)

So that was always accessible, the pleasure and joy she permitted herself. It is true, she had closed some doors. Who can blame me? How much can a heart be scarred and still go on beating? Because to stay open entirely means to stay open to all sides of things, to pain as well as pleasure. And some pains she could not absorb more of. The pain she already carried was always with her, it rose up like fumes and would not abate, like that night before she left for England, staying for a weekend on the Cape with Carol and John, the oldest of her friends, people she could be honest with. To. They had sat up late, very late, the three of them, remembering, the sorrow just below all their surfaces, until it rose through the liquor and the hour, and with no touch at all had poured out of Dolores like a geyser whose cap had simply worn out, had poured out and spilled over the room, silencing it.

14

4

THE MAN was staring at her.

She was sure of it. She had not turned her head towards him, she was still facing the window, but she felt something—an intensity. She slid her eyes towards him. And caught him! He was staring at her. He lowered his eyes instantly, and instantly she turned away to the window, but for a dot of time, their eyes had grazed each other's. His eyes were dark, almost black, with a pinpoint of light in them.

Or is that just the way she imagined they were? Because they were intense intelligent eyes, passionate eyes, just like the eyes of the man in the dream.

A cloud formed around her heart. Indigestion. Damned greasy eggs. Really ought to find another place to stay when I'm in London, but that place is so cheap and so convenient, a pleasant walk through Russell Square to the British Museum.

She gazed at a blur of landscape and puffed on her cigar. She got nothing. It had gone out. How ridiculous she must look to that person opposite her if he was looking at her and of course he was. She raised her eyebrows, hoping she appeared disdainful at this stupid cigar, and fished in her purse for a match. And as she did so, she let her eyes sweep the lower parts of him. Long slender feet, good shoes, tweedy brown slacks. Not at all a refugee's dress. Forget the damned dream. As she puffed the cigar to life again (ugh! stale and strong!) she slid her eyes up further. Tweedy grey jacket, flecks of brown in it, nice. A grey turtleneck sweater. And a longish face—looking at her!

(Don't panic. He doesn't know about your dream. Smile and say: Beastly weather, isn't it. But it isn't. Is it?) She looked out of the window to check. The sun had come out and had turned the canals a deep blue-grey, like the ocean at Gloucester in July.

Pressure was growing in the back of her neck. She could not control herself, she had to look at him again.

He was looking straight at her and for a courageous moment, she let her eyes meet his. She tried hard to move her facial muscles into something resembling a smile. Then her eyes, still operating under their own control, ignoring her directions, slid, or rather darted, back to the window.

He had not smiled back.

What a face he had! Long, thin, with deep lines running down the cheeks. It was a face that had felt. How often did you see that in a man? There was a kind of rumpled elegance about him, about his body, his clothes, his carriage, the kind you see in dancers or actors, people who are conscious of their bodies, people who use their bodies. Dream: he probably played tennis religiously, keeping the weight down.

She wondered what *he* was looking at, what he saw, looking at her. A woman of forty-five who looked her age but did not look middle-aged. Tallish, slender, very, maybe too thin, her shoulders always hunched forward as if she were trying to protect her breasts— or her heart. A face that was always—almost always— in control of itself. Why did he keep on looking?

She kept her eyes fixed firmly on the window, so firmly that she saw nothing. Then suddenly the train stopped. They were at Reading. And suddenly she panicked. Suppose he gets off? Suppose someone else enters the compartment? Good God. A drama I've made already. Shit. I want it. I want this tension, this intimacy without words or gestures, to continue. Oh Dolores, my dolores, idolores, what a fucking fool you are.

The Reading stop was always busy. People rushed past on the platform, getting off, getting on, meeting people. Shadows passed the windows in the compartment door, some swift, some slow, some jostling a piece of baggage that knocked against the door; people stopped, turned, moved on. Her face a mask of complete indifference, she smoked and gazed out the window.

The man rustled his newspaper. For the first time since they'd left London, he turned a page. The traffic of people slowed. A door slammed. The train started up again, slowly, then in usual tempo. A heavy pink-faced man, a late arrival, pulled open their compartment door, puffing. He was carrying a salesman's case that looked heavy, and he looked a little desperate. He glanced at their faces as they turned to him, both at once, bowed a little and retreated, slamming the door shut, trudging on down the corridor.

Is the air in here *that* charged?

Primly, Dolores looked out the window again, but her eyes, of their own accord, wandered back to the man. She had to check, to see if she had invented him, if he were a figment from her dream that she had decided to manufacture in the flesh. She caught a hand. Nice hand. Long, slender fingers, strong bones. Fingers presently holding a newspaper, but fingers you wouldn't mind . . .

Back to the window.

Back to him. Nice jacket, well worn, softened tweed.

Back to window.

Back to him. Sweater. Nice soft sweater clinging to the vulnerable flesh. What kind of flesh, do you suppose? Dead white? Hairy? Smooth and golden? Pimply?

Oh God, what am I doing?

Back to window.

Back to him. And this time she caught his eyes, caught them catching her, reluctantly. Yes, reluctantly. Was *she* the one directing this? Straight deep line between the brows. Anxiety. Puzzlement. Thought. Nice. Grey flecks in dark hair. Like hers. Nice. Was hers nice? Well, his was short, hers was long. Besides, everything was different for men.

Her eyes wandered off in search of something to look at. She puffed. Her cigar had gone out again. Damn! It was downright embarrassing. She tamped it out, and throwing all her rules to some wind or other, pulled out a fresh one and lighted it.

What an ass she must look. And he was watching her, clearly watching her.

It was intolerable. She did not know what to do with herself, where to put her hands, how to hold her legs, how to keep her face in order. She felt assaulted, invaded, adored, ridiculous.

Well, it was clear what she had to do. She had to look him straight in the face and smile a prim stiff

17

smile and say: Beastly weather, isn't it. And turn prissily back to the window.

That would do it.

The landscape was running in wavy lines in front of her eyes.

In a few minutes, she told herself, you will be in Oxford. You will stand up and turn around and lift your bags down from the overhead rack. Then you will turn sideways and walk through the door and turn left and walk calmly and quietly down the corridor and stand in the passage until the train has reached a full stop and then you will pull open the carriage door, descend two steps—one step?—and find firm concrete under your firm leather sole and you will walk to the stairway and descend (the escalator may be working but it will be better for you to use the stairs) into the cool bracing September Oxford air and you will walk home breathing deeply, and this figment, this passion you have invented, will blow away.

But I don't want it to blow away.

No?

5

YES, HE will remain seated and he will watch me go, longingly, and I will feel attractive for as long as the walk home lasts. And he will go on to . . .

It was not an Inter-city train, she suddenly realized. He must be going to Oxford too.

All right. He too will get off the train and carry his suitcase down, but he would use the escalator and run down it like ordinary stairs, knowing she was watching, sending her a message. Saying: I am running home to my wife and six children, you needn't feel so attractive, my wife is far more alluring. Alluring. Yes.

Having lived it all through, she lost her consciousness of self. She glanced at her watch and up at him, looking at him straight, with a little anxiety, telling him without words, well, this is it, and to be truthful, you know, I liked it more than not. Even though I didn't want you

18

invading my space, I rather enjoyed it. Good-bye. I'm sorry it's good-bye.

But he was looking back at her and saying something different. His dark eyes had brilliant spots of light in them, like fever. Yet they were embarrassed and reluctant. And they did not assert. They simply stood. There was nothing typically macho game-playing about him: his eyes showed nothing properietary, knowing, or superior. His eyes looked, looked at her: their assertion was their mere looking.

At least, that's what she thought.

My God, no wonder I have to be alone. Constructing such dramas out of air, what do I do with things that are more substantial?

Dolores Durer, what are you doing?

There had been other moments like this, she reminded herself. Tens of them. Sometime, back in time, hundreds of times, there had been beautiful men sitting across the way in airline terminals, in restaurants, or walking in Central Park or across the Common. Yes, beautiful, and the memory of the beauty lasts even if the memory of the faces does not. Beautiful because you do not speak, you do not ever have to find out who they were. Didn't have to watch that lovely mouth open and out of it come: Hey, Harry, whattayasay we go out on the town tonight, I know some real swinging places, and whattayasay we find ourselves some real great chicks and show them a real good time. Last time I was in Nashville, I dropped two big ones. Watch his head swing around, see the mouth open again, didn't look so lovely this time, "Hey honey, can I buy you a drink?"

This man hadn't said anything.

But he might. Think of all those who had: furniture salesmen wanting a little nooky, uptight actors wanting to impress, executives in fast food wanting to tell you about their degrees in philosophy, even once a Danish army general, slim and sophisticated and careful not to ask any personal questions, savoring the herring, letting his eyes take possession of you but drawing them back (is that how you run battles?) when you turned, and smiling politely, he lighted your cigar.

But this man wasn't any of them.

I should have smiled tautly and said Beastly weather.

The train was slowing now. It was over. He would get up, she would get up, and they would go their separate ways. In the freedom of that knowledge, she looked at him fully. His face was a dark intensity, staring at her. She let her eyes meet his, and promised him something, much as she had promised something to José earlier. No, fuck it, not promised, just answered. Yes, I think you're pretty too. That's all.

But when their eyes met, they locked, like two kids with braces kissing. Simply locked and would not let go. As their eyes met, her innards turned loose and liquid. Safe to feel now, saying good-bye. She looked at him and he looked at her and the message was unreceivable. Slowly, feeling her mouth to be a full moist communication, she tried to turn away.

And did.

Blanking out what she had seen, eyes full of such longing that she could not abide it, face full of such intensity that she could not resist it.

Calmly, competently, quietly, she looked down and closed her purse, then turned (what ease! what naturalness!) and glanced up at the overhead rack, and stood and reached for her bag and briefcase and he stood to get his bag and coat and the train braked hard and she staggered and he was behind her, holding her, and he reached up over her head and pulled down her cases (show-off! I could have done it myself! Did you think I couldn't?) and put them on the seat and for some reason she was still standing there and he put his arms around her waist, gathering his hands together in the front as if he had to tie them up or as if to tie her up. And something inside her sank, sank, and she let it sink, she surrendered, she let herself lean against him just a little, just a breath, as the train halted its way to a full stop.

The train stopped. Doors clanked open, luggage was bumping against the corridor walls, shadows of people passed the compartment window. They still stood there, his arms around her from behind, she with her head tilted back very slightly, her lips parted slightly, relaxed, and she knew she had to regain control, had to

20

move. And so she did, a good girl still; she moved her body slightly, just stiffened it, and he released her and she reached for her purse and reached towards her bags, but he snatched them up from behind her, and his arms were trembling (or was it her arms?) and he picked up his bag and coat and stalked out of the compartment expecting her to follow (me Tarzan you Jane?) and of course she did since he had her bags.

People were all around, greeting, being greeted, rushing to appointments, looking for a porter, and noises swirled around them as she followed him out of the train and onto the platform, and edged around the clusters of people, and to the escalator, and down into the station, and out, out into the cool Oxford afternoon.

6

ON THE street she stopped and turned to face him. "Thank you," she said formally, holding out her hand for her cases. She hoped he could not detect the tremulousness she felt: she felt like a child pleading with her father, begging for something.

He simply looked at her.

"I go up to the Banbury Road," she explained. Explaining what?

"Yes," he agreed, and began walking. She followed, she felt like a child trotting after her parent. He simply strode off. Damned male, sure of himself. She felt like shouting at him: What makes you think you can treat me like this! What made him think it was, obviously, that he could. She could dismiss him easily if she wanted to. All she had to do was get annoyed, or even just formal and controlled, ask for his credentials, inform him that she no longer desired his company. It wasn't true, though: she wanted his company. But she did not like feeling she was being preempted.

They did not look at each other as they walked toward the Banbury Road. What I can do, her mind rambled on, is turn and make polite conversation. Do you live in Oxford? Ah, the big house on the corner, the

21

one with all the little trikes outside? How nice. Why don't you and your wife stop in for drinks with me sometime? Lovely day it turned out to be after all. Such a beastly morning, wasn't it. But perhaps we'll have more rain later, don't you think? So kind of you to carry my bags. (They're so awfully heavy.)

Yes, I could do that. End it fast.

She remained silent.

Where does he live, do you suppose? Carrying a good-sized suitcase. His *Yes* sounded more American than British, although *yes* was hardly much to go on. The suitcase would hold enough clothes for a few days, a week even. If he didn't live in Oxford, maybe he was looking for a place to stay.

A jolt: she paused in her stride. NOT WITH ME! her mind cried, startled and appalled at a possibility she hadn't considered. Nothing had happened, yet she already felt invaded, crowded, imposed upon. No, no. He must already have a hotel. He'd have to be a fool to come here unbooked at term time. It did not occur to her to ask him.

Yes, he was an American professor spending a year in England, moving between the British Museum and the Oxford libraries. Just like her. Perhaps they'd worked across from each other in the BM, eyes not meeting. Perhaps he'd seen her there, perhaps she looked familiar to him and that was why he was acting this way.

No. He was a romantic, raised on novels of chivalry. He was like so many professors, all he knew about life came from literature. He would see her to her door, deposit her bags on her step, kiss her hand, and depart.

That had actually happened to her once, years ago, when she was lost in Manhattan, couldn't find the building she was looking for. She stopped at a construction site and asked directions of a burly red-necked man in his sixties, who was standing on the sidewalk drinking soda from a bottle. He put his soda down on a pile of two-by-fours, whisked her suitcase out of her hand, and set off without a word. She had trotted behind *him,* too, followed by jeers, whistles, obscene remarks hurled at them by the men perched up on the scaffolding. She thought to be nervous, but wasn't. She

22

trusted her unlikely knight, all two hundred fifty pounds of him. He was impervious to the workmen's cries, he walked proudly, silent. He stopped in front of her building, swept his arm out towards it, handed her her suitcases, then snatched up her other hand, kissed it, and bowed. Then disappeared.

She smiled, remembering.

So, now, she and this man walked in silence. The gardens were green on the Banbury Road; roses crumbled against the walls. Few people walked on the street —some teenagers, an old woman dragging her string bag of groceries and a huge black purse. She glanced at his body: no, he was too well-dressed to be a professor. She looked at his face. It was still composed, except for a tiny muscle twitching in his cheek.

And that startled her. He was afraid!

Afraid of me? Do I look like a mad rapist, a killer, a person who hits people over the head and takes their wallets? I'm the one who ought to be frightened. Of course, I am an experienced reader of faces, and he doesn't look like a rapist or killer either. But you never could tell with men. Charles Carson, the distinguished and eminent professor, beat his wife Nancy for years until she left him. And he had flecks of white at the sideburns and a superior kindly manner. Lots of sweet and gentle men ended up killing their mothers.

But no, no, that wasn't it. He wasn't afraid she'd do him bodily harm. It must be hard to act as he was acting, it cost something. He'd invested his ego in carrying this off, and suppose it didn't carry? Male ego was so fragile, because it made everything into a game and then has to win every game. Or shatter. That man who wrote a letter to *The New York Times* about his tiny children, and kept saying "She won," or "He won." Tiny children.

She was glad they weren't talking.

She came into my study and disturbed me at my work and she knows she's not supposed to, so I was going to spank her but she was so cute I couldn't: so she won. Man like that shouldn't have children.

Still, there was something about this man that wasn't like that, something that had . . . felt? suffered? Or was she inventing that? God knows she'd done it

23

before, looking at Anthony's sad face after they'd had a fight, such a sad face it made her heart mushy, and she'd go over and put her arms around him. "Honey, let's not fight." And he'd glare at her furiously and pull away. "Leave me alone, you bitch!"

They had reached her corner. "I turn here," she said, and stopped and he stopped and turned to her and looked at her and her heart bounded: he's going to leave me at the corner! She thought she could not bear it: to watch him leave, to trail down her street carrying her own bags, to return alone to the empty flat and stand there in the silent kitchen looking at the dirty dishes in the sink.

But he did not put her bag down. He did not speak. He just looked at her, and she realized after an instant that he was asking a question, and her blood began to flow again and she almost smiled looking back, answering it.

They turned together down the street of low stucco houses with their little gardens, turned again up the walk of Number 17, and she found her keys and let them in.

7

IT WAS after the door was shut that the discomfort began. She mounted the stairs to her flat aware of him behind her and wishing that they could just go on like that, mounting stairs one behind the other, and not have to look at each other, not have to do anything else. Because how was she to behave? She could talk, of course, could launch into her name, rank, and serial number so that he would have to launch into his. Then she could offer to make a cup of tea. But that would destroy the tension, the unknownness that made this encounter so marvelous. She did not know what else to do. She had lived always using language as a shield, and did not know how to live without a shield.

She unlocked the upper door and went in. Her tightness, which was beginning to turn to panic, blurred her vision so that she could not really see her apartment, only a patch of bright light from the living room, the afternoon shadow in the kitchen. She walked into the kitchen, simply out of habit. He followed, set down the suitcases, and stood there. She turned and looked at him.

"I'm Dolores."

"I'm Victor."

"Would you like a cup of tea?" Her voice was tense. He took her hand and held it with both of his. "Fine," he said tightly, but he did not let her hand go.

She could feel her body—not quite *move*—but *incline* towards him; it yearned, it leaned. And his body did the same, it merely inclined, but suddenly their bodies were together. And then they were pitched into the middle of a battle, or a battle began inside of them. Chemicals pulsed through thighs and sides, electrical impulses swept through bodies, fingers were charged, lips felt like victims of starvation, and the two of them clung together as if only holding fast to each other would save them from this bombardment, but of course, holding fast to each other only made it worse. They clutched and caressed as their hearts pumped, as the sparks fell, as fiery charges burned them up. She looked up and saw his mouth, full, sensuous, and a little wrenched (did he not want to be here? to be doing this?) and she raised her own mouth that felt like a melon that was ripened and wanted to be eaten, was aching to be eaten, and they kissed and the war was escalated, but they were the war, and they pressed their bodies together until they felt like a single unit melted together by the heat they generated. They clung together without moving, desperately, as if only this clinging, this being together, could keep them from perishing.

II

1

WHEN SHE tried to recall it afterwards, it was blurred in her mind, so fiercely had she felt their lovemaking, so little observed it. It had taken a long time. They could not get to fucking, so caught up were they by holding and embracing and kissing. Clothes were a problem, ripped off impatiently piece by piece as each was felt to be in the way. She remembered hearing a tear as one of them pulled something off in irritation. But at last they got down to bodies, simple smooth wonderful bodies, and they both uttered little sounds, as they rubbed their bodies together, and each stroked the other's.

Everything was extreme, shot with gold. He came to her at first with ferocity, with shudders that ripped through his whole body, and he stayed with her, inside her, and they played and wound around as if they were the one flesh the marriage service declares. A creature with twenty fingers, two tongues, two hearts, one body rolling over and around, interchanging its parts. Cries, sighs, moans escaped like animals from the cages of their ribs. They fit their bodies together clutching, clinging as if were they to let go, the world would return to the void. When, eventually, they fell asleep, they were still together, his contented penis still inside her contented complexities, both cool and quiet.

When they woke, the sun had faded from the bedroom window and the slate roofs across the back garden shone silver in the thin grey light. Their bodies were shadowed in the dim light; they looked long and smooth and cool and vulnerable. Always, caressing human flesh, stroking the beautiful lines of sides and

26

thighs, she thought about that vulnerability. It was peculiarly human: animals had things—fur, or feathers, scales, or carapaces—to disguise their nakedness. Humans had only clothes, which were removable, and when they were removed, you were forced to remember what nakedness meant, how a tiny bullet, a cloth the size of a grain of cereal, a sliver of flying glass could destroy all of it in an instant. A single swipe of a blade under a chin, and all the warmth and motion and color would drain away, the shapely flesh converted in an instant to stiffness, and all its expressiveness into rigidity, into stone that wasn't stone, petrifaction that rotted and stank.

He stirred, pulled up his torso, and leaned over the side of the bed towards his clothes.

Her heart bounded. Was he one of those? He couldn't be that bad, to get up now and dress! He couldn't be!

He came back up with a packet of cigarettes and a gold lighter. He offered her one and she broke her rule and took it. They sprawled comfortably against propped-up pillows, smoking.

He looked at her, glinting. "You know we don't even know each other's last names."

She smiled back. "That's kind of fun, isn't it. I mean, dramatic and mysterious and romantic and all that."

"It's fun until you have to look somebody up in the phone book."

"I'm not *in* the phone book."

"That's even more serious."

She looked intensely into his face: wonderful face, sculpted with expression. She put her hand on his cheek, gently, and held it. She did want to know, yes she did, what had made that face, what had lined it in that precise way, what had created such expression. He was looking love at her, and she lifted her head and kissed him lightly.

Even more serious. Did he mean that? He acted serious, he was looking at her with the same intensity now as before. All the silence between them on the train, all the intensity, hadn't it been designed to make this feel cataclysmic, a tremendous romantic ecstasy? And it had worked, their sex was extraordinary. But surely that was all, wasn't it? It had served its purpose, was finished now.

Then why did the thought of him getting up and out of bed, dressing, leaving, the flat vacant of him, vacant, make her heart ache?

"Okay, then," she said. "Tell me your last name. And everything else too."

His name was Victor Morrissey. He was a vice-president in charge of development for IMO, a company that made a whole range of things, but mainly electronic equipment for airplanes and experimental trains and buses and cars. He was in England to open a branch office, small to begin with, forty or fifty people. The present plan was that it would expand tremendously in the future. They were being given great help by the government, in its belief that IMO would help bolster the British economy.

"We're based in London, but I come to Oxford every few weeks because we work with the automobile companies here, in Cowley."

Aha: Wife in London, mistress in Oxford. I see what he's aiming for. R and R no matter where he is.

"Your turn."

My turn.

"My name is Dolores Durer. I'm a professor of English at Emmings College in Boston. I specialize in the Renaissance."

Actually I specialize in grief. I was apprenticed to it early by my mother, who was apprenticed to it by hers. You might call it the family business.

"I got an NEH—a federal grant—to come to England and do research on a book I'm writing. I work mainly in Oxford, that's why I've taken a flat here. But sometimes I go into London, to the British Museum, and work there. That's what I've been doing for the past couple of days. That's why I was on the train. . . ."

"Are you married?" He asked this with a special attentiveness.

"No. I was once. I have two children. And you?" She tried to seem indifferent.

"Yes." The look, the tone: she had known them before. Reluctant, apologetic, sad: intended to convey: poor me. I don't want to burden you, but it's a terrible

28

marriage, but I can't leave because of the kids because she depends because it's my third and I want to give this one a chance because because because. . . . But I am not happy, not happy at all.

"Do you have children?"

"Four: two boys, two girls. The oldest is twenty-three, the youngest is thirteen."

"'My son is twenty-two. My daughter is twenty-one."

There, that's done with. Name, rank, serial number. And the worst part over with: Yes, married.

He got up and went out into the hall and brought his suitcase into the bedroom. Surely he wasn't intending to move in! He laid it on a chair and opened it and rummaged around inside. He came up with a brown paper bag containing a Scotch bottle. "Care for a drink?"

"Sure," she smiled and he went into the kitchen to fix drinks.

And if *I* had said *Yes, married?* Would he have backed off? They used to call it honor, but it was actually territoriality: don't poach on another man's preserve. Doesn't matter what you do to women, though. Oh God. Why did I do this? I'm getting into that all over again, into the anger, the resentment. . . .

He came back and sprawled at the foot of the bed, facing her.

"'It's not that I don't like being next to you. But I want to see you, see your face," he explained, leaning toward her to hand her the drink.

Oh and I too. I too. That's why . . .

"Where do you come from? in the States," she began.

"I was born in a little town in Ohio, my father ran the local hardware store and dabbled in local politics. He was a roaring boy, that's what my mother called him. High-spirited, full of jokes. My mother had been an English teacher, but was forced to resign when she got pregnant. I'm the eldest, I have a younger sister and brother. Later, she went back to work as a librarian. She was the only one, I mean, there was only one librarian and a couple of college kids who worked part time. The town library was a nice old white house that had been converted. I still like it better than the new glass-and-steel places. It had odd little rooms, alcoves, always a surprise. And my mother turned that job of hers into a real drama. She was always giving battle to someone. Every night, it seemed, she'd have some new tale in the ongoing saga of Mame Morrissey to defeat the forces of ignorance and philistinism. She'd recount with relish her heroic struggle to get one more book on the shelves, or to keep one there that had shocked someone of importance, or to get some money to run the damn place. I think they expected her to heat it and light it on her housekeeping money."

Something they wouldn't have expected from a man.

"I did the usual things—high school, the army for a couple of years. They sent me to OCS and by the time I was finished, the war was just about over. At the time, I was disappointed. Maybe I still am."

"You think war is fun?"

"Well," he shifted his body, "it can be, you know. For some people, anyway. I had a great time in OCS— the camaraderie, the closeness, the drinking sessions, the particular kind of joking. It brings men together, you know?"

Yes. Too bad you need a war to do it. Need a war to cry for each other. To love each other.

"Yes, I understand."

"After the army, I went to college—Ohio State— and then to Columbia for an M.B.A. I got married just after I got my degree. Got offered a job in Dallas, hot-shot job for a green kid, well, I wasn't quite a kid anymore. We moved out there. After that, it's just the usual routine. You know, a couple of kids, a promotion, another kid, a move to another job, that one was in Minneapolis. We lived there for a few years, had another kid. Then I got an offer from IMO and we moved to New York. I've been with them for about fourteen years. We live in Scarsdale, in one of those houses that pretends it's English Tudor. But it's comfortable and it has nice grounds, and Edith likes it."

Edith. The most beautiful name in the world.

"And Edith is in London?"

"No." Looked for a cigarette, looked away from her. "She stayed in Scarsdale. Mark's in his last year of high school, we didn't want to disrupt him. He's president of his class, captain of the basketball team . . . you know." He smiled, proudly.

I know.

"And Jonathan's still a kid, only thirteen and in junior high. Just beginning to become peer-conscious." He grinned again. "It would be a bad time to move him."

"Yes." No mention of his daughters.

"Well, that's my life story, ma'am."

"And what about your daughters?"

"Oh, they're super! Really super! Leslie's in college, in her last year. She's very apt mechanically, I'd like her to go to engineering school. And Vickie," his face lighted up even more, "is terrific! Really bright. She has a master's in biology, she's interested in microbiology. She works in a lab outside Boston, she has her own little car, she shares an apartment with some other girls, and from the sound of it, they have a ball all the time. She's just great!"

President of class, captain of basketball team, peer-conscious—read popular—engineering college, microbiology, super, great, terrific, wonderful healthy wholesome American kids, Momma stays at home to keep them that way, Daddy hides his affairs to keep them that way, American dream, the right life. House in Scarsdale where they never have to meet those who are not their own kind. Stability, it's called. I'll bet they're Episcopalians and go to church. Oh, it's all marvelous if you get to be the Daddy, not so great if you get to be the Mommy, but some women like it, maybe she does, Edith.

"And does Edith work?"

His face changed, she couldn't tell how. "No. She has hobbies. Paints, does needlepoint, you know."

I know.

"So, come on, now." He grabbed her foot. "Tell me about you."

What should Cordelia speak?

"I live in Boston, Cambridge, actually. I was born in the area, I've lived there all my life. Momma sold real estate. Poppa drank. He was fun though, he liked to play. I felt very close to him. . . ." Her voice drifted off.

31

Don't get into that now.

"They got divorced when I was twelve, and Momma and I moved to an apartment in Allston. I'm an only child, and Momma gave me all she had—in terms of energy, attention, affection. . . ."

You might say she drove you. But you might also say she worked like a goddamn slave, day and night.

"We didn't have much money, but I was fairly bright in school, and I got a scholarship to Radcliffe. I majored in English, I always loved literature. I met Anthony at a party in Boston—student party—when I was in my junior year. He was at BU then, graduated before me. We got married after I graduated. I got a job, I was going to save money and go for a Ph.D. There wasn't money for graduate fellowships for women in those days. The best job I could get was as a clerk-typist. I remember I earned thirty-five dollars a week. I tried to save fifteen, but . . . well, before long I was pregnant, and then. . . . well, you know, the usual thing. I was bored because I didn't do anything else *but* take care of the kids, but I liked taking care of the kids. I really enjoyed them. And, I suppose, I wanted to mold them. Make them into what I thought they should be. It seemed to me a major project, fool that I was," she laughed.

"Why is that foolish?"

"Because you can't do it! Surely you must know that!"

No, he doesn't. President of his class, captain of the basketball team, engineering school, microbiology. . . .

"Well, anyway, *I* couldn't do it."

"I'm sure your children are wonderful," he said, squeezing her foot.

She gazed at him. "Anyway, when Sydney—my youngest—was about two, I went back nights for a Ph.D. To BU. Can't get a doctorate nights at Harvard. And then I got it and I began to teach, and I've been teaching ever since. I got tenure at Emmings a few years ago. I've had a couple of books published."

"Really? What about?" Eager.

"The Renaissance. My first book was on the underlying meaning of the moral images in the great poets—Sidney, Spenser, Shakespeare, Milton."

"Oh." His face closed down again. "I've read Shakespeare, of course. I read a little Milton, but recall none of it. My favorite writer of that period is Bacon, Francis Bacon."

Of course. Would be. Francis Bacon, the great experimenter, believed in science, believed in spreading the word, overcoming medieval superstitions. Beginning of scientific world, popularization, industrial revolution. Yes.

"The one who caught cold and died because he was experimenting with freezing food and went out into the snow to freeze a chicken?"

He laughed. "The one."

Her back hurt and she realized she was hunched over more than usual. She pulled her shoulders back.

"And what did he do? Your husband?"

"He had a series of jobs, couldn't find what he liked. He went into the mail-order business with his father, finally."

For years and years of discontent, he dallied while you played patient wife and worried about money: yes, I understand, Anthony, of course you should find something you really enjoy. After all, you will have to keep doing it for the rest of your life. Until Daddy got impatient and scooped him up: you've got to settle down, boy, you're a father.

"I wasn't happy in the marriage, and we got divorced. The kids and I moved to Cambridge—we had been living in Newton. And," she shrugged, "life went on. Both the kids went to Emmings. Tony's a musician, he plays about five instruments, but prefers the guitar. He's very talented. He works in a band out on the West Coast, in Berkeley. Sydney's a poet, also very talented, I think, although she's younger and it's more difficult to tell. She lives in a commune in the country, up in New Hampshire. Two artists. Don't know how I ever produced that. But I suspect Anthony had an artistic nature. He was never trained, his family had no sympathy with the arts, but I think he'd have liked to be a writer or a musician."

No need to say that neither of your children ever even finished school, that they are dropouts, dropouts from life as well. They wander the hills barefoot, both with their arms around women. No, that would shock him, he wouldn't know what to say.

Victor was gleaming at her. "It is pure miracle that you were on that train."

Yes. I know. Lovers' favorite game: when did you first notice, what was it about me, how could you tell I was wonderful?

But she gleamed back. "It's a miracle *you* were."

He reached for her hand and she gave it to him.

He kissed it, then looked up at her almost shyly. "You know . . . I don't want you to think . . . I don't, I really don't go around picking up women on trains."

She laughed.

"In fact, I had just . . . really, just yesterday . . . oh, there are these girls in my office, and I was thinking about, but then I thought, well, I decided, really, you know you decide things but then things sort of drift into your mind, and I decided again, once and for all, that I wouldn't, wouldn't have an affair.

"And then I saw you sitting in that compartment. I saw you from outside and I absolutely had to come in. And then I couldn't keep my eyes off you. . . ."

Oh, don't, don't hymn me. Beautiful, alluring, all the words we use to exalt something that is probably mechanical—electrical, chemical.

Oh, do, do, I want to hear. What was it, when did you first notice, how could you tell I was wonderful?

"Good God, why?"

He gleamed at her with intensity. "Don't you know how beautiful you are?"

She shrugged. "There are lots of women more beautiful." See how he lies now.

"Probably," he said, and she smiled. "But there was something in you—I don't know what it was—that drew me. But I really didn't want to do it. My head didn't want to. If I'd wanted to, I'd have spoken to you, tried to get to know you, tried to set something up. But I didn't want to and I determined I wouldn't. But I couldn't control myself. I kept feeling what I was feeling. I couldn't keep my eyes off you. And . . . it shook me up. And I kept thinking you must know what I was feeling, and then calling myself an idiot because how could you possibly know? And I kept expecting you to take control at some point, to rap me on the knuckles and say *down, boy*. Or something. . . ."

He sighed and leaned back and smiled at her in deep contentment.

"But you didn't. You didn't say a word, damn you," he grinned. "You could have said . . ."

"Beastly weather, isn't it."

"Yes! Something! You could have turned me off, you know, if you'd wanted to."

"Could I?" She grinned wickedly at him.

"Oh, you knew! You *did* know!" He slapped the bottom of her foot, lightly. "But you know, I was also afraid you *would*—say, *beastly weather* or something like that. In a prissy schoolmarm voice. Or look at me sourly and denounce the *Daily Mail*. . . ."

"Is that what you were reading? I should have!"

"But I hardly expected it from you, with your hair down and your cigar and that snotty snazzy look you have. And your clothes!"

"What's wrong with my clothes?" Laughing.

"Nothing, nothing! But they're hardly what my schoolmarm would wear. An Indian shirt and six strings of beads? I counted them!"

They laughed together, a low deep chuckle, pleased and contented.

"And then I was terrified you'd get off at Reading, or that someone else would get on and ruin everything, and then I thought that was exactly what I wanted, that everything be ruined, that we go our separate ways and just remember a chance encounter with someone who looked appealing. It happens all the time, after all. . . ."

Dolores was watching him tenderly. *He's like me. Maybe he'll understand me.*

"Sometimes I felt that even though I wasn't doing anything, I was going too far. And then I'd think that you were going to walk off the train into the arms of some waiting man, and I'd never see you again. And I don't know why, but that felt . . . unbearable."

His eyes appealed to her for understanding. She looked at him for a moment, then pulled herself up and across the bed to where he was lying, and took him in her arms.

2

THEY ATE eggs and bacon, which was all there was in the house. They had set the rickety kitchen table because the table in the sitting room was covered with Dolores's notes. She was wearing an old velour robe, a man's robe that the children had given her a few years ago when she complained about the cold and the scantiness of women's robes and their exorbitant prices. It was a little big for her in the shoulders, but she felt luxurious in it, all that fabric, deep pile, easy lines, nothing pulling or constricting or gapping when she moved her arms or her body. It had lots of room, easy room, and she loved it. Her hair hung loose and fell over her face when she bent forward.

Victor had put on his trousers and socks, and was padding around the kitchen trying to figure out where things might be in this odd little room. They had turned the radio on to the BBC, which was playing Prokofiev. Dolores hummed with it, to Victor's amusement, since she frequently went off-key.

"I can hear it in my head, I just can't get it out!" she defended herself, laughing.

Victor spent some time figuring out how to work the toast rack, and being slightly shocked by the British, who were so advanced in so many ways, but had yet to adopt the electric toaster. Dolores pointed out that they did have the electric kettle, which was far faster than any American kettle, but Americans had yet to adopt *that*. Victor had a number of reasons to explain that, among which was that electric kettles probably used more energy than ordinary kettles. She put her hands on her hips and stared at him, amused and challenging.

He put his hand up. "Okay, okay, you're right." He turned the toast. "I've only been here two weeks, and I'm still a hard-ass American, I guess."

She put her arms around his waist, standing behind him, and laid her head against his back. "I think you have a nice ass," she said.

He howled. "First time I've ever been told that!'"
Laughing.

"Mmm. But I'll bet you've *told* it plenty, though."

He turned to give her a snarky look. "And what about you, huh? I'll bet it's been both ways for you."

"Oh, not for years," she said airily, pouring the coffee. They sat down. The table rocked. Victor got up and fished in drawers and shelves, poked into little jars.

"What you are you looking for?"

"Something to prop up this table leg." He returned with a paper matchbook, tearing off its cover.

"It won't last," she warned as he placed the folded carboard under the table leg.

"It'll last long enough so that my eggs don't scramble on the plate." He creamed his coffee. "How long?"

"How long what?"

"How long have you not been told and not told that?"

Both of them giggled.

"Years. As I said."

"How come? Your lover unaffectionate? The strong silent type?"

He's really prying under the joking surface. Wants to know what the competition is. Would he be happier having some or not having some? Having some. Less responsibility.

"I've been celibate. For several years."

He put down his cup and stared at her. "Why? In the name of heaven, why?"

She laughed. "You know, the new American sin is nonsexuality, even though we haven't yet got rid of the old one, which is sexuality."

"I'm serious, Lorie."

Lorie?

"Well, I don't know exactly. I had a bad time with a man I was madly in love with. Or thought I was madly in love with. I guess I was a little raw afterwards, for quite a while.

"And just about then I began work on my second book, which was about images of women in Renaissance literature, and the moral and political meaning of those images. I was very caught up in it and I kept

37

getting angry. Angrier and angrier at what had been done to women. And besides, the book took up all my time—all the time I wasn't spending teaching, taking care of my kids, who were teeeenagers then, taking care of the house, cleaning, cooking . . . you know. I didn't really have time for anything else. I just drifted into celibacy."

"And never came out." He acted incredulous.

She shrugged.

"He must have been something, that guy."

She looked at him. Damn, if he isn't like all the rest after all.

"It wasn't just Marsh. You're married, you don't realize what it's like to be a single woman with children. You have a wife to take care of all your needs, to take care of your children. When you're busy with a project, you don't have to spend time and energy with your wife. You know she'll understand. I had to do all of that by myself. And I had only so much time and energy."

"Yes. But to turn you off in the first place. And so strongly that even though your kids are grown you haven't . . ."

I do not seek consolation in yet another pair of male arms, is that what distresses you? And when did I ever find it there?

"You know," she turned to him smiling, intending to be light, to joke, "you really want to believe that Marsh hurt me terribly. It pleases you to think that. I've never understood that, how men love to hear tales of women's abuse by other men. Especially if they can imagine the woman crying, bruised, beat up. I've never been able to figure that." She could hear the irritation in her voice, but she couldn't control it. "I don't know if they like to hear terrible stories because that is the only way they can feel good about themselves, comparatively, or whether imagining a woman pushed around titillates them."

"Women are the same way," he said defensively. "They love to hear that another woman has treated a man badly. They ooze sympathy; they coo and ooh. They stand there with open arms." His face was tight and he was staring at her.

38

Her back got very stiff.

"And women really enjoy hearing a man criticize another woman. They really draw you out if you do that. *Really,* they say, *she doesn't? Oh! Really? You poor dear.* And the suggestion is ever so subtle, or maybe not subtle at all, that they have exactly what the other doesn't have to offer."

"Well, not me!" She threw her napkin down on the table. "And I'm not going to sit here and listen to you malign women!"

"What is it around here, you can't say anything about women, even if it's true?"

"*You* can't say anything about women because you don't know anything about them!"

"Well, it seems to me you started this. And you *said* you didn't understand men."

"I don't understand male insanity. But I know men. And you don't know women."

He leaned back in his chair, his face very composed, his voice very controlled. She imagined this would be how he'd look at a business meeting, in an argument. He'd never raise his voice, he'd never sound really angry.

"I would suspect that my experience with women has been about equal to yours with men."

"I doubt it. Men tell women things, personal things. And so do other women. And women don't tell men everything."

"So no man can know either men or women as well as any woman?"

"No man knows either men or women as well as I do."

He pushed back his chair. "You are saying you are an infallible authority and my experience is simply invalid?"

Yes. That's what I'm saying. Just as men say about hundreds of things to women.

They stared at each other. The air was cold between them. She pondered. Logically, he was right. But there was something wrong with logic, something wrong with comparing the behavior of men and women. As if they were equals. So often she got into arguments like this. What was it that was wrong with his reasoning?

"I guess you're right," she said, coolly. He did not relax. He was looking at her from a distance. Well, so much for that. I've driven him away. Well, it wasn't supposed to be more than a casual screw anyway, was it? And if that little disagreement is enough to send him reeling off, good riddance.

But her voice was a little thick. "It's just that I have a thing," she said. He leaned forward. "I can't abide to hear men criticize women. I can't stand it. Oh, if you were to say, '*Alice* does this, *Betty* does that, and I don't like it': I'd be able to accept that. Not that I wouldn't be sympathetic to Alice and Betty. But I could accept *your* saying that. But I can't tolerate men making sweeping statements about women: Women do this, Women do that. Which men constantly do."

He smiled at her, shaking his head. "Do you hear yourself?"

"I hear myself." She turned away from him, and her face was a little wrenched, her mouth was trembling. "I can't help it. It's rooted in conviction." She turned back to him. "I suffer from deformation of character. It's a result of my past. I lost a fin in the war and now I swim at a list."

He was watching her intently. He reached across the table and took her hand, gently. "I think you swim just fine. And I'm sorry, not for pointing out your logical error," he smiled broadly, "but for defending men by attacking women. Cheap shot."

Her face softened.

"Truce?"

She nodded.

"I'd say armistice," he added, rising to clear the table, "except I suspect it ain't one."

3

AFTER ALL her panic, her long-standing fear of being encroached upon, invaded, crowded, imposed upon, she could not bear it when he dressed to leave.

"Stay!, stay!" she urged. Thinking she would take

half her clothes out of the tiny closet and store them in a suitcase under the bed. Thinking she would have to buy a few more glasses, perhaps some cups. Wondering how she could make room for his things in the small bathroom and deciding to buy a cardboard dresser and jam it between the sink and the tub. They'd have to buy him a bike, so the two of them could ride together on fine days.

"I can't. There's a room booked for me at the Randolph, there are people expecting me, probably messages. And I have an appointment early in the morning."

You could go and check in at the Randolph, get your messages, and come back here and spend the night with me. We could set the alarm to wake us up early tomorrow morning.

No. I won't say it. I won't beg. He could do it if he wanted to, he'd see it if he wanted to see it. The hell with him. He wants to go? Go!

He walked from bedroom to bath, dressing, combing his hair, finding his watch and his wallet under the bed where they'd tumbled. He was all business. She might as well not have been there. She could tell that he would just as soon she weren't there because he didn't need her now, didn't want her now. And he'd just as soon also not have to worry about her clinging or sulking at his departure. So, he dismissed her, although not in words. He blanked her out.

I will not say: When will I see you again? No, I will not say it. The hell with him.

She stood in the kitchen looking at the greasy frying pan, bacon fat solidified in it. The air in the small room was smoky and bacony, and she opened the window. It was chilly out, but she put her head out a little and breathed the fresh cold air. She gazed at the slate roofs, shiny in moonlight, the old chimney pots, black and homey against the blue-grey sky. She was holding her mouth severely together.

He came up behind her and put a light hand on her shoulder. "I have to go."

She turned around. He kissed her lightly on the cheek. Her body was stiff, her lips tight. He did not seem to notice. He pulled a card out of a leather case

—a business card!—and wrote *Randolph Hotel* on the back and laid it on the table.

"I don't know the number there, but I'm sure it's in the book. You can reach me there if you need me."

Does he think I'm an idiot and can't remember the Randolph?

He went out into the hall. She stood in the kitchen, arms crossed, rubbing her hands on her forearms. After a few minutes, he reappeared with his suitcase, wearing his raincoat. He was energetic, brisk. He seemed quite happy.

"I'll call you," he said, and kissed her forehead. "Don't bother to come down. I'll make sure the downstairs door is locked." And left the kitchen and went out into the hall and opened her front door and went through it without looking back.

Look not behind thee, lest thou be consumed.

And the upstairs door closed behind him and she could hear his footsteps on the stairs and then the bang of the front door of the house.

She stood in the kitchen.

Then she charged out into the hall. She pulled open the upper front door and slammed it again, slammed it so hard the dishes on the kitchen shelves rattled. The she locked it. Came back in and turned the radio up to full volume. Lucky thing Mary wasn't home.

She looked around the kitchen at the dirty dishes on the table, dirty pans on the stove, coffeepot still half full. She lunged at the table and swept off an armful of dishes, hurling them to the floor.

"Damn! Damn! Goddamn!" she screamed, but what came out was only a whisper.

4

DOLORES WAS down on her knees wiping up tiny shards of glass the broom wouldn't catch, bits of egg, cold coffee, and cursing with every breath: Damn him, the fucker!

Can't even get angry if you're a woman because

you always have to clean up your own mess. Damned fucker! She'd have to buy some new dishes tomorrow, an expense she hadn't budgeted. The flat had been only sparsely provided, and Mary Jenkins would miss what was broken. Women always end up paying.

She threw—not hard enough to break them—the dishes that had remained whole into the hot soapy water in the sink, along with the skillet. She scrubbed them until her hands were red and swollen and rinsed with boiling water. She heated the fat in the bacon pan and poured it off carefully, this being one thing she didn't want to happen, a fat burn, yes. . . . Then she scrubbed the skillet, which was still hot and burned her middle finger slightly. But she paid no attention to that.

She stormed into the bedroom, ripped the sheets off the bed, and remade it with clean sheets. She stuffed the used linen into the hamper, pounding it down as if she would crush it to ashes. Finally, she ran a bath and got in it and sat there and it was then she let tears come into her eyes, but as always, they came and stood for a moment, and then went back where they came from.

When will you learn? *Will* you ever learn? You were fine as you were, you were perfectly happy. Happy ever after. *You* let him in, *you* opened the door, *you* stupid! How could you let yourself forget that they never fail to hurt you? All women, they do it to all women. How could you let yourself fall again into the delusion that you can live in any kind of peace with a man? How could you forget that men are fuckers in all senses of the word?

Life was peaceful, no tumult. I didn't have a bleeding heart. "Dolores, honey, don't be a damned bleeding heart! Can't you see that Stevenson is a weak-kneed shillyshallyer? We need someone tough, someone who knows how to win." "Win what, Anthony?" "Stevenson's an ass, Dolores." "And you're full of shit, Anthony."

But he wasn't, about her, anyway. A bleeding heart, that's what she was, although not the way he meant it. Maybe the way he meant it too. But, God, what could you do? If you were one, you were one. Your only alternative was to avoid situations that would draw the blood.

"You can reach me there if you need me." Indeed! The way men assuage their guilt. They abandon you, but leave a phone number. What on earth could she need him for? To wash the dishes? To make the bed? No, it was in case you find yourself pregnant. Better find it out hurryupquick, baby, he may leave town tomorrow.

Was there a London phone number on that card? Probably. She hadn't even glanced at it when she ripped it up and threw it out. Well, anyway. He hadn't even told her how long he was staying, hadn't asked how long she was. Just: *I'll call you.* Oh, he probably will call if he's here for a few days. He'll call late at night, a little high after a rousing time with the boys at dinner, finding himself suddenly alone and not sleepy in his dull hotel room. Men can't stand to be alone. He'll want to come over for a quickie. Not because he's so horny: at his age he isn't. No, just because he gets the heebie-jeebies being alone in bed, alone in the dark. He'll come over and talk for a little while over a drink, rush us into bed, and leap up and pull his pants back on and rush back to the hotel to fall asleep quickly, before the relaxation wears off.

Damn.

Acting so emotional. Acting, talking even, as if it mattered! As if I mattered, we mattered. Why did he have to do that? I would have accepted it the other way, but no, he had to say things, act ways to make me think to make me feel to seduce not just my body but my feelings and why? Just so he could make me feel rotten afterwards, having led me to think it might matter, it might be something more than the usual casual screw. Oh god I hate men.

She got out of the tub and scrubbed it hard, then tied her hair back and put her robe on. It was chilly in the apartment, but she walked barefoot, not caring if she was cold, walked barefoot into the kitchen, not caring if she stepped on a sliver of glass. She hated herself even more than she hated him. She poured some jug wine into a chipped goblet, found her eyeglasses, went into the sitting room and opened her briefcase, spreading more papers on the round table.

The hell with him.

She began to code the notes she'd taken the past two days at the British Museum. But her mind wouldn't work, it fought her. After an hour, she sighed, closed her file, lighted a cigar, and moved herself with her wine to a comfortable chair.

What was it with men, that they could switch feeling off and on? As if they had separate selves, pieces not essentially connected to each other except by the fact that they inhabited the same body. One was full of desire and tenderness; it was vulnerable, needy, wanting. Another full of rage, vented at the slightest provocation. And another that was dressed in shirt, suit, and tie, and sometimes even a vest, crisp and ready for action. Body *and* mind in uniform.

They have compartments for things. Work. Buddies. Women. Sports. And they could act different in each room.

Whereas she had only one room. She was the same whatever she did. She was popular with students because she was a person with them, not a disembodied "teacher," an Authority. Her books had been called *humane*, which in her field, and because she was a woman, meant that they were taken less seriously than books one could never suspect of harboring such a quality. Oh, if she'd had a class to go to, an appointment, she'd have left, of course. But first she would have hedged him round with embraces, assurances of love, of her sorrow at leaving him, of her guilt. . . .

That was it, damn it.

No, it wasn't. It went beyond guilt. It came from thinking about others, not all the time or before herself, but thinking of them at all. Which was what men never did. She would have known, let herself know, that it hurts to be left under any circumstances, and would have reassured him of her return, complete with time and place down to the minute. And the whole time she was away, she'd have been anxious that she might be late returning to him at the time she had set. She'd rush back to the apartment. And he wouldn't be there. Not himself worrying much about deadlines, he would not expect her to keep hers. He might even have forgotten what she had said. He'd be gone for a stroll in the park, to pick up some milk, having a beer with a neighbor.

She put down her cigar. It was a rotten way to be, the way she was.

And what can you do about that?

She picked up the cigar again and puffed furiously. Well, maybe it wasn't such a great way to be, but at least it was a *kind* way to be. There was no excuse at all for the way *he* was, turning himself off as if he were an electric light. Acting as if he didn't even know her, as if she were a prostitute and he'd paid the bill.

Was it true that love was the core of women's lives and not of men's? It wasn't the core of hers, hadn't been for years and years. Yes, but the moment she did let herself feel even a little she was back in the same old morass. Men did things so that they protected themselves; women did things so that they protected others. It was grossly unfair, but all she had to do was stop doing it.

But I don't know how. Besides, I'm not sure I want to. What I want is for men to be like women.

Yes. Years ago—before I was celibate? Probably— Bruce Watler. An MLA meeting it was. So attractive, vibrant and dark, wrongheaded of course, but wonderfully so. We'd met before, we were on a panel at Penn. Intelligent. Sensitive. Didn't bother with academic nit-picking. Listed on the program as giving a paper on Elizabethan pastoral, a subject she was interested in, so she went to hear him.

Good paper, not pedantic: it showed feeling as well as thought. And she rather loved him for it: the prodigal son is always loved more than the dutiful daughter. She loved him, she was grateful to him because he was a man and sensitive. Whereas she would simply have *expected* sensitivity of a woman—not that one always got it. So she overlooked his receding hairline, his thick middle, his very large front teeth, and concentrated on his graceful hands, the elegance of his facial expressions, and the sensitivity of his gestures and vocabulary. She was seduced, finally, by his intelligence, which wasn't the brilliant firework variety bright men usually have, but a wholeness, an integration of feeling and thought. She sat through his paper and the deadly others in the hot smoky Hilton seminar room, and afterwards, she went up to say hello and compliment him on the paper. Her admiration no doubt showed as she praised him. In any case, she was not surprised when he asked her to have a drink with him later, at five, in the lounge in the lobby.

Perhaps she agreed a bit too fervently. One never knows what one's sin has been, but for women it is much more likely to be ardor than coldness. So she sat in the Hilton lobby bar alone for an hour, sipping Campari. He never arrived.

When she bumped into him accidentally the next day, she asked him about it lightly, very lightly. "Did we miss connections yesterday?" Smiling. (Always smiling.)

"Oh! Listen, I'm sorry. I bumped into an old friend and we got to talking and I completely forgot. But we'll have to do it sometime, soon." Squeezed her hand fervently and rushed off.

Forgot, my ass. I saw the way he was looking at me.

It was all perfectly understandable: a married man not wanting to get too close to a woman he finds attractive and has reason to believe is attracted to him —an unmarried woman, to boot. It made perfect sense, was fine. But they could have had a drink and talked and done nothing more. Or, if he felt he might slide, he knows himself after all, then he shouldn't ask in the first place. Why did they do this over and over again? He asks, and gets his ego stroked when I say yes. He has his moment of triumph, he doesn't need to screw, he's scored without the anxiety of performing further. And I get left sitting for an hour in the lobby, waiting. "Oh, sorry!"

When women did things like that, men called them prickteases.

Oh, he'd never thought it through, probably, never thought about it at all. More comfortable that way. Turn on, turn off, like Victor. Everything separate. Bow and scrape to the boss, bully the wife, play hearty rival with the buddies.

Still, she remembered, puffing on the last bit of cigar, that her attraction to Bruce Watler had not been snipped. She'd gone out and bought his book and would prepare to get in bed at night to read it by saying: I think I'll get in bed with Bruce Watler. She was a little disappointed in the book: it lacked courage. She feared for him: he might have gotten reviews that hurt. So she went to Widener and looked up and read all the reviews she could find, stretching her mind as hard as she could as she read them, trying to sense what he would feel, reading them. The reviews were not malicious, only bland. They did not notice the lack of courage. But bland reviews were the kind that bothered her most, and she wondered if he felt the same way. She wished she could talk to him, to know what he was thinking, feeling. But he probably wouldn't tell her anyway, even if she saw him again, even if they talked.

What an idiot she was. What man would do something like that for a woman? A star-struck kid, maybe, adoring an actress, might see her films over and over, might read everything about her. But he would be imposing his fantasy upon her, not trying to feel what it felt like to be her.

Dolores saw Bruce again, several years later. His book had brought him success, a major chair at a major university she would have had to write five books to get within calling distance of. He'd grown pompous. His hair was almost gone and he'd gained more weight. But she'd had some small success too in the intervening time, and he acted glad to see her. He took her hand in both of his. "We must have a drink sometime," he said.

She tamped out her cigar and rose wearily. Her body ached. All that athletic sex. I wonder if men get aches in their thigh muscles. Or anywhere. I wonder if we pay every bill. She turned off the lamp and walked to the bedroom, ruminant, tired.

Yes, he probably will call. Assumes that whenever he chooses to call, I'll be here, I'll answer, I'll be thrilled to see him. It will not occur to him that I might have meetings and dinners of my own.

Trouble is, I don't.

She got in bed, her teeth clenched. She was not going to let him do this to her. She would go out early tomorrow and stay out all day, all night too. The Bodleian closed at five. Okay, she'd go have a drink and then dine out. Or if she did come back, she wouldn't answer the phone. Perhaps—even better!—she would go to London tomorrow, she could do that. Stay a few days. See some shows.

If she did that she might never see him again.

Fine.

That was it! Back to London she would go.

5

BUT NEXT morning how was it? She woke late, after eight. She was tired. The sun, too, looked tired. That long trip to London, so tiresome. That lumpy hotel bed, those greasy eggs. Packing her bag again. Actually, she recalled, she'd never unpacked it. And she'd done what she had to do for the time being at the BM. She couldn't really afford tickets to more than two plays. And she was out of cash: she'd have to walk to the bank, carrying her briefcase and her overnight bag, then walk to the bus, or to the station . . . oh, it was just too much.

She was so tired she considered not going to the Bodleian at all. She had not missed a single day of work at the library since she had arrived. It wouldn't mean anything if she took today off: she would just not answer the telephone.

She wandered around the flat in her robe, feeling a little dazed. And all the while her mind was making excuses for taking a day off, another part of her mind was functioning at high speed on a rather different track.

It was really drab, this place. Of course the furniture was *real,* not American plastic, but you had to admit, no matter how much of an Anglophile you were, it was *ugly.* Wood, yes, but cloddy lines, chipped, scarred surfaces: what was called mission style at home, where it garnered high prices simply because it was made of wood and not foam. Cheap nylon rugs. Sofa fat and ugly and covered with a rash-producing fabric. Stumpy little lamps and damn few of them. Curtains à la Grant's.

It would be nice to buy a few things, liven the place up. After all, she was going to be here a whole year. Of course, she really couldn't afford it and she was fairly sure Mary couldn't. And whatever she bought, she'd have to leave behind. And it would take precious time better spent at the Bod.

Still.

She absolutely *had* to buy some dishes. So while she was in town, she could just look at fabrics, bedspreads, rugs, curtains, furniture. No harm in looking.

(Make it beautiful, warm, welcoming. For Victor. Who will feel the difference even if he doesn't see it.)

Shaking her head, grimacing at herself, calling herself hopeless, she dressed.

He will call. There is no question about that.

Where am I going?

Don't know.

She decided to let her feelings dictate her actions. She would move without thinking, do what her deepest impulses determined. She would end up at the shops or at the library. Or maybe somewhere else. Only not at the Randolph. No.

She picked up her briefcase and left. As she descended the stairs, however, she heard her phone ring. She stopped. Her Oxford friends worked all day and knew she did too. They wouldn't expect her to be home at ten in the morning. She fought a little skirmish with herself, but continued to descend, hearing the rings, expecting each to be the last, and sinking a little at that thought. The phone stopped ringing. In the lower hall, she wheeled her bike out the door, and got on it, and headed downtown.

She loved the ride down to the Bodleian, past little old houses with wonderful gardens, still blooming in September, past St. John's and Balliol. But she had gotten only as far as the Randolph when she realized: he couldn't call her, he hadn't asked for her phone number and she wasn't listed in the Oxford directory.

50

If he had had any intention of calling, he would have asked.

My God.

So he didn't mean it, not a thing he said, not a thing he did.

She had slowed down as she considered this, directly in front of the Randolph. Averting her head, she speeded up again and turned down Broad Street, The Broad, as they said here, towards the library.

Who could understand it?

Just forget it. Wipe it out, she ordered herself.

She set her bicycle in the rack and locked it.

Try to concentrate on something else. Look around you, isn't it wonderful?

But it didn't look wonderful today. Some days Oxford just looked like an elitist mausoleum. She mounted the old wooden steps to Duke Humfrey's Library with her head down, feeling tired, very tired. And her legs ached.

But once she entered the ancient library, her spirits lifted. She loved this room, loved working in it. It had been reconstructed with scrupulous fidelity to its fifteenth-century origins: it had old wooden floors that creaked when people walked down the center aisle, old wooden carrels filled with ancient flaking leather-bound volumes, huge things with dry heavy pages. There was a wonderful ceiling held up by carved wooden arches, and painted with ancient seals. The windows were arched, and decorated with roundels of pale stained glass. She always sat by the windows that looked down into Exeter Garden, not the best garden in Oxford, of course, but lovely enough for her, sun on the chrysanthemums and asters, on all the burning flowers of the fall.

She wished Victor could see it, this room.

Not going to think about him. He's not thinking about you.

But she did: as she waited for her books to be delivered; when she walked downstairs to look something up in the old handwritten book catalogue; each time she looked up from her book to glance at the garden or at some passing creaker.

She could not disbelieve the part of him that had

51

loved her. But she could not either disbelieve the part of him that had blanked her out, had turned her into a piece of furniture, or a servant from whom leave-taking is business, can be brusque. And she did not know which of these sides was dominant in him, although she guessed it was the businessman. The other side would no doubt surface again, perhaps tonight, perhaps not for a few days, when he felt the need, when it was convenient.

Convenient: Anthony's favorite word. It's more convenient if we go to my mother's: she has more room. It's more convenient if we stay home during my vacation. It's more convenient if I drive.

And the question was: did she want to be involved with a man who could turn her off when it was convenient for him, and who gave no thought to how she felt? Did she want to be even in the slightest degree involved with such a man?

The answer was clear: No.

6

So THAT was that. And even if she did see him again, there was no point in going into all of this with him, because he simply wouldn't understand. Men tended not to understand because of course it was more convenient not to. She'd have to work at it, explain, maybe even argue, to make him see. She might have to get angry. And she didn't want to get angry, to try to convert him. She was tired of that, sick of it.

So if he did somehow find her again, she'd say she was busy.

She returned to her books, forcing herself to concentrate. She reviewed the notes she had taken today:

No woman ever thinks abstractly. Man's intelligence is abstract; woman's concrete. Men love principles; women, persons. No woman ever really understands herself. (1899)

Woman was appointed by God to be inferior to man in authority and power. This arrived because Eve assumed a place which did not belong to her. And since Eve, the lot of woman was made hard and bitter by the oppression of man. Women's inferiority to man in respect of authority and rule is a memorial of past transgression. It is a proof that humanity is under a curse for sin, and it is a good reminder to man that he is not perfect. (1875)

Never forget that a man is a selfish being. Keep that little fact in view continually; and if you want to please him, pander to it. Don't cry, don't make a fuss, and certainly don't be quick-tempered. Be sweet above all, but your sweetness must be real. A man never wants to be controlled.

You must learn to hide your feelings. You must never allow a man to sacrifice his comfort for you.

Let this ever be in your mind: "I am a creature formed to give pleasure."

And never lose your temper: it ruins the face. (1895)

The sphere of woman's influence is domestic; she wins her master by sweet submission. (1844)

Woman is man's tempter and misleader. Her true place is at once the lowest and highest in creation. All women have an instinctive desire to be wives, even if they deny it. In being sweet servants to their husbands, they fulfill what is highest in them. (1878)

In Woman, weakness itself is the true charter of power; it is an absolute attraction. All independence is unfeminine. The more dependent, the more cherished. (1835)

She shut the last book, sighing. It was a strain to work on this subject. She kept being dragged into emotions she did not choose to feel. Still, she felt the subject was important, and no one else would write this book if she didn't: *Lot's Wife: A Study of the Identification of Women with Suffering.* This stage involved reading eighteenth- and nineteenth-century manuals and sermons which were concerned with women's role, either meditating upon it or prescribing female behavior. Many of the writers complacently justified women's suffering, even gloried in it. Some of them said that women's suffering was shameful, that it was unfair that men were so beastly to women, but alas! it had been decreed by God. Some said that women deserved it. Kindly clergymen had written these things. The writers were not strong in logic, but probably their readers had not noticed.

If only I had more distance, if only I were less involved.

Cal's voice, droning on and on. He didn't have to bother to make himself sound interesting, people followed him breathlessly. The Great Cal Taylor.

"It is, of course, in the highest sense *interesting,*" he gave *interesting* a special emphasis, a special expressiveness, it was his highest word of praise, "but it is, after all, part of a dead time. Your job—as a historian, which as a scholar you must be—is first of all to *see* the interest, and then to trace its connections. You should have no more emotion about it than a zoologist cataloguing toe shapes. *Your* work, my dear Dolores, is marred by your . . . well . . . *passion.* And your bias. Women, after all, were simply not important to the Renaissance, and your concentration on them, it seems to me, distorts the entire period."

"Women were important to Shakespeare. Science wasn't important to the Renaissance, but people write about that."

"But my dear Dolores, you write about morality! It is, you know, one thing to document the moral standards of the Renaissance—although one thinks that this has quite amply been done already—and quite another to treat that morality as if it were a living one, as if you had a present response to it, as indeed, you seem to. As if it affected you. That is historically naive."

He leaned back in his chair (How does he get a desk chair like that? All I have is a wooden one, with a hard seat) and smiled, his great pale forehead shining at her.

"I don't understand why you can write about any trivial subject—someone just published a book about animal imagery in Shakespeare—and it is respected. But if you write about women, you're being . . ."

"Ideological. Quite simply, my dear, because you are."

"But it is *not* ideological to write about men?"

He whooped a laugh. "I see you are becoming quite a fanatic!"

"I'm serious, Cal. I want an answer."

He leaned forward. He tossed her essay across his desk towards her, and his famous kindly face became a sneer. "I can only suggest that you send this to one of them feminist journals," he said.

She stood up stiffly, feeling utterly humiliated. How dare he speak to a colleague like that? How dare he speak to anyone like that? Everything was behind him, the weight of thousands of years of tradition. No one else would question his right to treat her this way. But where had he earned that right? Who conferred it upon him?

She looked at him coldly. "You know, Cal, you and your ilk will die too, someday," and strode out of the office with as much dignity as she could muster.

Cal snubbed her ever after when they passed each other on the campus. She'd lost the assistance of her most eminent colleague. She'd lost—nothing. Nothing he could do, even were he willing, could ever help her. His mind was set in a different place from hers, and it was a place that declared her point of view illegitimate.

She sighed and stood up. She picked up her books, standing for a few minutes in the soft pale light of the afternoon, wishing there were still sun, wishing she could feel something warm containing her, embracing her. Sunlight. But there was none.

She walked down the aisle and turned in her books, then turned around to look back at the room. The past ought to be burned, Ziggy said. Not just some of the books, but all of them.

Yes, if you could bury it that easily. But then you'd

lose this too, this room, soft and gold even without sunlight. What a room! Can you imagine building such a room for yourself? Built to house his library, Humfrey, the king's brother. It must once have held great scrolls, manuscripts. He could sit and read and watch the sun burnish the wood, smell the parchment, hold it in his hands, trace the illuminations with his fingers. He could watch the light shift from window to window as the day slowly died, see the blazoning of the stained glass. Silent room, smelling of true things: wood and wax and leather and parchment and ink and quills. And bodies and bat teeth, rotting in the mouth.

Still, there was something so human about its size, its proportions. Before man, *Man,* decided to transcend. Could transcend only in heaven. Oh, that's not true, Dolores. What in hell else were they doing, starving themselves, denying themselves sex when they were going mad for lack of it?

Don't sentimentalize. There was far more human misery then than there is now, the daily sort, cold wet hungry toothless smelly people walking around, losing legs, dying, dying all around you. Most of us have never known anyone hungry, really hungry. Most of us have never seen anyone die.

The lucky ones.

She sighed. She heard St. Mary's bells and turned and descended the wide creaky old staircase. Her whole body ached, her mind ached too. It came on her at moments, this depression, and felt like an enormous, wet, heavy canvas just sinking on top of her. As if everything were useless, as if life were misery for everyone in every place and at every time, and there was simply nothing anyone could do about it. You could delude yourself that you were aiding the cause of humankind by—what?—discovering penicillin, or writing a book. But it was only delusion. A delusion we'd invented, the way we invented the gods, to make things *seem* bearable. So as the torturer turns the rack that final screw and the body screams in agony, you can die with a smile on your face, dying for the glory of God. And, in truth, if you could do that, maybe you really didn't feel it, weren't aware of the pain. Transcendence. Invulnerability.

She unlocked her bike and wheeled it to the Broad Street gate. And only then did she remember her plan: to stay out late. But it was only five. The pubs around here weren't open yet. It was far too early to go to dinner. She was tired. And besides, she had her bike.

Christ, what did it matter? She could go home, she could answer the telephone, he'd come or he wouldn't, what did it matter? She wasn't going to see him again, that was that.

No. It didn't matter.

7

SHE WAS in her warm robe, sitting at the table in the living room, collating her notes, when the phone rang.

And she leaped up, her body did it, her mind wasn't functioning.

When she heard Victor's voice, her heart started to pound, further impeding her thinking processes. She realized she'd managed to forget about him, which was good, but also that his mere voice was capable of doing something curious to the hairs along her arms and back, which wasn't so good. And to her head. He had to repeat himself twice before she took in what he was saying.

Had to have dinner with the automobile people, had called earlier, had called on and off all day, had been thinking of her all day, but she was a gadabout it seemed, never home, and now it was late, he'd just got in, but he yearned to see her, was she tired?

"How did you get my number?" Her voice sounded cold, strange in her ears.

He was silent for an instant. "I took it from your phone when I was there. You said it wasn't listed. Why?"

"I just wondered."

His voice became more formal. "I suppose you're tired."

"What time *is* it?"

"After ten." Apologetic.

Late. Too late. He's tired, I'm tired. Not a good time for me to get my wits in order enough to explain to him why I can't see him again. Not a good time for him to understand what I'm saying. No. Won't see him. Besides, he's expecting me to say *no*.

"It's all right. You can come if you like," she said.

"You sure?"

She wasn't imagining the joy, was she? "Sure."

"Great. I'll take a cab. I'll be right there."

Oh boy. She went back to the sitting room and let herself down gingerly into a chair. I've lost control. I've given him entirely the wrong idea. All my body's fault. Damned thing insisted on having its own way.

Ever since puberty when she had first felt sexual longing, and sensed it as a surrender of the transcendent mind to the base body (so her philosophers taught her), she had resented sexuality as slavery to the body.

On the other hand, she had learned over the years of her life to trust her body. It was the only thing that always told you the truth. The mind lied; the body did not.

Sitting on a ladder, painting Tony's ceiling one summer Sunday, ten years into her marriage, a hundred years ago, when I was a young girl courting the boys, oh, a different person anyway, still sweet and soft about the edges. Hot day: sweat and paint dripping down her face, she rolled the nylon sponge over the stuccoed surface. Anthony suddenly appeared in the doorway: must be half time, or whatever they call it. When the commercials appear. He stood there for a minute, then said: "You're doing it all wrong!" His voice grew to outrage. "Jesus, you're leaving streaks!"

She turned to him coldly. "If you don't like the way I'm doing it, why don't *you* do it? I'd be glad of a break."

"Idiot! Look at that patch!"

"It's fine, Anthony, what are you talking about? It's perfectly all right."

He entered the room then, and walked around it, pointing wildly. "Look at that! And that!"

She sat back on the ladder and pushed her hair out of her eyes. Her fingers were wet and she could feel that she'd gotten paint on her forehead.

He kept screaming. "You're making a frigging mess!"

"Anthony," she said calmly, trying to calm him down, "there's nothing wrong with it. The paint will dry fine. Look at that wall, there's not a streak on it. I've done two rooms and I know how this paint works. It will dry fine. Look at Sydney's room."

But he kept circling, pointing, screaming. She watched him, incredulous. He saw streaks everywhere, when there were none at all.

"Anthony!" she yelled, finally. "Either shut up or finish the job yourself!"

He whirled around and shouted: "Bitch! Stupid bitch!" And stormed out of the room.

She sat on the ladder and cried, hating herself for crying, unable to do anything else. Why couldn't she be harder? Things pressed around her heart. Self-pity: here she was working so hard while he watched a stupid football game and he dares to criticize? Hot and tired and sweating, didn't she deserve appreciation? Oh, injustice, injustice!

But worse, and more frightening: what was wrong with him? Sweet Anthony, acting like this? Did he hate her? Why did he hate her? He'd been acting like this regularly, ever since his father died and his mother moved in with them. Was it his mother he hated? What could make him see streaks where there were none?

Something was terribly wrong. She cried for a long time, maybe just because she was hot and sweaty and daubed with paint. Maybe because she knew more than she could let herself know.

By nightfall, when she'd finished the ceiling and cleaned up the paintbrushes and the drop cloth and put the paint away, and made dinner and bathed the children and gotten them to bed—putting Tony in a sleeping bag on the floor of the girls' room—which upset Anthony: "Are you going to make him sleep with *girls?* What else are you going to do to make a pansy out of him?" but which she overruled: "It is bad to sleep breathing in the fumes of fresh paint"—by then, he'd forgotten. He never praised the job she'd done, but he never brought up streaks again either. One had to be grateful for small favors.

But indeed, there were no streaks. It was over, another little tempest. Anthony's rages came suddenly and left suddenly, and she was so grateful when they left that she did not sufficiently think about them. She did not want to think about them. Easier to tell herself, *that's over,* and pretend it would never happen again. Because if she had thought about them, she would have had to recognize that something was corroding him. It was inexplicable. She tried hard to be sweet to him even when she didn't feel sweet, to keep him calm. So another one was over and forgotten.

Except by her body. Forever after that, whenever he approached her, her body flinched a little. It was unconscious and probably barely perceptible, the way plants, they say, flinch at the approach of someone who has hurt them. She did not want him to touch her. As often as she could, she put him off sexually, and on the rare occasions when she pitied him or felt she owed him something, she submitted to his fuck the way she submitted in a dentist's chair: just get it over with fast.

Did he sense that, do you suppose? With the part of him that never came up for air, never made it even into his conscious mind? Did that, perhaps, make him worse? If so, he never complained. He even seemed more solicitous of her sexually.

She sat there remembering, shuddering. Was it her body that was going to make the final decision about Victor? Couldn't her mind have a little piece in the decision?

Because her mind had decided, firmly.

III

1

WHEN THE bell rang, her heart jumped a little, although she'd been expecting it. She ran downstairs to let him in. He looked pale in the dim hall light, and rumpled and tired, and he was smiling at her and she threw her arms around him and held him and he held her, and his body was heavy, he was leaning on her a little. She let him go and took his hand and led him upstairs and into the sitting room, and helped him with his coat and sat on the edge of the couch facing him as he lay there, and she stroked his face.

"Oh, you look so tired!" she lamented.

He reached up and pulled her down and kissed her and she lay against him. He stroked her back, and said, "oh, oh," softly, in his throat. She sat up again and kissed him lightly, kissed his cheeks and his forehead and his eyes and the hollows of his throat. He put his hands on her face and caressed it, gazing at her.

He revived, gradually, and pulled himself up against the couch arm. "I had meetings. All day. From nine in the morning until now. And all I thought about was you."

Despite herself, she gleamed. "What a lie!" she said. "You couldn't do your job if all you thought about was me."

"Did you do yours?" he asked, caressing her face still.

"Umm. Badly."

"Well, me too."

She smiled.

"How about a drink?"

"Oh. I don't know. I'll see." She jumped up and fished around in the kitchen cupboard. She came up with a little gin, probably there from the time she had the Carriers for dinner. She looked at it: nearly empty. What can you do with gin and nothing else?

Victor was standing in the kitchen doorway.

She looked at him mournfully. (Oh, how she wanted to please him!) "I've some gin. But no mixer." (But wouldn't I want to please any guest, man or woman? Want to please a friend as much as I want to please him? Yes.)

Victor held out a brown paper bag with a bottle in it. "Brought some, just in case."

"Do you carry little brown bags full of booze everywhere you go?"

"Yup," he said, and came in and got out the ice and reached for glasses, but there was only one. "Got another glass?"

And then she remembered. Yes: two glasses, a cup, and a plate. Broken. She fished around in the dishwater in the sink, where her day's dishes soaked, found a glass, rinsed it.

He poured drinks. She said nothing. She was biting the inside of her lip. He put his arm around her and they walked back to the sitting room. He lay back on the couch and drew her beside him. Her body went, it sat beside him, it leaned towards him, it yearned.

His eyes were milky with love. "I'm glad you let me come over. So glad."

She smiled unsteadily.

"I know you're tired."

"No, not really."

"You sounded tired. On the phone."

"Actually," she looked down at her drink, "I was angry with you." Never was anger conveyed in a milder voice.

His head came up sharply. "Why?"

"Well . . . it was the way you left here last night. It hurt me."

"Lorie," he took her hand, "I really had to leave. I had early appointments, I was tired—I'd stayed up late the night before I came, looking over the papers I was bringing. And I had to see if there were messages."

"You could have gone to the hotel, checked in, checked for messages, and come back here."

"Yes, I thought of that. But if I'd come back . . . we'd have been up all night."

Her face softened, but she forced herself onward: "But that's not what I'm complaining about, anyway. Not that you left, but the way you left."

"How in hell did I leave? I put on my coat and went out the door. How did you want me to leave?"

"You left like a businessman. The way a man leaves home in the morning, kissing his wife's cheek and reminding her to have his grey suit cleaned. You turned me off, you turned yourself off, you canceled me. I don't like being canceled."

He groaned lightly, and lay there with his eyes shut.

Canceling me again?

'You're sure I did that?" he asked, with open eyes.

"Sure."

He closed his eyes again. And opened them again. "I'm not much good at this."

"At what?"

"Whatever I'm doing. Introspection, I guess. I'm trying to remember how I felt last night, why I might have acted the way you say."

Well, he tries. You have to give him that. He doesn't just deny it, like AnthonyDougSaul. . . .

"I was feeling very good, I know that. And warm. And cozy. And comfortable. I didn't want to leave. I knew I had to get some sleep for today. I knew I had to . . . function. It's always like that when . . ."

"I know I have to function and I get up and get going. That's all. It never occurred to me that anybody else—"

"Existed?"

"No!" he moaned. "That it affected anyone else, that it might hurt anyone. I still don't understand why it did. Why you felt *canceled*."

"It felt, well, what I was thinking was that you had compartments in your life, and I was just one of them. On which the door could be closed anytime you chose,

63

even if I were present. It's hard to explain. Because of course people who live together spend long stretches without talking to each other, the way I do with my kids. I'm in my study working, they're reading in the living room or something. I mean, we're not in constant contact. But I'm always *aware* of them, not just as bodies taking up space or needing to be fed, but as people, people I care about, people who feel and think. And I felt canceled as a person: I was a body, that couldn't be denied, I had to be spoken to and kissed on the cheek and promised a telephone call. But nothing more. What I was feeling or thinking had been blanked out."

He gazed soberly into space, listening. "I'm sorry," he said finally, looking very gloomy. "I'm not conscious of doing that." He brooded.

"Oh, it's not that serious," she smiled at him tenderly. "Although it felt so last night." If he had seen her last night, would he have thought she was insane?

He tried to smile, but he was down.

Can't take criticism?

"The thing is," she began again, "it wouldn't have been so bad, I mean, I wouldn't have felt so bad, if you hadn't acted, spoken, as if what we have matters in some way. Isn't just casual. I couldn't see why you'd act that way and then turn around and act another way."

"But of course it matters!" He sat up sharply. "You had to know that. Didn't you?"

"Well, you led me to think so. But then, when you were leaving, I thought not."

"Now, wait a minute. You mean that if *I* thought it was more than casual, then *you'd* think it was more than casual? But if I didn't, then you wouldn't?"

She nodded.

"But what about *you?* What did you feel on your own, apart from me?"

A shadow passed in the back of her brain. She got up and walked across the room and sat in a rocker by the window. It was an ugly old chair, but you could curl up in it and rock, gently. It was comforting. She did this now, curled up in the chair, holding her drink, swishing it around in the glass. "There are times when

I only want it to be casual. Most times. Back then, back when I had a sexual life. But there are times when I'd like more than sex, when I meet someone who's interesting, someone I could care about. But I never let myself think about it, never let myself hope for more."

He put his feet on the floor. "I don't understand."

No, of course you don't understand WadeRansom-DougShaneSaulMarsh . . .

"You mean to tell me," he sounded indignant, "a woman like you sits around passively waiting to hear if a man is serious about her or not?"

"Well, it's pride, you see. I pretend I don't care. I never let anyone know I care."

"But underneath, you're doing what I said you were doing?"

"I guess so."

"But why, Lorie!?"

She looked at him mutely, then down at her glass. She shook her head. "What else can I do?"

"You tell *them*."

"Oh, Victor! You don't know anything about this. *You* go out with *women!*"

He laughed.

"Women are different. Women always—almost always—want more than casual sex. You can count on their wanting more. I can't count on that with men. You can't even count on men meaning what they say. A friend of mind, Jill, had a lover named Herbert. He told her how wonderful she was, all the time. They'd been together a few weeks, maybe a couple of months, and one day, in a tender mood, Jill murmured 'I love you' to him. She never saw him again. He turned white, and just dropped her."

"He was married."

"Oh, of course. Who isn't?"

"You aren't."

"Lots of *women* aren't. But men are, all of them who aren't gay. All of them who are over twenty-seven. Or so it seems." She was smiling and he shook his head.

"Quite a world," he smiled.

She gave him a little knowing look, cocking her

head. "You're pretty clever. You managed to pick up my attack on you and turn it into an attack on me."

He laughed. "I didn't intend that, I swear it!"

She smiled disbelievingly.

"Look, about my leaving that way," he leaned back against the sofa, and stopped smiling, "I don't know what to say. I'd like to say I won't do it again, but the problem is I'm not conscious of doing it at all. I can only say I'll never hurt you if I can help it."

But of course you won't be able to help it, will you. If I go on with this, I will be hurt. That's automatic: he's married.

And if I don't?

She raised her head to look at him. He was gazing steadily at her. And again, as in the train, their eyes locked.

He came to her and reached out his hand and she took it and stood up and they came together suddenly, violently. The violence was all inside, but both of them felt it. They embraced, they kissed, it was even more desperate than the day before, as if then they'd been separated for only a lifetime, but tonight was a coming together after a millennium. They felt looped together by some power outside them, larger than they, manipulating them.

Eventually they moved into the bedroom and lay on the bed, their hands filled again, palpable substance within their grasp, clothes, flesh, warmth, small throbbing vessels under the soft skin, curved bone. They undressed, rubbed part against part, cheeks rubbed until they were sore, chests rubbed together in something more primal even than sex, lying behind, beneath sex. Their fingers traced their faces, those written-on faces, with courses that could be followed, histories. And when their lips touched again, the violence inside them leaped and overwhelmed them. They were caught in it, not it in them, although it came from inside them.

It was a loving war, a way of flesh to get beyond flesh, to get to something not palpable. Grasping, twisting, holding, all intended to reach and keep something that could not be grasped, twisted, held. The iron loop surrounded them and as they surrendered to it, as it became the only reality, there flowed out from their bodies everything taut and selfbound, and the relief of that release came all the way from their bones, from the very marrow, it flowed out like a body melting into sleep.

Later, as he sat smoking and she lay half asleep, he touched her face. "I figured it out."

"Ummmm?"

"What I was feeling last night. I was feeling—I have to get myself together and get out of here, right now, fast. If I don't, I'll never leave. I'll stay and stay and turn into one of the pieces of furniture."

"Oh, Victor," she moaned. She sat up and took one of his cigarettes. She glanced at him. He was looking very pleased with himself.

"Feeling pretty good about yourself, aren't you."

He glinted. "It isn't often I psych myself out."

She grimaced.

"Well?"

"It's such a damned stereotype!"

"Oh God! The libber speaks!" He slid down on his pillow.

"Feminist, please." She poked his arm. "What you're doing is turning me into Circe."

He had pulled the sheet up over his head. Only his hand, holding his cigarette, protruded. From under the sheet, a muted voice howled.

"How in hell can I turn you into something I never heard of?"

Firm teacher's voice. "That doesn't matter. You know the stereotype even if you don't know the name."

Groan from under the sheet.

"Circe was a goddess who enchanted men to keep them with her. She turned them into pigs."

Sheet thrown off, body up. "And you don't like being Circe?"

"I don't like being *seen* as Circe."

"Well, I sure as hell don't like being seen as a pig!"

They laughed then, silly laughter, the kind that comes when it's late and you're tired and you love someone and you can afford to be a child. Victor slid down again and rested his head against her side.

"Listen, I have to know something. How long are you going to be here?"

"A year." Caressing his hair.

He sat up abruptly. "A year!"

"You?"

"A year."

They gleamed at each other like two children whose magnificent piece of mischief has come off without a flaw.

"Oh, Victor! If you could have heard my internal dialogue last night! You were killed, maimed, sent into an eternal iceberg! I walked on glass, hit my head, burned my hand, I was *so* mad!"

He turned his head and kissed her breast. Then lay back and stared at the ceiling. "I don't like you to be angry with me," he said, slowly, "but I do want . . . well, I want to know how you feel. I want you to tell me the truth. About that, I mean. I want to know how you feel all the time."

"Well, I'm feeling sort of warm, especially around the ass, and sort of hungry but too lazy to get up and fix something, and sort of tired but not ready to sleep."

He took her hand and kissed it. "I mean it, though."

"Okay." She slid down on her pillow and stared at the ceiling too. "Don't call me Lorie, okay?"

Made it a plea and not a demand.

2

EVENTUALLY, THEIR life together fell into a pattern, into the habitual that Dolores dreaded. But a month had gone by and she did not feel constricted. Victor had a flat in London paid for by his company. He spent most week nights there and came to Oxford to stay with her on the weekends. When Dolores had to work at the British Museum for two days, she stayed with Victor in London. When Victor had business in Oxford, he stayed at the Randolph and came to her flat evenings. He never took Dolores into the Randolph with him. She noticed.

Sometimes he would have to take business trips, to Manchester or Birmingham or Leeds. Perhaps even to the Continent. He told her this with delight. Wouldn't it be wonderful if they could go together? He'd rent a car and they could drive up together. They'd be together, they'd see some of England.

She drew back a little. "Yes. I guess. Sometimes."

"Don't you want to?" Incredulous.

"Yes, I'd love to. When I can."

"Well, why can't you?"

"Victor, I have work to do. I have only a year here and a lot of material to get through."

"Can't you take your work with you? You work here." He gestured towards the sitting-room table heaped with notes and file cards.

"Sometimes. It depends what point I'm at. Sometimes I have to work in the library."

He was silent, sulky. She was biting the inside of her lip.

"We have so little time," he said finally. "I want to use every minute of it, every minute we *can* use."

"So do I. But I don't ask you to take days off from work."

"That's different."

"Why?" It's always different for women. Whatever they do, it isn't important. Todd, begging her to type his paper for him. "I have exams to grade, Todd." "That's different. You don't have a deadline." End of that affair.

"I'm regulated externally: I have to be at certain places at certain times. You can regulate yourself."

"The work regulates me," she said coolly.

He got up and went into the kitchen. She could hear him preparing coffee. She turned back to her collating of notes.

He returned with one cup of coffee, sat across the room, and sulked.

She stopped working and looked at him. "Victor, what would you say if I asked you to take a couple of days off from work so we could go to Aldeburgh for a long weekend?"

"Where?"

"Aldeburgh. Anyplace!"

"I'd say I'd see. I'd try."

"Well, that's what I'm saying to you."

"Okay." Gloomily.

"What do you want from me?" Exasperated.

"Nothing. Nothing." A little martyred?

"You're used to women dropping everything at your call, aren't you. Do you own a whistle?" Vicious.

He glared at her. "I never needed one." Vicious back.

But she laughed, and he laughed too, wryly, abashed.

"Okay," he said. "You'll try. How about next Tuesday and Wednesday. I have to go to Birmingham."

"I'll see where I get to. I'll try."

Tight-lipped. "And just when do you think you can let me know? Because if you're not going to come, I'll fly. It's faster. And I have to make arrangements, reservations; rent a car."

"I'll know by this Friday. I'll see how far I get, how much collating there is to do."

"That's a bit late."

"Make both—plane and car reservations. Then cancel the one you don't need."

"I don't need your help in working this out, thanks."

Impatiently, she turned back to her work. He sat drinking coffee, his own papers spread out on the floor beside his chair, his briefcase on the footstool. He kicked the footstool.

She looked at him. Really this was too childish.

"I know, I know! I understand. But I'm not used to it. It's going to take some time for me to get used to it."

"Get used to what?"

"Oh, *you!* Your orneriness."

"Orneriness!" Having your own work to do was *orneriness*?

He smiled nastily. "Cussedness?"

She smiled nastily back. "All you have to get used to is being a little flexible."

"Okay, okay!" He kicked the footstool over. "I'm sick of this damned stuff. Let's get out of here, go for a walk."

Her back stiffened. She was in the middle of something and wanted to finish it. "Okay," she said.

They stood up, Victor walked toward her and put his hand on her back. "Honestly, Lorie, I don't mean to be a pain in the ass."

"I thought you weren't going to call me that."

"I like it. Can't *you* be a little flexible too?"

"About my name?" Men seem to think they can name women as they please, just because Adam did. That way they give women the shape and function they want them to have. "All the years I was married, my husband never called me by name."

"What did he call you?"

"Depended. Honey and sweetie. Or slut, bitch, whore."

He laughed. *"One* sin I haven't committed!"

"But you have! You are! *Lorie*. It's so diminishing."

"It's loving."

"Lorie. Judy. Jill. Pansy. Little girl names. We give women names they can't grow old with. Can you picture a ninety-year-old Judy? Jill with a bald spot and a walker? Dawn taking out her false teeth?"

"You can call me any name you like and I'll still come," he grinned in mock lechery, and walked to the hall for their jackets.

"How about Anthony?" she smiled wickedly.

"What was that?" Muffled among the coats. In the doorway: "What? Oh, your husband's name?" Looking at her grin, he began to laugh and went for her, wrestled her down, and that was the end of that walk.

3

IN THE end, she went to Birmingham with him. They drove along the motorways through rolling green English farmland. Cows rested on meadows velvety green, while in the distance white funnels rose—parts of electric generators?—and nearer, huge electric towers bore thick swaying wires.

"They do this better than we do," she said, nodding toward the scene. "Combine industry and farmland."

"In places they do. But their rate of production is nowhere near ours."

"It's easy to be efficient when you want only one thing."

He glanced at her briefly. "What do you mean?"

"If profit is all you care about, you can achieve it easily. But if you also care about the land you're polluting, the people you're posioning, the safety of the product you're making, then it's not so easy. You have many goals and have to be circular, not linear."

"And circular thinking never goes anywhere. There's too much of it—too many softheaded critics who don't know what they're talking about."

"Ecologists, you mean?"

"Among others. Academics. People without power who carp at those with it."

'Oh, Victor, do you really think that's all there is to it? That there isn't real ground for concern?"

"Sure, there's some. I guess. But what I know is that regardless of what people claim, their real motivation is to gain power. Power is what everybody really wants."

She tried to adjust her mind, to turn its gears to a place where she could argue with him. She had trouble. His statements seemed to her to come from a land so alien to the one she lived in that she could never find sentences clean and clear enough to break through the border.

"There are many kinds of power," she began falteringly.

"Sure," he agreed breezily. "And everybody has the kind that's right for him. The do-gooders ought to realize that. People know what they want, and they get what they want."

The border between their countries sprang a wall.

"Not everybody wants political power. Nor can everyone handle it. But everybody wants some sort, and everybody has some sort. Maybe it's only power over the wife and kids, maybe they roll a terrific boccie ball or play a mean game of Chinese checkers."

"This power of yours seems to be strictly male: power over the wife and kids?"

"Oh, women! God, have you seen them in action,

72

these dependent passive mommas? Never underestimate the power of helplessness!"

She gazed at him, silent. He was driving fast. The average speed on the motorway seemed to be ninety, but even driving on the left-hand side of the road, Victor was not flustered. His window was open, the wind blew through his hair, his right arm rested on the window ledge, his left steered with assurance. He looked beautiful, he looked as if he were steering a sailboat right into the wind. Beautiful and sure and precise. He knew what he was doing. He knew what he thought. He had language to say what he thought.

Easy to be beautiful, easy to be in harmony with yourself when you thought the same way as the powers in your world. So easy to be right and sure and clear if you were a man, white, interested in profit, successful. Whereas she, Dolores, could not even frame a sentence with which to argue with him.

She tried again. "There's power *to:* and everyone should have that, but everyone doesn't. Power to play Bach, or tennis, or boccie if you like. And there's power *over;* and no one should have that, but people do."

"Hah! Ever seen a world in which they didn't? You're turning reality into an academic subject, into political science or some damned thing. Everybody has some form of power over, as you call it."

"For god's sake, Victor, what kind of power over does a black slum kid have? An itinerant farm worker? An uneducated woman with a brutal husband and a job in a factory with an equally brutal foreman?"

"The power to rip somebody off, maybe. To pick more lettuce than anyone else. To cook up a great pot of stew. I don't know. I only know everybody has something."

She burst out explosively. "That is the most fucking complacent attitude I ever encountered! How nice to think we all have what we want, all have what we deserve! How nice to conceive of the entire human world as in a state of war—because that's what you're saying, really—when you already know you're among the winners! The fact is a lot of people never even get the chance to figure out what they want, much less to figure out ways of getting it!"

"It doesn't take chance, it takes thought."

"It takes *room!* The room to choose, the room to entertain possibilities. Some Indian woman in a sleepy Guatemalan town can't see beyond her own dusty village, can't see any future for herself beyond the one her mother, her aunts, her sisters, her friends must live."

"And what's wrong with that?"

"What's wrong with it is that she may be miserable!"

"Nonsense. Her expectations aren't great, so she's probably less unhappy than a middle-class woman with pretensions. And when your woman's sleepy Guatemalan town is ready for progress, it will find it."

Dolores clenched her hands so tightly her nails dug her palms.

"Apathy," Victor continued. "Most people live in apathy. I can't spare a sigh for them."

Nor spare a sigh/Though worlds of wanwood leafmeal lie.

She spoke calmly, sadly. "You sound as if you believed that all people need is ambition and will. But there are millions of people whose ambition and will have been sapped before they're five years old. Who will never have room enough to choose because they can't see enough, who don't have energy because they weren't fed enough. People are slotted into their positions in life."

"We're doing what we can about that." Coldly. "There are social programs. . . ."

He fished for a cigarette. She did not offer to help him. He found one, found his lighter, and tried to light it, but the wind blew out the flame.

"There are social programs," she repeated, cold too, as he waited for the car lighter to pop out. "Most of them are useless. Band-Aids. You can't cure a disease by cutting off the symptoms, you have to get at the root. And the root is our system of values."

"Capitalism, I suppose," he drawled nastily.

"No. Socialism is bad too. Better in some ways, worse in others. I see little difference between them.

Both see people as means to ends. If the end is called by different names, that doesn't make it necessarily a different thing. Production is the great aim, production and power. Not felicitous life."

"What the hell do you think the production and power are supposed to do but help people live more pleasantly?"

"Supposed! Supposed! In fact, the end of power is power and more power!"

"That's the thinking of a person who doesn't know anything about power! Goddamned ivory-tower academics! I'm sorry, Lorie, I don't mean to be unkind, but the people you work with have infected your thinking."

"Maybe I've infected theirs," she shot in angrily.

He ignored her. "Winning is wonderful! Success is wonderful! There's nothing like it! That's felicitous life!"

She rubbed her forehead. "Victor, this is hopeless. Winning is wonderful, yes—if you don't have to pay too much for it. To win money and lose your emotional life is not to win. Success too—it isn't success after all, is it, if it isn't an expression of your deepest energies? You know that old Greek recipe for happiness? Happiness is the exercise of vital powers along lines of excellence in a life affording them scope."

"Okay, okay." He nodded agreement, nodded eagerly. He *wanted* them to find some common language, wanted to agree. She watched him carefully. "I'll buy that," he nodded.

"But my point is that few people are permitted the scope even to discover what their vital powers might be. Scope is given to very few, and most of them are men."

"Now that's not true! It's just that most women don't want what men want! Look at you: you've had success, you've had books published."

"I haven't had success in your terms."

"My terms?"

"My books have earned me about five thousand dollars—if that—in the last five years. The best thing they did was get me out of The Swamp."

He looked at her puzzled.

"Place I used to teach. Our Lady of The Swamp."

He burst out laughing. "Really?"

"No. I just call it that. Intellectually, it's appropriate."

They smiled at each other. He put his right hand on the wheel and his left hand on her knee. He thought they were friends again.

"Anyway, Victor, I don't count. I'm one of the fortunate ones. I had a chance for an education, I grew up with lots of kinds of nourishment. That's not the case for most people."

"Jesus!" He removed his hand. "What do you expect me to do about that, Lorie?"

"Think about it! I expect you to think about it! How can you walk around in the world thinking the way you do when it's so patently false? How can you sit there complacently and say people get what they want? Just because you were slotted into alpha doesn't make you essentially superior, just luckier!"

"Listen, Lorie, I am aware of that. I also believe that people's disappointments are commensurate with their expectations, and that failure by my standards may not be failure by theirs."

"But maybe you're wrong. Maybe people's disappointments are commensurate with their essential abilities, abilities never fully discovered, never trained, unusuable, lying there atrophying year by year. I think that must hurt as much as the twisted feet of an adolescent Chinese girl back in the days when they still bound them. Every day the natural easy growth of her feet is stunted a little more; every day the bone is deformed a little more. Agony: years of agony. I've seen this happen in people's minds. They can't speak of it anymore than that Chinese girl could: they can only cry, like her, every night when the binding is removed for a few blessed minutes. What could she say? Whom could she complain to? It was the way things were. It is the way things are for lots of people."

He twisted his mouth. "Okay," he protested. "It's just that I find it distasteful to look down on people. That's why I hate the liberal party line, it's such a goddamned knee-jerk response. . . ."

"The bleeding hearts, you mean?"

He glanced at her swiftly. "I didn't say that. And I'm not talking about not having sympathy for people. It's just that to look at a whole class of people as if they were helpless children seems to me to harm them and to teach them to see themselves the same way. And it's bad for those who look down, too: it allows them such an easily earned superiority. In the short term, my view may seem hardhearted, but in the long term, you get better results if you expect people to take care of themselves, to produce, to be responsible for themselves."

"All the while conveniently overlooking the fact that the distribution of wealth and the laws that support it, the traditions and attitudes of our culture, make it impossible for some people to take care of themselves."

"No! I agree those should be changed."

"But they can't be changed unless we first look at people as classes and see that the different classes are permitted different privileges, and some no privileges at all."

He hit the steering wheel with his hand. He sighed. Dolores lighted a cigar.

"You never give up," he lamented.

"I can't," she said quietly.

4

YES, THEIR differences were wide, abysmal, even.

Dolores spent much time in the sitting room of her flat, thinking. She wasn't working as hard as she used to. It was almost as if she were intentionally leaving the collation, so she'd have something to do if he had to take another trip. . . .

Insidious, love. Not *his* fault, she was doing this of her own accord. Still, he'd been so disappointed when she said she wouldn't always go with him. That was pressure, wasn't it?

Yes, but she didn't have to give in to it.

She sighed and lighted her third cigar of the day.

One after lunch, one midafternoon when she needed a break from the books, one after dinner, and one before bed. Discipline. Victor was undisciplined. He smoked too much, drank too much, drove too fast. Those were the smallest of their differences.

The thing is, she thought, I couldn't take him home. And then felt shock at the thought. When was the last time you *wanted* to take someone home? Jack, probably. Ten years ago.

Dolores had spent most of her adult life not just in academia, but in *Boston* academia, which was a special world. Victor was a businessman, successful in the world, working for an American corporation which might, as far as she knew, produce napalm. A corporation which was controlled by a multinational corporation, and which was almost certainly producing industrial waste. Victor represented everything Dolores's society most despised. Although, heaven knows, MIT didn't quibble about little things like napalm or sending aid and assistance to the Shah of Iran. But her friends did.

Victor had a fine, if lifeless, London flat, an expense account that permitted them, when they traveled, to sleep and eat in whatever luxury a town provided. Dolores was used to cheap pensione, bed-sitters, a glass of vin ordinaire at the local. She suspected he cared more about money than he did about people. She only suspected this because it was not something you could ask someone: who would admit that they cared more about money—or power—than about people? Still, there were those who did. And perhaps Victor was one of them.

That's how insidious love was. It made you betray your principles.

Yes. And while he claimed he did not trust the military, he believed strongly in what he called a "ready defense." He had been known to vote Republican.

If she tried to take him home, no one would speak to him.

Of course, there were probably lots of people in Cambridge who wouldn't speak to *her*. Sin still existed in Cambridge, Mass., abounded, in fact, far more than grace. There were people who looked askance at you if you ate meat, or drank liquor, or smoked anything but pot. If you drove a big car, you were exposed to daily dirty looks. There were people who saw you as an Enemy Nation if you did not run every day.

Dolores had managed to slide through such standards, not having owned a car since 1970 (the real mark of a true believer), smoking only four cigars a day when she didn't cheat, and eating little meat. She drank mostly wine, and little of that. And she had never never never voted Republican. In the game of "how pure are you?" often played subtly at Cambridge parties, Dolores came off as at least not among the damned, if not among the chosen. But Victor, who had stocked her kitchen with a dozen bottles of Scotch, who ate huge steaks and roast beef, who chainsmoked, Victor would be outcast.

But that was not a problem since she was not taking him home.

If he took her home, it would be far worse. Dolores at the Scarsdale Country Club? With her hair hanging straight, its grey flecks showing? No makeup at all? And her funny clothes, Indian shirts and jeans, bare feet whenever possible, and never, under any circumstances, high heels? She owned two skirts: one, long and multicolored, which she wore to the rare formal affairs she had to attend; the other a mini, long out of style, in light pink cotton. She wore it in the summer because it was cool and she did not feel comfortable on the street in shorts.

At a Scarsdale cocktail party, she would be at someone's throat within five minutes. She had to admit she was not noted for her tolerance. She would attack something, anything. If she could not get a rise out of them (because of course they were terribly polite) yakking about recent Supreme Court decisions, the Bakke case, the First Amendment stuff, increasing withdrawal of federal funds for abortion, the policies of industry, spreading shit over the earth and sea and sky, no, not shit, shit was recyclable, poison; yes, if she could not get a rise out of them with any of that, she would attack their complacency, their elitism, their

79

easy assumption that they were entitled to their privilege.

No, it wouldn't work.

But it wasn't a problem, since Victor was not taking her home.

She had never in her life permitted herself to love someone who came from the world Victor came from. She had never even permitted herself to know such a person very well. Not only that, but when she was with him, she sometimes smoked a cigarette. And drank Scotch.

Worst of all: she missed him when he wasn't with her.

Principles compromised, all the way down the line. And after all these years. Not that being celibate was a matter of principle. It had just happened, but life was better that way. So it was a shock to be involved with a man, any man at all, but especially a man who was her opposite in almost everything. It was like consorting with the enemy. They shaved your head for that and paraded you naked through the streets.

How had it happened anyway, her becoming celibate? When did it begin, when did the faces start to fade, the mouths to open and close by themselves mindlessly, saying I, I, I, saying *my* car, that ball game, the best restaurant in London Paris New York Milwaukee, the same things over and over, hardware hardhat hardsell? When did my ears begin to close? Was it after Saul, who took two steps forward and three back, or Doug, who screwed with fervor and retired in shame?

Or was it that every time she had a bad experience with a man, she'd say: never again will I do *that*—drive someone to Princeton, listen to a boy's problems with his parents, not show my anger when I'm angry, make cassoulet. And each "never again" had led to longer and longer spaces between lovers. And finally to no lovers at all.

Because she was clever, she could read faces and manners, and she could tell when one of them wanted to be mothered, nursed, doctored, shrinked, educated, placated, fed, stroked, curried. Given given given to. Always.

Just as well. Slavery to the body, sex. And besides, it wasn't really sex women wanted men for. Do it better themselves. It was something else, it was wanting a body that stood there behind you that you could rest your head against, and trust not to move, not to slit the throat, or cut off the head, or pull the hair. It was to be together with someone who was there. Carol, saying in a dull voice: "Oh, yes, twenty-five years. It's a long time. It's not much of a marriage, it's pretty dead. We don't talk, we just inhabit the same house. But there's one thing that keeps me here, it's worth all the boredom, the routine. Lying in bed with John, I'm not talking about screwing. Just lying there together with him, his body warm and solid next to me. It's nice. It's comfortable."

Well, people had their own needs. For her, Dolores, nothing could be worth an empty boring marriage, nothing could be worth living with someone in easy, dead routine. Nothing.

And Victor?

Well, but it isn't easy, it isn't dead, it isn't routine. Yet. And never will be. It will end in a year.

She stubbed out her cigar in disgust. What's the point of thinking about all this? You can't eradicate your feelings by telling yourself you shouldn't have them. By dredging up principles. The fact is you're as tied to him as you are to your inner organs. Who knows, you may be tied to him *by* your inner organs. Call it love. Who knows, maybe it is.

Okay, okay. It's only for a year. We'll keep it light, we'll play, have pleasure. One's entitled, once in a while. Making love: pears in wine, peaches in champagne. Life was barren and arid enough. One didn't need to add to that.

Oh, yes, it was artificial. Two strangers cut off for a neatly demarcated time from everything they've known, from all the sticky roots and tentacles, all the mold and rot and mulch that builds up under stationary objects. An idyll.

Oh, Victor. Comfort me with apples, stay me with flagons. For I am sick of love.

Dolores was ardent about going to Aldeburgh, so Victor rented a car and took a day off and they went for a three-day weekend in October. She wanted to see Crabbe's ocean, his shingle, the grey skies of the Borough, its prosperous bursting farms, its shacks and hovels meanly protecting the Borough's abandoned wives and unwed mothers.

"Who?" Victor said.

"George Crabbe. C-r-a-b-b-e. An eighteenth-century English poet, a good poet. And a great human being. He wrote about the rich, people who mouthed moral pieties and turned their backs on feeling, suffering. And the poor, suffering, dying, suffering from guilt, feeling that it was their own fault they had loved some man and ended up pregnant and starving. In a culture where poverty was literally sin. Where they didn't even record the names of the poor in the village records. If a baby died, it was recorded as *Died: poor child.* I think Crabbe believed sex was sin too, but you can see him wondering about it all through his work. *Why* did these women have to suffer so much? He felt it. Felt their pain. It's in the poetry. I love him."

But when they arrived, they found a pleasant seaside resort, blue sky, blue sea, creamy beach, a fine boardwalk, and good hotels.

"It's supposed to be grey and bleak and barren," Dolores moaned.

"Gee, too bad, sweetheart," Victor laughed.

They signed in at a plush hotel overlooking the ocean. "It's a shame," Victor grinned, looking around. He was going to enjoy the weekend after all.

Hardly a sign of Crabbe in town. One woman, who ran a bookstore, knew the poet's name. His cottage, she said, had been swept out to sea long ago.

"Yes, there's something right about that," Dolores said. "He'd have liked that."

They had good drinks, a lavish dinner, and made love for hours.

"It doesn't seem right somehow," Dolores said.

Next morning the sky was still beautifully blue, the sea calm and broad and bluer than the sky. You'd think you were in Miami. They walked along the boardwalk. "It isn't supposed to be like this!" Dolores protested. "Oh, I wanted to feel it, feel into what he saw and felt, but this isn't it."

Victor spotted an oil tanker far out at sea.

"Poor old Crabbe's world is gone forever," Dolores said regretfully.

"From the sound of it, good riddance," Victor said. "I thought you were the one who wanted all that to disappear, all that poverty and pain."

Suddenly bells started ringing, loud bells. People came running from every direction to the beach. Victor and Dolores followed the crowd. It was converging on a lifeboat sitting on a slide set in the sand. The whole town seemed to collect there. Six or seven men wearing bright orange jackets were spooning up sand with shovels, in front of the lifeboat. Others, in the same jackets, were running around the boat doing things. Unfastening something—a long rail. They hoisted it off the boat and lifted it down to the beach and set it in the sandy groove the other men had shoveled. By now there was quite a crowd watching them. The thing took a long time, although the men were working as fast as they could. They'd glance out at the crowd occasionally, pleased with themselves, jaunty.

Eventually all the sand was shoveled away, the men on the boat were ready, the motor was running. There was a great boom, people gasped, and the boat shot out onto the rail and flew into the water.

Dolores cried out in delight, and clapped her hands. Other people in the crowd laughed and clapped too. But some were shaking their heads. A British woman with a kind face turned to Dolores. "By the time they get there, whoever it is that needs saving is sure to be drowned."

"Yes," Victor muttered angrily, "what a system!"

"But it was wonderful!" Dolores crowed. "So absurd! So funny!"

83

"Crabbe's primitive world isn't gone yet," he continued.

But Dolores danced. "Oh, those men, working so hard, so cocky and pleased at the admiration of the crowd. And that ridiculous little boat shooting out like a cannonball. I loved it!"

"You wouldn't love it so much if you were drowning."

"But I'm not!"

"Who's lacking in compassion now? People are drowning out there somewhere and these guys are going through this cockamamie routine."

She slid her arm through his.

"Wouldn't you think they'd find a better system!"

A few minutes later: "They could at least have the ramp permanently installed, with a roof over the whole business."

An hour later: "The whole thing should be set in concrete and walled off so sand doesn't blow over it. Roofed, doored, locked. Then all they'd have to do is slide up the door, the way you do a garage door."

"I'm going to be hearing about this for days, I guess."

"Well, damn it, Lorie, there's no excuse for such inefficiency."

She asked the desk clerk for news of what happened. An oil tanker had exploded in the North Sea. The lifeboat had picked up five men, saved them all.

She arched an eyebrow at Victor. "Well, now. . . ."

He grimaced. "There were probably twenty on board and the rest drowned." But when she laughed, he did too.

All they ever found of Crabbe was a tiny lane bearing his name, and a memorial bust in the village church.

Victor grinned at her over teacups. "I think you look for things to grieve about."

"Well, it's sad. What a face he had—if he really looked like that. So beautiful. I've seen pictures of him, but he wasn't so beautiful in those. Anyway, it does grieve me that he's forgotten. I can't bear it that art should die."

"It doesn't. It's still around."

"What's the use if nobody reads him?"

He looked at her kindly. "Why should art be immune? Everything else dies."

She looked at the table and played with her spoon.

He reached across and took her hand. "You know, sweetheart, what he did served its purpose. I'm not a worshiper of art. I like it, but I don't think it's sacred. It's a kind of food, it nourishes a culture, gets digested, and when it's lost its nutritiveness, it gets put into a museum—or a library. His poetry did what it could."

"That's a nice way of thinking about it," she said thoughtfully.

They walked out of the tea shop into the bright blue day. They wandered away from the main street into little lanes dotted with small old houses, nestled in gardens, comfortable looking, charming.

Not a hovel in sight. "Maybe his poetry did that," Dolores mused.

"I doubt it. I think it's called industrialization."

6

VICTOR WAITED until after their return to Oxford Sunday evening, to tell her he'd be tied up and unable to see her for ten days or so. He was sitting with his shoes off, drinking a Scotch for the road—he was driving back to London that night—and smoking a cigarette. His body had that brisk, businesslike look. His voice was flat, without feeling, a business voice. She hated the look more than she hated the news.

Some muckety-muck of the holding company that owned IMO was coming to London with his wife and expected to be wined and dined and ushered and catered to. For ten days. They'd never been to England before, they were not travelers, they couldn't take the unpredictable or the uncomfortable. They wanted to see Stonehenge and Canterbury Cathedral.

"They're High Church," Victor explained.

"Oh. I thought they might be druids."

"Don't be mad."

"Why in hell shouldn't I be mad? I'm going to miss you."

He gave her that look, the one that got her on the train, an across-the-room intensity she couldn't resist, so when he came to her, she held out her arms, and spoke no more of anger.

But she didn't like it.

It wasn't so much not seeing him for ten days. She saw him only on weekends most of the time anyway. It was all the other—the way he had waited until Sunday night to tell her, as if he thought she'd throw a tantrum and ruin their weekend. The weekend itself, in fact: had he dredged up a three-day holiday as a sop to keep her quiet about the ten-day absence? And the way he told her, turning again into his other self, the Businessman dealing with an unpredictable and emotional Circe.

Yes, that was it: She didn't like what she felt he was feeling about her, was seeing her as. As volatile, uncontrollable, someone who had to be handled gently. *Handled*. Possessive, dependent, emotional. Yes.

But you can't be sure about that, can you? It's only a vague sense that you have. Besides you can't tell people every little thing about them that bothers you, can you? So picky it would be. Such little things, vague suspicions.

So she decided to forget it and get lots of work done. She was way behind with her collation, and was coming to a point where she was ready to write a chapter.

Besides he probably wouldn't understand. He'd think she was making a fuss about little things in order to disguise her real anger at his absence. It would be very hard to explain to him. Not worth the effort.

No. So get on with work. And she did, finishing the last of one group of manuals within a week, catching up with the collation nights and over the weekend. Monday she would start to write a chapter. But as she laid things out Sunday night, she saw that she had forgotten to record a reference, so Monday morning, she bicycled down to the Bod to get it. She stopped at Blackwell's to order some books, then slowly wound back towards her house.

And saw Victor.

He was walking down towards Cornmarket from the direction of the Randolph Hotel, with a middle-aged man and woman, well-dressed in the American style. She stopped her bike at the corner. He did not see her, he was on the other side of the street. He was talking and being charming, but in his Businessman self, she could see that from where she stood. He had a map in his hand. He'd need it. What he knew about Oxford was mainly the way to her house from the Randolph.

The three passed into the crowded Cornmarket, and Dolores got back on her bike and headed in the other direction. Biting her lip. Victor in Oxford and he didn't even call. Didn't say to the muckety-mucks: there's an American scholar here in Oxford, perhaps you'd like to meet her, perhaps we could all have dinner. He could have disguised things.

No. He was hiding her away.

The thought made her heart stop.

She was, implicitly and beyond her control, a scarlet woman, a person branded illegitimate, forbidden to walk in the light. Victor was permitted to have her and even to keep her, on this condition. As long as he was secretive, furtive. That way he offers tacit assent to the prevailing morality.

But she, Dolores, did not assent to the prevailing morality. Yet she was in its power. She was the Mistress, the Other Woman, the woman with no rights, the one who had to be hidden away, like poor Rosamund, kept by Henry II of England in a palace that could be reached only by tracing a labyrinth, kept there forever out of the sunlight to serve his desire and his jealousy. . . . A prisoner.

No, no, I am not a prisoner, of course not.

She reached home with a throbbing head and sat down, just dumped her body in a chair, couldn't work. Lighted a cigar. Getting as bad as Victor. This is silly. There are terms, bargains. This is one of them. It's not that he wants to hide me, it's that he's worried about his job.

But why is it always the same old story? Always the woman who pays? Always, despite anyone's best intentions. *She* was the hidden one, not he. When the Carriers had invited Dolores to dinner one Saturday night, she'd asked if she could bring along an American friend who was visiting her. They'd had fun, Leonard with his grim ironic British humor, Jane with her equally ironic but livelier Bronx Jewish wit. Victor had, thank God, refrained from discussing politics. Yes, but the Carriers were sophisticated. You couldn't have taken Victor with you to dinner at high table in New College. Well, but that was on a week night, he wasn't here. And besides, *you're* not married.

Her mind whirled, and she could not get it in order.

Of course she wouldn't want him to flaunt her (but even the word shows bias!), to cause ripples of gossip in his company, to damage him, maybe even reach his wife, hurt her.

Maybe she, Edith, was loving someone else too while Victor was away. She should, after all, why not? But she'd have to be even more furtive than he, a woman, and living in a small town.

Yes, women always pay more.

She rubbed her forehead so hard that bits of skin began to flake in her fingers. She didn't want to *feel* this. But it wouldn't go away.

Victor did call, late that night, to say he was in Oxford and felt desolate that he couldn't see her. She was cool; their conversation was brief. "I'll see you this weekend, darling," he said placatingly. As if she were cool because she was angry at his absence. Just assumed she was eager to see him. Arrogant male.

But she said nothing.

7

AND NEVER did say anything. She was ecstatic by Friday, having written a rough draft of her chapter in just four days, having written with fire and conciseness, fueled, perhaps, by her anger. Yes: Women and Suffering. The right subject for her. A set of chapters on the way feeling, every feeling except anger, had increasingly been associated with women, and suffering above all. All those paintings of the Pieta, all those Hecubas and Niobes. At some point, feeling (except anger) had been declared unmanly. Then a set of chapters on the way women had been taught their suffering role, taught to accept their dependent status, subservience, patient endurance. And the way it had been justified, this role decreed for women. And the concluding chapters—the ones she was frightened of, hard to do—showing the effects of this dumping of emotion onto the one-half of the human race and declaring it off limits for the other half. No clear material there: she'd have to hunt and cull and pull things together from many fields. And there, she'd enter the realm of the subjective: always dangerous for a scholar.

But the thirty pages she had written were good, very good for a first draft, and she was high, dancing as she moved around the apartment. And Victor, almost as if he'd known, showed up without calling, at two o'clock on a Friday afternoon, and caught her high.

And was high himself, having turned some fine piece of business by getting the American muckety-muck's approval. "Worth the damned ten days of boredom!" he exclaimed. "If I had to listen once more to a complaint about the soggy English toast, the tasteless—read sugarless—salad dressing, the lack of American efficiency in the hotels . . . ! Once more, and I was going to puke. Let them go back to Howard Johnson's or the Ramada Inn, that's where they belong!"

High as she was, high as he was, and glad as she was to see him again, glad as her body was to have his body close to it, it was impossible to be angry. "What we have to do before it gets cold is buy you a bike," she said.

"I haven't been on a bike since I was sixteen!"

"Good for you." She placidly put on her jacket. "Put some air in your lungs instead of smoke. Tighten up your thigh muscles."

"Are they loose?" Worried.

"They're lovely. But loosening."

"Oh, those loosening thighs, those great big beautiful thighs . . ." he sang, and kept humming it, despite her elbow shoves, all the way to the bicycle shop.

And very shakily, anxiously watching the motor traffic, slowly, he rode back to her house on a shiny ten-speeder. By the time she had unlocked her door and wheeled her own bike out, he was riding in circles in the street with no hands.

"Look . . ." he began.

"You call me Mom and I'll Pop you!" she cried.

And in the grey-blue dusk, they rode off to the countryside, down curved lanes, to the river.

It was impossible to be angry.

Next day, he said: "You know, I don't know anything about this place. Oxford. I felt like a fool trying to show the Buswells around. Not that they noticed. How about giving me a tour?"

They rode their bikes to town, locked them in the yard outside the Bod, and looking at him with a just-you-wait glint, she led him into the library and up the old creaky wooden stairs. As they entered Duke Humfrey's Library, she kept watching his face. He glowed. She glowed. She took him past the railing that excludes guests, she whispered its history to him as he took in the wood, the stained glass, the ceiling, the old books. He kept glowing.

That mattered. Very much. Time she took Harry Hunter Harter Herter, something like that, to see the unicorn tapestries at the Cloisters and he hadn't seen anything. He just looked at them, smiled at her, asked *what else?* She refused to go out with him again, although he'd kept calling for months. He couldn't understand what was wrong, and how could you tell a person a thing like that? I won't go out with you because you did not respond, you did not stretch out and glow at something so beautiful, so wondrous. If you can't see that, the wonder and beauty of that, how can you see anything? How can you see me, who am not always wondrous or beautiful?

But Victor saw. She took his hand as they descended, and laid it against her cheek. He was still (mentally) in the library, he was talking about old books.

"I always loved them, I used to collect them. . . ."

He paused.

"I inherited a few from my mother's mother's father. I have a small collection. . . ." Again, the odd pause, but then they were out in the sunlight, and walking. Dolores talked, pointed, talked: teacher, a role she enjoyed, but wasn't sure Victor would. They went to New College Chapel to see the old stained-glass windows and the Epstein statue of Lazarus. Then to Trinity Chapel. Then to lunch at the Turf, a tiny low-ceilinged pub that was built in the thirteenth century. They ate sausage standing up, drank their pints looking at each other, unable to speak in the crowded, noisy, smoky room, people packed in, their heads nearly reaching the ceiling. Victor had to duck through a doorway, which delighted him, and he grabbed her hand as they left through the little garden, and out into a little lane that led back to the street. They walked holding hands, swinging them.

They walked to High Street—The High—and crossed and went down towards Christ Church, where they saw the lovely Wren "Tom Tower," and heard Great Tom, the great old bells inside it, strike the hour. They went to the cathedral, then walked over to Magdalen Grove and stood there for a long time watching the serene tender red deer, feeling serene and tender themselves.

"First time I came to Oxford, I hated it," Dolores said. "That was years ago, and in the summer, it wasn't term time, and the place was empty. And it seemed so fucking *monastic*. Boys on bikes with their academic gowns flying out behind them, soft-faced, protected, arrogant boys. All that tawny stone, the enclosed gardens, the spires, the gates, everywhere gates! Oh, that's still true—those buildings we couldn't get inside of, the windows I wanted to show you. Someone took me there one day, but one can't just walk in, one has to be taken by somebody who belongs. Well, almost everything is pure and white and austere on the outside. And rich and ornate and comfortable inside. You know, like priests taking vows of poverty, chastity and obedience and then going in to a banquet, five courses, each with wine. I went to an ordination party once, a huge affair and very lavish, and my friend John went up to the newly ordained priest and said, 'Bob, if this is poverty, what's chastity?'"

Victor laughed.

"'Anyway, I felt at that time that it had no place for me. I felt like a scarlet woman just walking around in it, as if I befouled it by simply being there, as if I were emanating sex all over the place."

"You emanate, you emanate," he teased.

"I felt as if," she went on seriously, unresponsive to him, "'I was the very person, the One the whole place had been built to exclude. And that my presence here was so serious a breach of its decorum that it was powerful enough to contaminate the whole university. I felt like a bad smell."

Victor was gazing at her in incomprehension. "Why? Why should you? I've never felt like that in my life."

She grimaced. "Of course you haven't, you're male!"

He shrugged, abandoning the discussion. He gazed around them, standing in Radcliffe Camera square. "Well, I don't know. The library's nice, inside. But on the whole the place seems pretty dead to me. It's a museum, that's all."

"Don't you think it's beautiful?"

"I thing it's great, tremendous! Magnificent, really. Impressive. But I can't imagine feeling that I could do anything to it—that you could do anything to it. It's so huge and impervious. The stone just stands, high, silent, dwarfing the people. . . ." He drifted into contemplation, and she observed him with a smile, thinking he must be exhausted and perhaps even embarrassed by his small foray into lyricism. She gazed at the Radcliffe Camera. High, silent, dwarfing the people. Yes. Built to do that. Built to testify to something conceived of as larger than the mere puny humans who walked in and out bearing their own smell of sweat and glands, bearing their own mortality. Blind stone, unwitnessing, nonsignifying. No. Not true. Testifying to something. She caught Victor's arm.

"Why *do* you like it? I mean, what do you like about it?"

He looked at her a little surprised. "Well, it's grand, of course! I mean, the glorious British Empire and all that. Created on the playing fields of Eton, you know. It's damned impressive, we haven't got anything that can compare to it, even though we've tried. . . ." He took her hand and pulled her arm, linked through his, close to his body, and began to walk towards the high iron gates. "Maybe I do understand, a little. It makes me feel a bit like a crude American, you know?"

"Oh, well, that's just an affirmation of a reality," she teased, and he squeezed her hand to hurt it, for just a moment.

"Breaking my fingers in a place like this would really prove your crude Americanism," she said, high and mighty but smiling.

He was reduced to glaring. Some young people, three boys and two girls, were walking their bikes through the gates. They looked pink and white and innocent and unintimidated. To them, all that white or sand-colored stone was simply the housing of rooms to which they went to listen to their betters, the Authorities. In lecture, or on the printed page, or turning the ancient heavy leaves of a manuscript: the voices of the past, wisdom. She stopped and withdrew her arm from Victor's. She looked at the buildings. The light was high, the air was still, the buildings stood, silent. Young people listening to their betters, their elders, learning from them how to be. How to be what? Victories of empire won on the playing fields of Eton, yes. The cruelties of patriarchal education vindicated, reaffirmed: they and only they could produce the hero-warriors necessary for the wars patriarchal society produced. Vicious circle.

She glanced at Victor. No, he would not understand. He was frowning. "Did I really hurt your hand?"

She leaned to him and kissed him lightly. (Was that forbidden in the square? Once, no doubt. Once her mere presence here would probably have been forbidden.)

"Of course not," she lied. (Lying so that he should not feel bad, or lying so that he should not feel powerful?)

They linked arms and left the square and walked down the street past the grandeur, towards the town.

Yes, testifying to all that. To the erection of permanences, the power and glory of God who was really the king, and those who did His work on earth, who were really the male aristocracy. To transcendence, erected on the backs of the undeserving poor, on the sinful bodies of women.

What did the young women studying there now feel? What did she feel for that matter, being invited to give a lecture, being asked to have dinner at high table? Uncomfortable, but flattered, yes, the truth now, tell the truth, flattered to be included at all.

God.

They walked in silence to Cornmarket. "Now I'll show you the real Oxford," she laughed. "Although you've already seen it." (Without seeing.)

Cornmarket is a street only two blocks long, and it is the real center of Oxford. And another world. It is lined with cheap shops selling clothes, handbags, shoes, books. And it is thronged with women.

"When I first came and saw it, I thought: so *this* is where the women are! The men get to have the colleges; the women get to do the marketing."

They stood, then walked slowly down one side of the street and up the other. They passed the crowded cut-rate drugstore, the five-and-dime. The street was dominated by young women who sauntered in pairs, arm in arm, conscious of their stylishness. They were shopgirls and secretaries, out for a Saturday jaunt. Almost all of them had haloes of frizzed hair, long full skirts in flowery cotton prints, frilly blouses and short jackets, nothing warm enough for this brisk day. They trotted along on five-inch heels strapped to their ankles. Their faces had blobs of rouge at the cheeks and dark, almost purple lips. They were all very thin.

Only after you got used to the girls did you see the older women scurrying from shop to shop carrying string bags. They were uniformly shapeless and dowdy, whether they were plump or thin, tall or short. They did not seem to look out at the world at all, they seemed driven by some inner meter that never stopped ticking (forty p, that's three pound ten, and I still have to buy a bit of fish for supper, Joe's shoes will have to wait until next week or perhaps a fortnight it's four o'clock already how the time goes such lines in the five-and-dime the children will be getting in and I still have to roll out the pie dough).

After that, you noticed that there were some men in the street, a few young ones: dark, rough, embarrassed. They did not walk together the way the girls did. When there were two or three in a group, they jostled and teased, they were uncomfortable with themselves, their bodies, their energy.

And finally, you saw the older couples. They walked together in a peaceful comfort one rarely saw in America, as if something important had been settled between them.

Or for them.

Still the girls dominated the street like brilliant-colored birds darting among sparrows and squirrels. And there didn't seem to be any in between. You were young or you were ageless; you were flitting or you were settled.

"This is where the women are. Over here the girls —an infinitely replaceable generation—shine for their hour and give the place its animation, its vividness. Then they turn into the anxious housewives."

"And over there the stone. Standing."

IV

1

ONE DAY after marketing they stopped at the Wykeham, a shop on narrow old Holywell Street, for a cream tea. It is a tiny place, with small tables placed close together.

"Clotted cream. It sounds disgusting."

"Call it Devon cream. Then you can like it."

"What is it, anyway?"

"Just cream that's been set near warmth and allowed to get thick, almost like butter. You spread it on scones. You'll like it."

A young couple sat at the next table talking in low voices. The boy looked like a student—he had that tender-faced pink-and-white protected look, toney. A bit sulky perhaps, but very genteel. The girl looked vigorous, healthy, not as toney as he. Her accent, when Dolores could catch her words, wasn't quite as U as his. They were both pretty, but distressed about something. Victor and Dolores glanced at each other with patronizing parental smiles: Sweet, aren't they? their smiles said.

The young couple's tea arrived. The waitress put the teapot down in front of the young man, the scones and cream near the young woman.

The two of them gazed at the things, then at each other. They hesitated. They seemed baffled. Then the young woman lifted the plate of scones and held it out to the young man. He looked at her in alarm. There was no room on the tiny table for the scones unless the teapot were moved.

He stared at the teapot.

Dolores and Victor glanced at each other with parental amusement: Funny, aren't they? their eyes said.

"Come on," the girl said, wiggling the plate.

Finally, with revulsion, as if lifting the pot would pollute him, he picked up the teapot and handed it to her, took the scones and set them down.

She poured the tea into their cups. Then she gazed at it, then at him. He gazed at her, then at it. Then at her again.

There were tea leaves floating in the cups.

They observed the tea. They looked questioningly at each other. He looked mortified, she looked uncomfortable. They sat.

The waitress passed their table, bringing tea to Dolores and Victor.

"Oh, miss," the girl called in a faint voice, "there's something wrong with the tea."

The waitress glanced at it. "Oh, sorry, luv, the teabag must've burst. I'll bring you a fresh pot." And took the teapot and the woman's cup.

The young couple sat. Victor and Dolores tried not to stare, and tried not to look at each other lest they break out in laughter. Eventually the waitress returned with a pot of tea and a clean cup for the girl. The boy watched, still mortified. The girl poured fresh tea into her clean cup, added cream, and lifted it, about to drink.

"I say!" the boy protested. He sounded near tears. "Gillian, why don't you take this one and let me have that?"

Dolores and Victor stared at him, and although he did not glance at them, he flushed, he felt their looking. The girl stared at him. There was no expression whatever on her face. After long seconds, she lifted her cup and saucer and handed them to him.

"Oh, no, don't!" he protested. "No, don't, don't. Don't be silly, Gill, it's all right, don't!" She kept holding it out to him.

"Take it, then, will you?" she said finally, and he did, his color rising, shaking his head at her, muttering about her foolishness, her silliness.

She poured cream over the floating leaves, and drank the flawed tea.

Victor and Dolores, no longer in danger of laughing, looked at each other.

"But I understand him," Victor said, cycling home. As they put the groceries away: "He's always been waited on—by mama, grandma, aunts, servants probably from the look of him. He was mortified when the teapot was put in front of him. He didn't know what to do. Life in his house has always been carefully ordered, graceful, proper. *Women* pour tea."

"Yes, and it was below his dignity to do a woman's job," Dolores said tartly.

"It was partly unfamiliarity. You get accustomed to things being a certain way and when they're not, it's a shock. It's hard to adjust."

"If a teapot in an unfamiliar place is enough to send him into shock, God help him when he gets out into the world. Selfish little bastard. It seemed to me they were talking about wedding plans. If so, I feel sorry for her."

"But she *did* it, Lorie, doesn't that count?"

"Count for what?"

"As a contributing factor. She participated."

"She felt she had to give in to him. He's used to coming first. Surely you saw that she thought he was behaving like a spoiled child."

"Well, why didn't she *tell* him that, then?" he yowled.

She stopped and looked at him.

"How's he going to discover that the things he does are rotten if she doesn't tell him?"

"Good God, an idiot would know that was selfish! And weak to boot! All he had to do was ask the waitress for a fresh cup. Just speak up. But that was below his dignity too."

"Oh, sweetheart, he's just shy. They both were. You could see they really didn't know how to handle the situation. I can remember when waitresses scared me, can't you?"

"Victor, what's the point of *us* arguing about it? You're right, he couldn't deal with it. He can deal with nothing. A nothing and a selfish bastard, that's what he is. Typical."

"Yes. He couldn't! *Couldn't!* Just like the people you talk about who are culturally brainwashed into inferiority, who can't overcome *their* backgrounds. He can't overcome his!"

They were sitting at the kitchen table. Victor was smoking furiously, drinking a Scotch.

"Are you feeling attacked?"

"Yes!" he barked.

"By me?"

He looked at her, then away. "It's just that I think there are mitigating circumstances, even for him. Of course he's a selfish little beast. But my point is that she helps to keep him that way by assenting to it. So that they participate equally. Share equal blame for it."

"No. Not equal."

"Why in hell not!"

So she got angry too and rapped it out: how she isn't responsible for his character, how you can't talk about equal responsibility or equal blame when there wasn't equal power. How you can't blame an underdog for submitting as much as you can blame an overdog for oppressing. How she'd listened to a white South African expert talking about Biko's separatist movement, and describe how he'd disapproved of it in the beginning, finding it "racist."

"*Rascist!* That's saying that if an oppressed people join together to overthrow the oppressor, *they're* the rascists! That's a Nazi mentality!"

"Jesus Christ! You can't say anything around here without being called a Nazi! I'm not exculpating him! You're so goddamned narrow about things, Lorie!"

Narrow. You have to be narrow when you're at war.

"If she's brainwashed, so is he. They both come out of the same cultural bag. In fact, it's more to her advantage to break out of the old mold, so in some sense, she's even *more* responsible than he is."

"What atrocious logic!" she burst out. "It is *not* to her advantage to break out! Society penalizes women who break out, in tens of ways! She pays the price if she stays in, but she pays a higher one if she breaks out!"

"Really? Are you penalized? You seem to me to get along pretty well."

"The punishment comes in the beginning," she said bitterly. "By the time you're my age, you are hardened to it. You can get beyond it because you don't let yourself feel certain things."

"Like sympathy for men?" he asked nastily, and she glared at him and got up swiftly and walked to the living room.

And broke her rule and lighted a cigar. All his fault. Oh God, all over again. All over again. Sick of this, she was. She didn't want to spend her life fighting, arguing, converting. Didn't want to ruin something that was warm and rich: an idyll. No, you couldn't do it, just go off to a desert island someplace and pretend the world doesn't exist. You brought it with you —it was in your brain cells, in your fucking genes.

I was stupid to imagine we could annul our pasts.

Why doesn't he see? Why doesn't he understand? It's all so clear, but so hard to understand. And beyond that, he doesn't understand why I have to hold so hard to my position, why I can't give an inch.

It's more convenient for him that way. Besides, he was never in your position.

She felt very tired.

Victor came into the living room with a very dark Scotch and a glass of wine for her. "Peace offering?"

She took it, said "Thanks" without smiling, sipped it. Tired.

He sat down opposite her. "I'm sorry," he said.

"For what?" Shrug. Tired, long-suffering voice. "You meant what you said and you said it."

"I'm sorry it upset you this way."

"Things do what they do."

"Well, can we talk about it?"

"Oh, Victor," impatient voice, speaking to a child. "Do you really think talking about this is going to help? When you don't see, you don't understand anything about my most profound convictions, and I can't seem to make you see them? Do you think the two of us aren't as ingrained with things as the two in the tea shop? Even more, because we're older. We tried to come together fresh and new, not dragging the past," her voice grew thick, full of tears, "but we couldn't. *Couldn't,* like your boy. So there we are. I can't accept your position. Can't." Her eyes were glistening and he moved swiftly towards her, and kissed them, wetting his lips on her tears.

The salt stung him, and he laid his head against hers, sitting on the edge of her chair, rocking her gently.

2

AFTER A long silence, she spoke in a thick voice. "Oh, I hear what you're saying. I mean, I heard. I understand. *You* were catered to, *you* were spoiled, by your mother, your wife. You've been selfish. Maybe you still are. And you feel you're not entirely responsible for that. So you don't want to feel the entire guilt. I understand. But I won't absolve you."

"If I want absolution, I'll join a church!" he yelled, pulling away from her.

"Sorry. I was confusing you with most of the other men I meet." Cold and snotty.

He sighed heavily and stared at the floor. He spoke in a low voice, slowly, very calm. "Okay, okay. What I'd like is for you to explain to me why you, an intelligent woman, deny, even get hysterical about a perfectly logical position."

"*I* get hysterical!"

"Well, what *are* you?"

"I'm furious, is what I am. And what were you?"

"Okay." Sigh. Change in voice, turns to her with appeal in his face. "Is it so terrible that I want you to understand my side of things?"

She gazed at him warily. "I guess not."

He sighed deeply. "Well, that's all I was asking for."

As if I didn't already know his side of things. Haven't heard it in replicate all my fucking life. As if there were, apart from a few people, any other side.

"All right," she said.

He turned eagerly, trying to see if she too were

101

eager. She tried to smile, but she felt tired, tired in her bones. "Your wife catered to you," she began.

"My wife LIED TO ME!" he shouted.

Oh, she was tired. She *didn't* want to hear, didn't want to have to listen. She'd heard too many sad songs of marriage, from wives, from husbands, sometimes from both together, or both in turn. She had reached the end of her tolerance—what did they say in business? Victor said it: the bottom line—yes, the bottom line of pain. She could not stand anymore. She thought how nice it would be to get up and take a bath. It would even be nice to get up and do the dishes. What she really wanted to do was get out her notes and work. But that would be too cruel.

Although husbands did that to wives all the time. Walked out on them when they were emotional, saying they had to work.

Well, the point isn't to get even, it's to be decent, isn't it?

Is it? You know being decent always puts you at a disadvantage.

Shit. Power, always power, crisscrossing with the other things, making everything impossible. And love was so hard for her, was impossible for her, because of what it meant to her. Being there for another. Not fidelity in sex. Not being a servant. But utter being there for the other, the way she was for her friends even if they called at two in the morning, even if they needed a place to hide out when she was finishing a manuscript. And for her children whenever they called, whenever they came, whatever they needed.

Why did she feel she owed him this? Would he grant it to her? She looked at him. He might. Then she looked again, shocked. He was gazing into space, he looked gaunt, hollow-eyed, drained of life. He looked old, spectral. He was a walking-around dead man.

She reached out and stroked his head, and he turned to her slowly, suspiciously. She did not try to smile this time, she merely gazed at him and stroked his head. "Your wife lied to you," she said.

"Yes." He relaxed a little, his back slumped. He took her hand and kissed it, then replaced it on her lap, and got up and moved to the other chair. He sat down and sipped his Scotch. He was facing her, he pulled the chair up close to her.

"You see: you go along for so many years doing things a certain way, thinking you're a decent person, well, average anyway, no, damn it, decent, because whatever you're doing, everybody else is doing too, or almost everybody else. And nobody seems to see anything wrong. So you don't *think* about it, really. . . ."

"What kinds of things?"

He shrugged. "Well, all kinds. You know. Little things, like opening car doors for women as if they were too weak to do it themselves. Or carving the roast even though Edith carves better than I do. Fetching drinks. Deferring to women in social situations. Taking out the garbage—whenever I was home to do it. Not ever, ever, dusting a table or clearing a table or washing or drying a dish."

She sighed. Dishes.

"But essentially what I mean is staying in a marriage that's been dead for years, simply because you are married and your wife is a good woman, and because it is wrong, wrong, wrong, to walk out on a woman just because you're missing something, some vitality. Especially a woman like Edith, who never worked, who's devoted her life to me and the kids, to taking care of everything, really. I say I did the 'male' jobs, but in fact, I was almost never home. She really did everything. . . ."

He was watching her face carefully.

Does he think this tale is going to upset me? Does he think I don't already know it, haven't heard it hundreds of times before, couldn't have told it about him?

"Well, so you decide that it is foolish and immature to walk out on such a solid good thing. That's what you call it in your mind. But you are hankering, there's an itch, you want more, it's not enough. She doesn't seem to be unhappy, she seems content with the way things are. So you tell yourself women are different. She has the kids, she has the house, those things really seem to matter to her.

"Whereas, they don't matter to you, much as you try. Oh, the kids are cute, sometimes they're even interesting, but not often. And it is a goddamned pain in the neck to watch them even for a couple of hours, if she goes out on a Saturday afternoon and leaves you to baby-sit. And you can't really grasp her total involvement with them, it seems strange to you. And you tell yourself women are a different species from men, and you shrug, and you accept it."

"Easily."

"Yes." He did not look at her. "And you're already spending two or three nights a week in town, having dinner with so-called important people, and it's not a difficult thing to expand that to four nights a week and cut back on the important people a little. And it's not a difficult thing either to get a little place of your own in town, you can even tell her about this, it's for nights when there are late meetings and you stay over in town. Or you can share one with some of your friends. I didn't though. Share it, or tell Edith. I just got it. But in fact I hardly used it, because they all had their own places, the girls. Wonderful girls—women. It seems an ideal solution. You get the excitement and vitality you've been missing, you keep the solid marriage, the house, the kids, wife's not unhappy, you're happy. It seems," he looked up at her bewildered, "the decent thing to do."

He lighted a cigarette from the stub of the one he was finishing. "It seems ideal, but of course it's not. You hurt the girls—sorry, the women. They get involved but you can't get really involved. You have to hide, be secretive, to some degree at least. Still you go on doing it because it makes you feel alive." He wiped his face with his hand. "And you think your wife must know. After all, it's obvious, isn't it? So many late nights in town, so many business trips that spill over into the weekends. You think she is giving you tacit agreement, saying just don't tell me about it and I won't complain. Maybe she's even grateful, getting the horny bastard to take his horniness elsewhere. She's been dutiful and unenthusiastic for years."

He swallowed a lump of Scotch.

"And then one day your wife, the person all this was for—"

"Or so you told yourself."

He gazed at her. "Yes, I suppose. But it was, wasn't it? She was the one who was happy with the marriage."

"Maybe. But if you'd divorced her, what would you have done? Turned around and married someone else, had more kids, maybe, get a nice settled life with her, and then start the running around all over again. Wouldn't you? I mean, 'all this' was for you, too."

He stared at the floor. "I'd like to think I wouldn't. But maybe. Anyway, Edith rose up one day and recounted a list of my sins a mile long. Seems she's never been happy. Says I kept her from having a career. My God, we got married right after she graduated from Sarah Lawrence, she never wanted to work, she never said a thing about it. And she has this list . . . things I did twenty years ago, for godsakes! Things, she says, that crushed her, wiped her out. But she never told me at the time! How was I supposed to know?"

His voice edged on tears of rage and frustration.

Dolores sat silent. A little sensitivity might have helped, she thought grimly. A little attention to her as a person in her own right, and not just as an extension of you.

"Can you understand how I feel?"

She nodded.

His head drooped. "I took care of her financially. Good care. She could have done anything she wanted to do, we've had a housekeeper for years. I fathered some children for her. I thought that was what she wanted. I thought that was what I was supposed to do. God knows, the kids were hers. . . ." He raised his head and his eyes glistened. "But she says now I've made her a total dependent, unfit for life!"

He lurched to his feet and went into the kitchen for another drink. She hated him like this. Swallowing Scotch in huge gulps, like some insatiable baby. She sipped her wine. And I probably look like some prim disapproving spinster, funneling my pleasures so carefully.

He returned with a fresh drink as dark as the last one, and sat down hard in his chair.

"Thing is," he resumed more calmly, "the sins she

threw at me were like the sins of that jackass in the tea shop today. Selfishness. Total self-absorption. And . . . I guess it's all true. But, Dolores, I swear to you, that's the way I thought things were supposed to be! Stupid, I guess. But as if God, really, or Nature, or something, had made women, my wife, to serve me, to cater to me, to spend her life caring for the kids and the house and me. And had made me, all men, to support her, all women, financially, to give them babies and get treated royally for it. It wasn't a question of believing that with my head. Because I never thought about it. At all. I just lived it, like everybody else."

Dolores was looking grim. Victor did not look at her.

"All those years I thought she was happy. She *acted* happy, damn it! She was thrilled about the job in Dallas. So much money. She was pregnant, that made her happy too. We bought a little house out there. She decorated it, bought all the furniture. Christ, I remember buying up every house magazine on the stands. Then twenty years later she tells me the move to Dallas broke her heart because it separated her from her family and friends. That she was lonely and bored and miserable in Dallas.

"But she never told ME!"

What would you have done if she had?

His eyes were wet again. He turned to Dolores. "She harbors grudges, she stores them up and pours them out in arguments like the stinking water that's left after the flowers in the vase have died."

She watched him suffer.

He hit the arm of the chair with his fist. "I'm sure everything she says is true. Said. But how was I to know? I acted like my father, I loved my father, I acted *better* than my father. My mother worked and did everything in the house too, he never raised a finger. She paid the taxes, mowed the lawn, paid the bills. I never asked Edith to do things like that."

"Too hard for her," Dolores said nastily.

He glanced at her and down. "Maybe."

She thought: he is changing before my eyes. Realizing. How happy that should make Edith. And he's good, he really is. He's *feeling* this, it matters to him. Most men would toss it off with a she's-a-bitch-and-that's-life shrug, not really caring. Go on finding their pleasures elsewhere—at work, with the boys, with other women. So he's better than most men. But does that make him good enough?

She said: "But you changed."

He turned his face away from her. "Yes."

"Is she happier now?"

She could sense his tightness from where she was sitting, sense his whole body as a knot of muscles. But she did not reach out to him. He was tied in the configuration of his own pain, in which she would be an intruder. And besides, she recognized with dismay, she did not at that moment like him very much.

"I've changed as much as she'll allow me to." He sat up straight and looked at her. "You know, if what happened to those kids at the tea shop had happened to Edith and me, she would have insisted I take the fresh cup. I wouldn't have had to ask. And years ago, I would have taken it. I wouldn't now. But it wouldn't make her happy that I didn't take it. You see? She wants it both ways." He was growling, glaring at the wall. "She wants to keep her old ways so that she won't feel guilty. But she wants to blame me for them, so she can justify her anger. But her anger is against the fact that she learned the old ways in the first place. And nowadays—she never shows her anger, never. She's always sweet, always smiling."

His face appealed to her. "Can you see why I feel a little—unjustly accused about all this?"

My foot you don't want absolution.

But there are women, you've met some, who stay in a marriage, especially in a wealthy one, even though they're stultified, and blame the man for that.

Ah, but it's because they're too frightened: poverty and independence are terrifying things.

His pain was like a fog, a dampness in the room. She had to say something.

"I understand what you say, how you feel. I'm sympathetic to Edith, too, though. It's too hard for me to give judgment on such a thing, and I think that's what you're asking me for. I mean, my suspicion is that you could have known what Edith was feeling if you'd wanted to. It was more convenient not to. Whereas if she'd told you what she was feeling, your marriage would have been in trouble. I'd guess."

He stared at her.

"But I can't stand all this, Victor. These situations. The personal. It's so harrowing. We all get caught in the world's traps and toss around in a web we've helped to weave, unable to free our arms and legs, tied in them forever. It's intolerable to me. And we look for someone to blame. And sometimes there's someone handy," she smiled, putting her hand on his arm. "Someone who maybe deserves a bit of blame. But I try, I guess I'm an emotional coward these days, I try hard to avoid involving myself in such things. I try to concentrate on the universal, the abstract, to look for the larger cultural patterns that make us so miserable, to get to the bases of these things, the sociological, psychological, intellectual bases. So I don't have to deal with this: with you, with Edith. With pain."

He was hurt. He heard her saying she didn't want to listen to him. And she was unable to think of a single thing to say that would soften what he felt, moderate what she'd said.

3

DOLORES WAS walking home from the bus stop in the teeming rain, when a car pulled over and stopped.

"Want a lift?" Mary Jenkins's head, shrouded in yellow plastic, stuck out of the car window.

Dolores got in for the half-block ride. The women were laughing. "I'm soaked!" Dolores cried. "The rain's gone clear through my raincoat, my jeans, even my underwear is wet!"

"Yes, rain is one thing the British do better than anybody else," Mary said mock-proudly.

They ran up the path to the house and shook themselves off in the front hall.

"You are a sight! You should get a slicker, like

mine. Why don't you get yourself dried off and come down and I'll give you a nice warming glass of sherry."

Mary's old-fashioned kitchen was primitive by American standards. No appliances except a tiny fridge and an old gas stove. A high-backed sink with two spigots. An electric kettle, a mesh basket to be placed over the gas for making toast.

But it was lovely. Light poured through the high windows facing the garden. An old wooden hutch held odd plates, cups, pitchers, all different, lovely old china used every day. Wooden table, well worn. Wooden cabinet with shelves above it, open shelves showing the few cans, the pound of sugar, the small bags of good coffee. And mess everywhere. Half a loaf of bread sat on the breadboard, a knife beside it, crumbs all around it. Open jam jar, butter soft and oozy from sitting out, soiled coffee cups, plates, an earthen jug and strainer that Mary used as a coffeepot.

Dolores felt completely at home.

Mary moved around the kitchen, doing things as she talked, but nothing she did seemed to clear the mess. She appeared to be constantly in motion—perhaps it was merely that she gestured a great deal, maybe it was her alert intelligent eyes constantly changing expression. For her face was calm and composed, yet she never seemed still.

It was quiet in the flat. "Where are your children?" Dolores asked.

"With their father. He has them most of the time. He has custody," she added in a thin dry voice.

"Oh." Pause. What on earth could she have done, that he got custody? Walked the streets? Taken drugs? Beat them? But maybe she didn't want them: she was so busy.

"You're so busy—always running, every time I see you."

"Oh, yes, frightfully. That damned qualifying exam, you know. Plus my surgery and the hospital work. I'm done in, really."

"I don't understand why you have to take a qualifying exam at this stage."

"Well, I'm trying to qualify as a specialist, you see

109

—in internal medicine. I've been studying for two years, squeezing it in between office hours and rounds and trying to see the children. It's very difficult, because there's an oral exam and the board is all male. They give women an extraordinarily hard time. If you try to be agreeable, they say you're not serious, and if you try to be serious, they say you're abrasive. There's not an awful lot of room in between. It might be a teeny bit easier if I were going for pediatrics or even gynecology. They could accept that more readily."

"Maybe you should put your hair in a bun." Mary's long dark hair hung midway down her back.

Mary giggled. "Do you really believe that would help?"

"You know men," Dolores laughed.

"Yes, of course. Someone my age with long hair might just . . . well, good heavens, might just do anything at all, actually. Smoke pot, or take lovers. And does, in fact. You're right. Bun it is." She sighed. "It's stacked against me anyway, though. One of the men on the board is a friend of my former husband's."

Another bad divorce. Don't tell me about it. Please.

"And Roger has great prestige in Oxford, great—what you Americans call—credibility. Ugly word, but useful, I guess." She laughed again. She had a tinkly laugh, silvery, like a little girl's. And her manner was gay and light and appealing.

"Roger Jenkins? The physicist?"

"That's the one."

"How long have you been divorced?"

"Four years. I had to, you see. He tried to kill me." Oh god. Please don't tell me.

But Mary did. She poured it out as easily and smoothly and quietly as milk from a jug in a Vermeer painting. She never speeded up, she never slowed her pace. Composed, a minuet, her telling. She paused occasionally to sip her sherry, or to pour more sherry into their glasses. Dolores interrupted her occasionally to ask a question, to get things clear. Mary was not always as coherent as Dolores would have liked, and it was only that—her hopping from thing to thing without providing background—that seemed distraught.

110

But she told her tale calmly, often smiling, her face impassive when she told the worst parts.

And there were lots of worst parts.

Finally Dolores burst out: "How can you sit there smiling?" She was enraged, she wanted to break crockery, or a head; she wanted to leap up, to *do* something, *something!*

"It doesn't do to get angry in this country. People hold it against you."

"Can't you appeal?"

"I have no money. They pay very little at the National Health. I had to borrow from my mother to pay for the last trial. And she's a widow and can't afford it, really."

"That judge should be disbarred! De-seated! Defrocked! Whatever they do to judges," Dolores stormed.

"Yes," Mary smiled evenly. "Extraordinary, isn't it."

Dolores put her head in her hands. Damned three sherries hadn't helped. Like having the dry heaves: wanting to cry, needing to cry, not being able. Pillar of salt.

"My plan," Mary said sweetly, "or at least what I hope for is that I'll pass the qualifying exam, and then I should get a bit more money. The National Health doesn't promote women often, but they'll have to do something for me. And then the rent from the flat. Gordon and I did it ourselves, created that flat. This used to be a one-family house. We put in a kitchen upstairs and a bath down, and walled off the stairwell. So I could get a bit more money. Then, perhaps in a couple of years, I'll have saved enough to appeal."

"And in the meantime?"

"I see the children as often as I can. Whenever Roger doesn't stop me."

Dolores's throat was full of pain, but there wasn't a tear in Mary's eye. Maybe there's something wrong with me. Certainly if she has to live this way it's better that she be calm about it, accept it.

I couldn't, though.

"The trouble is, they're so young, they don't understand And Roger turns them against me. Elise is only

111

five, she doesn't see what's happening, but Linton is nine. I can see what it's doing to him. He's angry with me, feels, I guess, that I've abandoned them. And then, Roger tells them I'm crazy, it's been his sole line of defense all along. And they start to see me that way. You know if you start with the notion that someone is mad—anyone at all—they begin to *look* mad. Whatever they do seems insane. If I drop something, or I forget something, they look at each other and roll their eyes. Of course, they live in a far more orderly household. Roger has a housekeeper. I have to juggle this"—she waved at the kitchen—"with a full practice and studying for the exam. I read all night, or nearly. I get only five hours' sleep a night. But it's all right, actually, I don't mind."

"Reading the books the judge damned you for."

"Yes," she laughed. "Extraordinary, isn't it. Anyway, every time I have them, it takes me a day or more just to get them to accept me, to act normal. Linton baits me, taunts me. He's unhappy. He doesn't understand that I want to be with them. He doesn't understand that it isn't my fault."

Dolores nodded heavily.

"So I try, but I have them only two days, three at the most, and then they go back with him. And I don't see them for another two weeks. Three now, thanks to the lovely judge. And then I have to start all over again."

Dolores put her head in her hands. *Her children! Her children!* She raised her head. Her fists were tight, her teeth were clenched.

"I'd kill. I'd kill."

Mary smiled at her with pity.

"Can you poison his food? Arrange an accident? Get a voodoo doll?"

"I can't even pray for him to die," Mary said quietly, "because you see, the children love him. He's good to them, he really is. Now. I shudder to think what will happen when they get older. But now . . . they'd be desolate if he died."

Dolores stared at the table. She wanted to be out of here. She examined Mary's pretty softly-lined pink-and-white face, her wispy long hair, her expressive, moving hands. Dolores searched for weakness, for something she could blame. Her storytelling *had* been a little incoherent, hadn't it? Maybe Roger was right, maybe she was crazy. Maybe she didn't really love her children.

Dolores looked at herself. She wanted to blame Mary, wanted to find something she could pin the blame on. She wanted to be able to say: this could never happen to *me*. *I* would never allow myself to get into such a position. She brought this on herself.

Knowing, of course, that this could happen to any woman, that it was just a question of luck. Some of us lose our children.

Her eyes filled with tears.

Mary sat calmly, smiling sadly at her. As if I'm doing her fucking feeling for her. Goddamned good manners. Well, I can have good manners too.

She rose. "Mary, if there's anything I can do, please ask."

"Of course." Mary rose too. "Do come down for dinner some weekend when Gordon's here, will you? I've told him about you. I'd like you to meet him."

"Lovely."

They embraced each other lightly, touched cheeks lightly, in recognition, in mutuality, in acceptance of a kinship far deeper than nation.

4

AND DRAGGED herself upstairs and poured some of Victor's Scotch in a glass and hauled herself to her bed and fell on it. Just lay there, head propped up on the pillows, sipping. Her breath was coming in heavy sighs, almost shudders. She felt as if she'd been beaten about the heart and gut.

The old salt pool. Can't get out of it. Every time I try, something heaves up from the bottom and drags me down again. My own private Loch Ness monster.

Terribly tired. Wanted to sleep, her body wanted to sleep. Forever. Never to have to wake up again, never to have to feel again. It was possible, of course. It was not difficult to kill yourself if you were determined to do it. She thought of it often, it was a good thought. Knowing you *could* end this corrosion of your innards, knowing that if you lived another day it was through your own choice, made life seem less oppressive.

Doomed. Doomed. It's me who's Lot's wife. She didn't even have a name, and she didn't have anything to say about anything. She stands there forever gazing down at the cities of the plain as the smoke rises, the brimstone falls. Stands there in Zoar, a word that means "scarcely anything." Yes, scarcely anything. Her husband, two daughters, a pack on her back. The daughters don't have names either, even though they screwed their father and continued his line. But not yet, not then. Still virgins. Only men have names in this story.

Lot's wife has trudged out of Sodom behind her husband, carrying what she can on a pack on her back: scarcely anything. The girls are there too, dawdling. Lot is smacking them on the rear to hurry them up. The old woman sighs, what is he doing now? This man, this very good man who is her husband. The night before this very good man had offered his daughters, *her* daughters, to the crowd of angry men pounding at the door. The men wanted the strangers Lot had brought home from the town gate, acting like a big deal, liked to feel important. He said the two men were angels. Angels already! The crowd wanted to bugger and roll the strangers. This good man had offered them his daughters instead. The strangers, he said, were more important than his daughters. Angels! Devils is more like it. Terrorist spies. Because look now, look!

Oh, but she's really too far off to see the cities burn. All she can see is the smoke. But she sees, she sees, in her mind's eye. She sees and she hears. She sees the marble pillars of the temple crack and disintegrate, she hears the crack, the terrible crash as the roof caves in and dust rises and blanks out everything. She hears the licking sound of the flames swiftly devouring the houses, the screams of children, the cries of dogs running on fire. They're being burned up, her two married daughters. They should be here, in Zoar with her, but their husbands laughed at Lot and his angels. What if he'd said terrorists: they might have believed that. But now they are burning, her Miriam, her Sarah, her five grandchildren. She sees the little ones running in circles, hiding their heads in their hands, crying *Mama!* Miriam is gathering Ben-ami in her skirt, she has little Piti in her arms, she is searching for Sarah, calling to her. But Sarah can't move, she was always timid, she is calling for *her, her,* calling *Mama! Mama!* Her children cling to her legs, whimpering. Miriam shouts that they should head for the palm grove, for the well, for someplace wet, someplace maybe safer. But Sarah can't move, and Lot's wife sees her drop, right there, on that spot, calling *Mama!*

Lot won't look. He has commanded her and the girls not to look. But she doesn't care what he says. Last night she divorced him in her mind. What should she worry about now? She should go on living on this earth? With *him?* After this? For it was those very men, his friends, his angels, who had brought this fire and brimstone, who were at this very instant murdering her Miriam, her Sarah, the five little ones, oh, my little Piti with the great black eyes!

Is it any wonder she turned into a pillar of salt? Nameless to this day, unimportant in the great male sweep of history, one who looked back, one who dared to see, one who dared to feel.

The old man and the daughters crept up to the hills and hid out. The story goes they waited until he was asleep and then crept to him and screwed him. What a crock. Impossible that he didn't know what they were doing. Trying to save their father from that fate worse than death: dying sonless. Story told by men, dishonest. Lots of daddies liked to diddle their little girls. And what can you do with a pillar of salt when you're horny?

She got up a little shakily and headed for the kitchen for more Scotch. Get drunk. Haven't been drunk in years. Victor's influence, blame Victor, she told the walls, throwing her arms out wide in a sweep of irresponsibility.

Fury. It was fury that was destroying her. But it

wouldn't go away. She stood stock-still in the middle of the kitchen and closed her eyes. She felt like a pillar of tears that wouldn't come out, petrified into salt.

There was a noise, a click, and she turned. Victor was coming through the door. He looked at her and smiled. She stared at him.

"Did I frighten you? I called, for a couple of hours, but there wasn't any answer. Then I had to run for my train. Is something wrong?"

He came in, hung his coat on the hall rack, and entered the kitchen. He stood looking at her. "Lorie? Are you all right?"

He wavered in front of her eyes. What was his name? Lot. Yes. Must be, since I'm Lot's wife. But I have a name. He doesn't know it though, he calls me something else.

He approached her slowly, he put his hand on her arm. "Lorie?"

"Go away."

He let his hand fall, but stood there looking at her. "Are you sick?"

"Yes."

"What is it?"

"It's my heart." She walked to the table and sat beside it, clumping her glass down.

He sat opposite her. He took her hand. "You're sick in your heart."

"Yes. It bleeds. There's no cure for it. And it won't go away, even when I ignore it."

"Sweetheart, have you been drinking?"

She nodded.

"Have you eaten anything?"

She shook her head.

"I think you're sick in your belly, too. It's after eleven." He got up and took some eggs out of the fridge and scrambled them. He made toast. Dolores stumbled around the kitchen making herself another drink.

"I don't want that. I'm not hungry," she said petulantly. But when he set the food in front of her, she gobbled it, she scooped it up. When she finished, he took her hands in his.

"Now. What's wrong with your heart?"

"I told you. It bleeds. All the time. Goddamned bleeding heart."

He lifted her up and put his arm around her and walked her into the bedroom. He undressed her and slipped her nightgown on over her head. He helped her to the bed and pulled up the covers and sat down beside her.

"What are you doing here anyway."

"There was a meeting called out here, last-minute thing. I told them I'd be coming out tomorrow, and didn't book the Randolph. So we could have a night together."

"I'm glad," she said and reached for him and held him. Then she pushed him away. "But you came here without calling! You're taking me for granted! How could you be sure I wouldn't be entertaining one of my other lovers?"

He smiled at her sadly. "If you were, I'd sleep on the couch. I did call."

"Oh, I was down at Mary's." Tears sprang into her eyes. "Oh, Victor!"

"Wait. Wait a minute!" He jumped up and ran into the kitchen, came back with a tall Scotch, and sat down again. He took her hand. "Now tell me."

"It's Mary. She told me the story of her divorce. It did me in."

"Her divorce did *you* in?"

"Yes, you see, that's why I can't. There are things I can't do, and I know it. I can't drink. And I can't listen to these stories. Like people who bruise if you even touch them, you know? Their skin turns purple if you just press your thumb on their inner arm. Well, I have a soul like that, it's raw. The only thing that can help it is getting angry, but who am I going to get angry at? I can't go and bash Roger over the head. There's nothing I can do with my anger, you know? It just sits around steaming. And eventually, it turns into this."

"Into what this?"

"This: the way I am now."

He stroked her head. "It's all right—the way you are now."

117

"No, it's not. You don't know what it feels like inside."

He held her against him, smiling a little, kissing her hair.

"Mary used to be married to Roger Jenkins, THE Roger Jenkins, the physicist, you know?" She pulled away so she could see his face. He nodded. His face was a little stiff. He doesn't want to hear this. Doesn't want to be dragged through it. Damn it, I had to listen to him, he can listen to this.

"Well, turns out this Jenkins, the great man, let out his excess energy not on the squash court but on his wife's body. He began by just sort of pushing her, the way Anthony used to do to me when I tried to leave the house during his tantrums. But Roger moved on to bigger and better things: slaps across the face, bloody mouths, a little arm-twisting. One night, after they came home from a party, they'd been married about eight years then, he was furious about something, and he punched her as she got out of the car. He knocked her to the garage floor. Then he bent down and picked up her head and smashed it down on the floor, over and over. She passed out.

"When she came to, he was gone, the garage was dark. He'd just left her there like that. She was bleeding and she felt sick, but she was afraid to go into the house. She believed he'd meant to kill her, and would if he saw her. She got herself up somehow and crept out of the garage and walked to a public phone and called a cab. She went to her mother's house, then to the hospital. She had a concussion. She said she'd fallen. Didn't want to damage the Great Man! Damned fool."

Victor lay back on the bed facing her, and lighted a cigarette.

"After she got out of the hospital, she stayed with her mother. She had no money, no job. She'd given up her medical practice when Linton was born, and had chosen to stay home with the children while they were small. Linton was four then, Elise was only an infant. When she was better, she went to see her children. Roger had hired a housekeeper with orders not to let her in.

118

"She got a job, saved some money, and took him to court. But all that took time. She rented a house as near to Roger's as she could—she couldn't really afford his neighborhood. And when she could, she'd walk there to see the children if they were outdoors. She went as often as she could. Roger brought charges against her for harassment. Harassment! Her *own* children!"

Her voice grew thick. "Elise had nearly forgotten her, and Linton was sulky with her, angry that she'd abandoned him—as he saw it. Eventually, they got a divorce and Mary was given the right to have the children for a weekend *every two weeks,* every *two* weeks, Victor! And ordered not to set foot in Roger's house. The judge said Mary had abandoned the children. Roger said Mary was crazy and had invented the stories of his brutality. Roger is a Big Name in Oxford, he has lots of money for lawyers, a big house, a housekeeper. He's legitimate and respectable. Mary isn't.

"Well, that wasn't bad enough, but then Linton got the measles and couldn't come to Mary's. And measles is a serious disease, and Mary is a doctor. So she went to see him, she went every day, she pushed the housekeeper aside and went in. (More crazy behavior, Roger claimed.) He brought charges against her. He mustered a strong case, and she didn't expect it, she didn't have things mustered against him. He brought witnesses to testify—her *friends,* Victor! Women don't stick together in this country—to testify that she had a lover. She does, but so does Roger, but she hadn't thought to get witnesses against him. He got her friends to testify that while the children were with her, she sometimes sat there reading books.

"And the judge found for Roger. He said any woman who would read books while her children were with her was not a fit mother. Mary said she was a doctor and could care for the children better than Roger, but the judge decided, in whatever place judges indulge their eminence, that she was only an 'embryo doctor'! I guess because she had given up her practice for a few years. And he reduced her access to the children from every two weeks to every three!

"All this has taken years. Linton is nine now. Elise is five. They're a little disturbed, judging from what Mary says. Roger tells them their mother is crazy. And she, poor thing, says nothing, she doesn't want to turn them against him, doesn't want to confuse them any further. Doesn't want to drive them mad. It's like Solomon with the two putative mothers—except the wrong mother won. Roger doesn't mind tearing his kids up if it increases his power against her. He must know that the best thing for them is to love both their parents, be with both of them. Fathers," she concluded bitterly.

She sipped her Scotch and looked around for her cigars. Victor found them, and lighted one for her.

"Thing is, I don't think she knows how to get angry."

"Roger takes care of that department," Victor said grimly.

"And so," Dolores's voice went high and funny, "she's lost her children!" Her mouth was twisted, her forehead was wrinkled, her hands were fists.

Victor sat down beside her again, took her hands in his, untwisted them, and chafed them lightly, as if they were cold.

"Can she appeal?"

"She has no money."

"Listen, Lorie: I don't want to see you suffer like this. Try to look at it this way: she *did* leave them."

She leaped up, furious-eyed. "She had no money! No home! And he is decent to the kids, she says. Although God knows how he'll treat them when they get old enough to talk back to him."

"Sweetheart." Patient. Calm. "It's terrible. But would you have left your children with Anthony when you left him?"

"Never! Never!" Fierce. Then she subsided. "But Anthony wasn't trying to kill me."

"Sure he was."

"What do you mean? You don't even know anything about Anthony."

"No." Head down, looking away, at the carpet, or at the baseboard. "But I know what I was like years

120

ago." He looked at her. "I think I might have tried to kill you—one way or another."

"Why!"

"To keep you."

"Pumpkin shell."

"Something like that."

She mused. "Yes, but it's not the same as physically killing somebody. He just left her on that garage floor. She might have bled to death, and he'd have been up on murder charges. He didn't even care. He's not a stupid man, he had to know. I think he's the one who's crazy. And besides, the reason you're saying that—well, I understand. It's because the whole thing is intolerable. So to make it more tolerable—to you, to me—we want to say: oh, well, her children don't mean as much to her. Or, she participated. That makes us feel better. But I don't think it's true."

Victor was staring at his hands.

She put her hand on his and he looked up at her. "I think I was drunk," she smiled.

"You certainly were," he laughed.

"I shouldn't drink."

"Well, nothing terrible happened."

"You should have seen me before you came."

"What were you doing?"

"Feeling. Just feeling."

"Because of Mary."

"Oh," she shrugged, "because of Mary, yes. But it's my own life, my own children I weep for, really, I think. Anthony. My mother. My father. My grandmother, for god's sakes," she laughed.

He stroked her forehead.

"Anthony was a terrible father. Of course, he couldn't be a decent father, he was only a little kid himself. Throwing tantrums all the time. He totally dominated the household, not by being macho, but by being a baby throwing tantrums."

"Maybe that's what macho really is."

She smiled at him, and interwound her fingers with his. "You know, you're really a feminist."

He smiled back. "I have two daughters."

"Yes." And I have one.

"They keep me on my toes."

121

Victor's face looked tired, the lines in it were shadowed, but his eyes looked right at her, he was being there for her although he'd probably rather be someplace else, anyplace else, or at least, making love or sleeping.

"Here you could have stayed in London and gone to a nice British comedy, and you had to come down and listen to this. Aren't you sorry?"

"There is no place in the world I'd rather be," he said, sounding as if he meant it.

She tried to put it to music. "Isn't there a song like that?"

He rumpled her hair. Hard.

"Anthony used to pick on the kids. Well, on Tony. For everything, all the time. Constantly. It happened as soon as Tony could toddle around, when he was still in diapers. And I began—it wasn't conscious, it happened, I slid into it—I began to stand between him and them. I tried to keep them separate. On the one hand, I tried to talk to Anthony, to tell him what he was doing. On the other, I tried to shield them from him, to feed them separately when I could, to ignore the punishments he laid on them like stripes, to keep them from doing things I knew would make him furious.

"By the time they were nine, ten, eleven, someplace around there, I had come to feel that my children were MY children. Mine. Totally. I didn't want him to have any part of them, I felt he didn't deserve them. I didn't want him to have any influence on them. I wanted more than anything in the world to nullify him. But I couldn't. They were nine, ten, eleven. They'd been listening to his screaming, his picking for all their little lives."

She wavered a little in her bed, her eyes closed as if she were dizzy. "I felt it passionately," she said with a thick voice, "that they were mine and he had no right to destroy them. And I felt that for Mary, you see."

"I see," he said. "But Mary's experience is different. You say she says her husband's good to the children."

"Yes," she sighed.

He nudged her. "Awake?"

She opened her eyes. They were wet. "Yes. But you see, I did what she did, too. I abandoned my children. Not physically, but morally. I should have taken them away from him when they were babies, as soon as I realized how he was, but it took me years to realize he was always going to be like that. But I should have taken them away. No matter how we had to live, it would have been better than that. But I didn't. I didn't," she whispered.

5

IT RAINED all weekend and they drooped around the apartment. They turned on the electric fire in the sitting room and closed the door so the room got warm, and worked—Dolores reading and taking notes in the big ugly rocker, Victor at the table, scribbling figures, studying a huge pamphlet of mimeographed notes. After some hours, they sighed, and turned to each other: "Want to play gin rummy?" Victor asked.

But that bored them too, in time. They kept falling into conversation, idle conversation, until Victor said: "You know, that's the third time you've mentioned Anthony today. After all these weeks with not a word about him. I think he's on your mind."

"Probably because of Mary."

"Why? Was he like Roger?"

"No. Not at all that I can tell, not having met Roger. Anthony was beige, blond, and blue."

Victor laughed. "And smoked a pipe."

"He did!" she exclaimed. "You peeked!"

"How did you come to marry him?"

Now, how could you tell someone that? So complicated it was, you couldn't tell yourself. How he lowered his head in a self-deprecating way and raised his eyes to look up at you, coyly, the way a baby does. How he talked baby talk and wanted to be fondled, all the time. But then held his head up like a little boy, an earnest little boy scout, saying that what he really believed in was honor, duty, country, and said it without the slightest irony. He believed it. Or, he believed that he believed it. For how could he believe anything when he didn't even know what he felt?

"It's boring. And complicated. I'm not sure I understand it myself."

How he wormed his way into your heart: sweet, adoring, playful. Looking at you with big baby eyes and biting his lower lip, keeping his teeth showing as he lost at cards, checkers, wrestling, running, at everything. Whenever we competed he lost. He said: You're so strong, honey. And I believed it. I believed it!

"Did you identify him with—Gregory Peck, or somebody like that? Did you associate him with someone whose image had enchanted you?"

She shook her head. "The only male images that ever enchanted me were Ivan Karamazov, but I always knew he was me, and Mr. Darcy in *Pride and Prejudice,* and then later, Laurence Olivier playing him. But I knew Anthony was no Darcy. I knew there *were* no Darcys. Why? Did you?"

"Did I ever! My image was a cross between Shakespeare's Rosalind and his Cleopatra, and June Haver. Poor Edith had her work cut out for her!"

"You imposed . . . ?"

"I," he paused, *"expected."*

"Poor Edith."

"Yes." Dully.

Darcy: proud, controlled, independent, graceful, sensitive, compassionate. Yes, but also *legitimate*: aristocratic, wealthy, part of Society. And under it all, passionate, as passionate as Heathcliff. But I think I invented that: I don't think Jane Austen put that in. And all I got in the end was Heathcliff.

"So why did you marry him?" Victor repeated.

"He was sweet. He loved me. He admired my mind. He knew I wanted to do scholarship and that seemed to please him. He was loving to his mother and to all the children in his family, his cousins. He seemed stable, except for an occasional attack of jealousy— entirely unwarranted. But I thought those would disappear when we got married."

And why don't you tell the rest? That you were in

the army and running an obstacle course. You had run the first hurdles: grade school, high school, college. After that came marriage, children, and happily-ever-after. It never even occurred to you that you had any other choice. Admit it.

"And under everything, under the beige, blond, and blue, under a certain childlikeness that Anthony had, I sensed a terrific intensity. Passion. Intensity still draws me, it's a magnet for me. And I also sensed that Anthony had a fidelity I didn't have. I had never—and still have never—felt that anyone, anyone at all, was the one and only person I wanted to be with. Except at moments; there are many moments when I feel that way. But I've never felt I wanted to spend the rest of my life with just one person.

"I can't help that, you know. I really can't," she pleaded.

Victor looked at her strangely. "I understand," he said, but his voice didn't sound right.

"It's just not my nature," she insisted. She stared at him. "What's wrong?"

He laughed uncomfortably. "I thought only men had that disease."

"Is it a disease? It seems normal to me, except there are people who aren't like that, who really are monogamous. It's always seemed unfair to me that the rules were all set up in their favor. I always felt there were thousands of wonderful people in the world and I wanted to know them all. And I wanted to screw all the beautiful, sexy men," she grinned. "Until awhile ago, anyway."

He smiled, but his smile wasn't right. "Well, with you, at least, I don't have to apologize for my past."

She gazed at him. "But you wish you did, don't you," she guessed.

He did not answer. "So he was going to be faithful while you screwed around."

Aha. Doesn't like the arrangement turned around.

"No." She was tired. "The point was that his fidelity would keep me faithful too. His leash was my leash: and he'd always have his fixed firmly in one spot. His passion and his possessiveness would root me to my place. Because in those days, I thought there was something wrong with me. I thought I was coldhearted, not like other people. Certainly not like other women. I thought Anthony's example would teach me how to be a decent human being, to feel what other people claimed they felt."

Song I loved then: Sarah Vaughan singing, "I'm not the kind of a girl for a boy like you." Or was it "You're not the kind of a boy for a girl like me"? Whatever, she was a tramp and he was a knight. Yes. And you loved the baby talk and the coyness too. Why don't you tell the truth? Anthony made you feel that he looked up to you so much that his admiration annulled the edge, the privilege men always have over women. Made you feel safe, made you feel you two could be equals. Not knowing then about what you have to pay for what you get.

Victor seemed to relax a bit. "So you enjoyed his possessiveness."

"I didn't know what possessiveness was. I knew he tried to come between me and my friends, tried to cut me off. But he had so many friends himself that I believed him when he said he didn't like my friends because they were x or y, which his friends weren't. I thought my standards just weren't as high as his. Although, in fact, I didn't like most of his friends. But I liked some, and that was enough to reinforce his message.

"And then, we did have ecstasy. I remember one night when I was still in college, and we went out late. The night was very black, and they were putting a building up somewhere in Cambridge. It was just scaffolding then, and Anthony said: Let's climb it! So we did. We took off our shoes and began. We mounted higher and higher, terrified, at least, I was. I'm pretty sure he was too. The higher we got, the more splendid the view was down below us. We could see for miles, the lights sparkled like colored stars: mostly white, but red, green, and yellow too. When we got to the top, we both took off all our clothes. We'd never seen each other naked before. It was ecstatic—his body gleaming, the lights below, the wide sky, velvet blue with a mound of dark clouds low on the horizon, more like a fluffy comforter than a threat. . . .

"And Anthony got along with people, at least it seemed that way then. He seemed humane and tolerant in ways I wasn't. I admired that."

Yes, he got along with his friends, not with yours. He seemed humane and tolerant because he tolerated fools. Such dopey guys he hung out with, fools who talked about nothing, laughed about everything. The most hilarious subject was drinking, I never knew why. And fuckups. Inadequacy. Men making fools of themselves. I didn't understand that either, then.

"The people in school with me were terribly intellectual. They intimidated me, but I always had this lurking suspicion that they were phonies. Something Anthony clearly wasn't. At least not in the same way. At least so it seemed then. . . ."

"You took his possessiveness for great love," Victor said.

"Yes. And his lack of intellectual pretension for genuineness."

"It wasn't?"

She shrugged. "What's genuine? I think the word ought to be reserved for describing leather, the way I think 'pure' should be reserved only for butter or milk," she smiled, shakily. "Oh, I think it was the Anthony of his stories that I fell in love with, really. And when I had to leave him, it was leaving that Anthony that broke my heart."

"Stories?"

"He used to tell me stories about his childhood. Not anything spectacular, just what happened to him when he was growing up. And I fell in love with that little boy, and sometimes Anthony was that little boy. But mostly he wasn't. It took me years to discover that the real Anthony, the Anthony of the stories, wasn't ever going to come out and play. And that Anthony faded, year by year. I divorced the Anthony I lived with, a person I disliked intensely. But it nearly killed me to give up the Anthony of the stories.

"So I guess you were right. It wasn't Darcy or Karamazov—it was a boy in a tale. . . . I remember one that wasn't a childhood story, or was just on the edge. He was seventeen or eighteen, and in the air force. Like you, he enjoyed being in the service. He was in

127

training, in OCS, someplace out west but east of the Rockies. He was very young, even for his age, and the guys in his unit called him 'Sweets' and took care of him. His best friend was an older guy, the unit Lothario, something Anthony admired enormously then. This friend would have a date every weekend with some woman in L.A. or San Francisco, and would have her get one for Anthony too.

"Whenever they had a weekend pass, and I guess that was most weekends, and there was nothing to do in the desert where they were, a bunch of guys would get together and con some pilot into taking up an old plane that was used only for training and couldn't go far. They'd talk him into flying them to California for the weekend.

"But the plane was really weak, it had trouble getting over the mountains. So whenever the pilot wanted to get the nose up to climb above some peak, he'd yell: BACK! And everybody would run to the rear of the plane. But then he had to level out, to get the nose back down, so he'd yell: FRONT! And they'd all run forward.

"He'd tell this story with a nice, gentle, self-deprecating laugh. It was his kind of story, it had just the right elements. A little derring-do, at least by my protected standards. A little risk. And considerable incompetence. All wrapped in humor. It seemed he was laughing at himself, and I loved him for that. . . ."

6

"WHAT DID he do?"

Tired. Tired. Why was Victor cross-examining her?

"I told you. He worked in his father's mail-order house."

"Oh, yeah. Did he do well?"

"You mean did he make money? He did all right. Nothing sensational. But I worked too, so we were comfortable. But that was later. In the early years, he dallied, couldn't decide, and we were always in

128

trouble. I remember being pregnant with Elspeth."
Tired, tired. "I was still working days as a typist.
Nights I was studying for my M.A. Anthony had quit
his job again, although the baby was due in a month
or so. The rent was due, so I paid it, and then realized
I had no more money. We had no money for food. I
got a little panicked, because the baby was due in
a month and I suddenly realized I wouldn't be working anymore for a while. And I tore into the living
room with my watermelon of a belly and I yelled at
him: 'Anthony, we haven't any more money! There's
no money for food!' He was reading the paper, and
when I said that, he threw the paper down and threw
me a disgusted look and stormed out of the house. He
came back a couple of hours later and threw twenty
dollars at me. He never told me where he got it. From
his mother, I guess. He got it from her ever after. To
the day he died. Even after his father died, he went
to his mother for money."

"Anthony's dead!"

She nodded.

"I thought you were divorced."

"We were."

"He died afterwards?"

"He died *when*," she said bitterly. "He didn't want
the divorce, you see. I don't know why—our marriage
was horrible. Constant arguing over the children. He
continually picked on them, to a degree of insanity,
really. And insane fits of jealousy in which he literally
turned purple, went into his own private night-
mare world. I had no respect for him, and no love
either, except for the boy who never came out, but
whom I glimpsed every once in a while through the
curtains. But I was like Edith, you see, I tried to be
decent to him, tried to smile. Still, I don't know
how he could not have known what I felt, although he
claimed not to.

"It was difficult to get him to leave. I had to get a
lawyer, had to go through some nasty business just to
get him to separate. And then, after we were separated, he'd come to the house every night, just at dinnertime. He said he was coming to see the children.
The children. He'd never paid any attention to them,

except to yell, when he lived with them. He'd come at dinnertime and watch us eat. It was unbearable. I didn't want to invite him to join us, didn't want to encourage this. But try to get your food down your throat in such a situation. I told him he had to stop. I told him that if he came only once a week, and on a night I'd name, I'd give him dinner. He agreed, but then started to come over a couple of nights a week *after* dinner. I told him if he didn't stop, I'd have him kept from coming into the house at all. I wasn't at all sure I could manage it, though. Legally I mean, or the other way: how can you keep somebody out of a house he half-owns? Then I said if he gave me a power of attorney for a divorce, I'd let him visit twice a week. He was so desperate he did it."

Her voice wandered off. Victor handed her a cigarette and she took it.

"I felt so goddamned sorry for him," she went on in a thick voice. "He was like a wounded animal. He kept coming back and coming back to the house, as if he couldn't imagine where else to go. The marriage couldn't have been much worse than it was. Why did he want a woman who could barely look at him without contempt? A contempt he'd earned, the hard way.

"On the nights he came, I'd go into my study after dinner. I had done that all through the later years of our marriage. The kids cleaned up the kitchen, he used to watch TV, and I prepared my lectures. It was a good arrangement, because he didn't pick on them nearly so much if I wasn't around to be hurt by it.

"But during the separation, although he knew I was working, he'd come down to the study. He'd sit there, arguing, pleading. He kept saying he couldn't understand why I wanted the divorce when we were so happy together. There just wasn't any way I could demonstrate to him that we weren't. The problem was, he said, that I'd never loved him the way he'd loved me. I said it was closer to the truth to say I'd never hated him the way he hated me. He insisted he didn't, never had, not even for an instant. It was impossible to talk to him. I'd say I had to work, and he'd begin to cry, get down on his knees and put his head on my lap and weep.

"It broke my heart. I couldn't bear his humiliation, but even more I couldn't bear his pain. Little Anthony had finally come out of the house, here he was, crying in my lap. I wanted to stroke his head, to say, 'It's all right, baby,' to tell him Mommy wouldn't go away and leave him again.

"But I couldn't. He was destroying me, destroying my children. I had to sit there coldly, telling him coldly to go away. 'Sweetie, sweetie, you're killing me,' he'd say, and I believed him because the ordeal was killing *me. And* the kids. I mean, they had to sit there at the dinner table with him, listen to him tell jokes in a hollow voice, trying to be social. They sat listening to him, trying to swallow their food. And then, of course, they knew or had some idea of what was going on in my study on those nights. The house was always very quiet on those nights, everything orderly, TV turned off early, kids in their rooms doing homework. With their doors firmly shut. Beware the quiet orderly house: something's wrong. They never said anything to me. I never said anything to them besides the bare facts. What could I tell them? That their father and I were tied together in some insane bond? That if our marriage had destroyed us, our divorce was destroying us too?

"I came to feel that we were at war, and all the winner would get was survival. If I gave in to him, we were all doomed. By then, I hated myself so much for having stayed with him so long that I would, I think, have killed myself if I'd gone back to him. Leaving the children with *him!* So I had to win, had to. For their sake and my own. But for some reason, I had to go through this ordeal, too. I owed it to him, maybe, or maybe I had to see if I could really abandon him, the fragment of the child left in him, Anthony.

"After an hour or so of pleading, he'd get angry. He'd get up then, and stand there, starting low, with bitter accusations that I'd never loved him, then mounting higher, ending with shrieking accusations: you bitch, you whore, you slut! He'd been calling me names like that for years, and I was able to ignore them now. Long ago, they'd made me cry.

"But I could deal more easily with his anger than I could with his grief. Except I was a little afraid of him. Always. He'd never done more than push me, or grab me hard by the arm to keep me from going out the door, but I was never sure of him. Anyway, that would last a little while, then I'd order him to leave, I'd stand up, I'd shout, and after some more expostulation, he'd go, slamming the door behind him.

"The whole house—you could hear it, it was like noise—breathed out when he left. But the kids stayed hushed in their rooms, didn't come out to see what the slam was. And sometimes they went to sleep without even coming out to kiss me good night. I'd go in to see how they were and the lights would be out, their eyes would be closed. Maybe they were pretending. They must have been angry with me as well as with him for all this disruption in their lives. They had no way of knowing how it came about, really. And the truth is, I permitted it."

She sighed. "I don't know why I did. I just felt I had to. I felt that endurance was my only weapon, that to call lawyers and cops was unthinkable. In fact, though, I did call the cops one night when he broke into the house late at night, smashed things, pushed me around. They were no help. The house is in his name, right, lady? Then we can't do nothin. Unless you want to come down to the station and fill out a form and charge him with assault. They'd heard it before, thousands of times. The fact is that below the surface, whatever it says in the law, a husband is seen as having the right to harass his wife, to push her around, even to beat her. And few people will get involved in a thing like that.

"Well, I waited until school closed, and told the kids we were going on a little vacation, to visit my mother on the Cape. I told him that too. And I drove the kids out there, then I hightailed it back to Boston and hopped a plane for Mexico.

"I had to be secretive because he could have annulled the power of attorney if he'd known what I was doing. And in fact . . . Anyway, I didn't want him following me to Mexico, to cause a scene. . . ."

Victor handed her a drink and she took it and

sipped it without looking at him, without seeing him. He sat near her, hands folded, hanging down between his knees, staring alternately at her and the carpet.

"But of course he knew. Hadn't he always known what I would do? Always. Even after we were separated he'd turn up where I was having lunch, come stumbling in on his crutches to the faculty club, or at a little hamburger joint we sometimes went to. I'd drive down to the beach on a beautiful spring day and walk along the sand, trying to get myself sane, and I'd turn around and there he'd be. I'd meet a guy and go out for drinks with him, something maybe pleasant, something to keep my heart up. And Anthony would be at the bar. Sometimes he started scenes. There were some pretty terrible ones. . . .

"So, of course he knew. And sent a telegram nullifying the power of attorney. Luckily, Mexico is so disorderly, they didn't get the wire in time. Or maybe it arrived too late. As it turned out, it didn't matter.

"I flew back and drove out to the Cape again. The time with my mother had been good for the kids. Peaceful. Regulated. They were feeling better. I stayed for a while and we played. Went swimming, riding, played cards. We laughed a lot, although there may have been a hysterical edge to it.

"Because I, at least, was terrified, and although I concealed it, they must have felt it. And eventually, we had to go home. They were very giggly all the way back to Newton. I had sent Anthony a telegram after I got back, telling him what I'd done. And now I imagined him sitting on the sofa waiting for us, sitting there with his rifle and knocking us off onetwothreefour as we walked in the door. It happens, you know.

"I couldn't tell the kids what I was thinking, but it came to seem so real to me that I insisted they stay in the car while I went in and got the door open. I didn't explain, I insisted. I said if there was any trouble, Elspeth was to drive away immediately, to go to Carol and John's. They lived only a few blocks away.

"They must have been frightened too, because they didn't argue. Although they knew Elspeth could barely drive, that all she knew about driving came from the few times Anthony or I let her sit in the driver's seat and go a block or two. It was bad. Later on, I wondered why I hadn't gone there first, why I never asked for help. And I concluded that I felt so *bad,* so *guilty*—a woman divorcing her husband for no other reason than that he is a bastard to live with —that I felt I wasn't entitled to ask for help, not even from my oldest friends. I had to suffer the consequences, and suffer them alone."

She laughed a little, thin, dry laugh—almost a cough.

"But Anthony wasn't there. What *was* there was a letter telling me he'd canceled the power of attorney, so my divorce wasn't valid. I was wild, lunatic. I don't know how to describe it. The whole thing had *cost* me so much! I don't mean just in money, although that too. It had been so hard for me—the deceit, abandoning him, leaving the kids, the fear of his revenge. And the knowledge that he'd never give me another one. That the truth is, you can't get away from an oppressive, tyrannical bully if you want to. You can't get out of a bad marriage unless both parties agree! It seemed horrible to me. I was looking at a future in which I'd never be able to get away from him!

"I called the kids in. Said I was worried the house might have been broken into while we were away. And Sydney said—she was only nine then—'You mean by Daddy, don't you.' That's how well we protect our children from the truth.

"We were all a little edgy that day. I guess we were awaiting a presence to descend upon us, purple-faced and shrieking. We went marketing together, we cooked together, we ate together, we laughed a lot. We giggled through dinner: no one was sitting there screaming about elbows or uneaten turnips or wrong forks or bicycles not put away. It was a sign, I thought, of how things would be when he could no longer invade us.

"I watched the kids' faces, and I thought: it was worth it. It was worth all the pain, the strain, the poor teaching I'd done that semester—it's hard to write decent lectures after such turbulent arguments. And hard to give good lectures when you don't know if some screaming meemie is going to meet you in the hall outside your classroom—as he sometimes did. It hadn't been worth the children's suffering, but nothing could be worth that. Nothing could ever redeem it, but perhaps they hadn't felt it as much as I had. And the best I could do—the most I could say—was that at least they won't have to suffer like that again."

There were tears on her cheeks that she didn't seem to notice. Victor wiped them away gently with his fingers.

"We sat around that night, the kids didn't even turn on TV, and talked about where we'd like to live, how we'd like to live, what we could afford. It was a good night. By ten, we all knew Anthony would not come. We were home together, *en famille,* for the first time in our joint lives. I sat up long after the kids had gone to bed. I was still worried and anxious, although I hadn't told them about Anthony's note. I sat there plotting my moves. I knew that if he had managed to bollix the divorce, I'd never get one unless I could somehow manage to frame him. That's what the law did to you in those days. And I wouldn't do that. So the next best thing was to get out of that house and get a place of my own that he wasn't legally entitled to come charging into whenever he chose. But I also knew that if I rented, I'd lose a tax deduction I needed, and if I tried to buy, I might have trouble—a married woman without her husband's signature—People say laws don't in fact express a culture's biases? Ask a woman who's tried to go it alone. And, in fact, he could have blocked my selling the house, because he did own half of this one. So there were all kinds of possible obstacles.

"But on the whole, I was feeling pretty good. I did have a set of divorce papers in my bag. Reminded myself to put them in a safe-deposit box in my name the next day. And the kids had been, if not relaxed, more so than they'd been in a long time. For the first time in many years, I had an intimation of . . . happiness. Lightness of heart. A future for my children in which they would be permitted to be gay, silly, light-hearted, noisy, obstreperous, whatever—children. To grow a little straight, after all the bending. . . .

"Next morning the kids were going to start summer school—a play-school thing, you know. I slept late, or intended to. And then I heard Elspeth sniffing. . . ."

Her voice went dead. Victor handed her his glass, but it was hard for her to swallow. She squeaked. Swallowed. Eventually she got her voice back, but it was a brusque voice, indifferent, hard.

"Yes. Well, she found him, you see. When she went into the garage for her bike. The motor was still running. Elspeth had enough presence of mind to keep the younger ones out, to cover her nose when she went in to turn off the ignition. And later they came running out and found him."

Her mouth was wrenched. "That's why I can't forgive, can't forget. He knew perfectly well the chances were they'd find him. He couldn't do it in his own car? At his own place? At his mother's, for godsakes? No. He wanted them to find him. He knew there was no way he could hurt me worse than to hurt them.

"And that's what I can't forgive men for. The Greeks were right to have the old man swallow his children. Oh, what men do to women is bad, but women are adults too, at least they can fight back if they have to. They can find ways. They're not babies, looking up to a parent. That's the profoundest, the most powerful love on earth, I think, the love of children for their parents. It endures even when the parents are abusive, rotten, brutal.

"Men put themselves before their children. At their best, they only try to mold sonny into more perfect versions of themselves—into the right schools, the right job, the right Little League team, for godsakes. At their worst, they use the kids as weapons against their wives. And here, they're relentless. Like Roger. How would it harm him if the children were happier, if they saw their mother more often? If they felt their parents to have at least a speaking agreement? But he wants to punish her. And he's willing to punish the children to do it."

She lighted another cigarette.

Victor stared at the floor.

7

AFTER A while, he cleared his throat. She turned to him, and he examined her face. It was less wrenched, less anguished, more controlled.

"I thought you had two children. Tony and Sydney. You never mentioned Elspeth before."

She turned away from him. Her face was a mask. "Elspeth is dead."

He covered his eyes.

"When she first died," Dolores went on in a monotone, "I thought I'd never recover. Some days I still wake up astonished that I'm alive, that I could keep on going after that. I guess every love has limits," she concluded bitterly.

"Do you think you shouldn't have survived?"

"How could I? How did I?"

He reached for her hand and grasped it. It was limp.

"When did she die?"

"An eternity ago. Seven years. She was sixteen."

"How did it happen? Was she sick?"

She turned away again. "It was an accident," she said thickly. "I can't talk about it, Victor."

He held her hand and stroked it. "I understand that."

"Do you?" Bitterly.

"You don't believe it, do you. That I could understand something's being so painful you can't discuss it."

"No. I think men don't feel the way women do. They learn all kinds of games and tricks to avoid feeling, and by the time they're fifty, they're emotional zombies."

"You think that of me?"

She was silent.

"I don't want to attack you," he began, "especially when you're feeling so low. But you get angry with

137

me, or you did once, for what you called canceling
you. Turning you off, acting as if you weren't there.
But you do this to me, too. At some point in our dis-
cussions, you stop listening to me, you act as if what *I*
say or feel is somehow . . . irrelevant."

She gazed at him sadly.

"You act as if I don't know how to think."

"On Sunday, years ago," she said, "I was at the
Guggenheim. You know how everybody takes the
elevator to the top and then walks down the ramp?
And the retrospective exhibitions are arranged that
way—the earliest pictures at the top, moving down
toward the present. Well, one day when I was there
with some friends, a man, a very beautiful and elegant man, a little precious perhaps, enough to arouse
nastiness—and wearing a salmon-pink suit, brilliant-
looking man—the man decided to look at the pictures from the bottom up. And proceeded to do so.
And another man watched him and said very loudly,
everyone tittered: 'Oh, look! A salmon swimming
upstream!' "

Victor gave her an uncomprehending smile.

"Of course, it makes perfect sense to look at the
pictures from the top down. But you might see something just as interesting and just as true if you looked
at them from the bottom up. And that's what's different about men and women. Because men always
look at things the so-called right way. And women
try, but whether they like it or not, the facts of their
lives force them to see things from the bottom up.
They never see the same exhibition as men. And
they're always swimming against the tide, upstream.
And alone, or so it feels."

"I don't see that. But even if it were so, what does
it have to do with this space between us, with your
shutting me out?"

"I don't shut you out, you just aren't in."

"That isn't true. You give up on me before you've
given me a chance. You turn your face away from
me."

She closed her eyes. Tired. Tired. "Would you say,"
she began with a deep sigh, "that you hate women,

that men are at war against women, that you and all men associate emotionality with women, and essentially, hate emotionality?"

He considered. "I'd say there's a little truth in that."

"And I say it's a portrait of our society."

He sighed. "That's too extreme, Lorie."

"You see."

"See what?"

"I can't talk to you."

"Jesus! Because I don't agree with every single statement you make?"

"Victor, would you say women are exploited in our culture?"

It was hard for him. "Some women, yes, I guess."

"Most."

"All right, most."

"And who profits from the exploitation of women?"

He put his head in his hands.

"You see. You don't want to see, don't want to know, don't want to think about this. And I know that. In society at large, I feel like an outlaw. With you, I feel simply alone—at some point."

"But WHY! I haven't failed you yet, have I?" He looked at his hands. "I don't abuse my children."

"I believe that. You probably have almost nothing to do with them."

Heavy sigh. "That *was* true. Not anymore."

"You write them regularly?"

He stared at her. "No, I write Edith and send them messages." He pulled himself up and together. "Besides, Lorie, it's different for women, I'm sure of that. The babies grow inside you, and that's profound. You nurse them out of your own bodies. You take care of them when they're helpless. You *sense* them. You see, you know what they're thinking, what they're feeling, what they need even when they can't speak. I used to be amazed at the way Edith could tell, just by the way a kid cried, whether it was hurting or sick or just tired and grouchy, or hungry. Whatever. And she could!

"Men just don't have that. *I* don't have it anyway. It's special, and it gives you—women—a dimension

139

of life that men don't have. So we have to find something that's special for us. I love my kids, but I don't think I love them the way Edith does. And they don't feel about me the way they do about her.

"In the last few years, I've tried to—well—get closer to them. I think I've succeeded. A little."

She hated this. Hated it. She wanted to say: how convenient for you all those years. How convenient to believe it's biological. If you'd taken care of those kids by yourself for three straight days, *you'd* have known their cries too. Known it all. It isn't magic, although you'd like to believe it is. Circe again: different aspect.

She said: "You feel close to them now."

Uncomfortable. "Closer."

"That's good."

"Yes."

Silence.

"But it's tragic, you know, this way of arranging things."

She was surprised. "Tragic? I thought you liked it this way."

He shook his head, twisted his mouth. "You know those movies, oh, mostly French, I think—*La Ronde*. Bedroom farces: A loves B who loves C who loves D who loves E who loves A. People running in and out of bedroom doors, closets; hiding under beds. Well: Edith loves the children very much but she's never allowed herself to be herself with them, never allowed herself to love them completely because she thinks she's supposed to love me more. And acts as if she does, although I can't see how she can. And I love Edith, but I love the kids more, but I love you more than that. And you . . . you'll never love me, never love anyone—it's clear from the way you talk—the way you love your kids. Something's wrong. Nature couldn't have meant us to be like this." He stared at the floor.

She gazed at him with her old untrusting eye. She examined him, and he looked up at her with moist eyes, and she decided to trust then, and so was able to feel. She got up and sat beside him, she held his

140

head against her breast. "Victor," she murmured, "I love you very much. Let's not measure." He was not consoled. The two of them sat together lightly clinging to each other, and gazed at the red electric coil that provided the heat in the room, that was supposed to be a fire.

V

1

VICTOR ASKED Dolores to come into London to stay
with him over the Christmas holidays. She told him
she would take two weeks off from her library work.
She was excited about Christmas, something she
hadn't been in years, not since Elspeth. . . . She'd
bought Victor heaps of things, strained her budget.
She'd even stinted—just a little—on the children: it's
only this year, she told herself. There was a Viyella
robe for cold British bedrooms in which his silk fou-
lard (a gift from Edith, she was sure) was inadequate.
an old leather-bound edition of *The Anatomy of Melancholy,* not precious, but beautiful, and little things
—some bright posters for his dull flat, some paper-
back books, each wrapped separately.

He was excited too, vivid and full of energy. He
left work early, came back to the flat stomping and
shouting: he wanted to tramp the streets with her, to
take buses to distant parts of the city and sit on top
and keep up a running sociological analysis. He
wanted to walk through all the parks. He bought tickets to plays, concerts, the ballet. They would eat all
their meals out, he said: "We'll try every restaurant in
London!" Her feet got cold walking, so he bought
her warm boots. He bought her warm gloves, so she
didn't have to keep her hands in her pockets, and a
money belt, so she didn't have to carry a purse.

She had brought her work with her. She settled into his flat happily, preempted the desk, and there she
sat each day during the hours Victor was at his office.
She was writing the second chapter. She worked well
but without haste, and wonder of wonders, she did not

feel intruded upon when she heard Victor's key in the lock, heard his footsteps coming down the hall. She looked up with joy as he entered, and his face glowed.

She wondered, sometimes, why he went on loving her, bristly and difficult as she was. When it was clear, given his attractiveness, his poise, his money, and his freedom, that he could easily have had fun with someone who *was* fun, someone young perhaps, lighthearted, not so weighed down with grief. It seemed he liked her bristliness: maybe he needed it, maybe he was suffering from guilt. In truth, he was pretty bristly himself. His voice shot off into yowls and yells at the slightest thing; his volatility might have frightened some women, intimidated them. But being, at least inwardly, volatile herself, she understood it. And after Anthony, rage never frightened her again. Direct rage, not like . . . Other people's rage, at least.

And Victor seemed to know something about grief, as well. Perhaps he would have been bored with someone who hadn't felt enough, seen enough, no matter how firm the body, how unlined the face. She herself had long since become bored with firm bodies and unlined faces that had not experienced enough.

That was it! That's how her celibacy began! It wasn't Marsh at all. It was all those young men, a series of them, yes, it was right after, yes, then, lots of men then, young and old, indiscriminate she'd been then, crazy really. The young men had been sweet as only the young can be sweet, but it was impossible to talk to them about anything without feeling old and tired. Which was a bore. Or ending up teacher/shrink/mother. And so self-absorbed they were! Obsessed with themselves, as young people frequently are. Understandable, but a bore too. Yes, little by little, she'd given them up. That's how it happened. Strange, how she'd forgotten that.

Yes, things were very good. She could forget, for long stretches, to guard herself against the hurt she knew would come. And it was remarkable how she didn't get angry with him. Just didn't. Oh, at moments. But it never seemed important afterwards. Didn't even need to express it half the time, it just vanished. That was love, must be.

Best of all, they could play together, be children together. They played games walking in the London streets, acting in accord with what they imagined was behavior proper to the characters they associated with Wimpole Street, Baker Street, Harley Street, Savile Row, Oxford Street, Regent's Park, Hyde Park.

The Serpentine. Once before she'd looked at it and turned quickly away. Now, with Victor, she was able to point to it, to say: "That's where Harriet Shelley drowned herself," and to wonder that it was possible, the water looked so shallow, so calm. But if you didn't know how to swim. Lots of people didn't know how to swim. . . .

They walked, they rode, they talked. When they got tired, they'd turn into a pub and have a pint. Then home, hand in hand, talking, always talking, for baths and cocktails and BBC music on the little radio Victor had bought, and out again "all dolled up" as Victor insisted on calling it, to the theater and dinner. Or to the ballet. Victor had compiled at list of restaurants from his gourmet British friends and they tried them at random: Wilton's, the Connaught, the Etoile, Stones, the White Tower. Victor tried things he'd never eaten before and found them edible: artichokes, escargots, frog's legs. He drew the line at liver, and would not even say aloud the word *brains* if it appeared on a menu. Dolores found it luxurious to eat at such rates, and had regular debates with herself, her conscience arguing that it was sinful to pay such prices for mere food, prices that could feed a family for a week; her senses did not argue at all, they merely enjoyed. And won.

At the end of the evening, they would curl up on the huge bed at Victor's place, drinking Cointreau or Drambuie or cognac or whatever Victor had chosen for that night, and discuss subjects of momentous importance: their dinner, their weight, and what they should do the next day.

On rainy days, and over the weekend, they went to museums. They turned their noses up at the eighteenth-century fluff (as they both saw it) at the Wallace Collection. At the Tate, Victor could not budge Dolores from the Blake engravings and the Turners and finally went outside and sat there smoking. They went several times to the British Museum, where Victor mused for an hour over the Rosetta stone, and (as Dolores had predicted) found himself unable to move from the Egyptian and Greek and Mesopotamian halls. Dolores would leave him there and go back to the main hall, to the cases of holographs, a handwritten poem by John Donne, Shakespeare's signature. She pored over these as she had many times before: she tried to drink them in, not sure what it was she wanted to imbibe.

After even the slightest separation, they came together tremulously, yearning after each other. They took hands, tender, as if there had been some reason to doubt they would find each other again.

Yes. Bliss. Not since Jack had she stayed this long with anyone. Wouldn't. Wouldn't permit them to stay with her either, longer than three days. But this was bliss.

Be sensible, she told herself. It wouldn't be like this if we were together all the time, if we didn't have foreknowledge of the ending. Death is the mother of beauty. You mustn't let yourself slide into romantic delusion. If we could hold on to this, all marriages made for love would stay glorious. It's the artificiality of the situation, she told herself, holding up her leg in the bath. Not a bad leg for an old lady. She lathered sandalwood soap on her shoulders: nice to be able to afford such luxuries.

No, if we were together all the time, I'd get to resent quitting my work whenever he decided to come home. And he'd get to resent my resenting quitting my work. And besides, if we lived together all the time, he wouldn't quit early. And I'd get to resent that he worked late. And then, if we were together all the time, it wouldn't be a holiday and he'd expect me to cook him dinner. And I'd resent cooking dinner every night, and he wouldn't be happy with a cheese sandwich, as I am. And of course, he'd expect me to do the marketing. He'd want, yes, he would: a wife.

She heard the phone ring in the bedroom, but remembered Victor was there. Anyway, she wasn't supposed to answer the phone here. So she soaped more, trying to figure out if there weren't any way out of this dilemma—not for her and Victor, necessarily (since they knew that had to end), but just in general.

Bliss, except for the telephone. Victor was afraid that if she answered, people who called would wonder who she was. Or it might be Edith. So if he was at the office and wanted to call her, he let the phone ring twice, then hung up and immediately dialed again. If there were a slip, if she picked up the phone without thinking, she was to pretend to be the cleaning woman. She imitated Julie Andrews' accent in *My Fair Lady* when she teased him about this, saying, "Aoh, HI'm just the char, guv'nor."

Yes, but that was really a small thing. Considering. Not a thing worth making a fuss about.

She came out of the bath pink, her hair piled up, her body wrapped in a towel. Hit the cold bedroom air and started to shiver, ran over and turned on the electric fire—Victor's flat had them in every room. Then turned and saw Victor's face.

"What is it?"

He was sitting on the bed, the phone on the table beside him. He looked tense, frowning. "My daughter Vickie. She's in London. She's on her way over."

A sudden decision: she'd been given a week off from work, Laker flights were available. And besides, she felt sorry for "poor old Dad spending Christmas all alone." And anyway, she'd wanted to see London for years, and here she'd have free room and board. She'd be there as fast as the airport bus could bring her.

Dolores let herself down into a chair. She'd let herself forget, in the luxury of tramping streets together, the other side of things, the furtiveness which was somehow all *her* responsibility. Only the telephone arrangements reminded her. They had dinner together, out in public, every night; and breakfast together privately, in their own kitchen, every morning.

But now here it was again: scarlet woman. She sat utterly still, waiting to see how he would ask her. Her feelings retreated to another place, her mind became cold and rational and watchful, prepared to grade his performance. Dolores, I hate to ask this, but . . . She waited. Victor was pacing. He left the room, she could hear him fixing drinks. Well, she could pack rather quickly, get out of there, and maybe get a hotel room somewhere if she weren't too choosy. But how? No travel agents open at this hour. She'd have to tramp streets with a suitcase. Or maybe find a place with a phone where she could sit with her suitcases, dialing, feeling like a waif. A hotel lobby, maybe.

Trouble was it was two days before Christmas, and London was overflowing with American tourists here for the theater. Maybe her dingy old hotel near Russell Square would have room—the place where she'd made a promise to José that she had not kept, not having gone back there since she met Victor.

So, say I find a hotel, then what? Maybe he can sneak over to see me sometimes, take some time away from Vickie, claim business . . . He would have to eat dinner with Vickie, of course, spend Christmas with Vickie. Spend all night in his own bed, with Vickie on the living-room couch.

No. No. She'd leave, but she'd go back to Oxford. Leave his Christmas presents on his closet shelf, a nice martyred touch, that. Go back and spend Christmas with the Carriers, they'd invited her, or with Mary, who'd invited her also. And try not to feel too resentful. No, she would not stay in London and be buried in some corner, waiting.

Victor came back in with two drinks. She looked at him and broke into a wail.

"No, I can't bear it!"

He came to her and crouched down and took her hands. "Can't bear what?"

"No, it's been too wonderful. I just don't feel like doing the right thing."

"What's the right thing?"

"Leaving."

"Well, I'm glad you couldn't bear leaving," he smiled, and kissed her hands. He stood up. "The right thing for who, anyway?" he said, pulling his trousers on.

She shrugged. "The usual right thing."

He put on his shirt and glanced at her. "Aren't you going to get dressed?" He tied the knot in his tie. "I'm really sorry, Lorie" (her heart slowed) "that we probably won't be able to get to the play tonight. I called about getting another ticket, but now I realize she won't get here in time. We'll go another night, okay?"

She stood up and dropped her towel and he looked at her with eyes suddenly lusty, and came and grabbed her, holding her very close. She put her head on his shoulder and her arms around him and stood there. When she pulled back her head, liquid-eyed, she gazed at his face.

What a face it was! It had everything in it: pain and pity, determination and fear, love and sadness. It answered her. She smiled. "I'll get dressed." She turned away and began to dress and felt something falling inside her, somewhere between her heart and her stomach, a hard thing, a kind of shield, like a sliding door covering a raw soft vulnerable place, unsealed and vulnerable as the center of a newborn baby's skull.

Then he said: "One thing . . ." and the door slid up again. She turned to face him, her face a mask. Yes? Would he, like Tom Harney, warn her not to say *fuck* or *shit* in front of his dinner guests? Or like Marsh, the day she drove him to Princeton, order her to stay properly out of the way? Was he going to pass her off as someone else, would he now tell her her cover story, a spy in the house of love?

He came to her and took her hands. She was stiff.

"Vickie's very much her mother's girl. They're close, and she's very protective of Edith. Vickie's twenty-three, but in some ways she's still a baby." (Twenty-three. Elspeth would have been . . .) "Anyway, if she *should* say anything . . . unkind . . . I hope you won't be hurt. It won't be personal, she doesn't even know you, it will be directed at the situation. At me, really. But it may spatter you. I'll try to deflect it," he smiled, but there were grim lines around his mouth, "but my deflector may not be as fast as her spitball."

He kissed her eyes and she clutched him, felt the shield falling, falling, thinking, oh god if it falls all the way how will I ever be able to let him go?

2

VICKIE WAS nearly as tall as her father, but strikingly blond, with a frizz of fashionable curls ringing her head. She wore large round pink-tinted eyeglasses that cast a pink light on her cheeks. And she giggled a lot. Beyond the giggle and the bland expression, Dolores thought she saw something watchful, thoughtful. But it was hard to be sure, since Vickie barely looked her way.

She hugged her father, jabbering with excitement at her adventurousness. She was wearing jeans and a heavy fur-lined jacket and she carried a backpack. Victor introduced Dolores as Dr. Durer.

"Dolores," she said. "Please." She stood and held out her hand. Vickie placed a limp cool young hand momentarily in hers, giggled, recited some pleased-to-meet-you formula.

Victor took over. Heartily. Not quite the Businessman, but the heartiness was borrowed from him. He was hearty about Vickie's bag, her clothes, her hairdo, her flight, the damp London weather, a drink, his rather swish flat. He got things into their proper places as far as he could. He could not prevent the girl from sitting on the very edge of her chair, at a right angle to Dolores, which allowed her to speak to him without looking at his lover. But when he brought her a drink —a vodka and tonic—he sat down beside Dolores, so she had to look that way. She managed however to look at him at such an angle that Dolores was relegated to Vickie's peripheral vision.

Dolores in her turn tried hard not to stare at the girl's backpack, which was resting on the floor near the door. She tried to look interested, tried to smile, wondering how many women had sat like her trying to look properly motherly and concerned. Who had decided on that proper, anyway.

He was asking about her job now, and she talked more easily, giggled less. He turned frequently to Dolores, trying to bring her into the conversation.

"Vickie's a microbiologist," he said.

"Yes. That's really impressive."

"Oh, I'm really just a lab assistant," she said to her father.

The job was fine, interesting, but after a year of it, she felt she'd learned all she could. She was thinking of going on for a Ph.D. "I could learn more there if they'd promote me, assign me to some of the zingier special projects. But I don't think they will. They don't take me seriously, I'm too young. . . ."

"Too pretty," Victor put in.

"Female," Dolores added.

Thinking: and you giggle a lot. But so what? Was that any worse than the mute shyness of young men? It was simply another form of shyness.

The girl's head swung around to Dolores. "Yes, that's it! There are a few women there in their forties, they're *still* lab assistants! The only way a woman can force them to look at her seriously is if she has a Ph.D. And even then there's no assurance. Unless you were ten times more brilliant than any of the guys. And I'm not. I'm as good as any of them, better than some, but not out-and-out superior. Yet three of the five guys I started with have been requested by the VIPs to work on special projects with them. The only special project I've been invited to participate in is midnight supper at the pad of the administrative assistant."

Dolores smiled. "Did you go?"

"No."

"Good!" Victor said emphatically.

"Oh, Daddy." She turned back to Dolores. "I didn't go because I knew we'd end shacking up—he's really cute. And I know that would hurt me at the lab. There's one older woman there, she has a degree but not a doctorate. She's been there for years, she's never gotten anywhere, she makes less money than the new guys, even. She smokes a lot, and she drawls, and

150

says: 'Don't follow my example, my dear. I slept my way to the bottom.'

"But he is cute, Maury, so it's hard." She turned back to her father: "I hope I'm not shocking you, Daddy." And turned back to Dolores: "My parents are so . . . old-fashioned. Moral, you know." Then realized what she'd said as Dolores and Victor both gave her the kind of smirks that are really attempts to control laughter, and she looked from one to the other and giggled and all three of them were able to laugh then, a long hard laugh of relief.

There were no problems after that. Vickie claimed to be in need of advice from her father. "I want to get an advanced degree, partly because I'm ambitious, but partly because I really want to get into DNA research and I don't know enough. There are still fellowships available in the sciences. What do you think?"

The two played family-style ring-around-the-rosy:

But of course I want you to do whatever you want to do.

I want to do it but I'm scared. Maybe I'm not good enough.

Of course you're good enough. You got straight A's in . . .

And I'd have to quit my job. I haven't saved much money. None, really. Suppose I don't get a fellowship?

Don't quit your job until you know for sure.

Then I wouldn't be making a real commitment. I'd be letting everything depend on some stupid fellowship.

Well, if you're sure you want to do it, I'll help you.

But I'm not sure I want to do it.

Of course you do.

They chattered on, Vickie describing at length the oddities of the brave new (to her!) world she was inhabiting. Finally, Victor asked: "How's Mother?"

She stopped dead, looked at Dolores, looked at him. "Fine," she said uneasily.

He shouldn't have done that. She feels she's betraying her mother. Should have waited until I was out of the room.

"Really?"

"Yes." An edge of irritation in her voice: "She's the same, Dad. You know." Her eyes crept around her father and his lover sitting there, his arm around her. And something happened in her eyes, something fell into place, a decision was made.

"And the kids."

"Fine. Leslie's home for Christmas. She can't wait to finish school, she hates it. She's bored. Says she wants to be a pipe fitter, and Mother laughs, high and gay as if it's a joke, but she's a little nervous. Actually, she's right to be nervous, but she doesn't know it. . . ." Her voice trailed off.

"Why?" Victor barked at her.

Dolores looked at him. "She's trying to be honest with you, not to challenge you," she said. Victor looked at her, and tried to soften his face. "The trouble with parents," Dolores said to Vickie, "is that they think they always have to be parents." Vickie watched them with wonder.

"What's wrong," Victor asked gently.

"Well." She looked at her hands. "Now I feel guilty, as if I'm, like, betraying her. But I'm a little upset. . . ." She looked up at Victor. "She's heavy into drugs. Pot and coke. Well, everybody's into pot, but coke . . ."

Victor glowered. "How did this happen?" Parental. Authoritarian.

Vickie shriveled. Shrugged. "At school, I guess."

Dolores was nasty. "*She* doesn't know and right now she wishes she hadn't brought it up at all."

"Oh, Vick, I'm sorry. Listen, is she in trouble?"

"Well, her grades are bad. But I think they'd be bad anyway, you know? She doesn't care about school."

"Well, what in hell does she care about?"

"Oh, she likes to go to bars with Reg and drink and then snort a little coke. I think, well, I think all she really wants to do is get married!" Disgust.

Victor sat back. "What's so terrible about that?"

"Get married? And end up like Mom?"

152

Victor looked as if she had struck him across the face. Her hand darted to her mouth, her eyes filled. "Dad . . ."

Dolores wished she could vanish. This was a private drama, she was an intruder. She could go get ice, pee, something. But she couldn't leave Victor looking the way he did. So she pulled herself back, drew her energy within. She became absent.

"I just meant," Vickie was babbling, near tears, "that being a wife isn't the greatest thing to do, you know."

"Maybe it could be different for Leslie," he said, looking at the floor, twisting his hands between his knees. "The young men today, I'm told, are more liberated."

"Oh, they're as piggish as ever," she exclaimed in disgust, then put her hand over her mouth again. "Oh, I'm impossible tonight!" she cried, in real dismay, and Victor and Dolores laughed.

Because for the first time in her life she feels she can tell her father the truth, she's really slamming it into him, Dolores thought. So the all-American healthy family isn't as ideal as it sounded. But he didn't know that. I wonder if Edith does.

The crisis passed with their laughter and other family news, less heavy, proceeded. Mark was driving Mom crazy because he was out in the car all the time. Jonathan was fine, on the junior-high basketball team, said it was only his height, not his skill, that got him there, didn't believe he ever did anything right, and Mom said he was just like her.

"I could kill him!" Victor smiled, grating his teeth at Dolores. "The one thing I can't stand is lack of confidence, and that kid has it to a fare-thee-well."

"He's also getting into girls," Vickie added, giggling.

"I hope you don't mean that literally," Victor grinned.

Vickie began to feel fully at ease.

"Say, how did you two meet?"

They both smiled broadly. "On a train," Victor said.

"A train. Yeah. I've met people on trains. Not at home, at home I hardly ever take trains. But in Italy last summer, me and my girlfriend were on this train together. We were going to go all over, you know, we had a Eurail pass. But the guys in Italy are something else! At the end, we bought umbrellas and carried them with us as weapons. Can you picture it? Umbrellas in Italy?" she giggled.

"Well, it must rain there sometimes too," Dolores smiled.

"Yeah. But I'll bet you didn't need an umbrella for my father!" And doubled over giggling wildly at the notion of her father as a sexual threat.

"Now, listen, Vickie," he whined in protest, but broke into laughter too.

"Well," Vickie sat back and wiped her eyes, "listen, you two. I gotta find a place to crash."

Pause.

"Don't be polite. I'm not going to intrude on you."

"I'll find you a place," Victor said, rising. "What's more, I'll even pay for it. It's only fair." He left the room.

"Great," Vickie glinted venally at Dolores. "Especially since I came over with my fare and my last hundred bucks. Spent all my savings on Christmas presents." Giggle. Then her face became serious, she turned to Dolores and Dolores knew it would be different now, woman to woman, the conversation entering areas not usually entered when men were around.

"How long have you known my father?"

"Since September."

"Do you live with him?"

"No, I live in Oxford. I came to London to spend the holidays with him."

"And I have to come bopping in."

Dolores smiled. "Well, to tell the truth, I wasn't too happy when I heard you were coming. But now I'm glad you did, and I can see he is. It's good for us that you came."

Vickie chose to believe Dolores, and flushed with pleasure.

"I guess he's in love with you," she said, rubbing the fallen cigarette ash into her jeans' leg. "I haven't seen him look so good in years."

It was Dolores's turn to try to hide her delight.

"But isn't it hard for you? I mean, he's alone here, so I guess . . . It's not that I have any of those ideas . . . oh, you know . . . that getting involved with a married man is *wrong*, particularly . . . I mean, I think that the arrangements made between married people are one thing and the arrangements you make with them are another . . . that, you know, it's up to them to decide how they're going to live, that *you're* not responsible for their moralities . . . you know." She leaned forward in Victor's gesture, her hands dangling between her legs, her face probing Dolores's. "But, if you're in love with my father, and I guess you are, you look as if you are, well, isn't it hard, knowing he's married and all?"

"You found it hard, I take it," Dolores said gently.

Vickie jumped back and looked warily at Dolores. "How do you know? Does my father know? How?"

Dolores smiled. "Vickie, you just told me."

"Oh." She settled down, but continued to look at Dolores a bit warily. "Yeah. He was my physics prof in grad school. When I was getting my M.A. He was married and he was bald and he had a yellow tooth, right in the front of his mouth," she pointed to her own white one. "But . . . I don't know, he was so . . . you know, I'd go to his office with a problem and he . . . it was as if he knew the answers to everything. Not just physics problems, but everything. As if he knew what I was feeling better than I did. Knew what I should do, better than I did. Like you, just now. . . ."

Tell me, Dolores, tell me: How can I live without pain?

"Yes," she said. "But I can tell what you're feeling only because you told me, or showed me, what it was. I don't know what you should do. I don't even know what I should do."

"Mmmm." Vickie was doubtful. "But you'd know better than I do. And he did too. And I really came to feel . . ." she leaned forward, and her face turned yearning, "almost as if he was God, you know?" She sat back. "It's bad, you know. I call myself a feminist —ever since I had this really great teacher in high school, I've thought I was a feminist. But," she lowered her voice, although they could both hear Victor's rumbling on the telephone, "the thing is," she was nearly whispering, "I *loved* doing what he said, I *loved* seeing him as God. It was just the way they say, the way you read—I found my greatest fulfillment in obedience to him. Is that sick? Surrendering to him in everything was the most happiness I ever had." She looked away, she lighted another cigarette, her mouth was quivering. "Do you think I'm some kind of masochist?"

Dolores smiled. "Listen, if I met somebody I was sure was God, I'd enjoy surrendering too. After all, what *else* can you do with God? But *only* with God, of course," she added, sarcastically. "I don't know if it's masochistic, Vickie. I do know it's not female. I've had young male lovers who acted like that with me. Those things never lasted very long, because I'm not comfortable in the role of God . . . but they were happy with it."

Vickie looked at her dubiously. "You think it's all right? I mean, not sick?"

"I don't know what's sick or well. I do think it's a *young* thing to do. And I think it wouldn't last forever."

Vickie sighed. She crossed the room to the little bar and made herself another drink, talking almost wildly all the while. She had her father's excesses. "I hope so. Because I really worshiped him. I had dinner at his house a lot, we all did, his research assistants, he had several because he got all kinds of grants and stuff all the time. And his wife—well, she was this tall woman, big-boned and skinny, and blond, and she wore her hair in a bun. And she was always good-humored, always nice to me, she didn't seem to mind cooking dinner all the time for two or three extra people. And she never deferred to him at all. And that freaked me out sometimes. I mean, how can you *not* defer to God? She sort of treated him like one of the kids. She ignored him completely when he sat at the dinner table giving . . . well, lectures, really. I'd be hanging on every word, and she'd be passing the mashed potatoes," Vickie giggled. "It seems funny now, but at the time it seemed *terrible*. I felt so *sorry* for him! Married to such a philistine, who didn't listen to his brilliant words! His pearls! Now, I figure she'd heard them all a thousand times before. And probably once upon a time, she'd listened the way I did. She was his second wife, and she'd been his research assistant too. Years ago. Now she takes care of their three kids, and on weekends the two from his first marriage as well. Quite a handful, I guess. There was a time when I would have given anything to supplant her, to oust her the way she'd ousted the first wife. . . ." Vickie's voice drooped again. "Terrible, I know."

"Then maybe you'd have had six or seven children to care for. A real communal family," Dolores said drily.

"Yes. They had this really great old house, lots of little rooms full of books. Books everywhere. And records. He must have had a thousand records. There were back staircases and little back bedrooms. Nothing like *our* house. And I'd go and have dinner there and then he and I would go into the living room and he'd play me Bartók or Hindemith, or somebody else I'd never heard of, while she put the kids to bed, and I was enthralled, but I was uneasy, I wondered what she was thinking, why she wasn't jealous. . . . She used to look at me with a certain expression in her eyes. I thought it was pity, and I hated her for it. I thought she was saying: yes, I know you think he's God, but I have him, he belongs to me. Now I'm not so sure. . . ."

Vickie sat back and was quiet for a moment.

"When I found out I was pregnant, he was furious with me. He said it was my responsibility to take care of things like that and to teach me a lesson, he wasn't even going to help me pay for an abortion. And I cringed, I apologized, I insisted I wasn't asking for money, if he'd only go with me. But he wouldn't. I got the money together, that wasn't a problem, but I had to go alone, and that felt awful. And after that, I was just . . . well," her eyes filled with tears, "I was *craven*, Dolores! He was annoyed with me, and I was terrified of losing him. And I was about to get my degree, and I just . . . I was like a slave. I'd do anything he said, I dangled on a string he didn't even seem to want to bother to pick up. I got the job in Boston, and I said I'd keep a weekend place near him, so I could still see him, he said that was ridiculous, I had my whole life before me. I found out later he was already involved with another grad student, a really brilliant girl. And then I understood his wife's eyes." She turned and blew her nose.

"Looking back, the thing is . . . it was so humiliating! I can't imagine I'd ever do a thing like that again. But still," she looked imploringly at Dolores, "I think I'm still in love with him. Even though I know what he is. Or, I'm not in love with him, but with what I thought he was. Which I know now he isn't. But which I go on feeling he is. Or that someone is. Or that, if someone isn't, I can't bear to go on living!" She turned her head swiftly again, but Dolores heard her cries. "Am I going to go on like this all my life?" Thick voice, nasal. "Wanting something that doesn't exist?"

Victor came striding back into the room, pleased with himself, glowing. "Well, don't ever say your father isn't a miracle worker! Getting a hotel room over Christmas with no advance warning at all! Come on, ladies! Let's go! Fast, before they change their minds. Besides: I'm starving."

3

VICKIE'S PRESENCE—and her confidences—totally changed their mix. Dolores found herself talking to Vickie more than to Victor, being solicitous of the young woman, pointing things out to her, touching her hand in silent messages of sympathy, support, affection. And although Victor too pointed out certain things to Vickie, and teased her benevolently, and although it was his arm she clung to as the three of them tramped the streets, increasingly it was Victor who was left out, as if the two women had something between them, something he had not been initiated into.

As was indeed the case.

Is this how it begins, Dolores wondered, mothers and children against the fathers? She didn't like it. After all, she wasn't the mother. When Victor went to pee one lunchtime, Dolores suggested to Vickie that she tell her father her story.

"'Oh, I couldn't. He'd be horrified. He'd go off and shout about killing the bastard or something. I know he would."

"'I don't think so," Dolores demurred gently. She could not be sure she knew the real Victor better than his daughter did. "Look, tonight, why don't I stay home and the two of you go out to dinner alone, and you talk to him?"

"On Christmas Eve? I wouldn't do that to you, Dolores. But thanks." Vickie eyed her ever more gently, trustingly.

Which made it all the harder for Dolores to discover that she was jealous of Vickie's presence. Even though *she* was the one giving Vickie her main attention. It made no logical sense, but there it was. She wanted Victor all to herself, and all of herself for him: with no distractions. She felt abashed, wry: so this is what it's like, jealousy.

But it all balanced out on Christmas Eve, when they decided to have a banquet in, and went to Harrod's and bought pâté and cheeses and wine and a stuffed goose and cakes. And ate before the electric fire, and went out near midnight, to hear a choir sing in a nearby church. And next morning—after all three had secretively and furiously rushed around buying gifts for the others—Victor's original presents for Vickie having been mailed to the States, Dolores not having bought one for Vickie, nor Vickie for her—with Christmas music on the BBC, and the electric fire warming them, and good coffee and pastries, they unwrapped hurriedly the lavishly wrapped boxes. "'I made out like a bandit!" Vickie said. "Double presents!"

Dolores and Victor had had their own private Christmas the night before, after Vickie returned to her hotel, with champagne and lots of other warming things.

And Vickie was sensitive, under that bland and

159

giggly exterior. At least, so Dolores concluded when she came tramping into the apartment late in the afternoon the day after Christmas and announced that guess what, she'd been walking down the Strand past Charing Cross and who should she meet but Toad and Vee and Boo and Ram and they were all going to fly to Paris and if Victor would "lend" her the money, she'd like to go with them, it sounded great, didn't it?

"Damn it, she conned me," Victor said after she'd left. "She did, that kid," he chuckled. "It's the old quarter routine they used to pull in the comic strips. You know, boy sits on the—what did they call them then—the davenport! waiting for girl and kid sister or brother comes slithering around offering privacy for a dime. Or a quarter. And gets it, of course."

Dolores eyed him reproachfully. "That's one way of looking at it."

"There's another?"

"You might consider it this way: the poor kid comes 'bopping' in, as she puts it, expecting a nice week with Daddy, seeing the sights of London, and doing the poor old man a favor, keeping him company over Christmas. And finds herself an intruder, and broke to boot. She knows that as long as she stays, both of us will feel obligated to spend our time with her. She knows I'm visiting you for the week, and that that is special, *our* holiday. What is she to do? I thought she carried it off bravely. I only hope there really are a Toad and Vee and Boo and Ram," she concluded, laughing.

Victor gazed at her without smiling, thoughtfully. "It could be," he said finally. Then, vigorously, hugging her, "But I am damned glad to have you back! It's, as Vickie would say, something else to find myself jealous of my own daughter!"

"Well, if it's any consolation to you, I was jealous too. Poor Vickie: she must have felt that."

"Well, I don't know." He leaned back comfortably, his arm around Dolores's shoulders. "Sometimes I get to feel there's some kind of conspiracy among women."

"There is, of course," she smiled. "Rather like the one among men."

160

"What did it?" He was smiling at her, but there was something hard in his smile. "What brought the two of you together so fast?"

She shrugged. "You saw. Just our experience of being women in a male world. And talking about feelings, I suppose."

"No. There's something you're not telling me. There was something between you, something more. . . ." He was still smiling, but the smile was fixed, there was an edge to it that frightened Dolores a little. She thought she would not like to be an employee of his, facing a smile like that.

"There *is* something I'm not telling you, but I can't."

His whole body seemed to rigidify, although he barely moved.

"Why?"

"It's Vickie's story. Her . . . secret, I guess. She'll tell you, I know she will. She wants to, but I think she's a little intimidated by you."

His muscles loosened. "Oh." Then tensed again. "She's not pregnant?"

She laughed. "Not that I know of."

He sat back again, looking grouchy. "Some man, I suppose."

"I suppose."

"You *know!* It's not right. *I'm* her father! What did the bastard do?"

"How can you be so sure he's a bastard?"

"All men are bastards."

"That's what Anthony used to say, too."

"Well, it's true."

"Why should any of us get involved with you then?"

"I didn't mean *me,* Dolores!" And took her in his arms. Later, he said, "Don't go back."

"To Oxford? I have to."

"No you don't. You could just as well work here. At the museum."

She considered. It had been a wonderful two weeks. She tried to remember her objections.

"I couldn't answer the telephone. If one of my kids needed me . . ."

"Christ, we'll get another phone!"

"And where will you hide me when visiting eminences descend who aren't your daughter? And what will you do with me when you have to go to Oxford? Take me to the Randolph with you?" A little nasty tone in that last. He heard it. An eyelash flickered, or a hair in his nose. Something.

"If another eminence descends, I'll introduce you. I'll invite you to dinner with us. Boy, will you be sorry!"

She smiled, took his hand. "Sweetheart, I think it's better if I have my own place. Where I don't ever have to hide from anybody. A place to go if I happen to get mad at you."

"Are you planning to get mad at me?"

"No, but it is conceivable. I have felt anger at you."

"When?"

But she could not remember. She searched her mind. "Well, that first time, when you left. . . ."

He dismissed that. "That was early. I didn't know you then."

"And you do now."

He gave her a look that said: don't be so uppity. I realize of course that you are immeasurably mysterious. But I know you well enough for all that.

"I have to have my own place."

He sighed.

"It's better this way. Really."

"Better for whom?"

"For both of us. For *us*."

"Somehow that sounds suspiciously like a parent telling a kid he's spanking him for his own good."

"But it stands to reason, doesn't it? that if *I'm* happier, we'll be happier?"

"Umm. And *that* sounds suspiciously like what I used to tell Edith when I wanted my own way."

4

DOLORES WENT back to Oxford. The sun rose late and set early; the sky looked grey and about-to-rain most of the time; and not a snowdrop appeared, poking its white fresh head above the tarnished grass, until the very end of January. But between Victor and Dolores, rainbows shimmered. They went cycling and for tramps through the woods; they ate out or in; they went to hear music in the Oxford chapels; they sat before the fire, holding hands; they talked; they made love. Their lips stayed wine for each other.

She was inclined to glint I-told-you-so at him; he was inclined to suggest that more of a good thing could only be better. But, he said, it certainly wasn't drab. Drabness and boredom were the two great curses, he said. Coming home night after night to the same old things—same old food, same old conversation, same old questions. Same kids having the same old squabbles, same old gossip about the same old neighbors, same TV blaring the same vapidities.

Nothing was worse than drabness and boredom, Victor said.

Dolores thought about worse things: death camps; gulags; torture cells in Iran Chile Brazil the Philippines Argentina Cambodia. Identification passes and black encampments in South Africa Rhodesia.

Boredom and drabness, Victor said, were the things he dreaded most.

Dolores tried to think what she dreaded most. Not death, not pain, bad as those were, because there was no point in dreading them, they were inevitable. Not natural catastrophe, bad as it was, because there was no point in dreading it since it was unpredictable. She knew what she dreaded most: the complete take-over of the world by a mentality she privately called Nazi. No relation to any political party in any country; found everywhere, indigenous on planet earth. And gaining every day.

The Nazis, after all, were only the epitome, the egregious example in her own lifetime of a common enough tendency, found on your own block, found maybe in your own house. Started from the belief that some people were inherently better than others, were by birth entitled to what they called rights, but were really privileges not extended to others. Color them legitimate. The "in" group then made nice neat (or not so neat) demarcations among the others: some

163

people were more entitled to respect by the legitimates than others. Color most of them white, and all of them male. There were even a few white Jews and some almost white niggers, if you looked hard. Not for some Nazis, of course. Some Nazis were more fastidious.

But everybody, and in time, everything, was ranked. And even the legitimates in one place became less so in another. The department head strode around like a martinet until he went up in the elevator to the top floor and met the president, and quavered. And the man on the assembly line had to take all kinds of shit from his foreman, but when he was with his buddies in the bowling alley, he was king of the hill. But all men had one unfailing area where they were legitimate, and that was with their women. Maybe with all women. Used to be, social class kept some men from daring to approach some women, but not anymore. Democracy had made all women open to anything from all men.

And the way you run this shop is through the brain: everybody is convinced that the people who say they are legitimate *are* legitimate. So everybody runs in fear, abject to authority. And everybody who has any hope at all aims for the top floor where the chairman lives. The chairman has no face and no body either. He has a uniform with a blank on top of it and he lives always at the tops of high buildings, or in fortresses on islands in warm waters. He goes up and down in private elevators and never encounters anything unfriendly, anything untamed—not people or weather or a hostile editorial. His underlings make sure of this.

And it is very scary to be in such a position, so you have to keep securing it. You severely rank the country. You put half the people in death camps or gulags or poverty or maybe you actually kill them— but for such a direct method, you may be called mad by other nations, as is Idi Amin. Then you put safe women in great houses where they can be inseminated only by those with the proper credentials, so you can raise a race of legitimates. The rest deserve what they get. Eventually, you tell your confidants, the world will be a great stall for a few black-jacketed or brown-shirted men to romp in, and everyone else will be dead or at-your-service.

But it is still scary, yes, because to secure your legitimacy, everyone else must be disinherited. And in time, the legitimate must hear the cries of the starving hordes just beyond the iron gates, and so must build higher and higher iron gates, pile more concrete around the bunker, must drink only bottled and tested water, breathe only canned and tested air.

Power held and loved and cherished in the hands for no other end than itself, yes. Oh, eventually, it dies, of course. It goes round and round, eating everything in sight, and never excreting, jealous of conferring, by accident, one magical bit of itself that might be seized upon and used by the unlawful to work a spell. So, bloated and glutted, it topples over, unable to control its own swollen body.

Except that now they were working on better and better ways to control—buttons and wires and wirelesses and computers that could reach not only the four corners of the earth, but even to space. And anyway, it is no consolation that the legitimates die, because there are always new ones to spring up and take their places, claiming transcendence, claiming invulnerability. And besides that, they always take us with them. Certainly. Look, there, that pink-cheeked boy with the tam and the rifle, standing scared on the street corner, he never finished school, and the army at least paid a decent wage, so there he is, but just behind him (he can't see them, but look and you will) are some children, not much older than eleven, sneaking up behind him, three of them, boys, with a bomb, just a little one. There! now you see the explosion, and the pink cheeks and the tam are in slivers, the boys didn't do much better, one ran faster and got away with one leg intact, the others lie there, their blood mingling with the soldier's now, in death, when it is too late.

Yes, and there is a slender golden-skinned boy with fair hair, who used to play with his sister on the veldt, and who always had to be reminded to brush his teeth, but who learned to obey because his father had a broad belt, and right this minute he is lifting his rifle, aiming it at a brown-skinned boy in a tree whom he takes for a guerilla, and who knows? maybe he is. CRACK! goes the rifle. DOWN falls the brown-skinned boy, the branches break as he hits them, his head clobbers the ground like a coconut and the brains spill out and the golden-skinned boy turns away a little ill, and pulls his illness together and molds it into righteousness and marches home and announces his feat. Never again will he cry: he will only shout. That's how the transcendents do away with pain.

Yes, and there, that one, he isn't very old, younger than Tony, he looks a little like Tony, same dark hair and sensual mouth and eyes. He too learned early to obey Father, and Father stands behind him now, Father-Commandant, Father-Superior, Father-in-Heaven, ordering him to do it, to do it, to place the electrodes on the woman's vulva, and he does, and the switch is pulled, and the woman shrieks and writhes and passes out, there is a terrible smell of burning flesh and the Father says *good* and the boy creeps back to his quarters and lies on his bunk with his legs drawn up into his stomach and tries not to think, tries to remember his village, but all he can remember there is hunger.

And if he grows up, he too will have to be a Father, for his guilt will permit him no other alternative.

Yes, yes, but maybe it's no worse now than it ever was. Maybe she shouldn't dread it as if it were the end of a livable world, maybe things had always been this bad only you didn't know about it.

Picture: a hovel in bare country, scrub trees and sandy soil, people bent and wrinkled and nearly toothless by thirty (even though they didn't eat white bread), bodies permanently stiffened into odd postures by work and cold, calloused feet wrapped in rags, minds nearly crazy with hunger and ignorance. Cold indoors and out; never enough fuel to do much more than bake the bread that is usually their only meal, and to keep a spark of the fire going. They milk the cow with stiff fingers, and bring it and their chickens indoors with them at night. The woman nurses her children as long as she can, or until they die. If they die quickly, she nurses herself into a cup and feeds the two who have somehow, miraculously, lived.

Their farm is in Cornwall, on the rough ragged coast, or in Crabbe country, perhaps. It is the middle of the fifteenth century. The country is falling apart, between civil wars and the plague. And one day up rides this band of marauders, wild, crazy-eyed kids out of the army because of missing eyes or limbs and no dole, but still able to ride. Come tearing up on hungry horses and rip the bread from their hands, kill the children, rape the woman, murder the man and then the woman, and burn the hovel. So mean it didn't require burning, it would have retreated back into the earth in no time at all.

Four skinny bodies wrapped in rags, two of them tiny, lie on the dirt floor as the straw flares and catches. The crazy kids yell crazily. They kill the cow and eat it over a couple of days until it begins to stink. Then they kill the chickens and eat them with the feathers still clinging in places. Then they ride off to find another hovel. It will be days before they do, and two of them will be dead by then.

"As our life is very short, so is it very miserable; and therefore it is well it is short." Jeremy Taylor should be resurrected and taken on a junket to Marin County.

Things are better, aren't they?

Still: who before the twentieth century could have imagined a long line of railroad tracks with connections to all of Europe, dotted all along the way with little white railroad stationhouses, decorated with pots of bright flowers and quaint signs bearing phony names? All designed to calm down people who couldn't get away anyhow, who were going to places that had signs over them saying *Arbeit Macht Frei,* where they would be forced to work. Slavery is an old institution, but what kind of insane slavery was that? It was the first wave, how many millions? the first line of the ridding the earth of the untouchables, the forever and irredeemably illegitimate. There were to be many more, but the giant toppled. It doesn't matter. He lives elsewhere.

And yet we forget. We forget it all, as we forget the Albigensians, the Amalekites, what they did to

Joan. Even though the signs are still there, we forget.

What lies beyond the signs is beyond imagining. You have to see it. You have to go to Theresienstadt, climb out the single lookout tower that is left, and gaze out at miles of silence. Not a single red patch stains the dry brown earth, for all the blood that was spilled there. The wind blows through and doesn't weep as it passes, for all the cries that were heard there. And for all the agony that was felt there, there is no monument, no bleeding heart set into the image of a god, nothing but the barren earth. Not a wall remains. No voice comes on the soft wind late at night and sings lamentations.

At Auschwitz the ovens stand empty, birds sing in the trees surrounding the compound, they peck in the earth. In a display case huge as a truck are shoes and boots taken from the prisoners. The boots crinkle and curl down, sad as bassets' eyes, but no sigh wrinkles the air. Even the visitors keep their mouths shut.

No depiction of human pain can ever suggest its reality. Even the earth doesn't remember, it doesn't want to remember. The world would drown in its own tears if it ever let itself feel its grief.

So maybe their way is better. Forget it! Onward and upward! Hey, young feller, pick yourself up (and wipe them tears offa your cheek), dust yourself off and GET OUT THERE AND WIN THAT GAME!

LADIES AND GENTLEMEN, HE'S COMING BACK! LISTEN TO THAT APPLAUSE! NOTHING CAN STOP HIM! Not osteomyelitis or his bad heart or his broken knee or his fractured collarbone or his ingrown toenail or his wife in the loony bin or his mother on the dry-out farm or his little baby kidnapped: NOTHING! HE'S DOING IT FOR THE OLD MAN, LOOK AT HIM, WILL YOU, LADIES AND GENTLEMEN, THE HERO'S FATHER STANDING UP! STANDING UP!

The hero is running off and off, into the future with a bomb in his arms.

Yes, but you had to admit it was a way of surviving. They deny pain. Is your way any better?

To deny pain you must deny all feeling. Denying feeling leads to insanity.

And who's the most insane person around here, huh?

It's true. Watching TV one night back in the States, the evening news. Report on a new weight-losing technique: Diet with Jesus. The women (they were, of course, all women) gathered weekly, were weighed, compared statistics, and read the Bible and prayed together. Sufficient faith, they insisted, would sustain them in their ordeal. The interviewer homed in on a woman who was not at all fat, even on TV.

Microphone in hand, hushed voice, reverent attitude, crock of shit: "You have just listened to a passage from the Bible. Tell me, what did it mean to you?"

The woman had a soft Southern voice, a sweet manner, a child's eyes: "That passage tells me that I don't need to eat to feel filled. It tells me that Jesus will fill me with His love."

Dolores had (naturally) burst into tears.

Everyone is a woman to somebody, but everyone doesn't admit it.

That nice Southern lady, there, she should have an affair. It was guaranteed to work, for a month or six. Of course she won't. Too pious: a good girl. Slowly, over the years, she will dry up, begin to say *Tssk* at movies with too much flesh in them, begin to feel what so many people felt, that sex was the deepest evil. (Forgetting the dry earth, not knowing about Theresienstadt.) She was a nice woman, she'd try not to turn vicious. She'd screw her face up into a smile and although somebody could see the trembling at the corners of her mouth, nobody would mention it, and she would say that she certainly did try to understand the young people of today even though she, of course, came from a different generation.

She might try tranks or booze or tennis or golf or bridge. She'd sit in a chair in front of the TV and her mouth would crinkle up and she'd read romances in which every titillation and no consummation occurred. Sundays she'd go to church and Thursday nights to the Ladies' Auxiliary.

Her husband believes he is different from her: she's a lady and he's a *man*—a *real* man. Fast and hard in bed, he's convinced he's a great lover, but his wife

just isn't, well . . . she's a good woman, you see. He'd
done his share of being wild, he wasn't no saint, he had
to admit it (but not to her), he had a bit of the devil
in him. But sittin there in church with her on Sundays
and listenin to that minister givin him what for, the
feelin creeps upon him that maybe it wasn't so good
after all, what he was doin, and that that Betty now,
boy did she have a pair though, well, she was fun, but
if truth be told, she weren't much better than a whore.

It was sex itself that was evil, like the Bible said.
So he gave it up. For the most part. He took to rifle
practice on Tuesday nights, bowling Wednesdays, and
poker with the guys on Fridays. Over the weekend
(Thank the Lord in His Mercy) there was football.
And he stopped, for the most part, just that any woman
that wasn't a good woman like his wife, that dressed
a little—well, you know—or walked out on the street
at night alone: well, she got what was comin to her.
But he was sure he had conquered the vice in his soul.
Just had to get these tramps, these whores of Babylon,
these temptresses under control.

But he, himself, he was saved! Hallelujah!

(Meanwhile, in Cambodia, government forces were
wiping out villages suspected of wrong thinking.)

He would not notice when he beat his son with his
belt for stealing money from his mama's purse to buy
candy with that he was hitting too hard, that he didn't
even hear the child's screams, that his wife was pulling on his arm, calling him, screaming at him. Because the kid wasn't getting the message, wasn't understanding him: Do not expect pleasure in this life!
Learn to obey!

He was pure and free from sin and he ought to
know.

Nor would his wife notice, when her daughter was
overjoyed with something that had happened in school
that day, was whirling around in the living room in
extravagant elation, and she went in with pursed lips,
hearing the crash, having expected it, and said: You
see there now! You knocked over the table! It's a
wonder you didn't break the lamp. Now you stop,
hear?: that she was saying, Don't move, don't expect, you'll bring everything down around you.

(In Argentina, at that very moment, the secret police whisked a young couple off the street and took them to a prison that had no official existence.)

Oh, what's the point of trying to sort these things out?

The point is that one has no choice.

But your truths are always so simple.

Yes. Bus ride somewhere, a conference, yes, near Chicago, all of us on the way to the airport. Professor Bickford, elderly and respected, had come to her lecture. He hobbled up the aisle from his seat to hers and asked permission to sit beside her.

He had listened to her talk, he said. Thought she was brilliant, profound.

He can't be coming on. I don't believe it.

He traveled a great deal, he said.

I don't believe it, he wouldn't. He's an innocent. Of course, I've been surprised before. Remember that kindly old toothless man in Assisi? Told you he was ninety-two, asked you how you liked his town, and then grabbed you with a wiry hand that felt like a claw.

And in his travels, he said, he met a great many interesting people. Fascinating people.

What do you suppose he wants?

And when he met these people, he always did one thing. He'd been doing it for years now, whenever he met interesting people. He asked them a question. Might he ask her that question?

Oh god. My favorite author. My institutional background: like Terence Malle, he has a theory of personality derived from whether you got your education on the East Coast (Harvard/Yale) or the West Coast (Berkeley). There weren't any other places, except Oxford/Cambridge, and they were unmistakable.

The question was: You are a scholar and a thinker who has read the great literature of the past and has thoughtfully viewed the life of the present: what, in your eyes, is the most profound truth of human existence?

He stopped and watched her, watching her very lips.

I don't believe this. And what's more, he's expecting long words, long sentences. He has his pencil ready.

171

She made a firm decision not to answer. He was a kind man, a good man, she could see it in his innocent blue eyes, his quivering white mustache, his nice plump smiling wife, his poised sharpened teacher's pencil. He represented what was best in academia.

And in his blindness, he represented the worst.

No, don't answer.

"Everybody fucks up," her mouth blurted.

He rose quickly and quivered his way back to his seat and his comforting wife after a thank-you that sounded more like an inhalation.

Sorry. Sorry. But you deserved it, with such a question. You wanted some nice abstract formula that would sound profound, didn't you? Besides, how could you know that Elspeth had just, that it was only a few months, that I was sick to death of words words words.

Sorry.

But he should have known. Because the horrors went on at home and abroad, in the kitchen and the nursery and the bedroom and the maproom and the conference rooms and the office of the high command and also in the field and the tiger cages. But everybody pretended we were living in a world where there was a clear right way to do everything. Everybody had a recipe. How to have a happy marriage, how to have a happy divorce, how to have a happy remarriage, how to stay thin, how to screw, how to make money, how to stay healthy, how to live forever. Yes.

Sometimes, Dolores had a dream. It was not really a dream, it came when she was awake, but not fully awake. Someplace in between sleep and wake. It came when she was troubled and it came when she was not troubled. It came when it chose.

She was lying in bed, near sleep, when she felt the heat, and opened her eyes. There was a glow and she looked and he was there, sitting at the foot of the bed, naked and gold-bronze and glowing. She recognized him because she'd been expecting him for years. His skin was shimmering in the moonlight that poured like phosphorescent milk through the bedroom window. His expression was utterly serene; he had just a little smile, not even a smile, just a loving expression. He was her angel, her animus, she knew that.

So she pulled herself up from the pillow and sat back against the headboard and crossed her arms, and said, "Okay, you bastard, now talk!"

He smiles. And talks. He explains everything, slowly, carefully. How the moon sun stars planets animals plants stones water people, how there was a plan for everything for all creatures with fur feathers scales dandruff, and it was glorious because it all made SENSE! SENSE! Even the pain inflicted by humans on humans, even the insanity of human culture as it presently existed, had a purpose in the overall plan.

She rapped out questions, trying to be tough. Little by little, her questions grow gentler, she is lulled into the beauty of it, it makes everything bearable. And little by little, her neck relaxes, and her head sinks back against the pillow. She listens in complete trust; he has hedged nothing, not the smallest thing. She doesn't have to scrutinize him anymore, she knows his face is telling her the truth. She doesn't have to look at him because his glow is everywhere, but she wants to look at him because he is beautiful and she loves him. She never has to think again, he has made everything clear. She never has to suffer again, because all of it makes sense.

And that clarity is the greatest bliss she has ever experienced. Her mind is in rapture. She feels herself glowing too. She is completely filled. (Jesus will fill you with His love.)

He pauses. He coughs a little. (Do angels cough? she wonders.) He says, hesitantly: The trouble is that now you know all this, we cannot permit you to remain on earth.

She nods. That seems to make perfect sense. Human beings have always lived in blindness, so of course they always will. Must. She doesn't question that. It doesn't occur to her to suggest that perhaps this would be a good time to change that. No, she just nods. She surrenders. (What else can you do with a God?) And heaven knows, when he leans forward to take her in his arms, she doesn't quibble: she leans towards him, wanting to be in such arms, against such skin. They melt together and they float upwards, off the bed, up and out into space, and he is hot and shining and she is hot and shining and their bodies come together in all that heat and they float out into space in a togetherness that knocks the rocks to orgasm.

5

DOLORES AND Victor were driving to Manchester in the rain. That is, Victor was driving and Dolores was watching the windshield wipers. And he was talking about his father, his fondness for his father, the bully boy, the roarer. "Except for one thing. He used to smoke a pipe, and he'd lay it down in an ashtray without finishing it, and it would go out. And the smell of that in a room literally made me vomit—when I was very small, anyhow. I learned to control it—but *I* had to learn to control it. *He* never stopped leaving those stinky pipes around."

Dolores rubbed his knee.

"It's strange, though, when I smoked a pipe, it didn't bother me at all, and I sometimes did the same thing. I tried not to, thinking it might make other people sick the way it had me. But sometimes I think we seize on one thing our parents do and hate that, use it as a kind of wastebin for all the other bad feelings we don't let ourselves feel."

"Yes. Anthony used to hate the way his father chewed. It really made him want to scream. Sometimes, when he was a boy, he had to leave the table and go into the john and recover."

"How did he feel about his father?"

"All he ever admitted to was love and admiration."

"And what do you think?"

She shrugged. "I'm sure it had to be terribly complicated."

"Tell me about Anthony. The boy. The one you fell in love with."

"Well. To begin with there was Jessie, who was

174

eighteen and very beautiful and madly in love with Aldrich, and a little pregnant. She and Aldrich got married. I don't know how he felt about her then. In later years he looked down on her. It was embarrassing to watch, you felt she must feel humiliated. If she did, she never showed it. But Aldrich was bright, and Jessie wasn't. When the baby was born, Aldrich fell madly in love with her, Laura, who had big violet eyes and an athletic body.

"They were happy. They had a little house, a car, nice clothes. I've seen the pictures. Everybody took pictures in those days. It's nice, I wish I'd taken more. . . .

"Times were high, money all over the place, Aldrich was rising fast in the Boston office of Blanchard Oil. Jessie got pregnant again. She didn't want another baby because Aldrich didn't want another baby. He was crazy for Laura. Jessie drank ergot tea, but it didn't work, and Anthony was born. But Aldrich went on being crazy for Laura, and because Jessie was crazy for Aldrich, she was crazy for Laura too. Anthony just tailed along. You can see it in the pictures: he's little and sad and sweet and his drawers droop as if he knows he's fringe. Laura is full-bodied, bursting with energy, her smile is like an Olympic medalist's. She takes up all the space of the picture.

"When she was nine, Laura fell ill with rheumatic fever. Jessie and her sister took their children to Florida to spend the winter. Laura recovered, and the next winter they stayed in Brookline. But when she was ten, she came home from a Sunday School picnic in a light rain. Jessie once said to me: 'I knew it was going to rain, Dolores. But I thought—what could happen to her going to a Sunday School picnic? God wouldn't let anything happen to her.' Well, God did, or somebody. She caught a cold and got sicker and sicker and was in a wheelchair for months, and one day around her eleventh birthday, she died.

"Anthony was seven, and playing ball in the back of the house with his friends. He saw his mother come out of the house with his aunts around her, he saw her get into a car, he ran to catch her to find out where she was going, but she was gone. He trudged back and

175

looked at his sister's wheelchair on the back porch and wondered where *she* was. It must have frightened him —his mother gone out and his sister absent? His mother never left his sister's side—because he remembers it, and that's about all he remembers for a long time.

"Aldrich and Jessie went away with Jessie's sister and her husband. They were millionaires, they had a yacht, and they took Aldrich and Jessie on a cruise around the world. They were gone for a year. They never said good-bye to Anthony, or explained anything to him. Jessie told me this. Jessie's mother came over and picked Anthony up and took him home with her; relatives and friends came over and closed up the house, put furniture in storage, sold most of it. Jessie and Aldrich never went back to that house.

"And Jessie never healed. She could never pass the street on which the house stood where Laura had died without getting the shakes. She never again, in her life, slept without chloral, or later, Nembutal. She spent her afternoons, after Anthony was at school, driving madly anyplace, every place, running to shops, running constantly. And for a long time, she would not let Anthony touch her.

" 'Every time his little hand would touch me, Dolores, I'd leap away from it, I couldn't stand it, it was Laura's hand, it reminded me of hers, but hers was gone.'

"Once, in a low mood, as close to the truth as he ever allowed himself to come, Anthony told me he used to wish that he had died instead of Laura.

"Well, they went on living," Dolores sighed. "People do. The Depression fell, but Aldrich was still doing well. Better than well, because to have a good-paying job in the Depression made you rich. He was smart and ambitious. He bought up real estate. Anthony listened to football games on the radio and planned to go to West Point, an ambition Aldrich fostered.

"Then, suddenly, Aldrich fell ill. It began as a kind of indigestion, but very soon he could not keep anything down. He was in pain. The first diagnosis was ulcers, but the treatment didn't help. They went to other doctors. They began a trek around the country, going from clinic to clinic. Anthony was left again, with Grandma. Nothing helped, no one could diagnose it. The only clear fact was that he was dying.

"Finally, Jessie left him, tearfully, at a sanatorium in Saranac and returned to her son. As often as they could, the woman and the boy made the long drive from Boston to visit him. Aldrich's illness was a constant subject of conversation, and Jessie always listened to suggestions. One day someone mentioned a clinic they hadn't heard of, somewhere in the Middle West. Jessie made arrangements, she drove to Saranac, she bundled the frail dying man in sweaters and coats and took him on the train to Wisconsin—or wherever it was.

"And this clinic diagnosed him. They said that Aldrich had eaten meat exposed to poison gas when he was in France during the war, and that he had developed tuberculosis of the intestines. I don't know how medically sound any of that is, but that's what they said. They operated on him and removed most of his intestine, and sent him home to die. They gave him five weeks.

"Aldrich weighed less than ninety pounds and was in constant agony. Jessie took him back to the big house in Brookline that belonged to her parents. She and Aldrich had lost everything or nearly everything they'd had, except for a few pieces of real estate. Blanchard had paid Aldrich's salary for two years and then stopped. The grandparents couldn't bear watching Aldrich's agony and they went out to the Cape, where they had a cottage. The big house was empty with just the three of them in it, Aldrich never leaving his bed. And Jessie tiptoed all the time, partly not to disturb him, but mainly so she could hear his every sound, his very breathing. He was still the center of the world to her, and Anthony had always had to adapt to that. She did everything for Aldrich: spoonfed him what little he could eat, brought him the bedpan and emptied it, cooked pots of soup, brought him liquids at pill times, which she never forgot.

"Anthony watched. He tiptoed and whispered too. There was no room for childhood in that house. At night Jessie would sit on the top step just below the

177

landing, sit there all night, listening. Anthony would creep beside her and slip his hand in hers. They would listen, not that Aldrich ever cried out, or often moaned. Jessie was listening to his breathing.

"The doctor came every day. Paunchy, tired, in a rumpled suit, he would examine Aldrich and talk to him briefly. Every day he'd ask again if Aldrich wanted a minister and Aldrich's answer was always the same, a growled 'Keep those damn fools away from me!' The doctor would nod. He would lay some morphine tablets on the bedside table and say: 'Aldrich, I've left you enough morphine to kill a horse.' And Aldrich would nod.

"Every day the doctor would descend the stairs heavily, tired in his heart, to the waiting woman and the boy. 'I don't know how he can last the night. I've left him enough morphine to kill a horse.' And the woman nodded too.

"Every day for a month this went on. Every night they sat on the steps. Anthony was only ten. Did he sit there imagining that when death entered the house, he would hear a rustle of wings, a sudden chill? Did he understand what his mother was waiting for?

"For that matter, did she? Because I've never understood what she was waiting for, adding to the death in the house, instead of trying to bring some life in it for the child.

"Well, Aldrich never reached for the extra morphine. Instead, he got better. Not well, but a little better, a little stronger. After a month, he could sit up in bed; after three, he could come downstairs once a day, for dinner. He would dress carefully, in Brooks Brothers' flannel trousers and a tweed jacket and a shirt with an ascot, and holding to the banister, standing as erect as an old general, he'd descend.

"Jessie was still very anxious. The three of them would sit at table, Aldrich's weakness making him nearly silent, Jessie's anxiety spreading round the room like fanned air. They all ate, in silence, the foods Aldrich was permitted to eat: never anything else. In silence, Anthony would listen to his father chew the same mouthful over and over: he had to, he had almost no intestine.

"And sometimes, Aldrich would be seized by a spasm of agony as he sat there, and he would clutch the wooden arms of the dining chair until his knuckles turned white. He never said anything about it. He didn't have to. At his slightest gesture, Jessie turned rigid and white herself. She would have leaped up, but sometimes he'd growl at her to sit down and eat her dinner. So she waited, but everyone had stopped chewing midbite. Sometimes the pain got so bad that Aldrich fainted. Then the boy and the woman would have to carry him back up to bed.

"In time he was well enough, Jessie decided, to travel. Her family owned a lodge on a lake in Maine. There were farms nearby, goats, horses. She decided the fresh air and openness would cure him. She made up a bed for him in the back seat of the car, packed their bags and they set out. Aldrich was shaken by the trip and lay unconscious through most of it.

"The lodge was stone, an old building with a stone fireplace large enough to hold a man lying down. There was a huge central room and a big kitchen, and several small bedrooms. Jessie kept a fire going in the central room all the time, even in the summer, to keep the dampness out of the room and the chill out of the stone.

"This was the one time of his childhood that Anthony remembered vividly. He talked about it often, told me over and over about the fireplace, the horseflies, the canoe—but that came later. He'd visit the next farm every day, and they let him feed the animals, ride the horses. He became a good rider. Every day he carried back goat's milk for his father to drink. He doesn't talk about feelings, ever, doesn't say he was happy, but you can hear it in his voice, in his lightness. You can hear sun and woods and rippled light through the leaves, and swimming in the lake and playing with animals, running, jumping, maybe even —God forbid—yelling and yodeling and screeching, if he were far enough from the house. He can recollect tiny details—the horses' names and colors, the color of the canoe, the color of the stone fireplace, the bends in the path that led from the road to the lodge.

"At first Aldrich sat out on the front porch in a recliner, wrapped in blankets. He was still in ghastly pain. His face was white and tight with it. Often, when Anthony came home, he'd find his father in the chair slumped over, and was not sure if he were sleeping or unconscious.

"Eventually, the supplies she'd bought on the way through town ran low, and Jessie had to drive to town to replenish them. Anthony was eleven now, a big boy, but not big enough to drive. So, she gave him instructions, and kissing Aldrich good-bye anxiously, she left to make the twenty-mile drive. Anthony sat talking to his father, but Aldrich wanted to sleep, so Anthony went indoors to read a comic book. He was through about five comic books before he remembered he was supposed to be watching his father. He ran outdoors. Aldrich was slumped over, and his hands were funny-looking. Anthony tried to rouse him, but couldn't, and his father's hands stayed stretched out and odd. He was dead, or dying, Anthony thought.

"He shouldn't have left him. If he'd stayed, this wouldn't have happened. Maybe his father wasn't dead, maybe he was just unconscious. Maybe there was something he could do to bring his father back. Standing there in what must have been guilty terror and panic, Anthony had a vision. He would take his father's pain into himself. If he had the courage to do that, his father would recover.

"Calmly, deliberately, he walked indoors and sat down in front of the fireplace that was big enough to hold a lying-down man. Calmly, deliberately, he removed one shoe, one sock, and rolled up his pants leg. He edged as close to the fire as he could, and then gingerly, slowly, lifted his leg and put it into the fire. He was frightened, but he was absolutely, unshakably convinced of the necessity of this act. He held his leg in the fire as long as he could bear it. He gritted his teeth, he tried not to whimper. His father never whimpered. Tears came into his eyes and he knew that in a minute he would scream and that would ruin it. Slowly, carefully, he brought his leg out again. It was very painful, he couldn't bend it. And then he cried, softly, not from the pain but from frustration. He was weak, cowardly, he was impotent. He could not stand

180

what his father stood. He couldn't help him unless he had courage, but he didn't, not enough, anyway. He cursed himself, he slapped his burned leg, but he could not get his leg to go back into the fire. He had intended to suck his father's pain into himself, draw it inch by inch from the sick man. But he had failed.

"In fact, Aldrich had only passed out from pain, and had revived by the time Jessie returned.

"In time, Anthony's leg healed; in time, Aldrich recovered. The goat's milk put weight on him and by the next summer he was out riding with Anthony and Jessie. He spent hours carefully building by hand a lovely red mahogany canoe. Anthony watched, but Aldrich would not allow him to help. Aldrich was a perfectionist. By next winter, the three of them were skiing. There are pictures. They all look happy now except Jessie, who won't smile because she's embarrassed about having no lower teeth, and hasn't the money to get teeth.

"They went back to Brookline, and Aldrich, uninsurable and too old now to get a good job, unwilling to take a poor one, started a little mail-order house, working out of the garage at first, and later from a building in Watertown. It was a happy ending. Of course, he died eventually, but he had twenty years of life left in him.

"Happy ending, I guess. Jessie turned sour after all, mean and bitchy, although never towards Aldrich. And Anthony never recovered. He reproduced his father, without his father's cause, every day of his life after the children were born. He had no feel for childflesh, could not abide child noises, his anxiety made mealtimes hell for all of us. There was death in his heart. He was a rather serious hypochondriac, and would nurse his slightest sty or boil—and get both frequently—as if it were a cancer. You'd think he wanted it to be a cancer. I guess he did. It's nice to have a reason to feel what you're feeling.

"He'd abuse me verbally to the point where I'd walk out of the room, or later, out of the house, or later, say I wanted a divorce. Then pull me back, desperate, clinging, helpless, saying I had imagined it all, he had never done such things, said such things, would never say such things to me, whom he loved. How could I imagine he didn't love the children?

"Maybe he did. Maybe he loved all of us, who knows? How can you tell what he felt, living in there with all his ghosts? He never escaped them.

"And perhaps," she concluded wearily, "none of us ever does."

6

HE PUT his arm around her. "You sound so awfully sad."

She shrugged. Her voice was thin, tight. "Oh, you know, I was such a fool. I accepted his cruelty, his craziness, thinking I could cure it, by love and fidelity and acceptance. I forgave him so much. And it did nearly kill me to leave him. One more abandonment. And in a way, my life ended then too. Not when he killed himself, but when I left him. I often feel that: as though that was the true part of my life, and all the rest has been a coda. Maybe because I suffered so much with him, although the worst part of my life was . . . was later. But also I guess because I still believed, then, still thought that if you took your life in your hands you could shape it. I went on believing until very near the end of our marriage that someday, if I just talked to him enough, showed him enough, loved him enough—even though by then, I'd stopped loving *him* (but never the Anthony of the stories, I never stopped loving him)—he would miraculously pull out of it, let the ghosts rest, let himself live. I never believed that again, and so I guess I never felt myself as fully *in* life again."

"But that's crazy," he said bitterly. "You're full of life. And why in hell should you break your heart over a selfish manipulative bastard?"

"Is that what you see?"

"Sure. I'll bet he had you all tiptoeing around the house on weekends for fear of one of his outbursts. I'll bet you were all supercareful not to do anything that had offended him at any time, because you were never sure what would trigger them."

"That's true."

"I'll bet he said he was glad you were teaching, but then yelled bloody murder if you came home late because of a committee meeting."

"How can you know such things?"

"It isn't hard," Victor said. He was hitting the steering wheel with the palm of his hand, not hard but regularly.

"Are you like that?"

"No. Well, maybe I was, a little. But I probably would have been more so if I'd been married to someone like you."

"Like me?"

"Someone who doesn't say 'Yes, dear,' and 'Whatever you say, dear,' in private *or* in public. A woman who doesn't even pretend to defer."

"He wouldn't have liked it if I had."

"Are you sure?"

She was silent.

Victor turned to look at her. "Am I upsetting you?"

"No. Well. It's strange. I'm so political in my thinking. But I never saw our problems, Anthony's and mine, as political. I saw them purely as psychological."

"But I should think you'd be the first to suggest to somebody else that psychological problems are also political."

"Yes," she agreed, surprised.

They checked into the hotel, but Victor had to go out again directly. A long meeting, it would probably run over into dinner, but he'd call if it did, would she mind getting something by herself in the hotel dining room? She glanced at her watch: it wasn't there. Broken, at the jeweler's. Right.

Something twinged inside of her, but she said of course not, and let him kiss her good-bye. She had the sense she ought to be deeply grateful to Victor, and was insufficiently loving as he left. Why was that? Yes, because he listens, he really listens! Most men let women's stories run off them like sweat. They *let*

183

women talk, they didn't listen. But Victor did, and responded thoughtfully, and had made her see something about her marriage to Anthony that she had never seen before. Odd as it was, unusual as it was, it too fell into a cultural pattern, it was not only her private memory of hell, it was a general experience. She remembered how other people had looked at her when she told them she was getting divorced: she had the distinct sense that even some of her women friends tightened their mouths at her. *She* wanted a divorce! Poor Anthony was the one who should have wanted it, married to a woman like Dolores! Even Carol confessed to having more sympathy for Anthony, at least in the early years of their friendship: "He always seemed so sweet, and you always seemed so jagged."

Yes, she was grateful to Victor, so why didn't she act more loving when he left, why did she turn her cheek to his kiss?

Oh, it was because she was internally disheveled, all this talk about Anthony, all the remembering. She had not told anyone about him since Jack, so many years ago. And ever since Elspeth, everything looked different, everything felt different. She was trembling, inside her skin; the tremble was not from the nerves, it seemed, but from the blood vessels, the bone. Could bones tremble?

She let herself down in the single chair. It was placed before a window which faced a warehouse. The hotel room was spare and drab. Drabness and boredom. . . . There was a double bed with a faded dark blue cotton spread, and a long wall of drawers made of plastic, above which was a long mirror, occupying the whole wall. There was a floor-length mirror on another wall: to make the room seem larger, no doubt. And the chair, with a low plastic table next to it. Three huge lamps, all ugly, and dark blue drapes that had once probably matched the spread. The walls were papered in a bland ecru pattern, and the rug was browny tweed. Ugly. Characterless. Was the characterless then ugly? No, because children were beautiful but their characters didn't show on their faces. Or did they? Did a baby have a character?

How old was Tony then? Just a year, probably, just

beginning to toddle. Certainly he had a character, even then. Yes, it was a Saturday, and raining, everyone inside the house, horrible, so Dolores had gone down to the cool basement to do the laundry, took a book with her and sat in a broken-backed wicker chair reading in the comparative quiet of the humming washer. For upstairs the TV blared the current sporting event, as it would all Saturday and Sunday afternoons. Anthony was lying on the couch watching; occasionally he'd open his throat and pour in some Coke, or pour out some blast at one of the children. Elspeth and Tony were in their room, scrawling with crayon on huge sheets of paper, and sometimes on the walls as well (hide it from Anthony!). Sydney was not yet born, was lying calmly in Dolores's belly.

Laundry done and folded, Dolores carried it upstairs to put it away in bureau drawers, and entered her bedroom to find Anthony crouched on the floor next to Tony, in front of her dresser. Tony was barefoot and naked, only a diaper around him. The backs of his legs were pink.

"Close it!" Anthony commanded.

"No." Not defiant, just stubborn.

SWAT. Anthony slapped his legs.

"Anthony! What are you doing!"

He turned to her a face white with indignation. "This kid opened your dresser drawer!"

"So what?"

"So I want him to close it!"

"Why?"

"What difference does it make, why? The kid has to learn to mind!" He turned back to the baby. "Close it!"

Tony's head was down, his back to his mother, his little pink legs growing pinker. He did not answer this time. He simply didn't move. He was holding on to the edge of the drawer to help him stand up: he'd been walking for only a couple of weeks, and could not stand for long periods.

SWAT! Anthony slapped again.

Dolores's throat was full. "Anthony, I want you to stop that! Stop it!"

185

Anthony looked up at her kindly. "Honey, just let me handle this, okay? The kid needs a father."

Dolores turned and swiftly left the room. She ran to her study and slammed the door, fell into a chair and cried.

Yes, I was young then, and tears came easily. Besides, I didn't know what was right. Was I right, or was he? Maybe I was too indulgent. Maybe children did need that kind of discipline. But what for?

Sounds of Tony crying came to her through the door, over the TV. She wanted to get up and go to him, but she gritted her teeth and sat. Anthony made him cry, let Anthony calm him down. But of course Anthony would do no such thing.

"You go to your room, young man, and you stay there!" he shouted.

Hah. Tony had not closed the drawer. He had defeated his father in the contest his father had created in order that one of them should be defeated. Perhaps he didn't care which one.

Anthony came looking for her, he peered around the study door as he opened it, smiling.

"That kid," he announced, smiling broadly, "is a real hoosher! Stubborn?" He began to laugh, then saw her face. "Honey, what's the matter?"

She sat up in the chair, not bothering to wipe her tearstained face. "You do that again," she said through her teeth, "you beat that child again, either of them, Anthony, and I will take them so far away that you will never see them again! Never! And I mean it!"

He just looked at her, he said nothing.

He never did beat them again—not when she could see, at least. Tony told her his father often kicked him in the rear—but never when Dolores was around. But he told her that only last year. No, Anthony never beat them again. He used his voice instead.

"Wipe your feet on that mat when you come in, do you hear me? Now you go back there and wipe them, young man! And no cookies for two days!"

"Did you do this? Look at me, I'm talking to you! You see this towel? Look at that! How many times have I told you to make sure your hands are clean before you wipe them on the towel? Your mother works hard [oh, please don't use me as your excuse] to keep this place clean, and what do you do? I've told you a hundred times! Now you go back and wash those hands! And no ice cream for three days!"

"You've already ordered no ice cream for the next four, Anthony, shall I mark seven on the calendar?" Sarcastic, but he didn't hear.

Mealtimes: Not that fork! Elbows off the table! Raise the fork to your mouth, not your mouth to the fork! Wipe your mouth with the napkin before you drink! YOU'RE SPILLING YOUR MILK! DOWN! DOWN! LEAVE THE TABLE!

Never did a Christmas or Thanksgiving or any holiday dinner pass without the children being sent from the table in disgrace. Never. Anthony sat like death at the head of the table, forbidding joy.

Eat those artichokes! You'll eat them or you'll have them for breakfast, lunch, and dinner, you won't have anything else until you've eaten them, you hear? And no dessert! You'll sit there until you eat them.

Anthony, I am clearing the table. Will you please let him get down?

He'll sit there until he eats them.

Anthony, I have work to do.

Well, go ahead, I'll sit here with him.

And did, until she insisted it was the child's bedtime. And got up early and served his son artichokes for breakfast.

Don't put the bread in the palm of your hand when you butter it! And break off a small piece first! Don't butter the whole thing! You hear? No cake, no candy, no ice cream, no cookies for a hundred and thirty-five days, you hear!

Dolores stood up and walked across the room to her briefcase. She pulled her notes out and laid them across the bed, which was the only place to work. Her throat was full, and her eyes were blurry, and she wanted to wipe that away. But the mattress was soft, and when she sat on the bed, all the papers slid towards her. She couldn't see the words written on them, anyway.

And how could the children tell, as the years went on and she got angrier and shouted at Anthony, that her anger was with him and not with them? They were ultimately responsible, anyway, they must have felt. While she knew better. But you can't haul ghosts up before the bar and accuse them. Besides, it wasn't their fault.

Oh.

She wiped her eyes, which were burning, then lifted her head up as if she were trying to breathe in deeply some purer air to be found higher, higher. But her throat felt as if she had swollen glands. She rose and opened Victor's suitcase, fished around for the booze and found it, and poured herself a Scotch, adding tap water. She went back to the chair by the window, facing the rain, the warehouse.

Letter from Tony this morning. He'd left Berkeley, had followed some girl to Omaha. Did they toss nickels and dimes in your guitar case in Omaha too when you stood in gateways and played? It might be cold in Omaha, his poor bare feet might need shoes. Did he have shoes? Twenty-two and still drifting barefoot through life. Sweet and gentle, self-deprecating always, he smiled his inadequacies at you. He was nothing *but* inadequacies. Even playing the guitar, at which he was very very good, he would be brilliant only in his bedroom: in public, he'd shy off, stop short of brilliant, and apologize. Always sure he would fail: and therefore, always did.

TAKE YOUR HAND OFF THAT WALL! HAVEN'T I TOLD YOU A MILLION TIMES!

Yes, you have. A million times at least. Certainly enough times that Tony got the message: You are worthless. Tony never admitted to his father having received the message; he was, as Anthony perceived, stubborn. But he never rebelled, either, never fought back. The message was received. But Big Chief never believed it, and never stopped sending it until Elspeth grew up and he could send it to her instead. Yes.

The whole house poisoned, the very walls reeked. Hated going back there at night after work, much as I looked forward to seeing the kids. Stomach would begin to churn about the time he was supposed to come home. Eventually, I got that ulcer. Not Anthony, though, he never got an ulcer. Friday-night blues: a whole weekend with him in the house in the house in the house. Never went out alone.

And I didn't go. I didn't go. I stayed and tried to reclaim the story-child, why? To make my fantasy come true? Why? Can you call that love? As well call it hate. We were emotional savages, Anthony and I. Between us, we plumbed every depth, he of rage and I of grief. Together we chewed our own hearts.

And destroyed the children.

No, now, don't give up on them, they have a shine on them still, Sydney, Tony. Yes.

And Elspeth?

Other people do it differently. Use a wastebin of emotions. Tina and Ralph, married thirty years and long since prosperous, go round and round still squabbling about nickels and dimes. Take a cruise around the world, come back and have a month-long bang-up fight because she wants a new washer. When she earns $30,000 a year on her own and doesn't need his permission to buy it. But wants it. Asks for it. Why was that? Or he yells about *her* garbage, as if she manufactured it. And she yells about *his* garage. But it's a happy marriage, they say.

America and Russia, guns aimed at each other for thirty years, bayonets fixed, ready to strike, tanks ready to roll, missiles poised. While in a gilded room, under chandeliers, our diplomats meet, drink champagne, sign documents.

Peace, it is called. Or domestic tranquillity.

Victor says power is the key to everything.

She stood up and crossed the room and poured more Scotch into her glass. It was going to be a very long day for her if Victor didn't come back for dinner. A very long day if she couldn't work. Horrible thought, life without work. Empty days, stretching. What could you do to fill them? Anthony in that wheelchair.

Anthony lying on the couch watching TV, scratching his groin. Me in the study, working. Kids getting ready for bed, squabbling. Always squabbling. Natural, of course, but was it worse in our house? Good reason for it, if it was. But Anthony didn't permit squabbling. He was the only one allowed to get angry in that house. He leaped up and marched down the hall, yelling the whole way. Then he cried out.

Dolores leaped up and ran to him. He was lying on the floor. *Another* phony heart attack? But he had those only when *we* were quarreling, he'd never pulled those on the kids. Yet.

"Anthony." Stern.

"I've broken my leg, you bitch!"

Said he'd slipped on the waxed floor and broken it. Tried to make it my fault, impossible, the kind of housekeeper I was. Floor hadn't been waxed in months. Never knew till last year: he was trying to kick Tony in the rear. And lied about it. Lied.

Tony, of course (what else?) felt guilty. He'd learned agility in avoiding his father's kicks, had ducked out of the way, heard the bone split, had started to giggle.

I looked at him lying there on the floor, cursing me for the break, insisting he'd get up and drive himself to the hospital, cursing me as I called for an ambulance, cursing me for months after that, whenever his leg hurt, whenever he needed it moved and I was the one to do it. I was gentler with it than I had been with my newborns, but he always shrieked.

I looked at him lying there on the floor, having broken the leg he'd put in the fire, listening but not hearing his curses, his orders, I foresaw all of it, knew how it would be, my life turned into a worse hell for months ahead now and the thing delayed, delayed. I knew he wanted to break his leg, wanted to break something, because he knew, how did he know? that the day before I'd gone to a lawyer to see about getting a divorce.

How can you divorce a man in a wheelchair?

Even if he is home all day, starts drinking manhattans at ten in the morning, spends the day listening to the call-in shows on the radio and spying on the neighbors with his telescope. Is furious drunk by the time the kids get home from school, drives them out and away. They spend a lot of time at their friends' houses. By the time I get home he is hungry, grouses and asks jealous questions for a while, but I ignore them, ignore him. I prepare dinner, holding my mouth in place, thinking I have to get through three more months, two more months, one more month.

The house is empty of children. I miss them but I am grateful. He wants affection, he wheels himself close to me, he puts his arms out to me, calls me "Honey." I shudder away.

Oh god.

Dolores got up for another drink. Her back hurt: her shoulders have been hunched over tightly. She exercises them, but they still ache. She pours an extra-large Scotch.

Sits down. On the bed this time. Stretches out, wrinkles her notes, doesn't care, sweeps them together carelessly. Head back against the pillow, neck stretched out, waiting for somebody to come and slit her throat.

If you had to have all that, and everybody had it, that pain from which nothing is learned, which changes nothing, if you had to have all that energy spent on suffering, at least it ought to mean something. It could run dynamos, that much energy. It could feed the world. If only your pain ran up brownie points in some great ledger somewhere, so that you wouldn't have to come back and repeat it all in some reincarnation.

But you do, you do. Passed on from parent to child, every generation going through exactly the same things, nothing learned, nothing changed.

It was intolerable.

Sydney's new poem, the one she sent last week, was really about hate. Sydney had thought it was about love, the pains of love. Well, maybe it was, but it was also about the pain of hating.

Dolores drinks thirstily.

Yes, and when all the tumult dies down, the dust settles, the car motor is turned off and the body removed under a canvas, and the police cars have taken their terrifying red turning lamps back to some dark garage where motors are not allowed to run, and you lay your cold body on a bed and try to sleep, you look out your window and the moon is high, it rides behind some clouds, and a sea gull screams out over the shore. The ocean is pounding, you can hear it from your window. Forgotten. Nothing remains. Cottage swept out to sea.

You needed a cause, some cause: Christ or communism or Israel. Something respectable enough to convince your mind, not just your passions. Something worth suffering for. You could bear anything if you had a cause. It wasn't the pain that was unendurable: it was the pointlessness.

It is getting dark out. She picks up her head and peers out at the rain. The streetlights are on. It must be late. She looks at her watch. No watch.

He won't be back for dinner. No.

Again.

She sat bolt upright. *That* was why! Why she hadn't loved him, as he was leaving.

She put her head back on the pillow, gently, her wits slowly coming together again. She put the glass down on the bed table. Her heart felt cold and hard as a rock, and hot, flaming, at the same time. Yes! He argues, he sulks, he gets angry, he pressures her into coming with him on these trips, and then what does he do? He leaves her alone in a hotel room, all day and all night. Leaves her to eat alone in a large empty cold hotel dining room, to wander alone the streets of some unfamiliar and uninteresting town. This was the third time. He'd done it in Leeds, and once in Birmingham, and now, again.

Of course. He brought her along so he didn't have to sleep alone, and could see England from a car, but not have to drive alone. Companionship when he wanted it, not when he didn't. How convenient for him! Brought her along the way he brought his bottle of Scotch, to be there when he wanted it.

And it never occurred to him to think about her. He wasn't *trying* to be selfish. He didn't have to try, it came naturally. He was involved with people, with appointments and meetings, trips through the works, meeting a new man, someone important, psyching him out, go for drinks, stay to dinner, fun, full of life for him. Yes. He had it all arranged for his pleasure: work, then Scotch, then her.

She'd become an appurtenance in his life. Like Edith.

The most beautiful name in the world.

Marsh, calling late at night from California: "I must

see you, darling, can you meet me in New York, I'll be there on the twentieth, god, it's been so long!"

She raced down to New York in the car, wearing the three-hundred-dollar leather suit she'd bought in Saks months before in sheer anticipation of his next visit. Couldn't afford the suit, but didn't care. It was splendid, white with black piping. Had the car washed before she went to the airport. Here we are all clean and new for you. She charged through the airport crowd like a blind woman, breathless. But didn't recognize him when he appeared. He walked over as she was still searching the crowd. He was fat: he'd gained thirty pounds.

She thought: He's eating. Because he misses me. And was not displeased.

He didn't like her suit, it was hard and it squeaked. He kept complaining about it. He didn't like anything. He complained about the paintings in the Modern ("a lot of crap"), the hotel ("I *told* you to book a single! They had me down for a double!" "I *did* book a single! They made the mistake"). They argued, finally dropped it. He never believed her. Thought she was trying to ruin him, unconsciously, of course. His secretary would see *double* on the bill, and suspect something. He could not afford to be under suspicion. What she really wants is for me to divorce my wife and marry her. Oh, she says she doesn't, but all women want to be married. Unconscious, of course, she doesn't mean harm. But I'll have to be wary.

Dolores saw what he thought. And knew there was no way she could convince him of anything else. She'd been very careful to book a single, he'd given her precise instructions about it. But he'd never believe that. He'd never believe that she didn't want to marry him, didn't want to marry anyone (he didn't know what marriage meant to her), but especially Marsh, a politician, what a life for a woman!

It made her feel strange that he didn't, wouldn't ever, believe her, though. As if for him she was a different Dolores, someone other than she was, someone who didn't really know what she felt, someone who needed a man to feel whole.

Over cocktails that evening (she having discarded

the hated leather suit and wearing plunging black) he asked: What's the most beautiful name in the world?

She looked at him: that was a question?

"Edith," he announced, smiling with satisfaction.

It was his wife's name.

She sat in numb stillness in the hotel room while he gave his speech. Why did he call me? Why didn't he say: I can't handle this, loving my wife on the West Coast and you on the East. That would have been honest, and she would have understood. Why didn't he say: My guilts are too strong, I can't go on with this. Why didn't he say: My political career . . .

Oh, god, what a coward he was! He couldn't admit to being a mere human himself, so he came and turned her into a subhuman. Came and found fault with everything she did, everything she said. Everything she wore, for godsakes. Came and unwound, ribbon by ribbon, my finery of love, stripped me bare so he could find nothing inside. And I, loving him, let him do it, let myself undergo it, and let myself feel stripped and empty, felt like the nothing he wanted to find.

But that night he was sweet and loving, the way he'd been in the past. He was going to Princeton the next day, would she drive him? It would mean staying over an extra day, but they'd have dinner at the Forum tomorrow night, have a chance to spend some time together.

She thought: Maybe it's just New York that makes him paranoiac, maybe he's right to be worried here, so many people who might know him. Maybe it's New York that's unnerving him.

So she called Carol and spoke to the kids to explain, and asked Carol if she'd mind keeping them an extra day. Then called someone to cover her Thursday classes for her. And rose early Wednesday morning and drove, nervously, the unfamiliar roads. They arrived at Princeton before noon. Then he told her there was a luncheon before his speech, and that she should go somewhere and have a bite and be back to pick him up around three thirty or four. And to park far from the building. He didn't want anyone to see her.

Chauffeurs are treated with more respect: at least you *pay* them.

He returned in high spirits, his speech had gone well, there were important people in the audience. He talked continuously, telling her everything, every detail, assuming she was fascinated. He didn't notice her silence. Then said that he was very sorry but he'd have to get up and be out of the hotel very early the next day, his plane left at eight, and he wouldn't get to see her at all next morning, unless, of course, she cared to drive him to the airport on her way back to New England? . . .

The airport? On her way *back* to New England? She smiled.

He saw her smile, and it was a full one, no sadness in it. He leaned back comfortably in his seat and smiled at her benevolently. "You know, Dolores, I think you're beginning to learn. To accept the way things are, the way they have to be."

"Yes, I'm beginning to learn," she said.

When they reached the hotel, he said, "Shall I have the boy park your car?"

"I'm not parking it," she said, and jumped out. She got the key from the desk clerk (forbidden!), and went up to the room and packed her things hurriedly.

When she returned to the car, he was still sitting in it, looking puzzled. "Where do you want to go?" he asked her, glancing at the suitcase in her hand.

"I'm going back to Boston."

"Boston? Now? I thought we were having dinner at the Forum."

"You have it. With your vanity, your superiority, and your stupidity."

He sat there gazing at her. She could feel a fire mount slightly in him, the fire he'd had for her in the beginning, before she'd shown herself docile.

"Get out, please."

He opened the car door. "Are you sure you won't reconsider? It will be dark driving to Boston now."

"Move!" she ordered, and took off, speeding into the line of traffic as soon as he was away from the door, but while it was still open. It felt good to do that, yes: action. Then reach over while driving and slam the door shut. Felt good.

For a minute or two. Because for the rest of the night and for months afterwards, she felt raw and scraped, felt she had swallowed a burr and it was stuck in her esophagus. Love, that was.

God loves you, He will fill you, diet for Jesus.

Tears stood in Dolores's eyes. She stood up, a little unsteadily, and poured another Scotch.

She never knew what to do when she felt this way, felt devoured by her own emotions, felt her stomach eating itself away. She wasn't given to physical violence. Jack used to knock over furniture, vases, throw things. It was a good way and she would have approved it had it not been *her* furniture, *her* vases. If she'd done that here, they'd cart her off to the loony bin. A man could get away with it, if he were drunk. They'd calm him down and put it on his bill.

Okay, Victor wasn't coming back for dinner. It was really dark out now, must be eight or nine. He said he'd call. Maybe he forgot that too, along with me. Well, I think I'll go back to Boston.

There might be a late train. Couldn't take the car and drive. Too many drinks. Must be late trains to someplace. Doesn't matter where, she'd go to Glasgow, Wales, anyplace. Just to go, to get out of this pumpkin shell. Leave. Show *him*. He can't treat me this way, the children are grown up and I don't have to stay here anymore. Just walk out of the house like that and not come back for days? What kind of thing is that to do, Martin, I ask you! Poppa, where ya going, Poppa? Can I come, Poppa? Can I come this time? Can I come *next* time? Poppa? Come back filthy and unshaven, Momma standing there looking at him with a face full of contempt. I love you, Poppa, little voice, hand slipped through his, he'd stroke my head, embarrassed, go to your room, Dolores, Momma would say, not unkindly. Lie there on the bed wondering why Poppa always goes away why Momma was always mad at him. . . .

She drank her Scotch down, got up for more. She had not turned on the lights in the room, because she could not stand all the mirrors, and she stumbled around finding her way by the light cast by the street-lamps outside. The phone rang, at least she thought it was the phone and not her ears, which were also ringing. She could not find it, she stumbled around, she tripped over something, fell on the floor, crawled toward the sound, it was ringing ringing ringing, and found it finally, picked it up and a man's voice said "Lorie?" and she said "Who?" and then he said "Lorie!" and she said "No," and then he said something else she couldn't understand and then there was a strange noise, a buzzing, it must be a bad connection all the way from California but if Marsh thought she was going to see him again after the way he'd acted, he was really oblivious, oblivious yes, oblivion. . . .

Well, she was sick of his rages! Sick, sick, sick! Slamming the phone down on her like that. Calling up to check on her, make sure she was home, it was a joke, he called wherever she went, everybody knew it.

Checking up on her while he was out there getting his ego stroked, telling her to park far away, or to stay in the room, hidden away, Rosamund. His wife too, plopped in her pumpkin shell and kept there. Very well.

> Jack, Jack, pumpkin eater,
> Had a wife and couldn't keep her,
> Put her in a pumpkin shell
> And there he kept her very well.

After the ball, after the finery, Cinderella's coach turns into a pumpkin shell. Yes, that was what that was all about.

She got up and stumbled to the bathroom and switched on the light. She returned to the bedroom, able to see by the bathroom light, and wandered around it, singing lightly under her breath, picking up her notes, her sweater, the shoes she'd kicked off hours ago. Bent and stood up and caught sight of a woman with a white face and disheveled hair and a strange expression. She moved back from the mirror slowly, and stood very still. There was something wrong with her. She could feel it. It was something serious. She'd have to be careful. It was going to be hard to live this way, she'd have to walk very carefully, a little at a list. She could do it if she tried hard. She'd slide by. She had to, because if they saw, they did horrible things to you, they grabbed you by the arm and stuck needles in you and locked you up and gave you electric shock.

First thing was to get out. But if she went out carrying a suitcase, they might stop her. Pay the bill, please, they'd say. She didn't have enough money to pay the bill and buy a railroad ticket. Where was this place, anyway. She stumbled over to the window and looked out. Melbourne, of course. Or was it Sydney? No, Sydney was in New Hampshire, learning to be a poet, growing alfalfa. She giggled at her brilliant pun. Sydney, running towards her over the grass, eyes bright, "You came, Mom! Isn't it great!" Smiling, leaping into her arms as if she was still six. Sydney with calluses on her hands from farm work. "I love it, I really do! Can I show you my new poem?" Shyly, flushed cheeks, trying not to care so much, but caring. Yes, Sydney was all right. And Tony, he was in Omaha. Do you suppose it's cold out there? Does he have a jacket? Well, by now he must know how to get jackets. He was all right, he was somewhere. And Elspeth too. She was dead, that's where she was.

Dolores stuffs all her things into her large canvas purse. Everything fits except a sweater and a robe. She'd leave the robe behind but she loves it, her children gave it to her. It won't go in. Solution: wear it! She pulls it around her, over her clothes, and looks in the mirror. (Terrible, terrible, to look in the mirror.) No, something wrong. It wouldn't pass. They'd catch her. She's clever, she knows they pick you up for the slightest deviation. Takes off the robe, takes off her jacket, puts the robe back on and the jacket over it. No. Even though fashionable clothes these days are layered. *Layered.* A very funny word. She says it aloud several times, giggling.

If she could pull the skirt of the robe up high enough so that it looked like those tunics they wear over pants, that would do it. Stuff the middle into the slacks, put the jacket over all. Oh, she is clever! Pulls up the robe, stuffs fabric into the waistband of her slacks. Takes time, effort. There's a lot of fabric and it's so thick.

She looks in the mirror. She buttons the jacket but the two bottom ones won't close. She looks odd. She is fat for Jesus. But she will pass.

Everything is ready. Except the sweater. She drapes that over her arm. She eyes the Scotch. Nice to have it on the train. But not much left. Leave it for him. But he doesn't drink Scotch, Marsh drinks bourbon. Anthony really is turning into an alcoholic, drinking from ten in the morning. If only she could lock *him* in a pumpkin shell whenever he is having a tantrum, lock him in and let him pound the door with his fists and cry until he was tired, then slump down at the doorsill, asleep. Yes, then the rest of them could be happy. They could smile and laugh even. They could play. The children out in the yard playing ball, voices light in the summer air, Tony and Elspeth taking turns trying to teach Sydney how to hold a bat, no, not that way you little Sydneybug, Elspeth would laugh, Tony pitching the ball to her ever so gently, not to frighten her, then racing around, bats dropped on the ground (pick them up before Anthony comes!), smiling, calling out, cheeks pink, hair falling in their eyes, Elspeth leaping high, oh, so high! little Elf, my little Elf, hair like a slow-motion wave against the green leaves, golden.

I don't know what trains there are.

Telephone. No. Doesn't matter. It doesn't matter what train you take, they all go to the same place. All trains lead to death, all children are born with cancer, born dying, the round soft faces, the sober straight clear eyes.

The eyes of a child look right at you. There's nothing between them and you. No veils. And when they laugh! Children in Fiji, splashing you as your boat passes them swimming in the river, eyes black and shiny as onyx, delighted with their mischief, delighted with themselves, delighted with you. Pure joy.

Little Johnny, Tony's friend, barred from the houses in the neighborhood on grounds of stealing. But he didn't steal. He simply took what delighted him—a pretty matchbox, a glossy magazine, a handful of long smooth shiny silver nails. And gave too, whatever he had: food, candy, money. He gave Tony his bike once. Same joyous black eyes. Probably in a penitentiary now. Penitentiary: sit and remord. You have sinned. You were born in sin and you will die in sin. All children are anarchists: *Anarchism verboten hier.* Sit and remord: Say twelve Our Fathers, and then go out and cut the ten acres with a hand scissor. Joy forbidden here. Joy not spoken here.

We kill the children.

She clutched her stomach, feeling a spasm, and as she bent, saw a person in the mirror. That was a pregnant woman there, holding herself as if she were in labor. But her face too old, no? Aha! It is a change-of-life baby! She approached the mirror, she touched it. It was *herself,* she was the pregnant one!

"Oн!" she cried aloud, her throat full of joy, "Elspeth, you've come back! You're coming again! I hoped, if I waited, you'd come back!"

She didn't mind the spasms, they were coming faster now, but it was joy, joy, joy, Elspeth was about to be born again, born again! And this time she'd do better, would know better, would do something, somehow, it won't happen the same way this time Elspeth, I promise you, this time I will try harder, and she was crying out loud, crying for joy as the spasms came faster and lower and it was going to happen, her baby was going to be restored to her as she had been in the beginning, before she was made to swim at a list, before she was bent, the way she'd been at the very first, round and pink and squawling and hungry and opening her eyes and beginning to see and beginning to reach, and then one day, opening her mouth and smiling, ah! what a smile and a gurgle, it was for her, for Mama. Say Mama.

"I've learned a lot, Elspeth, you'll see! This time it will be different!"

Then there was another thing in the mirror and she frowned, it was one of Them, yes, that suit and jacket and shirt and tie, she recognized the uniform, she knew Them, They would destroy her child, They all

ate their children, and she whirled at him, she
screamed as loud as she could:
"DON'T TOUCH ME! GET AWAY FROM ME!"

7

THE MAN came up to her and touched her and she
screamed and he backed away, staring at her, saying
something she couldn't hear. She looked back at the
mirror, she pleaded with the mirror.

"I won't let him hurt you, Elspeth, I know how to
protect you this time, I won't let any of Them get near
you, I promise, don't go away Elf, I'll take care of
things better this time."

He stood near the door watching her and then there
was noise, knocking, and the man went away. No, he
didn't go away, he was at the door, maybe he would
go away.

She turned back to the mirror, panting now as the
baby descended. She felt her belly, to make sure all
went well.

Something was wrong.

The baby didn't feel as if she were *in* her: she felt
extraneous.

And it didn't feel like Elspeth. It felt like fur. Elspeth had no fur. Elspeth was beautiful and delicate.
She had slender delicate bones like her mother and
great violet eyes like her father, except his were blue.
Her laugh was a piccolo playing early in the morning
on a lane into town.

And when she slumped and glared, as she had in
those last years, she was eerie blue light in a dark corner, electric, terrifying, a leaping laser of hate.

"Don't hate me this time," Dolores whispered to the
mirror. "At least, not so much."

She was pinching her belly between her fingers. It
was terribly wrong. She started to cry. "Elspeth? Elspeth?" And remembered calling like that night after
night lying in bed waiting for Elspeth to come, crying
because Elspeth

had died. Elspeth had died.

But she believed Elspeth's spirit would come back to her, would return to her mother who loved her so much, who had tried so hard, and who was so tired, would come back and lay her soft small cool hand on her mother's forehead and say Mommy it's all right, I'm all right

never had, the rotten kid.

Leaving me here, knowing how it is for me. Couldn't she have come just once, given me one soft touch, just a rustle of the air that I knew was her, just a sigh near my cheek so I knew she forgave

never.

Dolores pulled swiftly and roughly at the fake baby, a fake baby, that's all it was, put on her to torment her. She pulled and pulled and it all came out, it was nothing at all, it disappeared as she pulled, it simply vanished.

No baby.

Dolores fell to the floor and sobbed. No baby. No Elspeth. A trick, a delusion. Elspeth gone.

That person was back, he was standing near her, his legs loomed, and she reached out and growled and threatened to bite him and the legs retreated. She laughed. She was pretty clever. She'd scared him away all right.

Not that he could do much damage now. There was only she, Dolores. No baby to kill, warp, deform, beat, scream at, twist in his hands like a chicken bone. Swallow: chump, chump. She sat there swaying, weeping more softly now, calling softly, "Elspeth, Elspeth," feeling abandoned, why had she come so close and not come? "You still hate me," Dolores moaned, "you still blame me."

A voice answered her, but it was the wrong kind, it wasn't Elspeth, it was deep, one of Theirs.

"You're not Elspeth!" she accused it, and looked more closely. There was a man on the floor. He'd taken off his uniform, except his shirt and trousers. He was sitting on the floor over there. He was crying.

One of *Them,* crying?

Oh, he'd probably lost his job. Or his wife had left him. Wives kept doing that these days. Yes, Anthony never cried, not even when his father died, never cried until she left him.

"Don't tell me your problems," Dolores said. "I don't care."

"Darling," the voice said. That wasn't Anthony, he never called her *darling*. No, honey, or sweetie. Or the others. . . .

The figure inched closer. She held up her hand swiftly, hard. "No! No closer!" she ordered, and it stopped.

"Dolores," it pleaded.

"What do you want?" Impatient. "You always want something! I am busy tonight, you ought to be able to see that. I am communing with my daughter. I will not cook you dinner, I will not stroke your head, I will not listen to your problems, I will not laugh at your jokes, I will not screw you. So you might as well leave."

"Let me do something for you," it urged.

She sat straight and still, looking at it. "What could you *possibly* do for me? I learned long ago to do everything for myself."

"Let me get you some dinner."

"Dinner! Dinner! *Now* you want to get me dinner! Well, now, I am communing with my daughter, who has finally come back!"

The man put his head in his hand.

"You needn't cry!" she snapped. "There are lots of women who will give you whatever you want. Go find one!"

He slumped. He made her tired. She didn't want to have to worry about his pain too, it was too much, she had too much of her own.

"Anthony," she said in a dead voice, "go away." Her heart was breaking, she could feel it, it had been broken all along, but she had used egg and flour and glue to bind it up together like a hamburger, it seemed whole until you touched it with a fork, and then it all fell into pieces again. Damaged beyond repair.

Anthony was still crying. She loved him for that, that he could cry, that he could let himself suffer. She wanted to crawl over to him and hold him, hold his head against her breast and smooth his back and tell

203

him she loved him and it would be all right. But he had waited too long. If he had only cried before, everything might have been repaired somehow. But he waited until her heart was half hamburger, and that half was his. He waited until all she could see when she looked at him was a purple-faced automaton on crutches with his mouth open yelling yelling.

And it could never be all right again.

Yes, yes, baby, she wanted to say. Yes, you are my baby but you just don't grow up the way the others do, you stay a baby, and you're so noisy, and besides, you torment the other children. And they are smaller than you, they need me more. And there is more hope for them.

"Dolores," the voice said sharply, angrily, "I'm not Anthony, I'm Victor."

"Who?" She peered at him under her rain hood. It was raining hard.

He inched closer, but she couldn't hear what he was saying, the rain was so noisy, maybe it was the wind. Then he was next to her, he put his hand on her arm, she shuddered away, don't touch me, but then there was thunder and it terrified her, it was very close and he put his arm around her. Did he think that would solve everything, that he could pull her close to him and the other would go away, the rain and the wind and the thunder? Did he think that if he had his arm around her, she wouldn't still be frightened of the rain, the wind, and the thunder? How could he protect her from them? He couldn't. If the thunder came, if the lightning struck, it would get them both and his arm wouldn't mean a thing.

He didn't seem to understand anything, because he did it, he put his arms around her and held her and he did not smell like Anthony, he smelled like rain, maybe he was the rain, and she looked at him and there were tears on his face, what a crybaby, crying about an ordinary thunderstorm. She was terrified of thunderstorms, but *she* wasn't crying.

VI

1

WHEN SHE woke, there was light in the corners of her eyes. She lay like a trapped animal, not moving a limb but straining all her senses, lying still and quiet.

A floor. Yes, she was lying on a floor. She was bundled up in all her clothes, and had a pillow under her head and a blanket over her. On the floor. Some floor. She turned her head slightly. Victor was lying beside her, his arm was thrown across her body (why she felt trapped). His mouth was open a little and he was sleeping. There was a pillow under his head too, but all of the blanket was over her.

She moved a little and his eyes opened and looked at her. They were a stranger's eyes. He did not smile, he did not speak. Neither did she. Why did she feel some chasm had opened between them? He turned over on his back, pulling his arm away from her.

She got up and went into the bathroom to pee. For some reason, she was wearing her robe under her jacket, over her pants. It was strange. And she was hungry, terribly hungry. She looked in the mirror. God. She removed her jacket, her robe, her pants. Sleeping in clothes! They were stiff and smelled musky, like her. She returned to the bedroom.

Victor was standing up, buttoning his trousers. He did not look at her. He went into the bathroom and he closed the door. Closed the door! She went and sat in the chair by the window. She felt shaky. Victor came out of the bathroom and walked towards her. He did not like her, she could tell. He sat down opposite her on the bed, he looked at her.

"How do you feel?"

She looked at him dumbly. "All right," she said,

although she felt frozen, her face was frozen and her voice sounded frozen too. Could you have a frozen voice?

"Do you know who I am?" Voice low, but demanding. Oh, he was angry!

She hesitated. Why should she not know who he was? Something peculiar going on here. Retreat or attack? When in doubt, attack. "Of course I know who you are. Why shouldn't I?"

"Last night you thought I was Anthony."

Aha. Last night. Yes, she remembered. Anthony had come back, invading her space again, crying. Anthony had been here last night, but—Victor had not!

"*You* weren't here last night! You went off and left me! You beg, you plead, you insist I come with me on these fucking trips of yours and then you go off and leave me in this hideous hotel room, leave me alone, to eat by myself! Why do you want me! I'm just a convenience, something to come back to. You never think about me! Never again, never again, Victor!"

His face was saying *never again* to her, too. "Last night you screamed as if I was killing you. The hotel sent people up, I had to make up some story about your having nightmares. They wanted to come in here and cart you off to the loony bin."

"Maybe they came up to see if you were killing me. Maybe you would have." That's what they did. They knocked at your door, you opened it, you were glad to see them, you let them in and they walked in carefully enough, but in ten minutes they had their boots up on your cocktail table and in half an hour they were in your refrigerator. In an hour they were in your bed, and after that WHOOSH! they'd taken over your space, your life. Just like that. They did it because they thought they had rights over you because you are a woman. Didn't matter what you said or what you protested: they simply assumed that because you are a woman you are sitting there waiting for them to come and take over your life, to tuck you into a pocket of theirs, where, they assume, you will be very very happy. At least, they will be, knowing you're safely in their pocket.

There were steps: first, they crush your ego: streaks on the wall, creaky leather suit; then, they instill the behavior they want: park far away, Dolores. Then, when you had it down pat, they were satisfied: you were an appurtenance. But then they got bored because you were dull and docile, so they had to go out and find somebody whose ego was still intact and start all over again.

"Dolores?" His head was tilted, trying to catch her face, her attention. "Are you really all right?"

She peered up at him. It had been raining, she remembered, raining right inside the room.

"Elspeth was coming back," she said in a thin little-girl voice.

He jumped up and crouched in front of her. He took her hands. "Dolores?"

"I'm hungry."

He rose and went to the telephone. He said something into the telephone. She sat there, drooping, in her underpants. He brought her robe and helped her put it on. "You must be cold," he said. Then he picked up the pillow and blanket and threw them on the bed.

"Victor," she said uncertainly, and he turned immediately and came to her. She looked up at him, and he crouched down again, took her hands again. She took one away from him and stroked his face.

"You left me alone," she said in the same little-girl voice. "You do it all the time."

He bent his head and kissed her hand. "I'm sorry," he said in his throat. "I'm really sorry."

Somebody knocked on the door and Victor got up and let him in. It was a man with a rolling tray-table, lots of things on it, smell of coffee. The man went.

"Oh!" Dolores said, and jumped up. She sat on the bed, but Victor brought the chair over and told her to sit there. He sat on the bed. They opened the metal covers. There were eggs and sausage and broiled tomatoes and fried potatoes and coffee and toast and orange juice out of a can. Dolores ate like a starving woman. It was greasy, but she didn't care. She had four cups of coffee. Then she sat back and sighed.

"Feeling better?"

She nodded.

He handed her a cigarette and she took it. She breathed out and looked at him. "I was crazy last night, wasn't I?"

"You were," he spoke slowly, *"distraught* last night. You had, as far as I can tell, no lunch and no dinner, and you drank nearly a fifth of Scotch. You were angry with me, quite rightly. And you'd been talking about Anthony, and had stirred up old memories of distressing things." He spoke very precisely.

He is giving me my cover story.

"No, I was crazy. Do you never go crazy? I don't, usually. But sometimes, when I drink. That's why I don't drink. Still, I wasn't *really* crazy. Maybe I acted crazy, but the things I was feeling weren't crazy."

"I know," he said gloomily.

"I'm just like Anthony, you see," she said, gazing sadly at her cigarette ash. "I live with ghosts."

"Maybe we all do."

"Do you know who I am?" she asked suddenly.

"Of course."

"No, you don't. You know somebody called Lorie. That isn't me."

He looked down.

"You were crying," she recalled, dimly.

His face, as he raised it to her, was wrenched. She rose, and went to sit beside him on the bed, and pulled his face to her shoulder. He buried it there, clasped her, and sighed. They rocked for a while. Then he sat up.

"I understand . . . about mixing me with Anthony. And somebody else, I don't know. . . ."

"Marsh?"

"Maybe. Anyway, I understand."

"Yes." Dead voice.

"I'll take you home. We'll go home."

"Yes."

He got up and went to the telephone. He was talking to people over the telephone, he was saying *sorry, sorry, sorry.*

Back at Oxford, Victor opened the windows a bit to get the stale smell out, then turned on the electric fire. He sat her on the couch with her feet up, tucked a blanket around her, went into the kitchen and came back with a cup of tea for her.

Dolores thought: Mommy. It was nice to have a mommy. Everybody needed a mommy, once in a while.

Yes, that's what he'd been doing, she finally worked it out, canceling all the day's appointments in Manchester. Because of her. Because she was crazy.

She couldn't look at him. She wanted to take his hand when he brought her the tea, wanted to say, Oh, I'm sorry, Victor, sorry for putting you through all that when it wasn't your fault, no it wasn't.

But then you did turn me into an appurtenance. And all those other things, the hiding me away, all the little angers I'd stashed away and tried to forget. When you said that and then you didn't and you did do this and I decided to forget. Yes.

Yes, but you're not to blame for my whole rotten fucking life.

But she couldn't say it. She was too embarrassed.

He came and sat on the couch beside her, he turned her face, he made her look at him. "I'm going to the market. There's no food in the house. You sit here and rest, okay?"

She nodded. She heard the door close behind him. The house was very still.

It came to her that his face was scarred, covered with scratches. Her scratches. She had torn his face to shreds.

No. She had killed Anthony.

Yes, that's what she'd done. He was dead, he was lying on the front seat of her car, dead, and Elspeth was sniffing. *His* spirit wouldn't forgive either. He paced the corridors of her mind, asking her why, why. "I loved you so much," he wept. "You never loved me the way I loved you." He never hated her, he said. He was never angry with *her,* he said. He said he loved the children: how could she doubt that?

She tried to shut him in his room, but he kept wedging his foot in the door, he was so big, she couldn't close the door. He got out, he stormed into the living room. His eyes were great dark holes, devouring

209

her, trying to kill her. His face was purple and his mouth was open, it was a dark saucer, open and letting out noise like an air raid siren. She tried to get away, she tried to run out the front door, but he was after her in an instant, he pulled her back, he left black-and-blue marks on her arm, he smashed her against the wall and her earring flew off and scudded across the room and she never found it again until they were moving and the room was emptied of furniture. And she said I'm leaving, I'm leaving, you can't stop me, and she ran into the kitchen and got a knife and brandished it at him, and he stood there and looked at her and he was laughing, laughing, he was laughing so hard the tears came into his eyes, and she threw the knife against the wall, and she stalked off and he came after her, he put his arm around her, he said *Honey*.

She wouldn't have stabbed him, of course, but she wanted at least the respect of fear. He laughed. How can you threaten someone who laughs at you?

Still, in the end, I killed him. That's what Elspeth thought. She said so. Just once.

Dolores put her head back against the pillow, her throat was aching again, she waited for the knife, for the throat slit. Do it, do it.

The door slammed, Victor was back. He was in the hall, hanging up his coat, he was in the kitchen, putting down the parcels. She was afraid to see him. He opened the door and came into the sitting room. She would not look at him.

"Are you all right?"

She averted her face. "Did I scratch you very badly?"

"Scratch me?"

He came closer, into the circle of the lamp. "When?"

"Last night."

He sat down beside her. "You didn't scratch me, darling."

She turned her head then and looked at him. No, he wasn't scratched. But she could see the marks plainly when he was across the room, in the shadows.

His eyes were burning into her. Like Anthony's, when he was jealous, sitting across a room full of people, staring at her, she could feel him through the back of her head, and she'd turn and he was glaring, worse than glaring, eyes burning with hate.

Like Elspeth, later.

Was she so terrible? What did she do to make them feel this way?

"Am I so terrible?"

He held her against him, her head on his shoulder, her cheek against his. "Oh, you're terrible. As terrible as any of us, all of us. Oh, darling, Dolores, there's no justice, there's only love."

2

THAT NIGHT he simply held her. She was exhausted, she was grateful for the warm smooth body against her own, the feel of his arms holding her, they weren't imprisoning her, no, you could always tell the difference. Dinner party at the institute, Edmund Low's hand on his wife's knee, and she sat there calmly, Naomi, her own hands folded quietly in her lap. Beautiful Naomi, calm, placid. She had contempt for him, you could feel it, it pervaded the air around her when he was near, but he didn't feel it. His soft pudgy banker's right hand lay on her knee and it was a shackle. Yes. She sat there, accepting it, her shackle. Why? Her hands rested quietly in her lap, shackled in diamonds.

Everything was a matter of power, Victor said.

But now he was saying love. And he was holding her with love, holding her for her sake, holding her for his sake, holding her out of love, not out of possession. You could tell the difference, even across a room, even on the street, watching the young men's owning hands clamped on their women's shoulders. Did the women think that was love? Anthony's arm on her back at parties: light enough, but a clear message. No one would ask her to dance. Never touched her when they were alone.

Victor and she were breathing in rhythm. He was caressing her body, running his hand gently down her sides, her thighs, her buttocks, over her breasts, and she had her arms around him, and after a time she began to caress him, his thighs, his sides, his buttocks, his breasts, he felt good—smooth and cool and silvery. Oh, it was smooth and easy, they were together, they comforted the body for what could not be comforted in the mind, and it was all right, it helped.

Maybe it was possible to give up control, once in a while. Maybe one could give up control and the world wouldn't fall apart. All those years of staying in control (because disasters occurred when she didn't) when Anthony went off into a crazy rage, all those years of holding together when Elspeth, when Poppa, when Marsh said the most beautiful name in the world, when

yes, but here she'd gone and done it, for the first time, really, in her life, had given up control and acted like a madwoman. And nothing so terrible had happened. Here she was, in her bed. And here was Victor, stroking her, easing her, loving her.

Trust was what it was. Yes, to be able to go to sleep in his arms and know he would still be there in the morning, that he would not try to kill you in your sleep, and that, in the morning, he would not look at you as if you had baggy eyes and bad breath (even though you did) and therefore were no longer desirable. The way Phil did, looking at her in the morning as if he had suddenly discovered she was an old hag. Reverse of the fairy tale: go to bed with the princess and wake up with the frog. Frog*ess*?

She let herself down into it gradually, a warm tub. Down into it she settled, oh, delicious, warm and lapping and smelling of fresh herbs and sandalwood, all around her body the caress, the soft warm water, buoyant. She leaned in it, she turned in it, turned over and over as she did in the surf, the act of turning a joy, moving in water, with water, against water. She was swimming straight now, the list had disappeared. The water receded, proceeded. It wrapped around her, it enclosed her, it embraced her. She shot up, her head above the wave, then sank in it, surrendered to it. She floated for a moment, she drifted, then a kick of her legs sent her bounding off again. Joy, in the movement, in the power of her legs, in the feel of the water surrendering to her force.

She floated out to sea with Victor in a peace and surrender she hadn't felt before, not this completely anyway, as if her body had finally found itself, found the place where things meet, where they make sense, where you don't have to think anymore. Like finding the position, so hard for her to learn, that the body must sink into if one is to ski downhill. Bent at the knees, relaxed; bent at the knees, but not kneeling. Then go: the snow ruffles hair, face, jacket, snow flies up behind the skis, wind against, wind with, body against it, body with it, all at once, the mountainside whizzing past, a valley of delights, oh, last longer, last longer!

Longer and longer it lasted, and she realized they were making love after all. It was fine, it was what she wanted now, downhill faster and faster, the sky whizzing by, the water lapped her, she flew, she turned.

And then, suddenly, before she was ready, he was on her, he was in her, he was like a pole, she panicked. No, no, no! Don't! Not yet! Her speed broken harshly, she cried out in pain. Hard he was, and fast, angry fucking, she didn't like it, she cried to him to slow down. He tried. He slowed a little, but then speeded up again in moments, speeded up suddenly, harshly, ferociously, he was plunging into her, over and over, as if she were an enemy, as if his penis were a hand digging fiercely in foreign soil for a root to eat, for desperately needed food food food. He came in a spasm, he cried out in agony, he fell against her shoulder, his face wet.

"I'm sorry, I'm sorry," he cried.

Sorry. He'd been saying that all day. That was the trouble. You can't say *sorry* all day without finding some way to get even. He had to hurt her, because she'd hurt him. Couldn't forbear. Had to possess, get back his edge, to reassure himself.

"I'm sorry," he whispered, and tried to caress her,

tried to use his hand to start her up again. But she turned away.

"No," she said.

3

ONLY WITH a god, she thought, next morning, carrying her coffee into the sitting room and curling up in the rocker near the window. She had wakened before him. It was a dim pearly day, no sun visible, but the slate roofs opposite glistened as if they were wet with light. And considering the gods they've offered us over the past couple of millennia, not even then.

Her vagina was sore.

Yes, it was a lovely fix: you must trust lest you turn into petrified bone, but you cannot trust. Never.

Was it women and men, or was it all people?

It was clearly about power, Victor was right about that part at least.

She got up for more coffee, emptied the pot, thought of making more, then didn't. Let him make his own.

He did, an hour later; she heard him moving around in the kitchen, heard the clunk of the electric kettle being set down, smelled fresh brew. He came to the door of the sitting room. "Would you like more coffee?"

She nodded, and rose, went into the kitchen with him, and he poured it for her. He followed her into the sitting room, wearing his Viyella robe. They did not speak.

"Mad?"

She looked at him soberly. "What a way to get even. Why didn't you yell, I'd have preferred it. I'd even have preferred a little violence to that. At least then I could hit back."

He bent forward, lighted a cigarette, looked at the floor. "You know I couldn't help it. I couldn't control it, Dolores."

She sighed. "I guess."

"I *am* sorry."

"I wish you'd stop saying that. I feel that every time you say you're sorry, I have to pay something."

He half-smiled ironically. "I imagine you're right." He sat hunched over the coffee table, drinking coffee, smoking, gazing at the floor.

She got up and went to him, sat on the couch beside him, touched his shoulder. "Look, Victor, I'm not *that* angry."

He suffered her touch. "Yeah."

"What is it? You act as if you're angry with *me*."

He lifted his head, sighed, leaned back against the sofa, losing her hand as he moved. She replaced it in her lap. She watched him.

"I don't know," he sighed, "everything seems wrong, suddenly."

Her heart stopped. Her mad scene *had* done damage.

"*I* seem wrong," he concluded, miserably.

Her eyes spurted to life. "Have you ever seemed wrong—to yourself—before?"

"Once. Just once. But it was a long once. Or no, maybe twice."

"Want to tell me?"

"No. Yes. Both." He never looked at her. She rose and went into the kitchen. She made more coffee, some toast, and brought it out on a tray, with butter and cheese, and set it down on the coffee table before him. He was still smoking.

"Preparing for a long siege, huh?" he said, giving her his first full smile of the day.

"I think you've earned one," she smiled back, smeared cheese on toast, and returned to her rocker.

He buttered some toast, poured fresh coffee into his cup, lighted another cigarette. "The thing is, I don't know how I ended as I did. I don't think I started that way. It's as though I was meant to live on a branch line, but someplace or other got switched to the main line, and have been happily blindly shuttling between New York and Washington ever since. And not remembering. . . ."

He spoke with his eyes firmly fixed on a dark spot across the wall, never looking at her.

"I remember being fifteen or sixteen. I remember one day in particular, it was in the summer after my sophomore year of high school. . . ."

Long, thin, too thin, everybody said. Aunt Gladys laughed when he tripped—as he invariably did—on the little step up to her porch, and came flying through the porch door headfirst, arms outstretched.

"A skeleton with wings!" she'd announce, and laugh, and so would everybody else. After a while, he laughed too. It was better than blushing.

His long, thin, too thin body sprawled in the hammock, legs dangling out. Around him were the green hills of Ohio, overlooking a valley. Green for miles. Beautiful day, baby-blue sky of the Middle West, puff-ball clouds, warm sun, shady tree, green grass, garden in bloom. He lay there trying to think of one good thing. He couldn't. He hated this book, it was ridiculous. The ice in his lemonade was all melted. And then he felt a tingling on his chin, oh, no, oh, no, and put his finger up and it was, shit! it was a whole cluster.

"Don't pick at them, it only makes them worse," Mother said.

How could things be any worse? Everything was against him. The book slid from his lap and fell to the grass, knocking over the lemonade, which then trickled into the pages of the book. Shit! But he let it lie. Shitty book, anyway. Shakespeare, *Antony and Cleopatra*. Giant bestriding the world, winning battles with his own sword, not with bombs and airplanes and tanks, but with his own hand and arm, his own sword. He'd go on forced marches, days and days of marching, sleeping on the ground. When there was no water, he could drink horses' urine. He was the greatest soldier in the world, like Alexander in his time. The way Nelson had been the greatest sailor in the world. These people were real, not fake, like Superman or Batman. No one had made them up. People like this had really lived on the earth once. And women fell madly in love with them, Cleopatra, Emma Hamilton, the great beauties, they loved these heroes, they lived for them.

And here he was, Victor Morrissey, fifteen and a half, skinny and with pimples. He was as handy with a sword as with a battle-ax. They didn't even have a fencing team in their lousy hick high school. He closed his eyes and pictured himself in a tight fencing outfit, with a body like Victor Mature's, dancing elegantly across a polished floor thrusting, parrying, crying "Point!" In the small group of courtiers sitting in a circle was Dorita Haas with her black eyes and long black hair, watching him. She was wearing a rose in her hair and when he'd won the match and was bowing to the applause, she tossed the rose to him. He bent and picked it up, bowed to her, then walked off proudly, like a god, impervious. Elegant all the way through: no one could see what he felt. Maybe he wouldn't feel at all. Maybe he'd be like Clark Gable, who always looked at women as if he knew what color their underwear was, and exactly how they liked to be . . . touched. He *owned* them, he didn't have to be frightened of them. His eyes said so.

At school, Victor looked at Dorita only sidelong, when she wasn't looking his way.

No, there wasn't a single good thing. There were hamburgers, but so low was he, he couldn't even muster the energy to go indoors and cook himself a hamburger. He kept repeating to himself Antony's lines: A Roman by a Roman nobly vanquished. That's what he ought to do: kill himself. Leave a noble note condemning the tainted things of this world. Do it like Brutus, the noblest Roman of them all. Of course, he didn't own a sword. Or he could run away and join the merchant marine. The army would never believe he was eighteen, he knew that, but he'd heard the merchant marine wasn't so fussy, they took anybody.

There just wasn't any place for him in this jerkwater town. His father loved it here, his mother too, but they had small minds, that was clear. There were the jerky guys who spent their time outside of school—when they bothered to go to school—in roadhouses, drinking 3.2 beer, and conning some older guy to buy them a pint of bourbon every once in a while. And all they talked about was drinking and souped-up cars, and baseball, and broads and tits and asses, and they were stupid and boring. They all hung out with the town pumps and weren't even ashamed even though there were ten or twelve of them and only three or four girls. They'd meet the girls in the roadhouses and buy them a pitcher of beer, and the girls would get up and dance the polka with each other on the creaky wooden floor, while the guys sat there acting as if they were big-time operators, but watching the girls out of the corners of their eyes.

There was a small group of intellectuals, most of them seniors, a couple of juniors. They'd let him sit around with them a few times last year, and sometimes it was kind of interesting, they talked about books and poetry and it was because of them that he'd read *Man's Fate,* by André Malraux, and *Darkness at Noon,* by Arthur Koestler, and they were pretty good books, but they intimidated him. The guys. Because they seemed as if they knew everything, and although he, Victor, was perfectly aware that they could not possibly know everything, they *acted* as if they did, and somehow or other, that was the same as if they really did. And it wasn't just a matter of knowing everything, it was knowing where to *put* everything. Because it was clear that somewhere, somewhere far more arcane and rarefied than the public library, there was a master schedule listing the proper places of things. And some people knew it, and most did not, and those who did knew the rest did not, and it made them scornful. Victor would like to know enough to be scornful. Even his mother could trip him up, she read so much. But he'd bet his mother didn't know that Proust was heads and shoulders above John Steinbeck. Maybe his mother had never even read Proust. He, himself, had to admit that he hadn't. In fact, he wasn't even sure what the guy had written except something about a swan. But Proust, anyway, was good, and John Steinbeck was not, although Victor had read *Cannery Row* and loved it, liked it even better than *Man's Fate.* But he'd never say that with the intellectual guys. He'd learned his lesson, he'd blurted out one time that he liked Tchaikovsky, and there was a dead silence in the room. Then Leonard Masari said that no composer after Brahms was to be taken seriously, and the others agreed, and since Victor wasn't sure if Tchaikovsky came after or before, but gathered from the climate that it was after, he just shut up. Victor's fondness for George Orwell had endeared him to one of them, Bill Colt, but he was sort of tough anyway, not like the others, he wanted to become a newspaper reporter and was the editor of the school paper, and the others laughed and said it was all very well for the Rude Colt, as they called him, but Victor would do better to spend his time reading Yeats, Eliot, Pound, Williams, and above all, Wallace Stevens. One of them had given him a book with some poems in it by this guy Stevens, and marked one of them, something about some guy who was king of ice cream or something like that and Victor couldn't make head nor tail of it. He sort of stopped hanging around those guys.

Colt was all right, even though he had to act so tough all the time, walking around in the corridors with a butt hanging out of the corner of his mouth and the teachers not even making a fuss about it, just saying, Okay, Bill, douse it, but he'd just graduated and was in the army now.

Then there were the good boys. Nobody called them that, but that's how everybody thought of them. And they were lower than low. Victor had spent considerable time thinking about this. Because not too many people liked the jerky, wild guys, but the jerky guys thought they were hot shit and walked around like they were and so people might curl a lip when they talked about one of them, but the guys had a certain status all their own, especially the two who owned motorcycles. It was as if they'd made their own world and inside it they were kings, and other people sort of accepted that. And the same was true of the intellectual guys. Everybody dumped on them, I mean people really disliked them, but they were so above everything that it never touched them, and that fact meant that other people, no matter how they felt, treated them with a kind of respect. And of course everybody adored the athletes.

But nobody looked with respect on the good boys, not even the good boys themselves.

219

Most of them got good grades, but weren't geniuses, like the intellectual guys. And they didn't smoke, and most of them didn't go out with girls, and they went to church with their families on Sundays, and did what they were told. There was Bob Evans, who was going to be a missionary to China like his parents before him, and who was pink and white and sweet and kindly, and went out doing surveys to find out how many black people—called colored, then—were living in the county, and what their living conditions were. There were only twenty-three, but Bob got an A on his paper. There was pudgy little Joe Santorro, who giggled like a frog, and whom everybody liked because they could laugh at him. And other, less memorable, pale good boys who did moderately well in school and nothing at all with girls. These were the boys Victor was most at home with, but they were a bit too pious for him, and besides, he refused, absolutely refused to hang out with them, it was just too *low*.

Finally, there were the athletes. Some of these were also good boys, and one was even a jerk, but they comprised a separate group and it was this group that Victor aspired to. But no matter how he tried, he could not be a good athlete. He was okay, he had a batting average respectable enough to be mentioned in public, and he did not shame his team when he was sent in as end, second string, of course. But he was too skinny, too slight to be really good. His mother said his body had not grown up yet, and just wait, he'd be great in time. But it would be too late, he knew. He was best at basketball, but even there he didn't shine. Hanging around with the athletes, he felt second-rate, and felt, moreover that they treated him that way.

So he was mostly alone. He would have liked a guy he could be close to, tell things to, ask questions of. He wondered if other guys felt the things he felt. They didn't talk as if they did. So neither did he. He kept his lips shut and laughed at the jokes. He had laughed in eighth grade when he sometimes didn't know what was funny, but by now even if he did not

220

know what was funny, he knew what was a joke. They were always the same.

And mostly they were about girls. And alone as he was, he thought about girls. You never had to worry about girls looking down on you, like the athletes or the intellectual guys, because girls always looked up to guys. The problem was, he was even intimidated by the *girls!*

So there he was, lying in the hammock, unable to think of one good thing.

That morning, he'd gone to the lake to swim with a bunch of guys (mostly good guys). He always felt a little superior with them, since he also could be said to hang out with the athletes and the intellectuals (after all, no one else knew what he felt). But this day, the good guys had pulled one on him. There was a blanket of girls sitting next to them, and little by little, the guys got to talking to them. Only Victor and a small sharp-nosed boy named Heinz were too shy to join in. Eventually the guys were all on the girls' blanket, all except Victor and Heinz, who then looked at each other and decided to go home. They got up and Victor with bored bravado said he had a date, and Heinz glanced at him and Victor could see Heinz wasn't sure if it was true or if Victor was putting on an act, and so Victor looked over the girls on the other blanket with a look of scorn, as if they were dogs beneath his consideration, and then walked off, Heinz in his trail. They walked the three miles back to town not speaking, not even looking at each other. Victor would have liked to say something to Heinz, to ask if Heinz maybe felt the things he did, but he couldn't, after his bravado act, he had to keep the act up. He acted superior, as he had seen others do, and that shut Heinz up.

(Heinz, in later life, became an astrophysicist and quite famous. Despite the devastating fact that his height never went above his sixteen-year-old five-foot-two, he became the most acclaimed graduate of Cardon High.)

And Victor slunk home hating himself, hating the world, hating above all the new cluster of pimples erupting on his chin. And drank lemonade (iceless and now spilled) and read *Antony and Cleopatra* (stupid) and lay in the hammock concluding that the entire universe was a huge joke aimed at him.

So he was lying there watching the book get ruined by seeping lemonade, watching ants scurry up and occupy the pages, and his mother came out into the yard. It was Sunday, her day off. She must have seen, known, just from the way he was lying there, maybe from the way he'd acted when he first came home, that something was wrong. She sauntered out into the yard, it was a huge yard, not fenced, just acres of grass overlooking the valley, sauntered out checking on her flowers, then sauntered over to me, easy, nothing special, and tapped my behind and I slid over and she sat down next to me on the hammock and I wanted to scream at her because I knew she'd try to make me feel better and I knew she couldn't make me feel better and I couldn't stand her trying. Because she cared and that made it seem all her fault.

And she sat there and talked about how beautiful it was there and how she loved it there and how most people didn't get to live in places as beautiful as that and how we ought to be grateful. And I wanted to puke, she sounded so dreamy-creamy, god, but she didn't know anything, anything at all about what life was really like. And then she asked me what I wanted for my birthday, my god, did she think I was nine years old to be bribed out of a sulk by the promise of a birthday present, this wasn't a sulk it was despair, something she knew nothing about, always singing around the house and worrying about the stupid flowers and the stupid library. So I said that was months away and how was I to know. So she said I should think about it because she wanted to start saving for it, so I said *A car. I want a car.* Sarcastically. Even if they could have afforded it, there weren't many cars available then, in the midst of the war.

And she turned to me and said: "You think that will help?"

I turned away from her fast because I was going to bawl. I couldn't stand it that she knew, that she could *see*. It was humiliating.

Then she started talking, she had a meandering way

222

of talking, she went round and round and you never knew where she was going, but she always ended up where she wanted to, and she was stroking my back and reminiscing, and saying, "God, I remember being sixteen, it was the worst time in my life. My mother felt so sorry for me, she gave me a sweet sixteen party even though she couldn't really afford it. And I invited all the kids in my class, there were twenty, and you know what? Only seven came. We were really 'out,' because we were so poor. And Mom had gotten all that food in and worked for three days to prepare it. I was heartbroken for myself, humiliated in front of her, but my heart ached most because she'd spent so much money she didn't have, and I knew it.

"I think it's a bad time for most kids," she said. "Oh, there are always the roaring boys like your father, nothing ever seems to daunt them!" she laughed. "But I wish I knew what pill they took to get that way!" She moved her hand to my face and caressed it a little, and looked in my eyes, and her face was very tender, full of love and I wanted just to reach up and hold her but I couldn't because that would be a kid thing to do, but god, I loved her, and she said, "You know, honey, the only good thing I can say about being sixteen is that you live through it." And she laughed and then Shandy came bounding out through the screen door and she jumped up and ran with him awhile, zigzagging around the shrubs and trees, and Shandy was barking, and I watched her, her hair bounced, and she had a beautiful round ass and beautiful breasts then, she hadn't gotten plump yet, and she was laughing with the dog and as I watched her I felt the most tremendous desire I'd ever felt in my life. I sank down on the hammock, listening to Shandy barking, her giggling, then the bang of the screen door. My groin was hot and aching. Shandy came running over to me, he licked my hand and I lay there feeling hot and swollen and oh, god, I can't tell you, sick, deformed, diseased, filthy—there aren't any words.

4

"It's cold in here," Dolores said, and Victor got up and turned on the fire. She uncurled and rose and carried the coffee tray back into the kitchen, while Victor opened a bottle of beer, and took it and two glasses back to the sitting room. They did not speak. Dolores put the soiled dishes in the sink and stopped it up and ran hot water over them, put the cream pitcher in the fridge, and returned to the sitting room. She curled back up in the rocker, pulling a lap robe over her knees. Victor sat on the couch again. They were both still in their robes.

"I'm not talking about anything Oedipal: I was way past that age. Or maybe I am, I don't know. At the time I was convinced I was the only person who ever felt such a filthy disgusting thing. Ever after that, until she got old, whenever I saw my dad kiss her, I turned my face away.

"What it was, I think, was that I'd never before associated my mother with the voluptuous fevered images of my fantasy life. I used to work part time as a checkout clerk in a supermarket, and every evening as I walked home, they'd float in front of my eyes, women, girls, but not really: really, it was body parts I saw, boobs and cunt and asses and legs, I'd walk the two miles home with my head full of them and couldn't get them out. And I knew it was wrong— not church-wrong, but humanly wrong—to see people that way, as an accretion of parts, or not even as an accretion, just as parts. But just walking along the road, I'd get a hard-on.

"And suddenly, I saw my mother in the same way. Well, it was intolerable. And it was strange, because much as I loved her that day, that was the day I began to pull away from her. I felt too guilty. I tried to stop seeing *her,* I tried to see *Mother,* a notion of motherhood, I guess. In which she was pure and unsexual and saintly and occupied with compassionate trivialities. You know? I defused her. I could look up and down at her at the same time, but I never had to look across.

"Well, I can see that only looking back. But that was an important afternoon for me, everything began there, somehow. Because I lay in that hammock for a long time, feeling disgusting and filthy and powerless and isolated and scorned, and I made up my mind I would change things. I lay there working out strategy: I was going to be different. I decided to do what the little groups did, the jerks and the intellectuals and the athletes: to see *myself* as king of the hill, to force others, by my conviction, to see me that way. I spent the rest of the summer preparing. I got together a couple of guys, and worked out at the basketball court every day. I began to read the *Kenyon Review* and the writers it praised. I went back to school that fall determined to outsnob the snobs and to make the basketball team, and I did both. I learned to walk with my head in the air (like the intellectuals) and to talk down to people. It was fantastically effective. People may not have liked me, but they looked *up*. When I graduated, they voted me the class 'Renaissance Man,' the all-round accomplished one. Girls began to sidle alongside me, to flirt with *me:* I didn't have to do anything but deign to answer. I couldn't have predicted how easy it would be!

"And of course in the next two years, my body did fill out, as my mother had predicted, and the pimples vanished and hair took their place. Maybe, in some deep place in me, I was unhappy with what I was becoming, but my life was so much better than it had been that my new style seemed only a good thing. I developed then a determination to win, to win at any cost, and never to fall back into the shame and doubt of my early adolescence.

"And I went on like that, in the army, in college, and in grad school. Oh, the arrogant superiority no doubt was honed down a little with each step: I couldn't have gotten away in the army with what I got away with in high school. But it became my attitude. I was a winner, an egotist, confident and poised. I looked down on people who were not. And I had my choice of girls, always.

"I must have been an obnoxious bastard, but I didn't care; it had come to me that this was what a man has to be if he's not to suffer shame and powerlessness. Every once in a while my mother would eye me in a certain way, and I knew she was not liking this son she loved so much. But I didn't care about that either. By then, I'd completely put her down in my mind. Her trivial concerns—overshoes and jackets, the evening roast, the library board: 'Well, now, what do you suppose they've gone and done! They've taken *Lolita* right off the shelves! I went right down there, I said to Sam Hart, now listen here, Sam Hart, do you want to make Cardon County the laughingstock of the state?' And then my sister got married and had a couple of kids whizbang right away, and she would sit there for *hours,* literally hours, cooing and oohing over her grandchildren, talking to them and laughing at them and bouncing them when they were just, in my eyes, lumps of insentient flesh.

"She stopped seeming—*serious.* She was no longer someone I needed to please. She was irrelevant in the world of men, the world I lived in. She was nice, she was sweet, she cooked up a great roast pork, but that was all. You know?"

Victor wiped his hand across his face.

"By the time I got to college, I was a real golden boy. You ever run across one of them?"

"All the time. I advise them. They come into my office very soberly, prepared to be awed. They speak seriously, almost reverently, about 'my career.' They speak of it in exalted hollow voices as if the words were set in gold and mounted over the family china closet—which they probably are. They come in with a tentative schedule made up of heavy hardware: physics, math, and early Urdu.

"And of course, since I think learning ought to be fun and enlarging to the entire mind, I suggest a course in literature, art, or music. They are shocked: 'I don't know if that would be good for *my career.'* It's clear to me that his career has for some time been treated as community property—by parents, teachers, counselors of all sorts. He will look at you, this dewy-faced boy who still picks his nose when no one is looking, and masturbates himself to sleep, and hand it to you, *my career,* sure that you too will handle the sacred object with the proper deference.

"What I hear is the hollow rattle of someone who's lost his life and doesn't even know it. He thinks *he's* in control."

Victor leaned forward sharply. "Yes, but who *is* in control? Who? No one at all. It's a train running on a track with no one directing it, no one except the track itself which was laid long ago, and no one knows by whom."

He settled back. "I thought I was taking control of my life. It never occurred to me then that I was doing what society had determined I should do, that rather than taking control, I was ceding it."

"What would have been taking control?"

He shrugged. "Oh, who knows? Probably just suffering, going on as I was, feeling things, observing them. Until control came naturally, from inside, the power to act on what I saw and felt. Which would have been slow and hard and humiliating. But I wouldn't have become what I became. . . ."

He wiped his face again.

"What did you become?" she asked him, puzzled. He did not seem monstrous to her, who was super-sensitive to signs of monstrosity.

"Oh, a clear winner, you know? A go-getter. I got the peach of a job after grad school, and I moved ahead in that job faster than anyone could have anticipated. Even me. I was on my way and I could see it: I was going to be the next Mach."

"Mach? The head of Blanchard Oil?"

"Yeah. Why?"

"Oh, well, I know him. Sort of."

He looked at her amazed. "How could you know him?"

"I get invited, fairly often, to participate on panels here and there. I've met Mach several times—or rather, I should say, I've been presented to him, because he never once looked at me as we were being introduced. At conferences intended to get academicians and humanists to *communicate* with business and industry people," she laughed. "You know."

He nodded.

"You *can't* admire him," Dolores said.

"Not as a person. But he isn't a person, you see: he's Mach. He's power incarnate, the mover and shaker, the person who with one or two others moves OPEC chessmen around the chessboard that's the world. He determines the futures of countries, not just of one industry, or one corporation."

Dolores shuddered. "God help us."

"Well, I wanted that. Then." He lighted another cigarette, although he had two burning down in the ashtray. His hands were shaking.

"And what happened?"

"Well," he tried to laugh, but his face twisted a little, "there was this girl named Edith." He exhaled hard. "I met her toward the end of grad school at a party at the Long Island estate of some wealthy girl who was dating a friend of mine. She had class, Edith. She had short blond hair done in a pageboy, and big blue eyes, and she wore pleated skirts and cashmere sweaters and a single string of pearls. The thing about Edith was, the pearls were real.

"And I *think* what happened was that Edith fell in love with me. I can't, now, vouch for anything. What I felt, what I thought I felt—it's all lost in the haze of the years. I wasn't passionately in love with Edith. I've never been passionately in love in my life until . . ." He looked at her, then continued. "So I had no grounds for comparison. I thought I loved her. She would sit and listen to me talk as if—as if I were some kind of god. And it was genuine, then—her *awe* for me, I guess it was.

"And I thought life with her would be fine, just fine. She *loved* flowers, she *loved* babies, she *loved* dogs, cats, and spaghetti dinners in little Italian restaurants. And squooshy stuffed animals and the Staten Island ferry and Kahlil Gibran.

"Her father was a VP in Burton-Trilby, the ad agency, she was used to a certain standard of life, she lived it gracefully. She would not have to learn, as to some degree I would, and she could even help me.

All the while looking up to me for my superior intellect, force, and know-how. Who knows why? At the time, it seemed ideal.

"And it went on seeming ideal for quite a while. She was so much in love in the early years that our sex was terrific. I didn't know then. . . . I didn't know she was swooning with ecstasy even though she wasn't having orgasms. How could I know? Because she really was swooning with ecstasy. And things were going well for me, for my job, we had no money worries, she was creating a home, having a baby: it seemed the American dream come true. It was a comfortable life for me—she made it so. She thought I was wonderful. Do you know," he leaned toward her, "that there are men on this earth who have never been told anything else?"

"Or never listened to anything else," she laughed. "Of course! The Daniel Moynihans of the world."

"I don't know when things began to change. Maybe right away, maybe after a few years. It was all so gradual. It was years later that I was watching her— we were at some party and she was talking to someone else—and I noticed that she had this habit of smiling with only her lower lip and the corners of her mouth: she kept the upper lip stiff. And she hadn't done that when I'd met her, and I didn't know when it had begun, but there it was. She'd been doing it for years, by then.

"We had two kids and Edith was pretty busy with them in those years in Dallas. They were exciting years for me: moving up, power struggles, more difficult jobs. It was the game all over again, and by now I was an expert at it. But even experts get caught, trapped in infights. But it's the infights that teach you who you are.

"I remember one in particular, it was probably the first serious one I'd been involved in at the Highland Company, I'd probably just hit near the top of middle management. There were two warring factions. I liked one group—I liked the people, I liked their . . . well, what you'd call their *values*. But they were losers, all of them, losers in the political arena if not in life. And they were losers because they believed that the world

229

was divided into black and white and that if you had good values you always lost: good guys finish last. So they were always prepared to lose, and they were resigned. So they couldn't think up decent strategies for winning: the best they could do was plan a holding action. They could defend, they couldn't aggress."

"Ouch."

He ignored her. "The other group was the Reilly group—that's how I thought of it. A pompous shit named Reilly was its leader, and he believed that he was a wheeler-dealer who knew exactly how much ass to kiss, and who drew the line at nothing. I knew he was incompetent and hollow, but I also thought he'd win just because he was so entirely unscrupulous.

"For a long time, I managed to stay unaligned, treading a fine line, not appearing to favor either side. But you know, you can't keep that up indefinitely: the time comes when you're forced to take sides. And I was obsessed with all this, watching daily developments very minutely, and trying to decide which side to join—trying to decide on what grounds to decide, even. And right in the middle of all this, Edith decides to get temperamental. She is sulky, I find her crying in her room, she won't sleep with me. She hardly speaks to me in the mornings, at breakfast. I don't know why she's giving me grief, and I have no patience with it, I was caught up in a terribly important situation at work.

"Oh, we'd had little tiffs, I guess you could call them, before. Every once in a while I'd find her sulking, but if I asked what was wrong, she said, 'Nothing.' Or, 'I have a headache,' or, 'I'm getting my period.' She'd seem a little snippy, is all. And a couple of times—well, maybe more than a couple—I'd had late meetings and forgotten to call, and I'd come home at ten and there she'd be, a pursed mouth in a bathrobe sitting on the living-room couch watching TV and waiting for me. And then I'd realize I hadn't called, and I'd apologize, and she'd say, very snippy: 'Your dinner's in the oven if you want it.' Of course it was always dried up, but of course I'd already eaten. And then she'd get up and switch off TV and go to bed.

"Normally, she went to bed when I did—whether I went early or late. But on nights when I didn't call, she asserted herself. I never really cared. On those nights I really wanted to sit with a drink and think over what had happened that day. I enjoyed sitting there alone, quiet, not having to make perfunctory conversation about the kids or the house or the neighbors. That was my only time of solitude, those nights when Edith was angry with me.

"Anyway, the next day she'd always be herself again, smiling. She seemed to forget. I thought she had a sunny nature.

"But this time, it was a Monday morning, I remember, she got up in the morning with a frown on. I had no idea why. We'd spent a quiet weekend, I was exhausted and I'd sat out by the pool and read the papers and slept most of the time. I was getting ready to go to work, and she was tossing me dirty looks. I didn't want to get into it then. I had a demanding day ahead. So I ignored them, her. And as I was about to leave, she suddenly burst into tears. All the shit I had to face at work, I didn't need this. I yelled at her: 'What is it *now!*' As if she was always giving me grief. But truthfully, Dolores, that's how it *felt:* she didn't, of course, but it *felt* as if she did. I'd come home and the house would *feel* electric, on the brink of some hysterical outburst. But when I yelled, she just stood there blubbering, and I said, 'For God's sake, Edith, can't it wait until tonight?' And she opened her mouth and she screamed at me! What a shock! She shouted: 'You want to go, go! Go to your beloved office, go, go, go! But don't come back!'

"Well, of course, that was sheer idiocy. I grabbed my briefcase and stormed out the door. I didn't get back until very late that night, and I hadn't called. That was purposeful, though, to teach her a lesson. Except when I got home, the house was dark, and Edith and the kids were gone. There was a note, written in her"—he looked appealingly at Dolores—"don't get mad, now, huh? I'm trying to tell you how I felt then."

She nodded.

"Written in her large stupid female script, flowing

and careful, with a long swing up at the end of each word. On perfumed stationery with little flowers in the corners. You know? Well, I just picked it up and felt such contempt for her, such disgust. . . . I didn't know where it came from, what she'd done to deserve my feeling that way about her, and I hadn't even known I *had* felt that way about her until that moment. . . .

"She wrote that it was clear I didn't love her anymore, so she had taken the children and gone to her father's, in Scarsdale. I threw the letter down, I poured myself a nice big Scotch, and sat down in 'my' chair. I tried to go over in my mind what could have caused this, but I couldn't figure it out. I wasn't screwing around, I didn't drink too much, I provided for her and the kids very well. So there was no excuse, none at all. It was a power play: she wanted to get me under her thumb.

"She knew I was in a bad spot at work, that I was worried. She also knew that in those days corporation executives did *not* get divorced. So she was smart, she chose that moment to undermine me. I had to hand it to her for cleverness, whatever else I felt. I couldn't imagine what she wanted, though, except to get an upper hand over me, to—well, what I told myself was —castrate me. Make *me* the deferential one, like her friend Phyllis's husband Harvey. Well, I was damned if she was going to win *that* one, and double damned if I'd give in to *her*."

He started another cigarette, leaned back, put his hand over his eyes.

"I had it figured pretty well. She had two babies and not much money. I never left a great deal in the checking account, and she couldn't have touched the bank accounts because I kept the books in my office safe. Now that her daddy had retired, her parents lived in a five-room apartment—a *lush* five-room apartment, to be sure, but too small for two screaming kids and three adults. She had majored in art in college, but had never worked. She'd gone to Europe after graduation—her parents' gift to her—for a couple of months, and when she got back, we began to make arrangements for our wedding. So she'd never worked, and couldn't do anything—which is to say, she couldn't type. Even so, with two babies . . .

"The only thing would be if her daddy decided to subsidize her. But I knew the old man pretty well, knew how he thought about women—well, about what he would have called the *family*—although he really meant the place of women. And I thought there was little chance he'd support her in her flight from me, especially since I didn't believe Edith would lie, would say I abused her or ran around. Edith, I thought in those days, was strictly honest. I have to confess, I didn't even give her credit for that. I thought she was honest, not out of principle, but because she was naive and childlike and too simple to lie. Hah!

"Anyway, I thought she was in a weak bargaining position, and that every day she spent at her parents' house was going to make it weaker. I never even considered hopping a plane and chasing her to Scarsdale, where I would get down on one knee and beg her to come back. Not only because I wouldn't have done it for her, but also because I wouldn't, couldn't run out on the hassle at work, where such an act would have been interpreted as a failure of nerve. On the other hand, I couldn't just sit there and wait for her to come back, make no move at all. Even her old man would have found that pretty cheeky. So I telephoned, and he answered. I played it well, asking how she was and then, as if I were bewildered and bothered—well, hell, maybe I was, but I didn't know it at the time—asked him if he had any idea why she had left.

"It was a good ploy, made me sound innocent. Which, anyway, I was. He said: 'Don't you?' and I said *not an idea in hell*. And he said well, you know how women are and maybe I'd better talk to her, and she got on and we chitchatted for a couple of minutes about her flight and the kids, and then I said, 'Edith, why did you do this?' And she burst into tears and said, 'You don't love me anymore!' and hung up. Good Christ. I tell you, I was convinced all women were nuts. You couldn't understand them.

"A couple of days later, I wrote her a letter. I told her I loved her and didn't understand why she said I didn't. I swore there'd never been anyone else.

233

Strange," he said, moving, letting his hand rest limply on the couch arm, "how that was the way you proved love: by claiming sexual fidelity. Anyway, I said I needed her and missed her. And in fact, you know, that was true. It surprised me. So often I found her presence . . . irritating. But when she wasn't there . . . it was unpleasant, coming home to a dark house, no child noises, no food cooking, nothing. I'd eat out and come home late, but it felt . . . empty. And then I thought maybe this is what she'd been trying to tell me—that I did need and miss her, or would if she weren't there. Maybe she'd been trying to get me to value her more. And that's what I wrote.

"She never answered. But a couple of weeks later, when I came in late, I saw Vickie's tricycle in the driveway and Leslie's wagon near the front door. The house was quiet, the kids were asleep. Edith was sitting in the living room, but she wasn't reading and she wasn't watching TV. She looked sour. And I felt— *shit!* I was very tired that night, not up for a ringding battle. And then I thought: *women.* You can't live with them and you can't live without them. I missed her when she was gone, but I wasn't especially thrilled to have her back. But it never occurred to me that had anything to do with *me:* I thought—*women.*

"The three weeks she'd been gone had been hellish, but fascinating and exciting, really. I had discovered a lot about myself. I found I was good at maneuvering and I also found my inclinations were to act on principle. It was a good discovery, it made me feel strong. Reilly and his crew had won the battle, as I'd suspected they would. I'd backed the other side, who found themselves out in the cold. But without our knowing it then, Highland was being sold to a conglomerate and new management was coming in. What would happen—of course we didn't know it then— was that Reilly would end up with his little division, stuck there for the rest of his life, while the other group would move on, move away. Not all of them, but the leaders—including me.

"I felt strong. I felt . . . pure, I guess. I'd backed a side I expected would lose but which was essentially right, and made up of decent human beings. I didn't

234

then know what was going to happen to the losing side, except that Reilly got the division instead of Dawes. But I felt I'd discovered my real strength—not the fake superiorities I'd been parading around all my life—well, since I was fifteen—but real ones, strengths you can grow from. And I knew nobody could hold me back now. I'd discovered you never know yourself until you're tested and that you don't even know you're being tested until afterwards, and that in fact there isn't anyone giving the test except yourself. Unconsciously, you test yourself against your own standards. And I also found that it felt good to be among people you respected, even if you lost. And that I had some courage, some principle. I felt damned proud of myself. So proud that, I think, I never pulled the superior act again.

"Except on Edith. Anyway, all this had happened while she was away, and I felt changed and felt she was a stranger to the 'new' me. And I guess she'd gone through something too, although I wasn't thinking much about *her,* then. But we seemed strangers to each other.

"She was sitting there with a drink, which was unusual, so I poured one for myself, and sat down opposite her, heavily, sighing, telling her how tired I was. She just looked at me. She hadn't even smiled when I came in. I told her, rather bitterly, direly, that the Reilly faction had won. She didn't blink. I talked about it for a while, managing to suggest by my tone as much as anything else that it was largely her fault I was so tired, that she had been reprehensible in going off and leaving me during such a trying period of my life."

Victor broke off and put his head in his hands. "Oh god," he said, in anguish, deep in his throat. He lifted his head up again, and breathed in deeply. "I went on, full of gloom and doom, saying that I might be out of a job soon. And during all of it, she sat unblinking, without the little smiles and frowns and expressions of concern she usually showed when I spoke. Sat there like an iceberg.

"So then I launched into a little speech about love. I'd never even said I was glad she was back, but I

235

knew all about love. Looking back, it must have been pretty terrible, pompous and blind, but at the time I was full of a sense of my own rightness. I was telling her that love understands, love tolerates, love does not get impatient, love does not get angry and hold grudges.

"What I was really telling her was how she was to behave. It had never occurred to me that my way of loving wasn't perfect, so this break had had to come from her. And I was telling her I wasn't knuckling under to her, *I* was not going to be castrated."

"*She* was."

"Yes."

5

DOLORES'S MOUTH was grim. "She was defeated in a war you imagined, and by imagining, created. Once it was seen as war, there had to be a winner and a loser. And there was no question about who the loser had to be."

"Yes," he said faintly, leaning against the chair back, and reaching for another cigarette.

"But in seeing it as a war, you made it a war, and you never escaped from that, did you."

"STOP!"

She subsided.

His face was anguished. "I remember once, long ago, before we were married, we were walking in Central Park in the late afternoon, the sun was setting behind the buildings and the sky was deep pink and the trees were lush, and she, oh, she was young then, she had hair that flew when she turned her head, and she was giddy and happy, and she swung around and took my hands and brought her face up close to mine and she said: 'You know why I love you, Victor Morrissey? Because you have a name that sounds like freshly laundered sheets blowing in the wind!' And I laughed, and kissed her, but to tell you the truth, I thought that was pretty silly. But it has remained in my mind ever since. I'll never forget it. . . ."

It never occurred to me that I didn't love Edith as I was supposed to. She was set in my life like a wedge of pie. There was Edith and the kids; there was work; and there was relaxation, which came, increasingly, to be weekends of golf. It's true, I spent little time with her. But evenings, she'd watch TV, which bored me, so I'd go to my study and read. And weekends, there were always a million and one things to be done with the kids or around the house, so I just got out. So Edith wasn't the biggest wedge in my pie, but she was a permanent one. Maybe she was even the crust, the base that held everything else.

Anyway, I'm sincere when I say I did not know what more she wanted. I couldn't even imagine what more there was *for* her to want. I used to quote Freud to myself, in amused annoyance: *What do women want?* They were, I was convinced, unsure themselves what they wanted, and insatiable.

Well, anyway, I gave my little speech on love and she just sat there, cold and still. Then: "What will happen to your job?" I didn't want to worry her unduly. In fact, I wasn't very worried myself. So I told her I wasn't too worried, that I thought there would be numerous possibilities, although we might have to leave Dallas.

And *she* said: "Then it wasn't such a risk you took after all, was it. You could *afford* to have principle, *afford* to do what you felt was right, couldn't you. You had the luxury of feeling moral."

I was stunned. Someone I'd thought for years now was a part of, was inside *my* pie plate, had suddenly stepped outside, was looking at me critically from a distance.

"That's a very great luxury, Victor. It's given only to a very few." Her voice was as cold and hard as her eyes.

"Do you want to explain that?"

She looked at me with what I can only call contempt. Edith, look at *me* with contempt? She stood up.

237

"If you don't understand it, Victor, you're blinder than I thought. Will you be having breakfast at home in the morning?"

"The hell with breakfast! Where the hell do you think you're going! You owe me some explanation for your behavior, damn it! Now sit down, Edith, and explain!"

She had begun to walk out of the room, but she stopped and turned partway towards me. Her face was very white. She put her hands on a chair back and clutched it. She did not sit down, though.

"I left you because you care far more about your work than about me and the children. No!" She put up her hand to stop me. "Don't try to interrupt. This may be the last full statement I can get out without interruption for the rest of my life. And don't deny it. You spend the weekends lolling around here like a bored camel. You pay almost no attention to the children or to me. Then Monday morning, you're up and about stomping and pulling like a horse heading for the barn. You put on your suit and tie and you'd think it was wings," she added bitterly. The corners of her mouth were trembling. I was waiting for her to cry, because then I could get up and hold her and the whole thing would end. But she didn't cry. "You don't come home for dinner and you don't even bother to call. It means nothing whatever to you that I spend hours preparing a meal for you—for you! Because the kids eat almost nothing, and I'm never hungry. My time, my concerns, my care—all of it is just so much . . . NOTHING! . . . to you!" Her voice was getting higher now and I expected the break at any moment.

She turned her face away from me. I watched her back to see if she was crying, but I couldn't tell. Then she turned her face halfway back to me.

"All right. I am not stupid, although you think so, and I can see the way things are around me. You're all like that, men. My mother says my father was like that. I guess he was. I was always away at private schools, I didn't know. At any rate, I decided that the children need a father, and that I would do my duty. And so I came back. And I will keep my bargain."

She walked swiftly out of the room, so swiftly that

I didn't have time to yell *the hell with your damned duty!* And I sat there shocked. You see, she'd given the same speech I'd given, from the opposite side. I'd been telling *her* what love was—her love, not mine—and she'd been telling *me* what love was—her love, not mine. What I didn't know then was that we were saying the same thing in different ways. Because, indeed, from then on, Edith was understanding, tolerant, did not get impatient, angry, or hold grudges. I gave in on one point—I never again forgot to call if I weren't coming home for dinner. And I tried—I really did—to spend a little more time with the kids, and with her.

But something had changed. That heavy atmosphere I often felt in the house disappeared. I was relieved, it was less oppressive to come home. And Edith was always smiling, she never argued much, she *never* contradicted me. She listened when I spoke. She became rather quiet, although I'd hear her giggling and talking nonsense to the children.

And in the beginning, I thought—*good*. I'd won, I'd shown her who was the head of this house, and she wouldn't question it again. I saw her arranging everything for my comfort, and I thought *good*. Things were as they should be. But it was strange. And again, gradual. But over the next years—oh, we moved to Minneapolis and bought a new house and the kids started school, and she was pregnant again, twice, and there were two new babies to occupy her . . . but over the years I became aware of a kind of . . . emptiness. As though I came into a vacuum every night, a vacuum only I could fill. Like puffs of cloud that you walk into, that then shape themselves around you. I can't describe it except to say it felt empty.

And then, of course, Edith did her duty by night as well as day. Her duty and that's all. No more ecstatic swoons. We screwed less and less often, because I didn't enjoy that much either. And her face began to change. She developed little pursed lines around her mouth when she was only in her thirties, and her voice began to have a disapproving intonation. She seemed to disapprove of everything and everybody. I guess she thought (he added thickly) that everyone else was having fun in life except her.

And meantime, out there in the world, were all these beautiful, vivid, intelligent women, all for the asking. Warm affectionate women who lighted up when I entered the room. I was on the way up, I seemed attractive, I guess. I was a roaring boy in those years, everything I touched turned to gold. And it was easy enough to hide my new sex life—I'd always spent late nights at the office, and now that I was in the top executive bracket, there were business trips and even weekends away from home, meetings that did, in fact, drag on until one or two in the morning.

When we moved to Scarsdale, I got a little apartment for those late nights. So it wasn't noticeable that instead of having dinner with George, I was having it with Georgia. It wasn't noticeable to Edith, that is. And I was very careful, very discreet. I never went home without taking a shower first.

When Georgia began to hound me about divorcing Edith and marrying her, I stopped seeing her. Before long I took up with Lillian. Lillian got tired of having a married lover—of being alone on Saturday night, on holidays—and walked out on me. But there was always someone else: they are what you called the Oxford girls, an infinitely replaceable generation. It's pathetic, really. I don't know where the men are. But there are hundreds, thousands of them, I guess, beautiful, intelligent, sympathetic women who are grateful, really grateful for a good dinner in a nice place, a little attention, a little sex. Sometimes, when I could manage it, I'd take one of them with me on a "business" weekend—it was difficult for Edith to get away in those years, and she didn't enjoy business conferences.

Still, with all this, I sometimes felt sorry for myself. I wanted to come home to lovely Lauren in my bed instead of empty Edith—for I'd come to attribute the emptiness of home to what I saw as the emptiness of her head. But on the whole, I was, well not happy, but —well, yes, *happy* in those years. Yes, I was.

Well, life went on like this for a long time. But it ended, in 1973, in March of 1973. I came home about two one night to find Edith sitting in my study. This was unusual, first because she'd long since stopped

sitting up for me, but also because—and I didn't realize it until I saw the study light on—no one, no one
but me ever went into my study. Edith had made it
sacrosanct—the kids never even knocked on the door
if I was in there. I hadn't asked for that, hadn't de-
manded it. But it had been done.

Anyway, there Edith was, sitting in my leather
chair hugging herself and rocking herself back and
forth. I had a rush of remorse: something had happened to one of the kids and she couldn't find me! I
rushed to her.

"Edith what is it?"

She eyed me. Her face was viperous. There was a
glass on the table. I wondered if she was drunk. I
sighed. Drunk scene with charges of neglect. I knew
I had it coming, but I was tired. I poured myself a
drink and settled down wearily in the chair opposite
her, prepared for a long screaming siege.

She looked odd. Edith was always extremely neat,
every hair in place. Never a run in her stocking—she
always carried an extra pair—never a bra strap showing or a bulge. She was never overweight. I never saw
her without makeup—she'd get up early in the morning
and put it on before I was awake. The only times I
ever saw her hair in disarray were at the beach and
after the babies were born.

But that night her face looked different. It appeared
she'd been crying, because she was puffy. And maybe
had washed her face and had just not bothered to put
on makeup again. She looked—real. As if all these
years I'd been looking at a mask, and this was what
lay beneath. Her hair was tousled. And she *had* been
drinking, a little.

She smiled sweetly at me. "So did you enjoy your
little dinner at Hanson's, holding hands across the table?"

Oh boy.

Turns out she'd seen me there. And I was probably
the one who told her to go there. I never thought. I
was so convinced of her—I don't know—total powerlessness, I guess. Lack of will and power. She'd been
depressed for a while and she and her friends Jean
and Margaret, who also had husbands who were away

a lot, decided they would start to go out together one night a week. I knew about this, I thought it was a fine idea. They always stayed around Scarsdale, they didn't like to drive long distances at night. But that night they had tickets to a play and were taking the train to New York. Edith had probably told me about it. I paid so little attention to her. . . .

They decided to eat at Hanson's because Edith said I'd recommended it. And there I was, with Alison. Jean spotted me across the room and turned and tried to block Edith, but Edith peered around her and saw me.

She didn't tell me this calmly. She screamed, she cried. I knew she was hurt, but in a way I couldn't understand why. Surely she couldn't feel possessive about me sexually after all these years, after all her indifference? Twenty years. I wasn't possessive about her. I wouldn't have minded her having an affair if she'd done it discreetly. That's what I thought, anyway. It's easy, I guess, to think such a thing when you're positive your wife will do no such thing.

So although I knew that infidelity was one thing the world gives you permission to go into a rage about, I couldn't believe that she actually felt what she was showing. I thought it was an act, another power play. And this time, her motive was clear: she had a dull sex life, she was damned if I was going to have a lively one. Well, I was damned if she was going to lock me in a closet in my prime. Divorce wasn't such a shocking thing anymore. I was prepared to risk everything—what could I lose, after all?

She kept saying, over and over: "Right in front of my friends, right in front of them! Everybody will know about it by the end of the week!" I homed in on that. With impeccable logic, lighting my pipe, I pointed out that in fact she wasn't hurt for herself, that her main distress was humiliation in front of her friends, and since I happened to know their husbands were doing the same thing, she needn't feel humiliated. I added also that I found her motivation rather shabby.

Needless to say, this didn't help matters. She screamed, she went crazy. I sucked on my pipe, waiting for her hysterics to end. It took awhile, but eventually she calmed down and sat there sniffling. "Edith, I'm sorry if you feel humiliated. But you have to admit there hasn't been much life around here for years."

"Whose fault is that? Besides, how would you know, you're never here."

"Well, you must realize there's some reason I'm not here. You don't do much to keep me here, do you?"

"How would you feel if I'd done this to you?"

I shrugged. "After all these years . . ."

"Oh, don't lie! I can see you about to lie! Suppose everybody in Scarsdale knew I was . . . playing around."

I had to admit she had a point: *that* I wouldn't have liked. But I wasn't going to let her see she'd won a point. "Well, I certainly wouldn't be throwing a hysterical fit."

"Oh, wouldn't you!" she shrieked.

I got up and closed the study door. "You're going to wake the children."

"Let them hear! Let them know! Let them find out what kind of man their father is!" She jumped up and went to the bar and poured more whiskey in her glass. She wasn't much of a drinker, couldn't handle it, so I crossed the room to try to stop her and she shrieked: *"Don't touch me!"* She stood there holding her glass, clutching it. Her face was white and her hair was falling in her face. She looked like a fury and for the first time, in all the years I'd known her, I saw the Edith who lived underneath that stiff smile, that sweet manner.

She was unstoppable. "If you'd seen me with a man and your friends had been with you, you'd have charged across the room and grabbed me and hit the man if you could. Then you would have dragged me home clamping your hands down as hard as you could on my arms, leaving me black and blue. You might have hit me. You surely would have pushed me down in a chair and shouted at me, laying down the law. But the one thing you would not do is call *that* a hysterical fit! Oh, no! Only *I* have hysterical fits!"

She lowered her voice, which for some reason frightened me more than her shrieking.

"All these years, all these years! *You* used to throw hysterical fits regularly: or don't you remember, Victor! When the babies were little and it was all I could do to keep things going. You spat contempt at me if the coffee was too weak, if the meat was burned, if the kids were too noisy. Or don't you remember, Victor! And when they were older, you went into tizzies if your golf clubs had been touched, if your desk was disturbed. Of course, we didn't call those hysterical fits, oh no! We said Daddy's tired, now, shush, honey, or, Don't make Daddy mad, now, honey, he works hard all day, or Mustn't mess Daddy's desk, sweets, he has very important things on his desk. Oh, yes, you trained us all with your hysterical fits. You don't remember because it's been so long since you've had to throw one. We all learned to be quiet and give way before the great man. I tell you," and she turned to me a face full of anguish and sadness, so pained I nearly cried, "the day I came back to you was the bitterest hour of my life!"

She walked away, she laid her head in the angle between the wall and the bookshelves, and she spoke into the corner. Her voice was low and it reverberated.

"I had no place to go, no way to support myself and the children. And even if you or my daddy had given me money, I had nothing to go *to,* nothing to do with my life. It wasn't a question of going to another man: I saw you, you were all the same. *You* weren't even the worst of the lot, you weren't a drunk, you weren't brutal.

"My parents couldn't understand why I wanted to leave you. My mother, especially, I'll never forget that, never. She kept saying, 'But Victor's such a *good* man, Edith!' And I said, if he's good, god help other women. All my father wanted to know was whether you were fooling around. I said I was sure you weren't and then he said, solemnly, 'Edith, your place is at your husband's side.' "

She snorted. "Oh, I revered my father, I felt he felt I'd broken some terrible ordinance. If only I could have shown them a few bruises, told them about other women. . . ." She whirled around at me. "Why didn't you screw around then?" she cried.

Edith never used profanity, she rarely used slang. I was shocked, not at the language, but at her. She gulped some of her drink and sat down again. She didn't look at me, she looked at the floor. Her face was white and drained. I can't tell you how much I loved her, how much I pitied her at that moment.

"And so I saw," she said, her mouth a twisted line, "what life was for women. Women are body servants. The only difference among them is that some of them are lucky and have well-to-do husbands. And I was one of the lucky ones. I was lucky! Hah! And so I came back. I determined I would be a proper wife and mother, I would become the servant you wanted, but that I'd spend as much of your money as I possibly could. And I haven't done badly at that, have I?" she sneered at me. "That's what I was supposed to do, and I did it. It was a bargain: the terms of marriage. You pay me in goods, I pay you in services: neither of us is free. I didn't like those terms, but I wasn't strong enough to change them. I accepted. I bowed.

"And you, and you!" She leaned forward, whispering harshly, "You *broke* that bargain! It isn't enough that you had the best of it all these years! You want everything! You broke the bargain that cost me my life! My life!"

She was crying again. I sat there with bowed head, tears in my eyes. I wanted to go over and hold her, but I knew I didn't have the right. I sat there feeling ashamed and humbled. But I was also looking for a way not to feel ashamed and humbled, I guess. Because I said, "Edith, I'm sorry, I really am. But, darling, why didn't you *tell* me? Tell me what you felt, what you thought I was doing!"

She looked at me with what I can only call pure hate.

"And you would have listened? You wouldn't have said: 'Oh, Edith, don't be ridiculous! Don't you have everything you can want?' When was the last time you listened to me, Victor Morrissey? Not even last night. I *told* you we were going to Hanson's for dinner! I told you! You never even heard me!"

That last really ticked me off—at myself, of course, but I blamed her. I stood up, I shouted at her: "When was the last time you told me the truth! Who decided on this, that everything had to be what *I* wanted? Everybody's selfish! Why didn't you fight back?"

She stood up, too, furious. "And have the house in a tumult all the time? Have the children grow up in a house where their parents are continually fighting? A house like Phyllis and Harvey's? A madhouse? My parents never fought!"

"No. And your parents were just like us. They lived the way we live."

"My father never broke his bargain!"

"Oh, didn't he?"

She moved towards me, I thought she was going to throw her glass at me, she would have killed me at that moment if she could have.

"My father never . . ."

"Oh, Edith, for godsakes. It was well known. He had a woman in an apartment in the East Seventies. For years."

She shrieked and did throw the glass then, right at me, but I ducked. She just kept shrieking. It wasn't crying, it was cries, like the cries of seabirds. She was beside herself, she couldn't stand it. I was a little sorry I'd told her, but I figured it was about time she learned a little something about reality.

But I'd been in business too long, I guess. Sorry as I'd been a moment before, I went on seeing her as the antagonist in a struggle I had to win. And I knew that you press your advantage when your opponent is at a disadvantage. So I went on.

"Your mother knows about it, knew about it then. Ask her sometime. The woman came to his funeral, and your mother asked me to ask her to leave. She also asked me not to tell you."

The cries got higher, thinner.

"Look, Edith, I'm not saying I'm blameless in this mess. But you participated in creating it. In the name of domestic peace, you lied. You've lied for twenty years. You never showed me who you were, what you felt. You used the excuse of an orderly home to cover up the real truth: you're a coward!"

She stopped crying. Her eyes looked crazy, her face was swollen and blotchy. I thought I'd have to call a doctor and have him come over and give her a shot to make her sleep.

But she suddenly spoke more calmly. "You want the truth," she hissed, "I'll give you the truth. I hate you! I hate your pipe-smoking complacency, your complacent righteousness, your self-satisfied superiority, your utter unmitigated selfishness, your intellectual pretensions, your stupid dense insensitivity to anything that does not serve your interests, and your treating me like a ridiculous hysterical *Woman* every time I did try to tell you how I felt! *I'm* a coward! Your whole life is lies, you have never once in all your life seen yourself truly! You wrap yourself up in praise and look in the mirror and see god! *Your* cowardice makes *me* look like a hero!"

Suddenly she turned around and began to pull my books off the shelves and hurl them, anywhere, everywhere, not aiming for me or the lamp, although she got both, just hurling books. I didn't try to stop her. I thought that was as good a way as any to get her anger out. When she was finished, she'd come over and put her head in my lap and let me stroke her head and tell her I was sorry sorry sorry, because I really was. And then, I thought, we'd go someplace together, without the kids, Acapulco, maybe, someplace nice, and start over, start fresh, learn to tell each other the truth. Here she had all this passion locked up in her, all blocked. It fascinated me. I foresaw a revivification of our marriage.

I was standing there thinking this when I glanced at her and saw what she had in her hands. It was a first edition, 1605, of Bacon's *Advancement of Learning*. And she knew I treasured it, cherished it. That book had been in my mother's family for generations and no matter how broke they were, they never sold it. She knew all that. It had a leather cover, not the original, I'm sure, but very old and delicate, flaking. The pages too were delicate, the edges sometimes broke off if you just turned them.

And she turned and grinned at me and opened the book and with a sudden thrust, she broke its back!

247

Broke it! Pages fluttered down. She kept folding its back, and more and more pages fluttered down, and I went for her then, I was mad with rage, and she threw it across the room and ran in the other direction, and I went for the book, and she went out the door and I was gasping, flailing around trying to find the pages, I wasn't so sane myself at the moment, but anyway I never heard her leave, and at that moment I wouldn't have cared that she did, wouldn't have cared *what* she did.

I'd never forgive her for breaking the back of my book.

6

VICTOR HAD his head in his hands, covering his face. The ashtray in front of him was full and stank with cigarette butts. Dolores sat across from him, immobile, under a blanket, watching. When he lifted his head she saw clearly the scars, the scratch marks all across his face.

I don't know what I did in the next hour. Gathered up the pages of my Bacon, tried to put them in order. Set the lamp back up. I didn't sweep up the fragments of its broken globe. I remember thinking: Let her sweep up her own mess. I guess I had a drink or two, sitting there thinking about what she said. And I did think about it and even saw its justice. What I couldn't anymore see was a way to repair the past. I couldn't repair that, or my feelings, any better than I could repair my book. It could be rebound, but some of the pages were torn, and rebinding would come too close to the text. It was ruined. And so were we.

It would never be good again, and I would never forgive her for doing that. And even if I could, how could we change after all these years? The pattern of our behavior was set, twenty years set, unchangeable. I knew that my sin was that all those years while she'd been doing her duty, I'd been having fun. But what could I do about that? I couldn't make up for it; I couldn't erase it.

Divorce was the only answer, and at that moment it looked good to me. There was Alison, waiting in the wings—not that I'd marry again, not right away, anyway. I could live in my pied-à-terre in Manhattan until I found something better. And it might be good for Edith: older women were doing interesting things these years, going back to school, reentering the work force. Maybe that could rejuvenate her, help ease her rigidity. Jonathan, it is true, was only eight, but we had a full-time housekeeper and I wouldn't take that away from Edith. I'd give her a fair settlement, she deserved it for all those years. She could have the house and her car and a decent allowance. Mark was fourteen, nearly grown, both kids would be all right if she decided to go to work, or whatever. Be good for her.

Besides, every time I looked down at my ruined book, I felt such a spurt of rage that I knew I could never again lie in the same bed with Edith. I wanted to kill her for that, for the utter malice and cruelty of what she'd done. I would have loved at that moment to have her neck in my hands, to twist until the face turned blue, the eyes popped. . . .

Then the phone rang. It was the police. Edith had had an accident, a serious one, they said. She was in the hospital. I hung up slowly, my mind in a stupor. I had wanted to kill her and now she was dead. Maybe. Nearly dead. And for a second . . . no, for more than a second, I was glad.

He lifted his eyes to Dolores, questioning her.

"I understand. I often wished Anthony dead. It's such an easy solution to impossible situations. Sometimes I teach classes in creative writing at Emmings —whenever they can't get a name writer to do it. And in the beginning, the students, at least half of them, will end their stories with the main character— and sometimes the whole world—dying. It's so much easier that way. So nice and neat and final. So much simpler than living, having to work things out or work them through, or at least, live them out. . . ."

"Well, that's how I felt. But at the same time, exactly the same time, I felt a retching pain, as if somebody was digging my heart out of my chest with a garden hoe. Oh, it was guilt, yes, but it was also sorrow, sorrow that her life had been so . . . unlived, I guess. Sorrow at what we felt about each other, about how all this had happened and we hadn't been able to do one damn thing about it. . . ."

I got in my car and drove to the hospital. It was dawn, the sky was lavender, streaked with light. The branches of the trees were just budding, there were tiny green nodules, hundreds of them on each branch, that cast a green haze on the air, that made the narrow dead winter branches look complicated and alive. And the birds were beginning to wake up, to wake each other up. It was very beautiful.

And I thought: Edith will never see dawn again. And I remembered her saying that she loved me because my name reminded her of freshly laundered sheets flapping in the wind, and I knew she must have loved the smell of that, the sound and look of it. And that she loved me once too, that way, innocent and clean and fresh. I remembered her bitter voice saying to do what you want to do in life is a very great luxury, Victor. And I realized then that long ago she'd had a yearning, an energy, not perhaps for anything specific, not *I want to be a lawyer*, but for something. Having the children wasn't enough. There was something inside her she'd wanted to use, and never had, and now it had atrophied. And I understood her face then too, because to have an energy, a capacity that is never used, that dies a little year by year must be as painful as having your feet bound up, the bone learning to twist and stop, the flesh curling back on itself, stunted, crippled, the very blood kept from running. . . . And I remembered her standing there white and trembling, hurling my character at me like a hammer. She seemed at that moment very large in my imagination.

And then I thought of us at the bridge table. We used to play every couple of weeks, it was the one thing I could abide to do with her friends and their husbands. I'm good at it, better than she, although she's not bad, not really bad. But every once in a while she'd do something I thought was stupid and when she did, I'd mock her. Mock her in front of everyone, and watch her dwindle and pull up her face and try to smile and make a joke of it. And even as I watched her shrinking, I'd have contempt for her cowardice, and that became a self-fulfilling circle, you know? She deserved to be mocked, to be made to shrink, because she allowed herself to be mocked, to be made to shrink. . . .

I laid that, her behavior that I considered cowardly, against her determination, announced so long ago, to *do her duty*. And her duty, as she saw it, involved taking my mocking, taking whatever I handed out . . . I could barely drive, my eyes were tearing. For that was courage, greater courage than I possessed, but at the same time it seemed to me crazy courage, sick, directed at useless ends. . . .

Edith had driven her car directly into the wall of an underpass. Directly. The people at the hospital were suspicious, they asked me if she was suicidal. She was terribly smashed, but she was alive. She was in surgery, I didn't see her all day. And that was only the first. She'd have seventeen operations before they were finished. They told me there was no point in staying, they'd call me when she came out of the OR, but I couldn't *not* stay. I called home and spoke to Mrs. Ross, our housekeeper, told her what had happened and told her to tell the children some mild tale.

Edith didn't come to until the next day. She was lying in an oxygen tent swathed in bandages. I poked my head in every once in a while, and once I caught her with her eyes open. She looked at me and closed them again. She couldn't move her head, her neck was in a cast. But for the moment her eyes caught me, they spoke. *So I lived after all,* they said. *Wonderful.*

After that, I didn't bother her. I sat in the room. There were magazines and books there, I'd brought them, but I didn't read. I sat there aware of her breathing, and thought. About my mother, and how I had never told her how fine I thought she was, how strong, and in the end, how smart, much smarter than her cocksure smart-aleck son. Smart about life, about how you live a life. And about Edith, and our last argument, and how I couldn't resist sending her just one inch further down the road to madness, how I could not *not* give the rack one more twist. How winning had become, for me, all there was to life, and now I had won. The fruits of my victory were lying on that bed, breathing, with assistance. And I thought about that first time—the only time—she'd left me, and how, at the time, I read the whole thing as a power play directed at me. When in fact it had little to do with me. It was Edith's trying to get away from me, her attempt to try out her rickety undeveloped wings, to see if she could manage alone. It had to do with *her,* and her failure must have killed something in her, humiliated it, taught it bitter fear and inferiority.

I thought about all that, and I thought about the present, the future. Sometimes, when Edith was asleep, I'd go and stand near her bed, raise the curtain and look at her, as much of her as I could see. And I saw a stranger, a poor beat-up woman I didn't know now and had never known. Funny. When we were first seeing each other, Edith told me her mother was Catholic. I didn't know why she said that; I knew Edith was an Episcopalian, because I'd gone to church with her. Years later, I found out her mother wasn't Catholic at all, never had been. And I asked Edith about that. And she told me that she had thought *I* was Catholic—because of my name—and was afraid that I'd hesitate to marry a non-Catholic. So she'd made up a story, and I guess, if it had been necessary, she'd have gotten her mother to go along with it. Although in those days, there was much more anti-Catholic sentiment than there is now, and her old man might very well have vetoed a marriage to a Catholic. But I think—she really did love me once, Edith—that she'd even have defied her daddy to marry me.

Well, I'd stand there and think, but I couldn't come

to any calm place. I didn't know Edith, I'd never known Edith, but willy-nilly, we knew each other, we'd been married to each other for twenty years and that was that. We may not have known what the other felt, but we knew each other's smells, tiniest habits, manners. . . .

And I still couldn't see any hope for us, if Edith recovered. None.

7

FOR WEEKS they didn't know if Edith would live. There was so much internal damage, besides the external. I went home after she came out of the OR unconscious, and sat down with the kids and tried to explain. It was stiff, it was difficult. I realized I barely knew my children. Oh, I knew their names and ages and even what foods they liked, but I didn't know anything about their emotional contexts, about what they *felt* like—how they responded to things, how they processed things. I knew Mark had been a crybaby, and that Jonathan was given to playing quietly in corners alone. I knew that Vickie, who was eighteen then, gave me flak whenever she could, and that Leslie always covered me with kisses. Well, it was difficult.

At first I wouldn't let them go see her. I didn't want, if she died, that they should remember her that way, wrapped in all those bandages. The way I remembered my father, weak and weeping about my mother's death the last time I'd seen him. Six months later he'd had a coronary and died too, but I remembered a feeble crying old man, and I didn't like that.

Of course, later on, Edith said I was selfish and a bastard as usual. Because of course the one thing she wanted, if she could have asked, was to see the children. And it is true that after she saw them, she began to improve more rapidly. And kids are funny, you know? No manners. They walked into her room, after she'd somehow managed to communicate to the

253

nurse, who told the doctor who told me she wanted to see them, and stared at her as if she were a foreign species. She was out of the oxygen now, but she was still hooked up like a computer. They walked all around her, staring at the equipment, and Jonathan had a disgusted look on his face, he walked around pointing to things asking "What's *that!* and *that!*" about every appurtenance she was hooked up to. I'd explain, and she watched, and her eyes were laughing. She still couldn't talk, her jaw was broken, and she couldn't move her arms very well because they were stuck full of needles from the intravenous feeder, and strapped down to boards. But the children could read her eyes, and Jonathan plopped down on the bed next to her and said, "Mommy, do you *like* all those machines?" and I was about to stop him, to get him off the bed, and her eyes swung round to me and they warned me off, oh, did they warn me, and so I learned to read eyes too. And then the kids all flopped on her bed, the hell with the machines, and talked to her and she answered them with her eyes.

It was too tiring for her to have them all there for very long, but after that, one or two of them would go with me most nights on my regular visits to the hospital. She was glad when they came so she didn't have to look at me. Because what her eyes told *me* was: I hate you. I went every evening, for an hour. I don't know why, it was clear she didn't want me, but I had to go. And when I wasn't at the hospital, I was with the children. Because I was the only parent now. Mrs. Ross was wonderful, she kept things going, and she loved the kids and they felt and returned that. But she wasn't their parent. I felt terrible for them—orphaned, really, because I was hardly a parent. So I put a stop to most late-night meetings, and came home and helped Jon with his homework, and helped Mark with special projects, and tried to talk to the girls and to keep Leslie from continually sitting on my lap—she was sixteen and too old for that, I felt.

I had to break off with Alison, of course: there was no time for her now. I had lunch with her as soon as I went back to work and told her what had happened.

"Boyoboy, she was willing to do anything at all to get you back, wasn't she?" Alison said with a nasty ironic smile.

I wanted to strike her, whether for her nastiness or her accuracy, I don't know. Maybe both.

Things mended slowly, and when Edith had pulled some strength together, they always shot her back into the OR for one more operation. So it wasn't steady progress—it was three steps forward, one back. For a long time she wouldn't look at me. Then she'd give me a brief glare when I entered, and look away. But sometimes, as I sat there thinking, feeling rather dejected, I'd glance up and she'd be watching me. But then she'd look away.

When her jaw was mended, and she could speak, she was still very weak and could not talk much. She would ask the children some questions, smile at them, and by now, she could even lift her hands and caress them, although Edith was never given to demonstrative affection. But when I went alone, she never spoke to me.

One night, about three months after the accident, I went alone. I said hello, and kissed her forehead, as I always did, and she glared at me, as she always did, and I went and sat down facing her across the foot of the bed. And I began to tell her the little news there was, as I always did. I used to feel like a woman at a kaffeeklatsch, reporting the tiny events that made that day different from the one before. Vick wanted to buy a long dress for a dance. She had her eye on one that was low cut, with skinny straps, and bright red. What did Edith think of that? She shook her head *no*. The dog had gotten sick all over her beige Persian rug, but Mrs. Ross had cleaned it up fairly well. Jimmy Mehdvi, my old Iranian friend from grad school, was in town, did she remember him? Her eyes closed briefly, assenting. I'd invited him to the house for Sunday dinner, Mrs. Ross had agreed to cook it. Thought he might like a break from hotel food.

And suddenly she opened her mouth. "You mean you're not taking him *out* to dinner? You could get three nights of mileage out of him, Victor. But I guess you don't need cover stories anymore, do you."

255

I didn't answer. There was nothing to say. But her outburst had opened her up, and she continued, she went on with the long list of her grievances, a list kept for twenty years inside her mind, so deeply engraved on that mind that she didn't need a written record. She poured them out in a long stream, she dwelt on them with the pleasure of a victim who finally has a chance to hurl back the stones that have weighed her down all those years. I listened. I did not defend myself at all, even when I felt there might be a few words to be said in my defense. Most of what she said concerned things I did not remember, and that she could have been making up, as far as I knew —except, of course, she was not. She went on until she was exhausted, then looked at me, with her scarred pale face, expectantly, waiting for my refutation. I said nothing. I was sitting with my forehead resting in my palm, listening, thinking, trying to feel. Trying. But I couldn't. I knew that however true or false her specific charges were, the overall charge was true: I knew I was guilty. But I felt nothing—not guilt nor shame, and now, not even pity for her. It was as if we'd passed beyond such feelings, that now her survival was at stake, and maybe, mine too. I could feel only: All right, that's that, you said it all. What are you going to do now?

But she wasn't satisfied, she wanted more. She wanted me to suffer as she had, she wanted to rub my nose in every turd I'd ever laid. That's how it felt, and I questioned myself about it—maybe I was again turning something that wasn't, into a power struggle.

I wanted to give her what she wanted. I struggled with words, I tried to find some that would suggest I was suffering as she wished, and that I had learned through that suffering, and that I was now changed. But she knew better, of course: she scoffed at me. She stopped speaking, and I left. But I went back the next night, and the next, and the next. For days she continued this litany of my sins; for days I listened. It was the best I could do, it was all I had to offer— my presence, my silence. And in time, she accepted that—at least, she stopped.

I came in one evening and she said, *"Don't kiss*

me!" so I didn't. I sat down, but before I could launch into the evening news, she said, sharply: "Why did you prevent the children from coming to see me!" I explained, and she sneered at me: "Oh, thoughtful Victor! Who were you thinking of then? Certainly not me!"

Then: "Why do you prevent my sister from coming to see me?"

"I don't."

"She's been here once. Once in all these months! Why?"

I sighed. Whatever I did, I was damned. If I didn't tell her, it must be because I was keeping Kitty away. If I did . . . "Edith, you seem not to realize that Kitty is an alcoholic. She's not often fit to go out."

She glared at me and I prepared myself for an outburst like the one about her father. But none came. She fell silent. After a time, I began to tell her what was happening with the children. She listened in silence. Her face looked very thoughtful.

I don't know when the change occurred. She needed some special work done, and they shipped her to a hospital in the West where they specialize in that, and I didn't see her for six weeks. I went on as before while she was gone, spending most of my evenings and all weekends at home, spending time with the kids. I took Vick and Les and Mark out to the course and taught them to play golf. I took my vacation while Edith was gone, and the kids and I went camping. Which would have been a disaster if it weren't for them—I knew nothing about camping, but years of summer camp had given them a little knowledge. At least, Vick knew how to put up the tent, and Mark knew how to keep a fire going, and Les figured out how to make coffee for her fussy father. We got on fine, the five of us. We were very close during that year. . . .

Vickie went back to college, and Edith returned, not to Westchester, but to a hospital in Manhattan, where the remaining work would be done. So now the children had difficulty seeing her. I went every working day, and sometimes drove the kids down on a weekend. And she was different now. She was much like the old Edith, always sweet and smiling, but there was something frightened in her now, something . . . corroded. So it felt. There was panic under the old manner. She never called me out again, never maligned me again. She was quiet when I went, she smiled, she'd say, often: "Whatever you want, Victor."

It undermined me completely. It was so pitiful. So weak she was, having given up her anger, you felt there was nothing at all to her, that you'd have to lift a soft body with no backbone up in your arms and carry it, ever after.

I asked the doctors about it. They said she'd been so distraught out West, especially when it was clear she'd never be able to walk again, never be able to use artificial legs, that they had increased her daily dose of tranquilizers. She had no energy to cry and protest, but she also had no energy for anything else.

It felt as if her soul had atrophied.

Eventually, she came home. She was still this new person, but I was hopeful that being home, back with the children and in her own place, she wouldn't need so many tranquilizers, and would regain some energy, some force. The doctors had given her a present when they repaired her scarred face—they'd lifted it. She looked fifteen years younger than she was. In a dim light, she looked like a little girl. I guess they wanted to console her for the rest—the paralysis from the waist down, the stumps that had been legs.

I'd done what I could. I had my study completely remodeled, took out the bookcases, put in another big window so she'd have two large ones facing the garden. I put a wide sill below them, that she could use as a table or a desk, if she wanted to do something and look outdoors at the same time. I had the room painted in a light color, I bought bright new furniture, and turned it into a bedroom-sitting room for her. It was summer when she finally came home with her little-girl face, smiling, a bit teary, and I wheeled her to the window where the peonies and larkspur grew, and the roses she had planted years ago stood in beautiful formal rows in the next bed, blooming soft pink and salmon and creamy white.

The room smelled like the garden—the windows were open—and the sun spilled through the window.

I had the swimming pool enclosed with glass, and a physical therapist came every day to exercise her. I bought a VW van and a ramp, so even if I weren't there, the girls could roll her into it and drive her wherever she wanted to go.

I told her about all this, sitting opposite her in her new room, holding her hands. She let me hold them. They were soft and cool, her hands, as they'd always been. Nothing had happened to them, but they felt boneless, somehow, as if the accident had caused bone loss throughout her body. They were tender hands, yielding hands. They were, like all of her now, pliable.

I said: "You and the girls have to go shopping. You need some new clothes, you haven't had a new dress in a year! That's some kind of record for *you!*" I laughed. She didn't. "And Leslie's graduation is next week, and you have to show up for it looking gorgeous with your wonderful new face." She smiled. "And you'll need gowns for holding court in your new salon," I said, indicating the room. "Beautiful gowns. All colors." I kissed her cheek. "You'll get them, won't you?" She said, "Thank you, Victor."

Thank you, Victor. She didn't go shopping. She didn't go to Leslie's graduation. She didn't do anything. She sat in her wheelchair with her hands folded in her lap. She sat there patiently when the nurse came, four times a day, to take care of her . . . little bags. And drank the tea and ate the toast Mrs. Ross brought her, but not much more. And took as many tranks as ever. She just sat there. She didn't even spark up for the children as she had. She listened to them, she smiled sweetly, she said, "That's nice, dear." You had the sense she hadn't listened to a word they said. She sat and she smiled.

I spoke to the doctor, and he cut her dosage of tranks back a bit. After he told her, I went in to see her, and there was fear in her eyes, panic. I put my hand on her shoulder, I crouched beside her, I said, "Don't worry, darling, if you don't feel well, he'll increase it again. But try, at least." The panic remained, it hovered around the edges of her eyes.

But that worked, at least, it helped a little. She began to come out of herself a bit. She would take some interest when Mrs. Ross came in to speak to her about the weekly menus. She ate a few more things. She responded to the children more fully, more often. She'd turn on the TV set during the day, and at least appear to be watching it. And one night, when I came in, as always, with the one drink she was permitted, and one for myself, before dinner, she initiated the conversation.

"Victor, you don't suppose I could have another heart attack, do you?"

"Heart attack?"

"Yes, of course. It was because I had a heart attack that I ran into that underpass. Just a slight one, of course, but I lost consciousness and that was how . . ."

She had had no heart attack. But then, if you look at it differently, maybe she had.

"You won't have another one, darling," I said, sitting opposite her. "I promise."

I understood that I was promising to keep my bargain, forever.

She nodded. "And perhaps," she went on, "even though I'm . . ." she looked down at her body, "like *this,* we can have a happy family?"

"Of course we can." I know my voice sounded hollow, but Edith did not seem to notice.

"Yes," she sighed, lightly. Her voice had seemed to change with her face, it was girlish, light, as it had been when she was young. "So much violence, so much unhappiness, drinking, divorce, drugs. . . . Perhaps we're lucky, after all."

I nodded. I couldn't speak.

Then she raised her head a little. "And if this had to happen to me . . . if that was the price of us realizing how lucky we are . . . well, perhaps it is worth something, after all."

I just stared at her.

"To bring up the children in a peaceful and orderly and loving home, that was always my ambition. And *that* I have achieved," she said looking at me with tears in her eyes, "regardless."

260

I cried. I burst out crying. I put my head in her lap and bawled like a kid. I couldn't stop.

Edith patted my head. When I finally stopped and had blown my nose to oblivion and back, she said, "But, Victor, you must speak to Mark about the noise he makes in the yard when they play Indians. It gives me a headache."

I said I would.

"And, Victor." She turned her head a little away from me, it was almost a coy gesture, although she didn't intend it that way. "I know men can't . . . I know," she faced me then, "you need . . . sex. And I don't want you to . . . suffer. So, even though I feel nothing there now, well, if I feel nothing, it can't hurt me, can it? I want you to have what you want," she finished, blushing. I swear she was blushing.

Victor broke off. His face was wet, with tears or sweat it was impossible to tell, and he looked like a man being strangled, his head was poked up, his neck stretched out as if he couldn't breathe at low altitudes, and his muscles stood out, neck muscles, under-chin muscles, hard and tight. He stood up and strode into the kitchen. He returned with the Scotch bottle, two glasses, and a bowlful of ice. "I figure you might want one of these tonight."

Indeed, it was night. They were sitting in the last light of dusk, without electricity to warm them, except from the fire. Dolores nodded, and he poured two drinks. She did not move. She was locked in the rocking chair, legless (her legs curled up on the seat), with a blanket over her lap. Victor gave her a drink, then turned on the small lamp beside her, and another beside the couch. He sat down again, sighing. His voice was different now, his usual voice, strong and in control.

That was four years ago. Things are much the same now. Edith never goes out, well, almost never. Mark uses the van, for fun, not for her. When the girls think she needs or could use some new clothes, they buy them and bring them home. She wears a straight

261

size eight, just as she always did. She accepts whatever they—or I—bring her, accepts it with that same sweet smile she always uses. She asks for nothing. Nothing. The only way Mrs. Ross discovered she was tired of lamb chops was that she began to leave them on her plate. She never asked for something else, ordered something else. She did take up painting again, but even there, the kids and I keep an eye on her supplies. We have to be sure to replenish them. Otherwise she'll paint in only a few colors and when we ask if she's changing her style, she'll say oh, no, she'd simply run out of cobalt blue, or whatever. Or she'll sit there with her hands in her lap until we discover she's out of watercolor paper.

She sits at the big sill gazing out into the garden, and paints pictures of dumpling-happy babies and little children doing cute little mischievous things, like dumping water on the dog, or spraying water on each other with a garden hose. Or trying on Momma's or Poppa's clothes. That sort of thing. She doesn't mind repeating herself. She does a couple every week, and every week Bob Minelli stops in and visits with her and picks up her latest productions. He has a —well he calls it an art gallery in town. He frames pictures, sells gifts and the work of some local painters. Edith's pictures sell like hot cakes, people love them. And why not? They have the same dreams. Anyway, all the money she earns goes into a special account, and when there's enough in it, she gives it to a local art museum. It's a paltry affair, an old house with some bequests in it, but thanks to Edith, it's improving. They're planning, although it's a secret from her, to rename the museum after her on her next birthday: she's given them thousands and thousands of dollars. In fact, she does them well, those paintings. She does them well because she believes in them, those dumpling children and their happy harmless mischief. . . .

Sometimes an old friend will stop in to see her. But she doesn't encourage it. We never entertain in the evenings, never go out together—almost never. It's just us, the family. Smaller now, because the girls are gone. And over the years—something else happened.

After she came *to*—came back—to whatever degree she has. Oh, it was my fault too, I'm sure. But she helped.

I'd gotten so close to the kids in that year she'd been away, as close as she'd been, maybe even closer because I wasn't always shushing them, telling them their father was tired, or busy, or not to be disturbed. And I loved that, it was terrific, it was like a gift, late in life, of something you'd been missing without knowing it. . . . But once she was home—well, I stopped spending so much time with them. I went out to play golf with my old golf buddies, not with the kids. I didn't take them to the beach or the movies or anyplace, as I had, because that would have meant leaving her home alone. I pulled away.

And Edith—oh, it took awhile before I realized what was happening, but by the time I did, the damage had been done—Edith almost never spoke of them to me without complaining. They were noisy, or they were getting grease on their clothes that Mrs. Ross couldn't get out, or they were leaving the TV blaring so loud she couldn't hear herself think. And I had to do something about that. I had to scold them. And whenever anything went wrong with them—when Jonathan came home with a poor report card, for instance—she'd say: "Well, I hate to think what your father is going to say about that." So that even though I didn't say much, the experience had already been lived through, he'd already felt my disapproval, my anger. . . .

So I lost them again. At some point, I saw, and I tried to repair the damage. I asked them if they wanted to go to the movies; if Edith didn't want to come, she could stay home alone. I asked them if they wanted to go to the beach. But they were older then, they had their own friends. And they'd, well, they'd lost their trust in me. I'd betrayed them twice. Once when they were born, and again after Edith came back.

"And I felt," he put his head in his hand again, he stared at the floor and his mouth was grim, "I felt that she had done that intentionally." He raised his head. "And that makes me think that maybe all of it's intentional. Because the kids are growing up, Mark's in a local prep school but he'll be starting college next year. He'll be gone too. And Jonathan will be home only for a few more years. In fact, Edith's already talking about sending him away to prep school, says he gets on her nerves. Which he well might, he gets on mine too, he's so jagged and nervous and—hysterical, really. A lot like me at his age, if truth be told.

"And then there will be just two of us. No friends. No family to speak of. My sister and brother live in Ohio. Kitty's in and out of the dry-up farm. . . . So, just the two of us. Sitting there together. The kids at a distance from both of us now, for they are. The two of us, sitting and looking at each other, Edith smiling sweetly, as she used to do. . . ."

He stopped, breathed out deeply, stared at the floor. His voice changed again, it was quiet, reminiscent. "One day I was walking towards the restaurant where I usually have lunch, and I was alone, and I bumped into Alison. She looked different, but splendid. I asked her to have lunch with me, on the spur of the moment. I had no intention of it going any further: but what harm could a lunch do?

"Well, she came, but she had changed. She'd joined one of those women's groups, she told me about that as if I had had something to do with it, as if she were flinging a punishment at me. I don't know. God, maybe I hurt her too. And she asked about Edith and how things were, and I told her. I told her the truth, all of it. I didn't put a slick surface on anything. And I finished—maybe a little solemnly, I don't know. But it occurred to me she might think I was complaining, that I was asking for a little love and affection from her, when in fact I wasn't up for that at all, I had given my word and intended to keep it—so I finished by saying: 'I made a cripple out of her and it's my turn for duty now.'

"And Alison raised an eyebrow. She'd always been sharp. And said; 'Oh, how nice! You have what you always wanted! A woman with a child's face and a child's dependency. You don't have to worry about her running around because she's numb, and you don't have to worry about her running away because she has no legs! She's utterly housebound, utterly subject, and utterly passive. Just what you wanted! How nice to get what you want. Just what you deserve!' "

VII

1

"JUST WHAT you deserve," he repeated bitterly. "Does anyone deserve what happens to them? Anyone at all? I thought about that a lot in the year Edith was hospitalized. And I've thought about it since. You talk about people who suffer deprivation from the social system. And they do, I know that, I admit that. But in the end . . .

"I don't know that one fate is necessarily worse than another. People's expectations are different. Some little peasant in Chile doesn't expect out of life what I expected: if he gets something, he's happy. If something is taken away, he's miserable. And it's the same for all of us. And there is no justice, nowhere. Talking about justice is like drawing lines in air.

"And I thought: only love can fill the place where justice ought to be. Only being held and cherished, holding and cherishing can make up for your lost inheritance, your tortured brother, your sainted mother who died when you were six. Only love. And I made up my mind that I would give Edith that. Not that it would replace her legs, her broken spirit. But that it was all there was except for emptiness, bitterness.

"But," his mouth twisted, "that's not so easy. You can't just order up two loves, medium rare. I try, but . . ."

He fell back against the cushions, exhausted. And stared with deep-set eyes at the glass in his hand. Dolores sat across the room, utterly still. After a few minutes, she got up and went to him and sat beside him. She did not touch him, she merely sat there. He did not move.

The rocker was still swaying slightly from Dolores's motion. She stared at it, seeing a woman in it, a woman with yellow hair and a blue hair ribbon, rocking, smiling, calculating how to capture him, this elusive husband of hers, how to tie him to her forever with unbreakable bands. She knew him, oh yes. She'd seen him when he wasn't seeing her; she had read him, whereas for him she had remained always an unopened book. Helplessness and passivity: oh, yes. Anger he could deal with, anger he could leave.

But isn't that what he'd wanted from her?

Dolores tried to brush it all out of her head. She touched his hand. "I'm going to cook you up something great. Want to help?"

He shook his head, and she got up and went into the kitchen. She was halfway through peeling potatoes before she realized she'd never, that day, gotten dressed. Neither had Victor, for that matter. She shrugged. She took him some cheese and crackers, she urged: eat something. He was sitting on the couch like a boneless dejection.

That night he made love to her desperately, over and over. Next morning, as he was leaving to return to London, she caressed him, she held him, she tried to console him with her body.

But after he'd gone, and she was not totally occupied with him, with trying to give him love and space and quiet for his wound to reheal, she had time for herself.

That day she did not go to the Bodleian. She dressed and cleaned up the flat, and gathered her pads together, but then she sat down in the rocker, and simply didn't get up again.

She kept seeing a woman with a girl's face and a blue hair ribbon in her yellow hair smiling and nodding: "Victor says the economy will not improve for a while"; "Victor eats only the filet, so we never order any other cut"; "Oh, do you like my gown? Victor bought it for me"; "Victor says that book is trash." From across the room the woman smiled at Victor, smiled sweetly, secure at last in the indomitable power of weakness.

Victor, the expert on power.

Dolores sat there rocking, remembering an argument they'd had one rainy weekend. It had begun genially enough with a discussion of the political situation, but at some point their real differences had emerged and turned them hostile. Dolores had made a remark about the insanity of those who dealt in international power, and Victor had steamed up inside—she could recognize the signs by now.

"You know, for a smart woman, you're awfully stupid about power," he said.

He could have used a different word. He had to know by now, he must, that being called *stupid* would gall her. So there was an animus, a personal arrow in the answer she delivered.

"I don't claim to know anything about it. I despise it and the people who hold it. I manage fine without it, as do my friends. We have enough money to live, but not a lot of money. We don't have fancy cars and houses, but we have tons of books and records and we travel all over the world and our minds range everywhere. We don't *need* power. Only the poor in spirit need power. It is the bankrupt in mind and emotion, the Nixons of the world, who want power."

"Oh, that's lovely," he drawled. "Lovely. You have no power and don't care about it. Well, in the first place, you *do* have money, make no mistake about that. You and your friends may not be millionaires, but you're not scratching crops out of the earth with your bare hands. You may have a lower standard than most Americans of what constitutes necessity, but you have money for luxuries—books, records, concerts, theater, travel abroad. What do you think money and education are, but power! You sit there in your comfortable ivory towers deploring the behavior of politicians and industry, feeling virtuous because of your clean hands. But who do you suppose permits you to keep your hands clean?"

"I suppose you're going to say you do."

"I wasn't. But I could. But that's beside the point, I'm not trying to say you're as guilty as the rest of us. You aren't, directly, at least. My point is that you and people like you sit in your puddle of virtue and spatter contempt and scorn on government, on the 'military-industrial complex' or whatever you call it these days, as if your disdain could shrivel it. When in fact your dismissal of it only lets it thrive without impediment."

"All right, I'll accept that. But you tell me what else we can do. We write our letters to senators, send our telegrams to the White House, we vote, some of us even work actively for political candidates. We went on the marches when there were any. The letters get counted and shredded. Voting is a joke, a choice between twins with different names. You vote for a man who promises to end a war, and he escalates it. You vote for a man who promises to reduce the arms budget and next year it goes up three million—or maybe it's three billion, for all I know—dollars. People in power make dire speeches warning us that the Russians are getting ahead in the arms *race*. Race! Well, what *is* a race? It seems to me races have goals, ends, winners and losers, but I can't see any goal to what they call the arms race, can't see any winners either. The winners will win themselves the same grave as the losers. Everywhere you look, insanity rages, all over the world. Because the whole world is infected with that way of thinking, believing in winning and losing, never thinking about just what it *is* you win or lose. Immediate power is all they think about. But power for what? What good is power if all it means is survival for another day? You can have that without power.

"What else can you do in such an insane world but turn your back on it and try to find what happiness you can in your own small world?"

"Cultivate your garden, I know. It's no good, Lorie." He was still calling her that then. "Because as you retreat from the implications of your own prosperity, your own position in the world, retreat out of guilt or wanting not to be responsible, you give them free reign, you leave a vacuum, and they step in, the very people you fear, the bankrupt in spirit, in mind and feeling."

She was silent.

"The only hope for the world is for every power to have an equal and opposition power. That's the notion our country was founded on—a balance of powers. I'm not a monster—I think. I hire people, hire people who hire people. I make the rules, to a large degree, in the place where I work. But don't imagine for a minute that if I were permitted by law to hire seven-year-olds to work in a factory twelve hours a day and pay them five dollars a week, and that if everybody else was doing that and I had to do it to stay competitive, I wouldn't do it too. The labor unions put a stop to that, back in the days when they were an opposite force to industry. Only an equal and opposite power can keep human beings honest."

She stared at him. "Victor, now who lives in an ivory tower? I agree with you, oh, I agree. But how are you going to manage that?"

He would not allow he was idealistic. "It can be managed. But not until you and millions of people like you who live with their heads in the sand move into accepting power, to see it as a positive thing, not something tainted and corrupting. See power as the wonderful, liberating thing it is! As a creative tool. If people start thinking that way, solutions will bubble up, will simply emerge naturally."

"Well," she said sadly, "I wish that were true. But I can't see much hope for it. Even in the smallest unit, the family, there is no equality of power. Men have the greater economic power—and beyond that, even if they don't, they have the moral power. The force of a tradition which declares them the boss, and declares any woman who denies that subversive or a castrating bitch."

"Oh, Lorie. There is *no* power greater than the power of passive dependency."

Months ago he'd said those things, Victor. She'd argued. Passive dependency works, she said, only when it is operating on a guilt-ridden antagonist. Try passive dependency on General Trujillo. Or Marcos. Or Idi Amin.

She hadn't known then how well he understood the force of passive dependency.

An image flared in her mind: Victor, gaunt and hollow-eyed, standing with his arms dangling loosely at his sides, behind a doll-faced woman in a wheel-chair who nodded and smiled.

She tried to brush it away, but bits of it clung, like cobweb dusted from a stuccoed wall.

She saw Victor close his book, take off his reading glasses, lean back, and light up his pipe. No, he'd told her he'd given up pipe smoking that night. He was lighting a cigarette, sitting in a French-style chair covered with brocade, on one side of the fireplace. He was smiling across at Edith, who was sitting in her wheelchair opposite him, the mate to his chair having been pushed at an angle close to the other side of the fireplace. There was no fire, they had central heating. Edith sat at a polished wood folding table, laying out a tarot pack as if she didn't already know her fortune.

No, no. She was embroidering. No. She was reading too, a Gothic romance or a best seller full of horrible apocalyptic cataclysms. Those, after all, she had some experience of. She'd feel his glance, his closed book, and she'd close hers, except she'd keep one finger in her place. She'd look up and smile. And he'd ask her if she wanted a nightcap and she'd smile with delighted surprise just as if he didn't ask her every night and she'd say "Oh, that would be nice, but make it light for me, please," and he'd get up and go to the bar and make two drinks, one light, one dark, and carry them back and bend to hand her hers and go sit down again and sip his drink, then clear his throat and ask her if she'd like some music and she'd say if you would and he'd get up and go to the stereo and put on some Vivaldi and sit down again and say, "Mrs. Ross tells me you had a nice long swim today," and she'd say oh, yes, her arms were getting a little stronger. And he'd ask her if any more of her watercolors had been sold, and she'd say that Bob Minelli had called yesterday to say that six of them went over the weekend, had she told him that? She had told him that. Oh, well. Oh, there was a letter from Vickie, she'd forgotten to tell him, it was lying on the worktable in her room. And he'd get up and go and get it and sit down and put on his reading glasses again and read it, laughing at parts, reading parts of it aloud to Edith, who already knew them, but she'd smile or laugh, and then Victor would take his glasses off and lay them on the end table and sip his drink and Edith would say she hoped this new beau of Vickie's worked out, here she was twenty-three and single, she ought to be married, twenty-three and she'd never even had a steady beau, Edith couldn't understand it, certainly Vickie was pretty enough. It was all that macrobiology or whatever of hers, it scared the boys away. And Victor would listen and not argue and not correct her, even though by now he knew that Vickie had had several lovers and one abortion, even though he had read between the lines of Vickie's letter and could tell that when she said she was moving out of her apartment because one of her roommates was off to California and another was getting married and besides it was time to get a place of her own, what she meant was that she was moving in with this guy, whoever he was. Strange name, don't you think? Edith would say: Ram? What sort of name do you suppose that is? Maybe it's short for Ramsey, I knew a Ramsey once, Ramsey Hollister, he came from Darien, although his family was originally from East Hampton. And Victor would not say he thought Ram was an Indian name, no, he'd let Vickie handle things in her own way in her own time.

So he'd try to change the subject. He'd start to tell Edith about an incident at the office, but her eyes would glaze over, not because she couldn't understand but because she didn't want to hear. That was one thing she didn't want to know about, his life at work. Didn't want to know, didn't want to think about it, didn't want to have to imagine him striding into the office full of energy, rapping out orders and jokes, sitting down behind that huge desk of his dictating, calling meetings, telephoning the chairman of the board, letting his mind work on what it liked to work on, going to lunch at the best restaurants, where the maître d' bowed at the sight of him, said, "Good afternoon, Mr. Morrissey," led him to his table himself.

No.

Joined there by two or three like him, perhaps below in rank, perhaps above, all of them sitting there drinking, eating, plotting, talking, dramatizing everything that occurred, full of pleasure. Talking about all of it as if it were eminently serious. Once she'd believed that too, that Victor's work was highly serious; he'd convinced her of it. But now she knew better, now she knew it was only a game that men in their egotism pretended was world-shakingly serious, when in fact it wasn't, nothing was serious except losing your legs, nothing whatever.

No.

So her mind would glaze along with her eyes, and eventually Victor would notice and he'd get up and change the record and ask her if she wanted another drink and she'd say no thank you, sweetly, and he'd pour himself another, and while he was doing it, Edith, glancing anxiously at him, would open her book again, her finger red-lined from holding her place all that while, and when Victor came back she would be reading and he could sit down and read too. Free.

Oh god. Dolores closed her eyes. No. No. She didn't want that for him. She wanted him charging bareheaded out into the rain, poking, pointing, laughing, getting angry: amused at the spectacle of life, delighted by the London streets, standing with her, arm in arm, admiring the displays in British greengrocers' shops, sitting on top of a double-decker bus, spouting hot-air sociology on British customs, tramping through the streets alive alive-o. In London. In New York. Anywhere.

But of course there *was* no human spectacle on the neat, gardener-tended streets of Scarsdale, was there. All indoors there. Quiet suffering, lower your voice you don't want the maid to hear, you know how these girls gossip.

No. She wanted Victor the way he was at his office, the way he came Friday nights to Oxford, bounding up the stairs with an armload of booze, talking a mile a minute about what happened that week, getting impatient after her fourth interruption, saying he guessed she could have five minutes if she wanted to talk. She wanted him with an equal and opposite force. Yes.

Which Edith was not.

But whose fault was that? Hadn't Victor himself pressed down on her harder and harder until she was

273

a crumbled powder under his thumb? And didn't he have behind him the weight of the entire culture, while she didn't even have her parents' help? So that even without pressing he would have had the advantage?

Yes: you could not in any way talk about equality between men and women. Someday she would have to find a way to explain that to him. How you couldn't do that because women were always salmon swimming upstream. How no matter where women went, they always found the old tradition in which implicitly men were important and women were not—in paintings, in books, in the laws and the customs. Women existed *for* men: their bodies for men's pleasure and rage; their emotions to provide the suffering witness to men's identities.

Pick up the paper, any paper, she wanted to say. Any day. For instance, the other day I read an account of a woman who accused a man of rape. It was a tiny report on a back page. And the man was tried and acquitted and the woman stood up in the courtroom and protested, cried out, damned the jury. And the judge sentenced her to thirty days for contempt of court. Sentenced *her!*

Pick up the paper, she wanted to say. You will read about John Smith and *his* family, *his* house, *his* taxes, and *his* car. You will read about the working-*man*, the *men* in industry, about *man* and his great destiny, and prehistoric *man*. The only time *man* isn't used is in talking about mastectomies and hysterectomies.

Did you read, she wanted to say, about the whole monastery and school that picked up and left the Episcopal Church and joined the Greek Orthodox Church because the Episcopalians had ordained a few women as priests? A handful of women priests was enough to send them reeling into apostasy! To renounce their religion! What could that handful of women mean to them? What were they seeing in those people whose bodies were different? Putrefaction? Blood? Sin? Flesh? What horror could send them flying into foreign arms?

Yes. You have a fight with your wife and you go to

your local bar and sit there staring in your glass and somebody starts talking about the Red Sox and pretty soon you start telling him about your wife and he sympathizes, he shakes his head, he knows, oh he knows. Yeah, all the same, broads, dames, bitches, cunts, squaws, whores, cows, dogs, WOMEN. Yeah, yeah, he shakes his head in agreement. Sure, he'd been there too. Somethin, ain't they? Every man in the bar will agree.

But I, she wanted to say, have a fight with my husband and I don't dare go to the local because I'll get dirty looks or dirty hands, I'll get something to diminish or enrage me. And if I try to tell my women friends, five of them will look at me askance, will priss their lips, will assume there must be something terribly wrong with me to have such trouble, *they* don't have such trouble, they say and I think: Wait until next week. They shake their heads as if I were a bug in their ear they are trying to shake loose.

How there are only the other five women, thank god for them, who understand, and who know they are the only ones who do. And how we have to hold hands and form a circle and stay together because there is only we, there is no one else, and we're alone in our world.

Because, she wanted to say, look at the world! Look at the cracks, the jokes, the whistles, the pawing hands, the rapes, the judgments, the ads, the movies, the TV, the books, the laws, the traditions, the customs, the economic statistics, the government, the Catholic Church, the Jewish tradition, the Moslem beliefs, the rulers of the socialist countries, the rulers of the fascist countries. . . .

Yes, she wanted to say, the whole world goes the same way. There is a word for hatred of all people: misanthropy. There is a word for hatred of women: misogyny. But there is no word for hatred of men, males. Apparently such a thing is inconceivable. Oh, there was a war all right, but it wasn't women who declared it, it was men, thousands of years ago. They declared women invalid and built that illegitimacy into the laws, into the very dreams of the human race. That division lies curled deeply at the very root of our whole power-hungry, industrial, nature-crushing, ambitious, structured, patriarchal, hierarchical world. But when women started to fight back, men threw up their hands in horror and screamed in hate and fear about man-hating women! Yes!

So that—and now she would soften her voice, be a little kind to him because he is fragile—so that men who don't go as far as others in their misogyny, men who are willing to admit that perhaps women can do "men's" jobs, can think, can act, men who are willing to admit that perhaps men haven't been entirely fair to women over the ages, men like that feel virtuous and pure and large and generous and expect women to fall all over them with gratitude. Yes.

But a woman who protests—and she would have to insist that he grasp this fully—a woman who blames men or male society for anything, who complains, is seen as a nut, a freak, an aggressor, humorless, petty-minded, a shrew, a virago, a castrator, an Amazon, a ballbuster. Yes.

And because she has to raise her voice to be heard at all over the dominant machinery, because those who will listen to her are so far away and so few, she is shrill, abrasive, strident, yes. And she must speak largely, because people will shrug off small things. And loudly. Whereas a man can whisper and the maître d' will seat him.

Men can take their bad feelings about women anywhere they go, because everywhere such feelings are accepted. But women must keep their bad feelings about men locked up, the outside world is hostile to them. They sit in silent kitchens, simmering, wondering if they are insane, knowing they are alone. To be a woman in such a world is to be an occupied population, with the Nazis in control everywhere. To be a woman in such a world is to be an outlaw. By birth.

Victor wouldn't like that. He would say: Are you saying all men are Nazis by birth? Is that what you're saying?

And she would say: Any man who profits from the exploitation of women, profits in any way at all, is responsible for the exploitation of women.

And Victor would say: Are you saying all men are Nazis?

And she, because she was swimming upstream and therefore couldn't give an inch; because she was engaged in a war not for the survival of her body but for the survival of her self-respect, couldn't give an inch; she would have to say *yes*. When that wasn't exactly what she meant. But she couldn't say *no*. No.

Victor would get outraged, and would barely listen as she tried to explain more clearly. He'd shout: All right! All right! But can't you find some other word?

And she would smile at him wickedly and glint: No other word would be as effective, though, would it.

Yes, that's what she wanted to say.

2

YES, SOMEDAY she would, she'd tell him all that. Someday when he wasn't feeling so wounded, when the scar he'd dug around in to show her had healed over again, when the blood was not there in his eye. Tell him that he couldn't judge Edith the same way he judged himself, because she was a lonely fish swimming upstream and he was surrounded by respectful if not friendly fish, and swimming with the current. Tell him you cannot judge equally things that have different contexts, and that no man knows what it is like to live as a woman. Tell him that you can't equate passive dependent power with assertive power because the dependent kind isn't fun, it doesn't give you a kick, it just allows you to survive. Whereas the assertive kind, as Victor says, is wonderful, it is using yourself in the world, doing, being, achieving.

And tell him, finally, that Edith was not calculating her behavior, was not consciously planning to dominate him any more than he had calculated, in the early years, had consciously worked to grind her down. Oh, he had consciously planned to dominate, yes. But he hadn't then known what that meant, what it would mean to Edith. People think that if they can just rule you, you will remain the same, except that you will defer to them, your rulers. But that is not true. The state of being ruled changes you, hones down your edges, softens your bones, kills the spontaneous anarchic spark.

No, Edith was not consciously plotting against Victor. She was simply going along with the tide, as Victor had twenty years before, going along with what her world permitted her, taking that as her "decent allowance," the only allowance she could have.

Dolores knew, of course, that Edith would have been among those who would protest her analysis. Mild in voice and manner, uncertain in judgment and inclined to fall silent with pursed lips, she would talk about complementary roles, about people being helpmates to each other. After all, where would be her maid, her nurse, her swimming pool, her car, her paints, without Victor?

And without Victor, she might have kept her legs.

Dolores sighed deeply. Her stomach was burning, there was a hole in it, or so it felt. She went into the kitchen and poured a glass of milk and drank it down. She stood there, motionless, looking at nothing. Something had come into her mind that she did not want there, and she pressed her temples as if she could shoo it out that way.

She was recalling Edith's complaints. The young wife had been unhappy—oh, how many years ago! —at her brilliant young husband's energetic preparation for work, his uniformed taut Businessman self emerging from the chrysalis of his slack homebody self. Yes. You don't love me, she's said, all those years ago. You go to work as if you had wings, you fly out of here in joy and come back to sleep. Had she added to screw? How many years ago did she say that? It was only a few months ago that Dolores had said the same thing, the same complaint. September, after the first night Dolores and Victor had spent together. It was indeed.

You don't even call when you're not coming home for dinner, Edith had complained. Never dared, probably, to complain about the nights he did call but didn't come home for dinner. Didn't dare say—you leave me alone, you don't want my company. Un-American to say that to a man on the rise. But Victor did neglect her, all the time, her, Edith-Dolores, whom he left in hotel rooms for long hours after pressuring her to come along on his trips. Yes.

Don't touch me! Edith had screamed, like Dolores herself. And Victor had said: Why do you throw hysterical fits? to both of them.

Dolores, in a daze, poured a Scotch, a dark one, like Victor's, and returned to the sitting room. It was a grey day, midafternoon, but it looked like five, no rain, but the air was thick with moisture. It was the first time Dolores had neglected to go to the library. She sat in the rocker, her feet firmly placed on the floor, her body leaning forward, her shoulders hunched over as if they would protect her heart.

A scene formed in front of her brain. It was the conference for businessmen and humanists, the first time she'd met Mach. Victor might even have been there, she might have seen him. And if he was? What would he have been like, there, across the room from the observant academic spy, Dolores?

There was a piano tinkling in the room, soft, un-demanding, meandering diminished chords, no climaxes, music that flowed and went nowhere. And there were people, very well dressed in a conservative way, standing all around the huge room with the glass wall looking out at a garden, standing in front of the glass wall, or in front of the huge paintings on the other walls, paintings of yellow or pink, sometimes with a black line or a splotch. The people all smiled a great deal, even the men.

There was Victor, tall, tanned from golf, showing just the right amount of joviality, the right degree of control, no hearty backslapper he, no pincher of bottoms. Indeed, none of the men at this party would think of pinching or patting or slapping a bottom (at this party). Victor was talking to a man in a plaid jacket, a man who had less class than he, was paunchier, cruder. Victor manages to convey—oh, so subtly: is it the way he stands? the position of his head? the tone of his voice?—manages to convey that he is aware of the difference between them, but because of Bitlow's success with the OXI program, he is willing to offer him, Bitlow, his, Victor's, respect. Bitlow is flattered, seduced. He will become one of Victor's ardent boosters, and claim friendship.

There is Victor talking to Mach, who is seventy-two and still powerful, thick red mottled neck, red mottled face, full-bodied, eyes like yellow creases, mouth a thin straight line. He talks without inflection in his voice, and without moving his lips more than necessary, and he looks at men, when they speak to him, like a wary animal, his eyes watery blue thin slits with a cold yellow light. He listens as if he were a machine, and everything that is said to him must go through a certain number of coils and bobbins and gears and printouts before he can respond to it. He *never responds* to anyone's face. It is one secret of his success.

Mach never looks at all at women. Once in a while you may catch him appraising an ass or a pair of boobs, and it may be upsetting if the boobs are yours because the eyes look only at your breasts, never raise themselves to the face. But he does not look lustful, merely appraising. If he wants anything, he can have it, he doesn't even have to pay, his name delivers it to him. But he rarely wants anything.

Someone brings up Suzanne Hein, the great physicist, to be presented. Mach does not look at her, does not listen to what she says. It is just as well, because she is protesting something, some chemical process which is having a bad effect on the atmosphere. In the middle of her words he turns away to say something between his teeth to a man standing nearby. It is Victor. Mach turns to speak to Victor, and his body turns strangely, all at once, without any give at waist or knee. He sleeps the same way. He doesn't turn fluidly, movement rippling through the flesh and bone, the dreaming body murmuring, snoring a little, hands coming up to slide under the pillow. When Mach turns in his sleep his whole body turns at once, suddenly. His body lifts, turns, and hits the mattress hard and becomes rigid again. His snores are like drumbeats.

Maybe he is afraid, who knows? But what does he

have to fear? It is well known that Mach never wears a coat because he never needs one. He has a chauffeur to drive him to the front door of wherever he goes, a man to walk behind him carrying the briefcase and the cash and the credit cards and Mach's cigar case, a man to pay the bills and give directions to the driver and open doors and close them: for Mach. This man will tell the chauffeur to be waiting at twelve thirty to drive Mach and him and a few deferential, anxious corporation presidents to lunch and to pick them up afterwards. The chauffeur will be kept waiting half an hour to drive them, half an hour to pick them up from lunch. But he doesn't care, he's being well paid, he had to go through a security check to get this job, he drives one of the most important men in the world, and he knows it, on cold days he tucks Mach's knees under the lap rug with such solicitousness that Mach growls at him. Besides, he's used to waiting. The aide pays the lunch bill and scribbles the amount down in a little lined book, or signs the charge slip. Everything will be charged to the corporation.

Mach lives in a penthouse apartment in Houston, owned by Blanchard, and takes his vacations in Aspen in a glass-walled house surrounded by a chain link fence and guard dogs, owned by Blanchard, or in an island in the Caribbean, rocky island set in azure and turquoise waters that play in white foam around it, covered with trees, lianas, bananas, orchids, the very air is perfumed, and the house is a fortress, Spanish style, cool promenades under stone-arched cloisters, heels resounding on the tile floors. Island and house owned by Blanchard, and Mach flies there in his jet, owned by Blanchard.

Mach never has to worry about facing the unfamiliar, about encountering an unpleasant word or gesture, about being caught short in the middle of the desert. He is more protected than a collar-wearing priest in a world full of devout Catholics. He is more protected than East Germany with its layers of chain link fences and lookout towers, its patrolling soldiers with guard dogs, its mined fields.

Why then is he so rigid, so anxious? Why does he look at every man who approaches him as if the man were a potential enemy? Why does he seem never to relax, to enjoy, to have pleasure? Why does he sip his martini carefully, and stop at two?

Dolores watches him. Maybe he thinks everybody is talking about him, that everybody knows about the deal he made for Blanchard Oil with I. G. Farben back in the thirties, a deal that kept Germany going strong all during the war that killed both German folk and American folk and lots of other folk besides, but that left Farben and Blanchard absolute victors when the war was over, so loaded with money they didn't know where to hide it. But the truth is, everybody knows about it, or has chosen not to know, or has chosen to forget. And in the circles that surround Mach, he is admired for it. He doesn't need to worry about that.

Wherever Mach is, the circle around him is quiet, waiting for the great man to speak; it is still, like the eye of a hurricane. But Mach says little. He listens, selectively. Only to men.

And there, standing a little behind Victor, is Edith. Dolores sees her too. Talking to Bitlow, Victor has forgotten to introduce her, and Bitlow too (he learns quickly) has forgotten to introduce his wife. The two women stand beside, a little behind, their men. They are both perfectly groomed in neat but not gaudy and certainly not sexy cocktail dresses. Their hair is styled and blonded identically. Both are drinking something a little sweet, in a pretty glass with a stem. They glance at each other and venture a formal half-smile. They glance at the men and pretend great interest in the serious and important conversation. They know it is serious and important because their husbands have told them so. They gaze upward—for these men are invariably taller than their women—at their men, and then across at each other. Their smiles say that they understand how important and intelligent and powerful their men are and that they are grateful, oh, so grateful, to have such men. They try to laugh at what they think are jokes (sometimes inappropriately), but in fact they are not at all sure what this conversation is about. They smile uncertainly at each other. Bitlow's wife, Edna, does know the name of

Victor Morrissey, and is a little intimidated by his wife. Edith knows this and enjoys it.

The men are talking about Oil. And the Alaska Pipeline. The women's heads bob energetically. They may not know much, but they know the Alaska Pipeline is a Good Thing and Should Be Permitted to Proceed. For the Good of the Country. Otherwise there will be an Energy Crisis. Their husbands have mentioned this in Dire Tones, Often.

The women do not know that such crises can be engineered, that, in fact, one is being engineered under their very eyes. No, that's silly. *Their* husbands? Who just two weeks ago Saturday went out on the lawn and played Frisbee with the kids? Never!

The conversation moves into more opaque areas —shipping, markets, prices. The women's eyes glaze over, although they keep smiling and nodding their heads as if they understood everything. They are not embarrassed at not understanding what is being said. They know they are not supposed to understand what is being said. They know exactly why they are there, standing in the room beside their taller husbands. They are Respectability. They are the living, walking, talking, laughing proof that their husbands are good Family Men, no matter what hanky-panky they may occasionally indulge in, good Family Men who support The American Way of Life. They are not pansies or queers, these men, they are reliable, not bohemians or artists or hippies or anything else subversive of The American Way of Life. Anyone looking at these women can tell that they sleep only in their husbands' beds, and not especially happily there, since they know that sexuality is the work of the devil, and that Children and the Home and the Family are the work of God.

Even if they don't believe in God, they know that. But most of them do not know whether or not they believe in God, because that is a dangerous subject, better not thought about.

Knowing why they are there, they are extremely careful. They know they have no power to improve things, to make an impression or advance a deal, but utter utter power to destroy their husbands, to say the wrong thing, or get angry and throw a drink, or curse out loud, or frown at the wrong woman, or . . . oh, the list is endless! of the harm they are capable of inflicting. So they are very careful. They don't dare move, they don't know how things are progressing in the conversation, or what is going to happen next.

Suzanne Hein and Dolores are watching together.

What happens next is that Victor puts his arm up and lays his hand lightly on Bitlow's shoulder, easily, seemingly in comradeship. Edna Bitlow's eyes glow. Is it greed or ambition or relief that tonight her husband will be in a good mood, will be expansive and perhaps even kind, after his success? Perhaps he will even approve her, Edna, for her excellent behavior? Or is it that she is looking at Edith Morrissey, who is calm and cool and blond and assured and who does not have a single ripple of flesh along the lines of her svelte body, and imagining that someday she, Edna Bitlow, will be in the position of Edith Morrissey, and will look like her too?

Victor turns Bitlow's body without force, like a man leading a woman in a dance, with a light touch, fingers on a waist, hand on hand. What he is doing is turning Bitlow to face the great man, and Bitlow gasps inwardly, his heart sends gushes to his brain, his brain sends gushes of gratitude to his heart, gratitude towards Victor Morrissey, who is doing this for him. And there he is, the great man, Mach himself, peering at the two of them out of his watery blue-yellow slits. The three men are talking together, Victor is introducing Bitlow (Bitlow!) to the great Mach (Mach!) and their backs are to the women. (Didja see that, Edna? Me, Billy Bitlow from Nohank, Arkansas, talking to him, Mach!) Edith moves a little closer to the men, she pushes herself against Victor just slightly, and smiles, fixedly, at Mach. She keeps smiling, looking directly at him, waiting for a moment of recognition, but she doesn't get it. She has never gotten it, although she's been introduced to Mach at least five times. She has mentioned this to Victor, who shrugs and says, Come on, Edith, he has important things on his mind, and who thinks, Good god, women and their petty concerns.

284

The women are totally cut out and are feeling a little humiliated, but they will never admit that to themselves or to each other. And in a way, they also feel liberated. That conversation left them only glazed in mind and body. They smile at each other more humanly now, and begin to talk. Such a lovely party, yes, and the weather so fine for this time of year, yes, they had taken a drive to Connecticut recently, Edna and her husband, and the foliage was really gorgeous! To see their son, yes, broad smile, pride coming up now, well, why not, to see their son who is a freshman at Yale. Yes.

Edna does not of course mention that the reason Billy was willing to take time off, was willing to drive so far, is that son has had a breakdown and is now in the Yale clinic, and they drove up to see if he needed to be driven back home to Washington. Her face shows it, trembling in tiny lines around the smile. Edith sees this or doesn't see it. She knows the rules and would be shocked if Edna mentioned such a thing, shocked to the point of smiling and saying Ummm, and moving away and telling Victor later that she did not think the Bitlows were to be taken up.

But of course Victor already knows that and has no intention of doing it.

But Edna knows the rules too, and doesn't mention it. Yes, the buffet was magnificent! Such huge shrimp! And the pineapple mousse! A *really* lovely party!

Yes, we drove to Connecticut to see Billy, Jr., just a freshman, you know, first time away from home and a little homesick. Isn't that sweet? I think that's sweet.

Edith thinks: No prep school? She *knows* the Bitlows are not to be taken up.

Both women perceive, out of the corners of their eyes, a woman standing behind a pair of men, talking. Her body is slightly turned towards them. She glances at the men and nods and smiles graciously, you can see she is thinking that, thinking *gracious,* I am *gracious.* Only occasionally does she glance over at Edith and Edna. And Edith and Edna recognize her moves, and inch a bit closer to her. At an appropriate moment, when the distance between them is just right,

Edna turns to the new woman and smiles (she's the superior here, after all, the one in charge) and says hello, I'm Edith Morrissey. And the woman's face brightens, she knows the name Morrissey, and reaches out and puts her hand lightly, very lightly, very briefly on Edith's arm, and Edith bristles, but then the woman says, Oh, I'm happy to meet you, I'm Eleanor Howe, my husband's with EGC. And Edith knows *that* name, and so, awed, does Edna, and the reaction could be measured by an instrument that was sensitive to the vibrations and intensity of air, and in moments there is gay laughter in that little group, laughter betraying joy and gratification in the company, such exalted company! Yes, the three ladies stand in their neat but not gaudy cocktail dresses, one dark blue, one light blue, one beige, and their hairdos, two blond (one dyed) and one brunette, and hold their pretty glasses with something sweet in them, and smile and talk and praise, yes they praise the food, the drink, the men, the corporations, the view, the windows, the decor, the paintings, the weather, the music, the company, the woods and gardens beyond, the beauty of the entire created world! Hallelujah!

Party over, Victor drives home abstracted but with a lively glint in his eye. Edith glances at him, decides to talk, tells him about Edna Bitlow and her untakeable-up-ness, Eleanor Howe and her eminent takeable-up-ness, trying to please him with her perception, her understanding of the rules. He barely listens, says Umm, and if he catches any of what she says, he thinks how petty women are.

He's right. The women imitate on a petty scale what the men do on a grand scale. Or at least, what the men think is a grand scale. (Oh, Mach!) Edith's mouth twitches, because something like this comes into her mind, but she can't bring herself to think it fully, much less say it. So she smiles and subsides and tries to think of something pleasant to wipe away the other and as they pull into their driveway she thinks how nice it is they have a circular driveway when everybody else on the block has only a straight one.

How CAN you love a man like that? I ask you, how can you?

He's not like that anymore. He's suffered, he's seen. Suffering makes a person more human.

Indeed. Does it occur to you that even Mach has probably suffered, that once upon a time he was four years old and had a round freckled face and eyes that looked straight at you? No doubt he did. No one escapes pain.

She hummed: The man I love belongs to somebody else. She rose. Not to Edith, no. To Mach and his machine. Victor's machine too. Edith was in a wheelchair invented by Victor's machine. How can you love a man like that?

Poor Anthony. Always wanted to belong to the machine, to feel he was part of it. Never quite made it. Why he hated me. But I loved what it was in him that woud not allow him to become part of it. Always throwing a tantrum at the wrong time. Still, it's failure for a man, not to belong to the machine.

The machine always wins. When World War III is over and the world is a huge pile of steaming rubble and the people are all dead, there, on the horizon, there, with its chimneys still smoking, will rise I. G. Farben and the robots it invented to save the cost and unpredictable behavior of human labor. Computer-controlled robots jerk across the floor pushing ingots into ovens with long shovels. The robots don't know everybody's dead. Even Mach's or Blanchard's Caribbean island is an ember now. Even Mach is an ash.

So are the rest of us.

Equal and opposite power, Victor says. How?

Still, he's right. We're all part of it, there's no purity, only milk and butter can be pure, not people. What's pure? One hundred percent pure TNT, napalm, margarine.

Who's pure? The farmer, injecting his chickens to

make them grow faster, giving them electric shock to make the egg happen? The clerk, stamping in quintuplicate forms to permit nerve gas to be transported across country in a rig? She, teaching in a college that owned stock in Blanchard Oil? She, whose books were published by Crosscutt, a company owned by a conglomerate that pushes sick white bread on America, that pushed nerve gas while it was legal, that still, in one of its subsidiaries, manufactures napalm?

Where can you go to get clean? Some little island in the South Pacific, white beaches, coral reefs, natives living by pulling taro from their front yards, shellfish from the coral, breadfruit and pineapple from the trees? Toothless by thirty, ignorant, yearning. For what? For a TV set, a washing machine, a refrigerator. Yes. And to make enough money to buy an occasional piece of cloth to cover your body, you have to work for one of Them, the Dutch traders, the Aussies, the New Zealanders, the Americans, the Germans, who trade, who wheel and deal, who complain as they sit in their air-conditioned offices about the lazy natives, as the thermometer outside registers 100 degrees and the humidity reaches 99 percent. The natives intelligently slouch from shadow to shadow in the midday sun, while on the beach a white-skinned visitor with no visible fat jogs on the beach, and later collapses of heat prostration.

Victor had spoken to her one day about right and wrong, explaining his frustration.

"The holding company was thinking about buying a strip-mining firm and I was supposed to look into it. I ordered a set of studies, from every possible point of view. The company wasn't worried about the morality of strip mining, but they were worried about getting flak from the ecology freaks, and the increasing numbers of lawsuits being brought by citizens' groups, people whose farms—they claimed—had been ruined by strip-mining operations. The company did not want to spend a lot of time and money in court.

"And I'm not going to say I was terribly concerned with the morality of it when I began either. It was a question of investment and risk versus possible profit:

it was my job to analyze that, to evaluate it. But I got dragged into the morality of it, willy-nilly, because there's no way not to.

"Well, I read the studies—they took months to complete—and I went down to Tennessee and West Virginia, out West to Colorado. I looked at what had been done, I even spoke to some of the farmers who were complaining. And there's no question, none at all, that some of those mining operations left utter devastation behind them. Barren land, not a blade of grass to keep it from eroding at the next rainfull. Farms nearly buried in mud that had slid down from the mined slope. People's wells full of mud, no water to drink. Unreplaceable plants and wildlife destroyed. Some of the flora in Appalachia is ancient, and exists nowhere else. I looked out at miles and miles of bleak sandy terrain, it looked like the moon. And at once-productive little farms, homes of independent self-reliant people, destroyed by the strip mines.

"I heard about fishy contracts and forceful take-overs by some of the mining companies, cheating the farmers who sold out, pressuring those who wouldn't. The evidence seemed clear to me—although it wouldn't easily hold up in a conservative court. I know how corporations work. There had been deceit and political power involved in getting them what they wanted.

"And then I looked at statistics about under-the-surface mining—the number of lives lost every year, the incidence of black lung and other diseases, the bad conditions in the mines—healthwise and safetywise. And the cost of getting a ton of coal out of the earth.

"And then I looked at the political situation and the problems we are going to be having, increasingly, with foreign oil, and its cost, and the consequence of its cost to the American dollar. And what that meant to the average American, not even people like you who travel abroad, but average people, in terms of buying power. Knowing that if money gets tight it will be human programs, the social programs you support, that will be cut back, not the budget for the military.

"And when I was all through, I tossed all that out and made my recommendation on a basis purely of possible risk, possible profit, possible loss. There was no way to do it otherwise."

"But those were your priorities in the first place."

"And in the last place."

She grimaced.

"Some people say we should have no growth. They say a little poverty is better than destroying the earth. But a notch in the belt for those people is the loss of sustenance for people lower on the economic scale than they are. They don't think about that. They think poverty is having to drink jug wine. Even those who live really simply don't know what poverty is because they've *adopted* it. My father's father lived in a shack with five sisters and brothers and his mother. Every morning the mother woke up the three oldest kids—my grandfather and two sisters—and sent them out with sacks. They lived near the coal mines, and they'd go to the slag heaps and fish through them finding tiny bits of coal that had escaped the sorter. They knew better than to go home without a full sack. They'd get home hours later, black and ashy from head to foot, and sometimes she'd smack them anyway, their mother. She was so desperate, so frantic. . . .

"She used the coal the kids found to heat the shack. She and the next oldest children would spend the morning in the woods, finding edible plants, something to eat. The littler one tagged behind. One of them died from eating a poisonous mushroom. I don't imagine she wept too long. One less to feed.

"All of the children except my grandfather grew up to be idiots. Stupid benighted bigoted hateful people. Poverty is not good for the soul or the body or the mind. My grandfather ran away from home, he found shoes somehow, he got a job in a factory, he got someone to teach him to read. He drove, he was a bit of a bastard, I guess, at least to his children. But he became a storekeeper, he married a woman who had a store, and they ran it together and they fed themselves and their children.

"And when it comes to things like that—to survival, to sheer enduring—morality is a joke, a middle-class luxury, like white gloves and silver coffeepots. As far as I'm concerned."

"Yes," Dolores agreed, "I understand. But that's because of the kind of morality you're talking about. A true morality, an honest one, would begin with that, survival. Survival, not the luxury of deciding on moral grounds that you will not have iceberg lettuce this week. With what people really need and really feel. When you talk about survival, sometimes it sounds terribly close to sounding like the survival of the world's highest standard of living, not real survival."

"Ah, Dolores, who knows what people really need, really feel?"

Yes. Who knows? Antony drank urine of horses if he had to. Whereas she, Dolores, felt deprived if someone entered her compartment on the London to Oxford run, and intruded on her privacy. And Victor would have had what even he would have to call a hysterical fit if he ever ran out of Scotch.

There is no way to be right, Dolores knew that. But there is righter and wronger, isn't there? And to be able to say that, you had to have some notion of what was good, what was bad.

She tried to smooth out her brow with her hand.

How could you love a man who had done that to his wife?

How could you live in a world that did what this world did to its people?

What other world could you live in?

Join a nunnery, say beads all day, blank it out, say AAAUUUMMM.

And even then, how could you live with yourself?

Victor called the next day, sounding extremely gloomy. (How could he know? When I caressed him, when I smoothed his forehead, I smiled.) He had to go to Brussels, it would be a terribly busy trip and he couldn't promise he'd be there for her much, but would she like to come along? It might mean dinners alone in strange hotels. He had to see important people, money people, he could not fudge this one.

He did not want her to come: she would be a burden. She sensed it. Did he sound relieved when she · said she was just this moment in the middle of an important segment of her work and could not leave it? Or did she want him to sound relieved?

He accepted the refusal easily. He would call when he got back, he said.

A week later, he had not called. Two weeks later, he had not called. She, nervous, developed a rash on her hands and wondered what she would say when he did call. Then, when he didn't, the rash got worse.

Images kept flashing in her brain: Victor, scolding Edith across the bridge table, mocking her. Victor, scolding Edith about an unrecorded check, an unbalanced checkbook. Victor, coming home late from a rendezvous (clean, showered) and finding Edith sitting in bed reading. She looks up, smiles, takes off her glasses. She asks him how the meeting was and he has to recall quickly what meeting it was supposed to be, says fine, fine, offhandedly, the way he would if there had really been a meeting. He finds it easier to answer her in monosyllables, he's tired. I'm tired, Edith. Long day.

The trouble was that when these pictures appeared in her mind, it was she, not Edith who lay in the bed, who sat across the bridge table, who had tears in her eyes over the checkbook. Because it was so hard to maintain yourself, so easy to slide back into seeing it his way, their way, the dominant way. To stay true to yourself, you had to hold yourself erect and stiff, you couldn't give an inch. No.

By the middle of the second week, Dolores began to talk to Mary. Mary couldn't listen very well, she was terrified, her oral was in two weeks. Her hands fluttered across the table, she kept repeating the same things: "Yes, well, this all-male board of doctors, the kind who belittle women, who even when they think they're being kind, automatically look down. And who don't test women the same way they test men, although they think they do, but they can't because they don't *see* the genders the same way. They claim they use the same standards, but how is that possible when your mind shifts gears depending on the body shape of the person entering the room? They failed the last three women who came up."

"Did they deserve to fail?"

"It's so hard to know, you see. The women seemed intelligent to me, and I know they worked hard, but who can tell? I mean, you're not *there*, in the examination room, and even if you were, you can't see the pressures in their heads, the fear of failing just because they're women, which might *make* them fail, you see. . . ."

"Is there no recourse for them?"

"Oh, they can take it again. But it's so devastating, you see, to fail at all. After all those years of study, all that effort, feeling you've tried as hard as you can. . . . It undermines you, makes you think perhaps you're really not clever after all. And then that damned examiner who's Roger's friend . . ."

"He should disqualify himself."

"Yes, but of course he won't. They are so bloody sure they can keep things separate. So sure they're fair, objective. When any woman, any woman at all, can see they're not. All you have to do is listen to them talk. But they have the power, there's no way you can convince them. . . ."

Mary gazed at her. "But listen to me babbling on, you must be sick of listening to this. You're upset, I can see it. Is it Victor?"

So Dolores told her the whole story.

"Oh, dear," Mary said in a little sad voice. "Oh, dear."

Dolores stared at her drink. It was late Friday afternoon. Mary had neither children nor Gordon coming this weekend. Dolores had no one coming this weekend.

"Would you like it if he divorced his wife and married you?"

"No. Not at all. He'd be the same to me, in time. Anyway, I'd never marry again."

"Nor I. Gordon comes on weekends twice a month and it's quite wonderful. The other weekends he spends with his children. When he had a sabbatical last year, he came and stayed here for the entire time and his children visited him here. It was lovely. But marriage—being a wife—the very thought is appalling."

Dolores laughed. "I heard the same sentiments from

a young German woman in a railroad carriage one long dark journey. We were together for twenty-four hours on that train. We barely spoke the other's language, but we were able to communicate *that*. Maybe it's a new international movement!"

"With three members," Mary laughed. "Still, I think one wants to have been married. Once."

"To have laboratory-tested the recipe for happiness-ever-after."

"Yes. But have you quite turned against him, then?"

Dolores gazed at the table. "I don't know. I can't tell you what I'm feeling, they haven't invented words for it yet. It's a mixture. It's as though I had one picture of him and I liked it, it was the centerpiece of my present album, you know? And he came to visit and ripped the picture out of the book and tore it up right in front of my eyes and substituted another, one I don't like at all. . . ."

"But he is the one you had at first, isn't he?"

"Is he? He is, yes. But he's also the other. People don't change so completely that the old person isn't always showing through, like old paint. And even the new Victor deals with men like Mach."

"Someone has to, I suppose."

"That's what Victor would say."

"Yes, quite. Because even if the man is the incarnation of evil you feel him to be, he exists. Isn't one's only course to deal with him and try to defuse as many sticks of his dynamite as you can?"

"If you don't get polluted by him first."

Mary laughed. "Is he *that* contagious?"

"It isn't just Mach. It's the whole system. It's poisoned. You suck it in from the moment you enter and you develop a kind of immunity, like people who take a little arsenic every day. After a while your body can tolerate large amounts of the poison without even noticing it. But you are infected. You just don't know it."

"But we all live within the system. Even hermits do. If there are any hermits nowadays. We must all be poisoned."

"And so we are. That's why it's imperative that we work against the current all the time, to the highest degree possible."

Mary sighed. "Ah, well, Dolores, I can't see things as clearly as you do. For me, everything is murky. Or perhaps it's just that I see things in more personal terms. If the person Victor is lovable, I'd love him. It sounds to me almost as if you are . . . well, taking a position in a certain square. And saying, because I stand here and I am opposed to that and that, I cannot love this man. Because it's politically against your principles. Everything you say makes so much sense, you know," she laughed, "that I can't deal with it. I don't have that much sense. I live in a far more chaotic world."

Dolores smiled sadly. "Yes, you're right except for one thing. I stand in my little square and I am opposed to that one and that one. That's true. But I am not saying that I cannot love this man because I'm standing in this square. Those two things happen at once, they are the same thing. Recognizing fully, for the first time, where he does stand, has destroyed my love for him, because I stand where I stand."

"Ah," Mary said softly, "so then there's no conflict, is there. No reason to grieve."

"Am I grieving?"

Mary smiled at her with soft eyes. "Perhaps a little."

4

SHE WENT upstairs that evening, after a dinner of cheese and tomatoes with Mary, feeling warm and cared for, feeling mommyed, as she sometimes did with her women friends. She missed them, her beloved Carol and Barbara and Suzanne and Letty. She prepared for bed remembering how good it always felt to talk to them, not just because they were cherishing and funny but because they *saw*, with clear intelligent minds, and saw as she did. She did not have to fight with them, explain things to them, struggle against a current. Nor did they with her.

Even Mary, whose sight was not quite as focused, had *seen*, had been able to say it: Dolores's politics were ruining her love affair. It was true. It was sad. And there wasn't a damned thing she could do about it. You could give up a love affair, but you couldn't give up a political stance that had grown out of your very gut, out of your entire experience of life. That would be giving up your integrity. It would be like Edith pretending to be Catholic.

She worked hard that following week. All her energy and her attention were directed at her work. She did not even miss Victor, and she wondered if love weren't just another of those things we tell ourselves is important, when in fact it is about as important as having a delicious meal every once in a while.

She did not miss Victor until the weekend, that is. And then, the library closed, wandering around the apartment, she felt . . . well, some lack. So she was grateful that Mary had invited her for dinner on Sunday, to meet Gordon and the children.

She went downstairs with a bottle of wine. Mary threw open the door at her knock, bent over a pile of something, her face damp and pink, her hair hanging over it. Dolores had to climb over the pile of something, which appeared to be chair cushions and turned-over furniture.

"Oh, hullo, Dolores, come in, won't you, sorry about the mess, yes, do step over if you can, thanks so much, children, this is Dr. Durer, Dolores, this is Linton, and," Mary lifted her head a bit and nodded in the direction of the front room, "that is Elise."

Linton was beautiful and delicate-featured, with large intelligent eyes. He stood beside his mother, he was exercised about something. At the introduction, he looked at Dolores, full face, straight, for a moment and then returned to arguing with his mother. Elise was sitting crouched in a corner of the front room. She had long straight red hair and was very tiny. She glowered from her corner, but said "Hullo" when her mother bade her.

Socialization already begun. Male and female created we them.

Mary was picking up toys and carrying them into the front room, which was the children's playroom and bedroom. She glanced at Dolores again, breathless and unkempt, and said, "I'll just get this picked up a bit, you don't mind, do go in and say hullo to Gordon, I'll be in in a jiff."

"Why can't we? Why can't we then?" Linton was complaining. "It was a good fort!"

Mary, breathless, said, "Pick up those cushions, then, Linton, and return them to the sitting room, that's a dear, Elise, I want you to come out here and turn these chairs right side up and put them back where they belong. Come along now."

The children argued, complained, whimpered; Mary explained, cajoled, pushed; her voice was calm, but Dolores could hear the exasperation just below the calmness.

Dolores stepped down into the kitchen. A large man with a big bushy black-and-white beard was standing at the sink washing dishes. He turned slightly when she entered.

"Hello. I'm Dolores, and I expect you're Gordon."

"Hello." Cool British manner. He returned to the dishes. He was, Dolores, knew, a mathematician, had written a book or two in mathematical theory. He taught at a college on the east coast of England. Mary clearly thought he was a genius.

She set the bottle of wine on the cluttered kitchen table. The mess, it appeared, was from breakfast. "Can I help?"

"No, thanks, we're fine." He finished the dishes, dried his hands, and sat down in a chair beside the fireplace. He did not look at the food and crumbs still covering the table. He picked up a newspaper and began to read.

Dolores sat. She looked out at the garden. She would have liked to clean up the mess on the table for Mary, but Gordon had made her feel that would be intrusive. She stood up and went back into the hall. Mary was crouched down with the children, who were standing beside her. Her arms were around them and she was explaining something in a soft voice, nuzzling them occasionally. They listened to her soberly, but Linton pulled away when she kissed his neck.

"I brought some wine," Dolores said. "Shall I open it now? Would you like a glass?"

"I'd love some!" Mary smiled.

"You're not going to drink *wine,* are you, Mother?" Linton said disapprovingly.

"I am, why not?" she answered lightly.

"And would you mind," Dolores went on, "if I cleared your table a bit?"

Mary looked guilt-stricken. "Oh, Dolores! I'd forgotten. It must be a mess."

"It doesn't bother me. But clearing it would give me something to do," Dolores smiled.

"Oh, dear, thank you," Mary smiled gratefully, and turned back to the children. Elise moved and rested closer to her mother, leaning lightly against her body.

Dolores returned to the kitchen. "Is there a corkscrew handy?"

Gordon looked up from his newspaper. "Oh, yes, of course." He fished around the shelves over the cupboard and came up with it. "I'll do that for you," he said, taking the bottle from her.

It's okay, I can do it, she wanted to say, but the bottle was already in his hands. He handed it back to her. "Presto!"

Oh, you are a marvel.

"Thank you. Are there glasses?"

He searched the top of the old hutch and found some wineglasses behind an old china pitcher and sugar bowl. Dolores let the wine breathe for a moment, and began to clear the table. She put the butter in the fridge, and the cream pitcher, and the jam, although she wasn't sure that's where Mary kept it. She put the cut loaf on the cupboard, and wiped away the crumbs. She left the sugar bowl and salt and pepper, but carried the ceramic coffee jug and strainer to the sink and washed them.

Gordon had returned to his newspaper.

Dolores poured the wine and carried a glass across the room to him. She glanced down the hall, but Mary was gone. In the children's room, probably, dealing with problems, problems. Dolores's stomach twisted for Mary: how could you have any authority at all with your children if they believed you were mad? You had little enough normally, unless you wanted to act like a tyrant. She would not bother Mary now. She sat down and sipped her wine.

"Thanks," Gordon said, and put the paper down. He put it down reluctantly, not as if he were finished with it but as if he would pick it up again at the first opportunity.

"I understand you're a mathematician."

"Yes." Bored. Didn't want to talk about it? Didn't want to talk to *her* about it?

"I teach English," she offered.

"Yes."

They sipped their wine.

"Mary tells me you've written two brilliant books. Can you explain them to a layman?"

"Not really, no."

Silence.

"I understand you and Mary converted the house to two flats. Put in the kitchen upstairs and the bath down. You did a good job."

"Actually, the toilet was already in downstairs. But, yes, we did the rest. It was fun, actually."

"I can understand that. You get sick of using only your head all the time. It's good to use your body."

Silence. He frowned, ever so slightly.

"At least, that's the way I feel," she added quickly. "I like to go out bike-riding."

"Umm." He looked out the window, and slowly, reluctantly, returned his eyes to her. "Yes, we quite like riding our bikes."

Maybe she was just a stranger to him? Maybe he was shy? Maybe he was wary of people after what had happened at the hearing. For Roger, Mary had told her, had mustered her *friends* to testify against her, to testify that she read books all day and had a lover.

"Mary's told me about the situation with Roger. The hearing. The decision. The children. It's appalling."

His mouth twisted a little. "Beastly."

"Mary's remarkable. I wouldn't be able to stay so calm. I'd want to set bombs in the court, shoot Roger, at least shout and scream."

His head raised and so did his voice, just a trifle. "But I don't *want* her to get angry, you see. My

former wife was angry all the time. I abhor anger,"
he finished, mildly enough.

"But she must *feel* angry."

He gazed at her coldly, then away.

Mary came in bustling, pink, laughing. "Well, I
think that little crisis is resolved. I have the chicken
in the oven, so that's fine. I hope you aren't starving,
Dolores."

"No, not at all. I don't usually eat my main meal
in the middle of the day, so I'm not suffering from
delay. If there is one. But I'd be glad to help."

"No, no, the kitchen's so small, but do sit there
and talk to me."

She ran around the kitchen, or rather she seemed to
fly around it, so light and swift were her movements.
And although her gestures appeared ineffectual, somehow she was getting everything done, she was washing
broccoli and cleaning and chopping it, she was peeling
potatoes and cutting them, she was checking on the
chicken, she was making a roux, she was grating
cheese, setting the table, stirring the cheese into the
cream sauce, testing the broccoli, the potatoes, slicing
tomatoes, finding serving dishes, a platter, some serving
flatware, brushing hair out of her eyes, testing the
chicken, drinking her wine, talking, laughing, pink.

Gordon had returned to reading his newspaper.

"Oh, I feel guilty, you shouldn't have to do all this,
you have your oral this coming week, isn't it?"

"Monday week. But good heavens, we have to eat,
whether you're here or not, you know, it's no trouble,
none at all, Dolores!"

Monday week. Couldn't Gordon cook the dinner
so she could study?

Mary was telling her about a case. ". . . and she
said it was because she'd been raped and I suppose,
you know, that makes sense, it must be terrible, but it
had been two years, yet on the other hand the rape had
left her pregnant and she'd had to have an abortion,
and I know the man who performed it, they shouldn't
let him do them because he hates women and he
butchered her, he really did, he's cruel and tried to
hurt, and *that,* on top of the rape, must just have been
too much.

"Still, it was awhile back and the examination revealed nothing out of order now. And her husband was such a lovely man, Dolores, really *sympathique,* and know? He was graceful and kind and he made so much sense: all he wants is to have his wife back, to have her sleep with him again. He loves her. It seemed . . . so *little* to ask, you know? I mean, he was perfectly sane and loving and kind. Whereas she seems so . . . oh, I don't know. She's *difficult*. She whines and she complains and she bursts out with the most extraordinary statements. She's *jarring*. She's very pretty and quite young. I can see why he wants her, but she's really, I feel quite impossible.

"And that's a problem, because after all *she's* my patient, yet I find myself so much more in sympathy with her husband. She is a little alarming, really. What do you think?" Mary turned and faced her, stopped her constant movement for a moment.

"I think," Dolores said slowly, "that the rape and the abortion have driven her over an edge. She's probably had other bad experiences in her life and everything has come together and right now she can't stand men. I think that to tell her to go home and be a good little girl and let her husband screw her is to violate the very fibers of her being."

"Yes," Mary mused, "but her husband is such a *nice* man."

"It's easy for him to be nice. He's not fighting against anything. He probably feels very virtuous that he still wants her after the rape. He wants her back and feels he has every right to her body.

"Whereas she knows she's doing something wrong. I don't know about British law, but it may even state that a wife owes her husband rights over her body. Some American states have laws like that. So in addition to the hatred and rage that's all bottled up in her, she has the burden of feeling wrong towards her nice, kind husband. That's enough to drive anyone to distraught behavior."

Gordon, Dolores noticed, had stopped turning the pages of his newspaper.

"I suppose you're right," Mary said thoughtfully. "I just wish I could *like* her more. . . ."

She returned to her preparations.

Mary called the children in to dinner. She went with them to see that they washed their hands, returned, shepherding them, seeing that they were settled comfortably at the table. Elise needed a cushion under her, Linton could have used one as well, but he disdained such baby things. Mary carved the chicken and set it on the table, then brought the potatoes, sprinkled with parsley, the broccoli covered with cheese sauce, sliced tomatoes. "Gordon?" she said lightly, and he rose, carrying his wine, and came to the table. Dolores poured more wine into their glasses. The children sat looking at the table. Then they looked at each other, and away. Mary sat down. Her face was flushed, her hair was askew, she acted a little confused. She was talking to the children, asking them what part of the chicken they wanted, helping them to vegetables.

They stared at her. "You've forgotten the napkins," Linton said coldly.

She started. "Oh, have I? Indeed I have!" And jumped up and fetched paper napkins from the cupboard and folded them and laid them at each place, but she was uneasy, Dolores could see it.

"What's *that?*" Elise said with a curl of her lip, peering into the broccoli bowl.

"It's broccoli, darling," Mary said. "Will you have some?"

"It's yellow."

"That's cheese sauce, sweetheart. It's very good."

Linton put some chicken into his mouth and chewed it warily. "This chicken tastes funny."

"No, it doesn't, dear." There was an edge of hysteria in her voice.

"Yes, it does!" He spat what he had in his mouth onto his plate.

"Linton!"

"It tastes funny!"

She was near tears, Dolores knew it, but she did not show it, she smiled, she laughed a little, she said, "I've put some tarragon on the chicken, Linton. It's a herb. It is supposed to go well with chicken, and it does taste good, darling, if you'd only give it a chance."

Tried to produce a special dinner. For me. Poor thing.

Linton looked at his mother suspiciously. "It tastes funny."

"It's only because you're not used to it. It's very good, really," she smiled nervously. She swallowed some wine. "It's really very good."

Linton looked at her, at his plate, and considered. He picked up a small piece of chicken with his fork, slid it slowly into his mouth, and chewed, slowly, considering.

Mary smiled across the table at Dolores. "Children's palates are so bound by habit, aren't they," she said, and Dolores, near hysteria herself, launched into a series of little pointless tales about her children's early love for canned spaghetti and Big Macs, and about the night Anthony would not let Tony get down from the table until he had eaten his artichoke (although Anthony himself had never eaten an artichoke until that same night) and Tony had never eaten it at all, and Anthony had served it to him for breakfast the next day, but then Anthony had had to go to work, and she had gotten up and Tony was sitting there at the breakfast table looking at anything except the artichoke before him, and she had swept it up and hurled it down the disposal and had cooked him bacon and soaked bread in the drippings and handed him a huge sandwich of bacon, which he'd gobbled down and run off to school and and and . . . she ended nowhere, in confusion.

It was all right. She had appeared an idiot, but her noise had covered Mary's embarrassment. The children chewed slowly, as if they expected glass in the next chaw, and stared at the table. Linton left most of his chicken. Elise left most of her broccoli. Dolores could barely eat, could barely swallow, despite the fact that the food was delicious. She finished her dinner with relief. Gordon had thirds.

Eventually, dinner ended. Dolores sat over Mary's wonderful coffee, sighing. It was three o'clock. She could go back upstairs soon.

"What shall we do this afternoon?" Mary inquired gaily.

Where does she get the energy?

"I want to build a fort," Linton said.

"No, dear, it's not a good idea. You simply can't take all the furniture out of the rooms, and block the hall that way. It's too much work for me, dear."

"I want to go out on our bikes!"

"Oh, Elise, darling, that would be lovely, but the weather looks so grey."

"It's good enough," Gordon said. "It won't rain for an hour or two."

Mary turned from the sink, where she was scraping the plates into the garbage. "Oh, do you think so?" As if he were a deity and had decreed the weather.

Elise jumped down from her chair and bounded around the room clapping her hands. "We're going to go out on our bikes! We're going to go out on our bikes!"

"I'm not going on any stupid bike," Linton said sullenly, slipping down from his chair and out of the room.

"It won't rain until evening," Gordon pronounced.

Dolores stood to help Mary. Mary told her to sit down, but she refused to listen. She did what she could without intruding on Mary's ways.

"I suppose it would be all right, if we don't go too far. Elise can't ride too far."

"I can so! I can!"

Linton was absent.

"We could go up the back lane to the river."

"I don't want to go there! I want to go to the woods, the big woods!"

"Well, darling, we'll see." Mary left the room in search of Linton.

Dolores took over, scraping plates, putting food away, then washing the dishes. Gordon puffed on a pipe. Elise and Gordon were arguing about where they should go. Mary came back into the room, breathless and pink, behind her son, who was insisting stubbornly, "I don't want to go."

"I'll show you how to do that trick I do, Linton," Gordon said.

Linton eyed him. Silence. "Well, perhaps," he said,

his nine-year-old face an arrogant mask of suspicion and pride.

Elise ran up to her brother and clasped his waist. "Oh, *do* come, Linton, it'll be fun!"

Mary was smiling at Gordon, her face was soft and pink and yielding. She was smiling at him, her eyes were sending promises to him. Thank you, she was saying with her eyes, her smile. Her face was like a kiss, a gift, a surrender. Thank you, she was saying. Thank you for paying some attention to my children. Thank you for paying some attention.

5

DOLORES CLIMBED the stairs to her own flat wearily.

Yes. Because of her politics, she, Dolores, was ruining her love affair. But *that* is what comes of *not* sticking to your politics.

Ah, well. We all do what we can do. The best we can do.

Her heart ached for Mary, but she refused, absolutely refused, to drop down into the salt pit for Mary again. Mary was an adult, she made her own choices.

When you swim upstream, there isn't any right way to do it. There isn't any right way to do anything, but at least when you went with the current, you could be graceful, poised, assured. Going the other way, everything was catch-as-catch-can.

She let herself down in a chair. Her bones were tired, and from what? From having Sunday dinner with some friends.

It was three weeks now since she had heard from Victor. She understood. He had told his tale, he had laid himself out on the table for her to stick darts in, but he couldn't do anymore. He must have seen something in her face, heard something in her voice over the telephone, that made him hesitate. And she had not called him, although he was surely back from Brussels by now. Feeling like a moral monster, he looked in the mirror and saw only deformity. Seeing himself so, how could he call her, ask for love? Seeing himself so, he would be sure she saw him that way too, worse, probably, given her politics.

But she felt rather like a moral monster too. For when she had sprawled her pain and rage all over the floor for him to see, he had remained, had been steadfast, had been angry and had found a rotten way to get even, but he had not flinched. Whereas she, right now, did not think she could bear to look at his face. Rotten, it was: no justice. Poor Victor.

She remembered Victor saying, late one night: "I know what you mean when you say your life with Anthony was truer than anything you've lived since. Because you were young then and didn't have the defenses you have now, and you allowed him to hurt you in terrible ways. He bruised your soul, he damaged your dreams, as well as your heart and mind. You wouldn't let anyone do that to you now. You wouldn't let anyone even get close enough to you to do that."

He was right, she supposed. But here he'd gone and let *her* get that close to him, opened himself up to her, and what had she done? But there was no use castigating herself for it, because she could not control what she felt. If she called him, if they got together, he would sense her distance, her new vision of him, see it in her eyes and mouth, hear it in her voice. You couldn't lie, couldn't pretend, about a thing as strong and deep as her present aversion to him.

You can't salve your conscience by going through motions, pretending that everything was as it had been, pretending she liked him as much as ever. That was the terrible thing about an honest conscience: you couldn't cheat. You had to live with the knowledge that you were rotten, that you were betraying a person who had been dear to you, that you were closing a door in the face of a man who had been utterly honest with you.

Yes, but on the other hand, was he so free from rottenness? Wasn't he slowly, slowly, trying to put you in the same pumpkin shell he'd finally locked Edith up in? Oh, you were quick to catch him in the beginning, calling him on his Businessman self, but then habit sets in, and affection solidifies, and you got slower and slower, you let him leave you in those hotel rooms three times before you complained, and then you had to have a hysterical fit to do it. Other irritations, disturbances, you buried, and then you slid, slid like mud right down into your own yard, your own well, muddying your own waters. You fell in with the dominant force, you gave up your critical distance. And he was not unhappy with that.

But Dolores was not certain that her motives were simple. She gave herself examinations, probing. Are you sure, she asked herself, that part of what appealed to you about him wasn't a tinge, just a tinge mind you, of white-knightliness? That his desire for you felt just an iota like being snatched from the jaws of a celibate withering monster, and carried off to lush playlands? Saved for the forces of sex and mutual affection, all warm and wet and, these days, morally proper.

Are you sure, she continued, that he didn't come close to reminding you of Anthony in the picture of himself he drew? The tyrant-child's breath, cold and dreadful, was perceptible at the edges of the room when he talked, wasn't it? The difference between them was that Victor was married to someone who said *Yes, dear,* the kind of woman she used to think poor Anthony should have married.

Oh god. She got up and went into the kitchen, heated the kettle for tea, put the breakfast dishes in the sink to soak. She took her tea and went back to the sitting room and began to work at her notes. But she had no concentration. Writing on the reality of women and the images of them purveyed in culture, she put down her pen.

And I have probably done that to him. Made him up. Maybe I made them all up, Anthony and Marsh and poor sweet Jack with his eyes that looked as if the light came through them. Had she done to Victor what men did to female characters in novels, made him one-sided? Powerful but without malevolence, without a single dire consequence issuing from his power; bringing joy but not pain; beauty without a single bad smell; generosity without the expectation of repayment. Yes, had she done that to him? Because if she had, there was no alternative but to kill him off at the end of her novel, because such a creature cannot be moved from romance into marriage. That's why all those dead heroines . . .

Yes, if she had created a fantasy figure, it was inevitable that she would turn away from the real one. Whereas he, when he had seen her naked—or partly naked—had accepted her. Had learned her true name, and called her by it. He was better than she was, larger, kinder, more generous.

He could afford to be. He was a man in the full flush of success, enjoying his life, having a glorious time in London, while his wife . . .

His wife sat in her wheelchair.

He had broken his bargain again.

Even as he laid his sorrow in Dolores's lap, even as he suffered from his past and his present, even as he asked for sympathy, he was breaking the bargain which was the reason for his plea!

She breathed in sharply.

Oh, Victor.

Spring was arriving, the daffodils were beginning to bud, there were crocuses and violets and bluebells. The gardens were beginning to be a joy again. Dolores worked well and swiftly. She had three finely polished chapters and material for another two. She figured she would have all her research finished by the end of June, which would give her three weeks free. Perhaps she'd take a holiday, fly down to Greece or Spain or Italy for that time. If she had enough money left. Maybe one of the children would like to join her. But they were always broke, and she was too.

Tony was back in Berkeley without his lover. Omaha was a drag, he wrote. Berkeley was beginning to be a drag too, in fact. What did she think about his coming back East and trying to get into Juilliard to study composition and scoring? If he could get in, if he could raise the money. But he thought he might be able to, a friend of his was working at a café in the Village, and his combo would be needing a guitarist soon, the present one was leaving.

She wrote back instantly, a one-word letter: Go!

Sydney, proudly, shyly, you could see her face through her language, sent along two poems she had had published in a little magazine called *Avanti*. They were about animals and they were sparse and tough and fine. The women in her commune were about to do their planting, she wrote, and were gearing up for a hard siege. But this year they were going to borrow some mechanized equipment, so perhaps it wouldn't be as bad as last year. They were going to plant a little corn this year, along with the alfalfa.

Dolores went to a party at the Carriers and met a good-looking young man who talked to her all evening, and asked if they could have tea someday. They did, their eyes playing and teasing a bit. He had a nice body, and Dolores thought of inviting him to the flat for drinks. But he was terribly boring, so she put it off, thinking she could call him the following week. She wasn't sure she would be able to tolerate listening to him even if he should prove to be a good lover.

She went home after tea, faintly tremulous, and at home, tried to bring up what was bubbling below her surface. It had to do with the young man, with screwing him. Dance music played in her ears. Of course: yes. She was dancing with a boy, a young man, dancing close, teaching him to do the two-step, but he was holding her tight against his body, his body and his eyes were telling her *I want you* and he thought her body and her eyes were telling him the same thing. But they weren't: her message was similar to his but not identical. She knew this because it had happened before. What she was saying was *I want, I long*. It was a general, not a specific, yearning that she felt, increased by the profound sexual longing in the jazz they were listening to. And their two longings would come to-gether, and explode in fireworks that would last for a week, or two.

At which time, she would have to find a way to send him off feeling hurt but not too hurt, would have to spend energy and time and delicacy in finding a way to do that. Because she hadn't wanted *him* at all, she had merely *wanted*. Which would have been all right if he, if they, were her age, or even near it, if they had had a few callouses. But they were young and tender, they bruised easily.

Each time this happened, she disliked herself more; each time she wondered how she could manage the thing better. Until one day she decided the thing simply wasn't manageable. It wasn't that they were younger than she that bothered her; it was that they equated sex with love and believed themselves in love, and were therefore devastated at her rejection. And that would have been all right—it was with Jack—had she loved them, *them,* and not just sex itself.

The responsibility, the guilt, and the self-dislike that followed were too much for her. She stopped. Period. And since her choices of lovers lay between married men, who after Marsh were more unappealing than ever, and very young men, whom she ended by hurting, there was nothing for it but to move into celibacy.

That was it! That was how it happened.

She mused. She had reversed the usual male-female pattern, getting involved with young men. But the reversal had not worked for her. The young men were boring, callow, they had no rich, convoluted depths, and Dolores found that a good body and a good screw were not enough. One didn't require love, but one did require interesting conversation, at least for as long as breakfast lasted. Although her young men had a habit of moving in, lodging themselves in her flat, so that she had trouble dislodging them. She could not, as men could, did, screw, then slap an ass and say *shoo,* I'll see you again late tonight, baby. She could not do that because to demean them in such a way would have made her hate herself.

That was probably better morally than what men did, but it left you not getting what you wanted, while they got, men like that, exactly what they wanted when they wanted it.

No justice.

Mary took her oral and passed, and the house rocked a little that weekend. It was a nonchild weekend, but Gordon came out, and all Mary's friends gathered to celebrate including the good-looking young man, whose

310

name, interestingly enough, was Tony. And Dolores felt a little teary because Victor should have been there, he would have been a great celebrant, he liked Mary and he loved parties. The young man hung on her, but she did not invite him upstairs for a nightcap when the party was over, she smiled and kissed him good night and went up tired, feeling old, feeling that perhaps it was time she accepted that she was old, and that there were more and more things that she would never do again. She lay in bed staring at the ceiling, wondering how many more years she would have to live.

Riding to the Bod, she pulled back her rain hood and let the fine rain fall on her hair and looked around her at the gardens coming back to color. The grass was turning deep green again, and the birds were making a clatter. Since they had returned, she no longer needed her alarm clock: they woke her up mornings.

She remembered a garden party at Carol's house just before she went to Mexico for her divorce. Ten or twelve people sat around on Carol's fine patio, thick grey stone meandering around flower beds and trees. The sun was setting and the sky was resplendent. People spoke in low voices, desultorily; ice clinked in glasses. Then it was dusk, the sun was gone, but the horizon was still streaked with pink and red and salmon and lavender, it was still light. Carol lighted bug candles. Faces were beginning to grow dim, shadowy. There seemed to be a hush in the air that all of them felt, for the patio fell silent. Dolores watched the dark patterns of the leaves on the grass and thought about connections.

Birds began to call to each other. Louder, louder. Getting shrill. "Watch this now," Carol said. "They do this every night."

And suddenly the air was full of birds, they were a huge dark cloud over the treetops. They flew in by the hundreds, wave after wave, coming from the west to settle in the great cedars at the foot of Carol's garden. They called to each other, and more rose up at a distance and joined. So many there were that she imagined she could hear their flying, hear the flap of delicate tough wings against the delicate tough wind. They swept into the cedars, barely ruffling the leaves, and disappeared. Stragglers followed, calls from the trees directing them. Patches of sky were dotted with groups of latecomers, and behind these there were a few single birds tailing the tardy ones, coming home really late. Then, suddenly, another great wave arose, beat the wind, and settled in the cedars, followed by their own stragglers and the really late singular birds.

It lasted ten minutes and was over. The birds disappeared into silence, into the dark cedar leaves, into the sky, blue, royal, preparing for darkness. Not a leaf rustled, not a chirp sounded. The locusts began their saw, their timbre rose swiftly, they sang high, a drone, monotonous and comforting.

"Oh, god, how I wish I could fly!" Dolores said. "I'd like to get one of those tanks the army has, that you strap on your back, you know? And just take off."

"Like to be free as a bird, huh?" Bert Janes leaned towards her. "Well, you will be soon."

She glanced at him. He was giving her a USDA standard-brand lecherous look. She looked away.

"They are free and singular, but they all gather together at night, they all sleep together," she said.

He slid an arm around the back of her chair. "And so can we!" he laughed.

"Knock it off, Bert," she said, and rose and walked down to the cedars and stood there looking up. She could see nothing, yet there were thousands of beating hearts up there, thousands of small creatures, soft and delicate for all their power, you could break one in your hand if you chose.

She stood there until the mosquitoes had bitten her ankles to shreds. They had it knocked, those birds. Free, alone, arching air, soaring with the wind, against it. Then together, settling down, tucking a head under a wing, all of them close together on a branch, perfectly poised on a thin limb, no fear of falling. No insomnia. No bad dreams. Perfect balance. Together, friends, calling out to each other, knowing if one was missing, calling out to the straggler.

She turned and looked at the people on the patio. They were gathering up glasses and ashtrays, they were preparing to retreat indoors. Bert Janes was slumped in a chair, looking dejected. He'd been dejected ever since Mildred had left him. He was right, she thought, they could all be together, they had been together for some minutes there, as dusk settled. It was imaginable, people acting like birds, all cuddling up together on a giant bed, sleeping with their arms around each other, over each other, touching a hand.

She would not have minded curling up on a bed with Bert Janes, even alone. Just lying there feeling body warmth, hearing another's breathing. She wasn't sure she'd want to screw him, but it was possible. Had they been lying warm and comforting to each other, it was likely.

But she would never do it. Because Bert Janes didn't want *her;* he didn't *want* her. Or maybe he did want, but didn't know he did, had long ago lost the capacity to express, and perhaps even to feel, simple yearning. So he thought and acted as if what he wanted was to score. He wanted nooky, he wanted brownie points. He wanted to win. One more notch in the gun belt.

So of course she could not lie on a bed with Bert Janes. Women did, sometimes, lie together with men like that, hoping they can get the real longing to show itself, but meanwhile taking the winner for a lover. And they always ended being manhandled; well, what can you be with a winner but a loser?

The birds were twittering in Oxford now, all this many years later, and Bert Janes and Charlie Roberts, who had also been there that night, were dead of cirrhosis. And Binnie Walsh had taken too many sleeping pills. And beautiful elegant Mina was dead of cancer. Yes. So short, so short. The life of man is very brief and very miserable and as it is miserable it is well it is brief.

Mina's mother-in-law was a vegetable in the hospital. Mina went to see her every day. She would come into Dolores's office at lunchtime and they would walk to lunch as Mina reported on the woman's condition. She was paralyzed and nearly blind and deaf. The nurses had no patience with her, they left her food in front of her but she couldn't feed herself. Mina went, on the days she wasn't teaching, to feed her lunch and dinner, and on the days she taught she fed her at least dinner. "Otherwise, she'd starve," Mina said, her mild rich voice registering a dignified outrage.

"Why doesn't your husband feed her?" Dolores asked crudely. "It's *his* mother."

"Oh, he's so busy. And I don't mind. I like to watch her. I think she can see a little light, perhaps peripherally, but I think she's conscious of sun. And she enjoys her food, she relishes it, I can see that. And when I take her hand, her face warms over, it's beatific, really."

"That's all? Food, a touch, a bit of sun? God, I'd rather be dead. She'd be better off dead than living like that."

"Never say that!" cried Mina, mild, elegant, dignified Mina. "Never!" said Mina, who had had cancer of the uterus, but who had recovered. She went on passionately. "When they wheeled me into that operating room, I knew I might never come out. Alive, that is. And my heart was breaking, as they wheeled me. It was clinging to all the things I was leaving. Some of it clung, wisps of it, to the sunlight, and the trees down below, outside my window. And some of it would not let go of my nurse, who was a dear. And gobs of it clutched onto Tom, onto his body, to the smell of him, the look of him, the feel of him. I tell you, Dolores, if you can see the sun and feel its warmth, if you can taste a spoonful of food and roll it around in your mouth and find it good, if you can hear a human voice and let it embrace you, oh, the gold of sound! I love your voice, you know. If you can find anything at all to love, to enjoy, then you want to live. And you will want to live.

"They took out my uterus, they said if the cancer grew back they'd have to take out my vagina. My vagina, Dolores! But I won't let it happen, it can't happen. I want to go on fucking until I die, I want to go out fucking. I want life, I want it all!"

She had died of cancer of the breast. Quietly, elegantly, considerately, as she would.

I don't have a picture of her either.

There was a beautiful garden on the west side of the Banbury Road, and Dolores rode across to look at it. She stopped her bike and just gazed. Blues and yellows and whites, unusual tulips with stripes, iris, daffodils. She looked at it for a long time, thinking about Mina, wishing she could talk to Mina now, just pick up the phone and dial heaven. Hear her laugh.

Then she got up on the seat again and stepped on the pedal and rode on down towards the Randolph, and there was a man standing there waiting for something, a man in his early fifties, tall and gaunt and dead-looking, but with a face you could cherish, a face that had felt.

She stopped dead. Victor didn't see her. The car he was waiting for pulled up, there were two other men in it, and Victor got in the back seat and the car pulled away.

She began to pedal again, slowly, seeing the car vanish in the distance, then turning left into The Broad, her head in a daze, in a place that was numb and distant and dying and crying and yearning and full of sorrow.

6

THERE WAS nothing to be thought, nothing to be said. She would stop at the Randolph on her way home from the library and leave a note for Victor. In spite of everything, anything.

He might not want to see her, and she would not blame him if he did not. She had turned her face away from him when he showed himself naked. She might go up and touch his arm and say "Victor!" and he might turn cold eyes on her, and say "Hello, Dolores," in a calm tone with a composed mouth, as if she were someone who used to work for him.

But there was a worse possibility. Suppose she left

a note and he met her and she went up to him and at the moment of meeting realized, heard her body saying that she was repelled by him, that she could not bear saying that she was repelled by him, that she could not bear to have him touch her. Oh, she could cover that over with social forms—"I'd like us to remember each other as friends"—but he'd know and she'd know that she had hurt him even more. And that seemed unforgivable.

But it didn't matter, she had to do it. Had to risk hurt and guilt, remorse.

Late in the afternoon, on her bike, riding towards the hotel, she composed notes in her head. "Saw you this AM by chance; would like to see you some PM by intention. D."

No. Too peremptory.

"Would you like to get together some evening? Call me. D."

No. Promised too much.

"I would like to see you. Dolores."

Yes.

Parked her bike and walked into the hotel head down, thinking about what she would write, pushed through the hotel door and bumped into Victor.

And it was the same as it had been that day on the train. They did not touch. They did not speak. But their bodies cried out, sent out and received messages on the same line. Chemical, electrical, or romantic; delusion, illusion, or penetration to the basic truth: whatever it was, it was so strong that when Dolores moved to allow a couple who were leaving to pass between her and Victor, she could physically feel herself breaking a field of force. There was a snap, she heard it and looked around to see if others had heard it too.

They stood facing each other, bodies clamorous, faces speaking. She knew her face looked like his, soft with longing and pain and desire, hard with anger and knowledge and the past.

"Excuse me, sir but would you allow me to pick you up? I'd like to buy you a drink."

"Madam, I'd be honored."

"I don't, of course, ordinarily pick up strange men."

316

"Of course. I realize that I am extraordinarily attractive."

They walked into the lounge and he ordered drinks. "Will you excuse me for a minute, Dolores? I have to make a phone call."

"Was it hard to explain?" she asked when he returned.

He looked at her startled for a second, then expanding, his face moving into a broad smile. So there you are, he was saying. I've missed you, you old sharpie. "A little," he laughed.

They sipped drinks.

"How have you been?"

"Miserable. And you?"

"Numb, mostly."

"Work going well?"

"Very. And yours?"

"Fine, fine."

"Have you been traveling?"

"A little. Brussels. And I flew back to New York for ten days."

Silent pause. Caught breath, expelled. "Oh, how nice. And how are things there?"

"Fine. The same."

They will always be the same.

"That's good. How's Vickie?"

"Fine. Good. We had a long talk, it was really good. She's applying for graduate school."

"Oh, that's good."

"And your children?"

"Fine, fine." Like to tell him the news, but then I'd have to tell him the truth of them, show him my barefoot children, my babies.

"You never called," she began.

He stared at the table. "No."

Silence.

He turned a wrenched face to her. "I felt . . . well, I know how you think, your . . . politics, I guess. And I felt . . . well, I didn't want to pressure you, to embarrass you. I knew if you wanted me, you'd call me."

"Yes," she sighed.

317

"Well," he lifted his glass to her, "and here we are!"

"Here we are," she smiled.

They finished their drinks.

"Would you like another?"

"Umm. What I'd really like is to see your room."

"My room?"

"Yes. Don't you have a bottle up there?"

He grinned then and reached out his hand and pulled her up and they walked as swiftly as they could, careful not to run, to the elevator, and she bumped her knee on a chair in the lobby, but paid no attention, although it made her limp a little, and she followed him to the elevator and they went up up up up up.

And down the hall and he unlocked a door and she saw a blur of pink around a lamp, dusk at the windows, a bedspread pinky-red, salmon. And him, his body, his face, and that was all there was then, him holding her, her holding him. Holding, standing still, just holding for a long time. Then there was rubbing and feeling and their bodies spoke. They did not tell *about,* they *told,* like counting coins. They held, they felt the fine rough wool and the silky cotton and tissues of silk and cotton smooth and cool as water, buttons cold as pearl. They held, they felt, they rubbed and smoothed and caressed.

Oh, so good, so good to lie down, to lie down together, warm and solid and fitting. And, oh, so good that golden shining place just beneath the opened collar, smooth as cotton or silk but rippling with intrusions, mountains of bone around a valley as vulnerable as a wound. Around it the throbbing landscape of body, ear against it, hear the throbbing, like hearing the earth's heartbeat when you lie against it, the other side of silence, absorbing its rhythms into your own, harmonizing them.

Smells: of melon and strawberries, fresh sweet cream, cheese of the goat, cool lemon, salt everywhere to give it savor. Softness of lips, bodies like ripe fruit hanging with only curled leaves caressing it, fruit aching to be picked, held, turned over in the soft firm palm, rubbed against the cheek.

Arms tired of hugging themselves hugged other

bodies, cherished them, lavish in pleasure, treasuring the soft places, the hard places, places that were soft and hard at once. A strange hand, a strange mouth, sighs of a strange throat that seem to come from your own. Deep breath, from the soft-hard place far back in the cave of the mouth, warm and wet.

Moving, so good to move, to bend, to twist, to encompass, to be encompassed, knees, arms, thighs, calves, hips, moving, clasping, pressed together, interwound. Which are whose? Lying together, around, over, under, rubbing softly, bending, flexible, warm. Alive. Feet cool and damp and smelling of the earth they walk on. Hands, masters of arts, doing, feeling, being, all at once. Giving, taking, in one instant; strong and delicate, hard and weak. Fingertips stroking lightly, being stroked, shivering satin flesh, silken flesh, flesh like the finest sheer cotton shimmering in the sun.

Heat builds up in the engine of the body. Hot channels pump it all the way to the fingertips, while the feverish damp source aches with longing, hot and wet and silently crying, agape or athwart. Picasso mouth and tongue wanting each other, bodies almost violent trying to absorb, assimilate, meld together, wanting to become fluid and melt together, wanting to possess and control, wanting to be possessed and controlled, both at once, wanting it all, having it all, both swooning under hands, powerless, both making to swoon, powerful.

Power meets power with both engines running, two eagles fornicating in midair, wings flapping lest they fall, head-on collision, joy in the power and the motion, joy in the powerlessness and the surrender. And all at once it is both, taking and giving in the one instant, and then it floods, the release, the relief, tension flooding out, away, giving in. Everything resolved.

Contraries exist simultaneously. Paradoxes are simple truths. Pain and pleasure equally mixed impossible to differentiate. Solids turn liquid, filledness is emptiness, you are the fruit that is plucked and held and caressed and bitten into tantalizingly. You are the plucker who picks the fruit from the branch, holds it, caresses it, takes a tantalizing bite, then bites deep, the juice squirts and runs down your chin, you eat it all, hungrily.

Smell of lemon, smell of salt, salt fish swimming upstream in eager encouraging waters. Hands holding, smoothing the fine damp silken flesh, holding firmly the firm soft bodies, lost and found, familiar and strange, filled and insatiable.

7

IT WAS Saturday night and they had decided to eat in for a change. Dolores cooked, made a *blanquette de veau*. Victor peeled onions and carrots and mushrooms, but mostly he sat at the kitchen table watching her and drinking wine.

She told him everything, told him she had been confused and still was, but she couldn't think anymore, couldn't work it out so that it made sense. And that she couldn't help feeling what she felt, and that she was sorry. All those lost weeks. But she couldn't help it.

Yes, he said. Yes.

Knight on white horse, perhaps.

Yes, he said, I understand.

Political differences, she said.

Yes, he said, I understand.

Poor Edith, she whispered, and he lowered his eyes and whispered too: Yes.

And then: I don't want you to live with her because it is killing you. But I don't want you to leave her because that will kill her.

He put his hand on his forehead: Yes.

And Mach, she said. You work with him.

Mach. Yes, he said. "But you know, darling, Mach is only an ant. You know, the soldier ants, who are hierarchical, like humans. The avant-garde goes out early in the morning and does the spying, then comes back and tells the rest it's okay. And then they march. And the forward group marches out with banners flying, the rest plod behind. And they come to a river, and the forward group charges bravely in. And drowns. All the ants plow in behind them. And drown. By the millions they drown, until their minute bodies form a bridge, a human bridge, no, I mean an ant bridge; they drown, Dolores, one on top of the other until there's a solid line and the millions who are left can walk across it, can get to the other side where there is food, where the race will continue.

"What I'm trying to say is that Mach isn't a person, he's a vehicle of the culture, he carries on the ideas of the culture, he's its DNA. He has no ideas of his own. He plods along, he and his kind, creating napalm and penicillin, employment and deployment, food and starvation. He hasn't any moral standards; to him napalm and penicillin are equally valuable because they make money. He's an automaton, a machine."

She stared at him, her knife in air. "Yes," she said. "Yes, exactly. And that's the problem."

"But," he said hesitantly, "don't you think we're better off with a Mach, simply because he has no moral priorities, than we would be with a man like . . . Hitler, say, who had clear plans for the human race?"

"Better off? I don't know. I suspect if Mach had Hitler's power, he'd be as bad. It's true that one man's moral priorities are another man's oppression. But I believe we have to get beyond that, have to find a more humane set of priorities. Oh, god, Victor, why is it so easy to be a monster and so hard to be human? When the very word human, as I use it, as others use it, means superhuman."

He stared at his glass, he fiddled with it. "Yeah. I can remember the moment when I realized I'd become inhuman. It wasn't that night with Edith, wasn't even when I sat there in the hospital waiting for her to come out of the OR. But it was that same day, it was the late afternoon of that day.

"I went home, having seen Edith, knowing she was unconscious and would remain so for some time. I knew I had to tell something to the kids. I thought that maybe I'd even have to tell them the truth. And I had no idea how to do that. I'd been thinking about it for hours, sitting there in the hospital waiting room. Not knowing then if she'd come out of the operation alive. Wanting to tell them the truth, sick of deceptions, but not wanting to shock them into horror, to hurt them beyond recall.

"I got home a little before dinner. Mrs. Ross was in the kitchen, there were warm food smells in the house. She came running to the door as I came in, she put her hands on my arms, she cried, 'Oh, Mr. Morrissey, how is poor Mrs. Morrissey?' So genuine, so concerned that I couldn't answer her, couldn't even swallow."

He swallowed, remembering. "I told her I didn't know, that we'd have to wait and see, but she was in bad shape. And Mrs. Ross began to cry, softly, gently, like a light spring rain. 'Ah, the poor lass!' she said."

She told me the children were in the den, and I went in there. The children were all sprawled around. It was a big room, paneled, with a fireplace and a TV and couches and tables and a set of French doors leading out to the garden. The children never sat all together in the den. They stayed in their rooms, or a couple of them might have been in there watching TV, but they didn't usually hang around together. But they were together that day, and that's how I knew how scared they were.

Vickie was sitting curled up in a chair reading a magazine. Leslie was watching the TV, filing her nails. Mark was making paper airplanes and sailing them across the room. There were tens of them lying around on the floor. And Jonathan was lying on the floor on his stomach, watching TV with Leslie. They looked up when I came in, they were silent. Leslie got up and turned off the TV set. "How's Mom?" Vickie said.

There was a paltry little fire going in the fireplace. They must have built it themselves. I was getting more and more stuffed up, my throat felt as if it were going to burst. I walked over to the fireplace and began to roll and twist newspaper and put it into the fire.

"We don't know yet how she is," I said.

I began to pile kindling on top of the newspaper.

"Is she going to die?" Mark said in a thin high voice.

I poked the fire into life and sat down in an armchair. "I don't know," I said. "Nobody knows, yet."

Mrs. Ross came in with a tray bearing a bottle of Scotch, a glass, and a bucket of ice cubes. She almost curtseyed, she was so anxious to please me, so anxious to make me feel better. She caressed Vickie's cheek on her way out. "Oh, ye poor lassies and lads," she said.

And Jonathan stood up, he began to wail. He was eight then, and he just wailed, he had no control. He started out of the room and I leaped up and tried to catch him, to hold him, but he wriggled out of my grasp, he fought me, he hit my arms, pounding them, and then he ran out of the room. I was dazed, I had tears on my face, the fury of him, the rage, the fear!

I looked around at the other children. They were lying or sitting as they had been. Their faces were blank. I sat down again.

"How did it happen?" Vickie said.

"She ran into an underpass. On the parkway."

"When?"

"Early in the morning. Late last night."

"What was she doing out, early this morning, late last night?"

"We'd had a quarrel. She was angry, she ran out, she drove away."

Silence.

Then Leslie picked it up. "Why did you quarrel?"

"Oh, Les, it's so complicated. We quarreled because we live together and living together is hard."

Vickie's voice came in cold and hard. "In other words, she finally gave it to you."

My head jerked up. "What?"

"For never being here, for never being really nice to her, for never paying any attention to us."

"Oh, Vick, Vick!" I cried then, it had been a long day, I couldn't help it. And they stood or sat where they were, I couldn't see them but I could sense the stillness in that room. Then Vickie got up, she moved towards me, she stood a foot away, she watched me. She must have felt terrible, it had probably never occurred to her that I could be hurt by anything, that I could cry, that I could be defeated. She inched closer. She put her hand on my arm. She laid it there very lightly, then removed it, as if I might jump up and hit her.

"I'm sorry, Daddy," she said in a thin little voice.

The real fall from innocence: realizing her power, realizing that she could hurt, she could make me cry.

"It's okay, Vick," I said, wiping my face. "Where's Jonathan?"

"In his room, probably," Mark said. Mark and Leslie were sitting there on the floor, as erect and trembling as catkins.

I got up, I staggered to my feet. That drink had hit me, I was exhausted. I left the den and went to Jonathan's room. The kids trailed behind me.

He wasn't in his room. We searched the house. He wasn't anywhere. The kids went outside, they looked all over. Jonathan was nowhere. I went back to the den and poured myself another drink. I thought: just what I need, a runaway kid. I was about to go out to the car, to drive around the neighborhood searching for him, when Vickie came into the den.

"It's okay," she said. "He was sniffling in his closet. I heard him. He's in his room."

We went to Jonathan's room. He was curled up into a ball on the floor of his closet, in a corner, sniffling. I pulled him up, I pulled him out, I carried him to the bed, I sat down with him on my lap, I held him, he laid his head against my shoulder, he bawled. I sat there holding him, stroking his back, stroking his head, kissing his hair, saying, "Okay, honey, it's okay," and as I did that I felt him, his little body, felt his backbone, his vertebrae under his shirt, such little bones, so fragile. And I smelled him, he smelled of sweat and dirt and lamb chops, child smell, smell of flesh, childflesh, sweaty hair sweet as corn. His body was warm and his heart was beating very fast and his sobs were coming more slowly, were dying down. And I felt his body, the delicate ribs, the delicate vertebrae, thinking how fragile he was, how fragile we all are, Edith in the hospital with her fragile body smashed to smithereens, ruined, ruined, all of us ruined, and I rocked him, I laid my head against his and I let myself cry too, twice in one day, some record, but I was tired, I didn't care, let them see. I let the tears run down my face, I knew the kids were standing there gaping. I didn't care.

And he fell asleep with his arms tight around my neck, fell asleep out of pure emotional exhaustion, and I looked up at the kids to say I think we'd better undress him and get him to bed the hell with his bath tonight, and then I saw Vickie's face, she was staring at me, she looked at me as if she were watching something inconceivable.

And I knew, oh, well, we weren't close, Vick and I, when she bothered to talk to me at all she shot a nasty crack of some sort, and I didn't like it, and I'd told Edith she had to do something about it, but I didn't really pay that much attention to her. But here she was, looking at me as if I were a stranger, as if it had never occurred to her that I might do something like that, comfort a baby. As if men never did things like that. As if—the way you feel sometimes—as if men were an occupying army that marched around shouting *Achtung!* Now hear this! And shifted their rifles and shoved the barrel at a kid's butt, pushing. But couldn't, ever, possibly, sit there rocking a baby.

She didn't know I'd done that to her tens of times when she was a baby. She couldn't remember back that far. Because along the line I'd stopped doing it, I'd rocked Leslie a little, Mark once or twice, Jonathan never, I think.

Anyway, I saw her looking at me and I understood that I'd become inhuman for her a long time ago and she couldn't quite grasp what she was seeing. And I thought about how good it felt to sit there holding Jonathan's little body, feeling him needing me, feeling me needing him, feeling us tied together by bone and flesh and heartbeat and the rhythms of life. Love. I understood love then, at that minute. For the first time.

And I said to Vickie, "Where are his pajamas?" and she found them, and we undressed him, gently, took his little body out of his pants and shirt and slid the pajamas on, and we all kissed him, asleep as he was, and stroked his head and tiptoed out and turned off the light.

And Vickie didn't remember with her head that I'd

rocked her like that once, but maybe she remembered with her body. Because after we closed the door, she turned and put her arms around me and held me and said, "I'm sorry, Daddy."

Dolores was silent when he finished. She stood there, her knife dangling in her hand, chunks of veal sweating on the cutting board before her. No, he was not Mach if he could *see* Mach; was not Mach if he could tell this, if he could say *his need and mine.*

"And to think I wanted you on a white horse," she said.

He turned his head sharply, startled out of his mind's place. And she went to him and held his head against her, embraced him, saying, "When you're so much better off it, so much better."

And let herself forget, for a time, what Edith had had to do to get him that way, what Edith had had to pay.

VIII

1

DOLORES HAD not gone on a business trip with Victor since the terrible night in Manchester, but when he said he had to go to Paris in April, she cried "April in Paris! I've never seen April in Paris!" He grinned, and said he had a week's work there, so if they spent the surrounding weekends, they would have nine days of Paris in April.

April in Paris proved to be damp and chilly most days, with some rain and not a chestnut blossom in sight. But it didn't matter. Dolores loved Paris, and knew her way around the central part of the city without a map, something she never mastered in London. She walked continually, never tiring of Paris streets. She probed and poked into little neighborhoods that were unfamiliar to her, always finding a fine little café in which to sit and rest and observe. She went to parts of the Louvre she hadn't visited before, gaped at the startling new Beaubourg, and browsed in the little art shops facing the river on the Left Bank.

At night, she and Victor would go out in raincoats and walk along the Seine on the lower path, something she'd never done with a lover, something she'd always wanted to do with a lover. They walked with their bodies close together, holding hands, speaking little. They spent all their energy savoring the scene, storing it up against dearth. They went to a café on the Ile, opposite Notre Dame, and stared up at the different cathedral revealed by the spotlights—spare, stark, eerie, and angular, it was beautiful and overpowering. It was inhuman, Dolores thought, thinking too that humans had made it, just as humans performed the behavior they called inhuman, humans had made it purposely to dwarf the human, to awe it. They sat looking at it, drinking café filtre, holding hands, drinking the scene in too, cellaring it, like camels, against the desert.

One Saturday they went to Chartres by train, and stood for hours at the portals and the windows, Victor enraptured by the blue madonna, Dolores, as always by the gargoyles. And by some happy chance, an organist was practicing for a concert to be held in the church the next evening, and Victor and Dolores were able to sit down and listen to him rehearse, hearing the whispering shuffle of the tourists' feet, a tap of heels on the marble floor, low conversations, sudden sharp orders to children. And they watched the arches rising and the light flooding in through the clerestory, dim light radiating around the stained glass. And heard the Bach that comprehended it all, that grumbled with the tired feet, was sharpened with the smell of bodies damp and soiled from use, that soared up from the floor and sang, touching with delicate fingers the highest point where the arches met, tingled against glass, which trembled and sang too.

Body and minds heavy with lading, they took the late train back to Paris, sitting opposite each other so they could see the other's face, silent, eyes and mouths speaking without words, saying nothing new, nothing startling, only the same utterness, the emotional-totality of their bond. They could not bear to take their eyes away from each other, yet they did, turning to gaze at a wistful figure, to listen to a man berating his wife, to watch a middle-aged couple sit in the silence of years of marriage. And they commented, continually, on these events, with tiny twists of mouth or eyebrow, with flickers that seemed mere light rippling on their faces. Their delicate communication ranged from amusement and malicious delight to pity or contempt or simple interest. It was fun and a luxury, this silent communication, it hung on the reverberating air between them and took up all the space around them. And through it all they were gazing at each other's faces as a portraitist would, limning them inside their own heads, etching them on the inside of the eye against absence.

Dolores insisted that Victor go with her on the boatride on the Seine (too touristy, he said). "I take it every time I come to Paris and I love it every time and so will you," she said. They had a sunny afternoon, and they sat with the Germans and the Italians and the Scandinavians and the Americans and the crackly loudspeaker offering multilingual incomprehensibilities, and sailed down the river, under the bridge, along the Iles, past the heroic buildings of old France.

Victor insisted that Dolores go with him to the top of the Eiffel Tower ("and you called the boat trip too touristy?") because in all his trips to Paris, he had never been up, his trips being business trips, leaving little time for pleasure of that sort. The lines were not as long as they are in the summer, and they got there within an hour. But the view was disappointing, because the day was overcast and they could not see far. So Dolores tugged at Victor's hand and led him to the Arc de Triomphe and they climbed that, and then they stood in the magic circle at the very heart of the old city, gazing in wonder at the broad tree-lined avenues spoking out and away, and turned and there was the Bois looking like a great forest in the middle of the very civilized and most beautiful city in the Western world.

Both wanted to go again to Sainte-Chapelle, the little chapel built by Louis the Saint and connected to his palace. The room glittered with the dancing light of the stained-glass windows, and Victor said it was as if religion had merged with Merlin, and this was a faery place. Dolores wondered what the world had seemed like to him, to Saint Louis, what the world out-of-doors had seemed, that he could have built *this* indoors.

Victor wanted to go to Versailles, but Dolores put her foot down on that one. He was adamant, he said one had the right to see it once, that she had, after all, and so she was forced to give in. He found it fine, impressive. But Dolores kept muttering, "No-wonder there was a revolution." He'd point to a gilt frame, a painting, a vase: *Ugh,* Dolores said. The only things she liked were the carpets.

Victor launched into theory. The monarchy may have been selfish, but look what it left behind! *Ugh,* Dolores repeated. Art, Victor continued, ignoring her, always flourishes in cultures that have an elite, an aristocracy, a class with the leisure and wealth to appreciate and foster it. "Since we got government by committee, look at the stuff we get, look at Soviet art."

"If this is the sort of art aristocracies foster, I'll take anarchy any day," Dolores said. "And I think American art is fine. It's vital, it's thinking."

"You like yellow canvases?"

"That isn't all there is to American art...."

"The trouble with American painting is that it thinks too much," Victor said. "And artists aren't taught craft. Look at the work on that gold hand mirror: there's probably no one alive who could do that today."

"And why should they? That's part of a different vision, when men declared themselves gods and ate up everybody else's dinner. Our artists aren't aiming for anything like that."

"You're right. They're aiming for art without content."

Their disagreement was total: it was aesthetic, moral, and political. But they liked it. Both of them were inclined to be contentious and both of them usually won their arguments. It was a pleasant change to argue with someone who responded strongly and would not give in, to argue in a closed circle, knowing you would never win. It made the argument *play,* which was liberating to the mind and the spirit.

"Victor," Dolores was snarling with a smile, "sometimes I think you haven't read a piece of history since you were in high school."

"Dolores," he snarled smiling back, "I sometimes wish I could get inside your head and see what broken gear in there is making an intelligent woman say such stupid things."

"I get pretty sick of being in my own mind," she admitted. "It's so convinced, so relentless, so grim."

"Okay, let's change," Victor decided, as they entered the Hall of Mirrors and Dolores said *Ugh* for the fiftieth time. "You use my mind and I'll use yours. Mine is quite brilliantly full of facts and figures, names and dates. And in the place where your mind is grim, mine's a blank."

"I wouldn't mind," Dolores said. "For an hour a day, anyway. Like airing out the rooms."

"We start now," he announced energetically, and looked at his watch. "Three ten." He looked around the hall, opened his mouth wide and stuck out his tongue. He said, "Uuuuuuuggggggggghhhhhhhhh!"

She broke into a giggle. "Not here!"

"Bbbbbbbbblllllllllaaaaaaaahhhhhhhh!" Victor continued. People were turning to look at him.

Dolores walked away from him and tried to pretend that she didn't know him, but she was giggling so hard she aroused as much attention as he did.

"No, no, no escape." He chased her and grabbed her arm. He made her stop while he gazed theatrically around the hall. "Ugh! This place is grotesque!"

Dolores pulled her arm away and spread both her arms out, gesturing at the mirrored walls. "Ladies and gentlemen! Before you are fifty thousand mirrors, which took five billion tons of sand to produce, and several thousands of lives, as well. The workers, you see, kept drowning in the sand. However, the king thought it was a noble thing for the workers to give up their lives for their country, especially in such a magnificent cause! The Hall of Mirrors, ladies and gentlemen! The hall is twenty feet wide and a hundred feet long and every day five thousand four hundred and thirty-five tourists pass through its . . ."

An American in blue jeans and a beard applauded. A party of German tourists looked at her confused, while their French tour guide sent darts of outrage at her. Victor grabbed her arm and pulled her along roughly. "That's not my mind," he said, *very* grimly.

She could not stop laughing. Her eyes were tearing, her face was wet. She pulled away from Victor again and spread out her arms: "Oh! What a gorgeous palace! This is the way kings should live! This is the jewel in the crown of the monarchy! Long live the king!"

And to the curiosity of passersby, Victor swooped her up in his arms and kissed her wet face. She giggled through that too.

Leaving for the airport, they looked out of opposite cab windows, sitting far apart but holding hands across the space. They looked out of different windows and so saw different things but the same thing, a different city but the same city. Dolores tried to absorb, assimilate this city she loved so much and would return to but never with Victor, wanted to absorb it with him in it. It made a difference, his presence, the air seemed differently salted or sweetened, motions were directed by a different pace. Both of them wanted to remember it this way, treasuring not just their experience of the city, but also their experience of each other. They looked out as if they were hungry, as if they could eat it, lardering their minds with the way it had been for them, was for them now, together, stocking it up against a winter of deprivation.

2

BUT OF course they could not live in peaceful coexistence for very long. There were rhythms to things, and even harmony palls and requires discord and new development if a bond is to remain a living texture.

They were back in Oxford, later that month. They had had a happy dinner at home, Victor having decided that he wanted to make moussaka, and having spent the entire day doing it, leaving the kitchen a dishwasher's despair. And of course, since he cooked, Dolores had to wash the dishes. She gritted her teeth and promised him next time she cooked it was going to be cannelloni. *Three* sauces! Watch out!

But the dishes got done, eventually, and Victor even helped, and they were sitting quietly in the sitting room with cognac, and something triggered her memory, and Dolores launched into her lecture on women always having to swim upstream. Victor listened more and more uncomfortably, and when she got to the Nazi part, he looked extremely dour. But he said nothing.

"You don't like what I'm saying, do you."

"I don't mind what you're saying." Short.

"Why don't you like it?"

"I didn't say I didn't like it."

"But you don't. Why don't you admit it?"

It came out in an exasperated burst. "What do you want me to do? Fire all my male managers and hire women? I try. We do appoint women at the managerial level, Dolores, and nine times out of ten, it just doesn't work! Women don't think like men! They don't! I'm sorry if that sounds chauvinistic to you. I can't help it. It is simply true!"

There was a little hard place in her stomach. "It doesn't sound chauvinistic to me. I agree, most women don't think like most men. They think *better*. Men get caught up in status and games and winning, and they lose sight of everything else. Women see things in the round, they see the totality of things, and so they have different priorities. I'd say yes, you'd better fire all your male managers and hire women if you want your company to be decent."

A long, heavy exasperated sigh. "Oh, Dolores."

"I'm serious," she lied. "That would humanize your company. If it wants to be humanized."

"You're not serious. You're simply trying to challenge me."

"I'm not serious because of course I know you won't do it. But if you could keep your women managers, it would be a sign you were doing something right. Really. I mean this. Women are the touchstone. If they can tolerate your policies, that means your policies are decent."

"Oh, god. Really, Dolores. Sometimes you speak such arrant nonsense!"

She glared at him.

"Look, let's talk realistically, okay? Given the competitive intense profit-motivated world we live in . . ."

"Country we live in," she corrected him.

"Don't delude yourself. The Soviets may not allow profit, but they're motivated in exactly the same way we are—everybody wants status, money, and power. You think the Chinese are any different?"

She shrugged. "No. They're all male-dominated, male worlds. Male worlds are all the same, the differences are only in degree."

"Jesus!" he breathed. "Do you realize that you are a monomaniac? You see male domination everywhere and it's all you see and you talk about it constantly and you are constantly on my back about it!"

"I see it everywhere because it is everywhere."

"So is death, but I'd just as soon not have to look at every corpse that's buried."

"Oh, what a ridiculous metaphor! In the first place, death is inevitable, male domination is not. In the second place, if you saw every example of the ugly consequences of sexism, it would take you the rest of your life just to examine this block, the people on one side of this street!"

He relaxed his shoulders. "Okay, look I don't want to do battle over this. It's just that . . . it gets tiresome. Because not only do you see it everywhere, but it's *all* you see. You go down and have dinner with Mary and her lover, whatever his name is, and you turn a Sunday dinner into a goddamned feminist drama! I get sick of it, Dolores!"

"Oh, you don't want to do battle. But you sit there and tell me I bore you."

"I'm not saying that! I'm not! It's just that you're constantly on my back!"

"I am NOT!"

"And you probe into the damnedest things! People's private relations. You know, what people do in the privacy of their own homes is their business, and things are equal there, you don't realize that, well, I suppose you had an especially lousy marriage, but you don't know how much power women wield in the home."

She nearly leaped out of her chair. "Things are not equal there!" she shouted. "What do you think I've been telling you? They can't be equal there when they're not equal anyplace else! The genders are subject to different conditions. . . ."

"Okay! Simmer down! The point is, anyway, that those things are petty, they're not worthy of your attention, you have too good a mind to be sitting around thinking about what Mary said to John and what John said back. Who the hell cares?"

"Oooooh!" she screamed and stood up, holding her temples with her hands. She went to the wall, she banged her head against it. "Oooh! Oooh! Oooh!"

"Dolores, for godsakes!"

She whirled around at him. "Petty, is it? Beneath consideration? It's the fucking future of the world, you dolt! On the relations between women and men rests everything else: the well-being or not of the children, the character of the children, the character of the society, the future of the society, the character of the entire culture! It just happens to be, Victor Morrissey, the most profound subject there is! I suppose you think oil lines matter more! Well, that's because you're a *man!*" Her tone made *man* synonymous with *stupid,* at the very least.

He glared at her and puffed hard on his cigarette. He pulled himself into composure. Then he launched his attack. He leaned forward and gestured at her with his hand, the cigarette in it flailing ashes on the carpet. "And *this* is the thing I hate most about you. You get hysterical and then you go into a goddamned sermon! You are constantly preaching at me, trying to teach me. Well, I don't need your preaching, I've gotten along pretty well for fifty-one years without it. You act as if you're challenging me to completely rethink the way I live, the way I fucking *think!* Nagging at me, all the time, to redecorate my moral house, rearrange it, or maybe even abandon it and get a new one."

She was stiff and cold. The little place in her stomach was a knot now, small but tight as a fist. She sat down, hurt. The *nagging* had got her. Only the powerless nag. Only the powerless *have* to nag. The powerful command.

"Well, it isn't possible for me to change the way I think, but even if it were, I wouldn't do it. I don't want to do it. I like the way I think. I like my work. I like myself."

"Sometimes," she shot in nastily, and he glared at her.

"Well, *that's* mutual," he retorted and it was her turn to glare.

"You want me to adopt your way of seeing, your way of thinking, your way, period. I'd have to change everything in my life. I'd have to give up my work . . ."

"I haven't tried to get you to give up your work."

"No. You just spatter it with sarcasm continually: corporations, capitalism, organization men."

She was silent. That was true.

"You see everything that's bad about those things, but nothing that's good."

"That's because there isn't anything good."

"That's NONSENSE! Dolores. Jesus! I don't know how you can be so blind! No system is perfect, can we say that? But capitalism allows greater freedom to a greater number of people than any other system . . ."

"And requires a slave class if it's to operate smoothly."

". . . and corporations are structures designed to maximize efficiency, and because of them the United States has a higher mass standard of living than any other country. . . ."

"That's industrialization and rich natural resources. All coporations permit is legalized robbery and exploitation. . . ."

"ACCCCH!" he shouted. He stood up, frustrated beyond bearing. He began to pace the room.

"You see!" His voice was shrill. "You refuse to see, you will not give an inch! You want *me* to give feet, yards, miles, for godsakes, you try to make me question everything I do or say to see if it's pure enough for the puritan Dolores, which is not only goddamned self-indulgent, it's sick! Sick!"

"I don't have the power to force you to do anything," she said coldly. "If you do it, you do it for yourself. Don't lay the blame on me."

He whirled around. "Look, I get along fine in the world. Better than you, if the truth be told. I don't need your help!"

"You get along fine in the world because you think and feel and act the way the world thinks and feels and acts. Talk about Mach being an ant! You're just

336

an automaton, that's all. But you don't do so well in your personal life."

"And you're an expert on that, I suppose!" Savagely.

Elspeth.

He didn't mean that, he doesn't know about that.

She was shivering from the cold hard tight place in her belly.

He was pacing, he looked hot, he was sweating. His pacing annoyed her. She clenched her hands in her lap.

"You might get along a little better if *you* went along with the world," he said. "You women complain all the time that you're left out. All you have to do is join. If you have the brains for it."

She grimaced. "That was cheap and stupid. Give me one reason we should want to join you. Become hollow men like you, wear uniforms, never have a thought that isn't in the service of the system? Never!"

"What in hell *do* you want!"

"Oh," she mocked him in a mincing voice, *"Was das Weib will?* What I want. Victor, is to change the world, what do you think? To make it a place where women's way of seeing, thinking, feeling, is as valid as men's. Where maybe even men will join the women because they will see that women's way of thinking is more decent, more humane, and in the long run, Victor, more likely to preserve the human race!"

"Well, *I* don't want to change the world! It never occurs to me, since I'm not megalomaniac, that I can! And that's exactly what I object to in you, that you're constantly trying to change the world. And since you can't do that, you spend your energy trying to change me!"

"You seem to *object* to a great many things about me," she said bitterly, hurt now, tired.

The thing I hate most about you, he'd said.

His voice became milder, he sensed he had hurt her. "I'm only objecting to the fact that you constantly try to change *me.*"

"And you? What do you do? What are you doing now? You're trying to shut me up, to tone me down.

You've already accused me of getting hysterical, but I assume you wouldn't call yourself that. When women get angry, that's hysteria. You pulled that on Edith too, didn't you? And what are you doing now but trying to tame me, domesticate me so I won't gallop around rooting up *your* yard. You are trying to turn me into Edith, for godsakes!"

Silence. Only the whites of his eyes shone in the dim room. His arms were rigid at his sides. He wanted to hit her, she knew. The room was very cold. No lamps had been lighted, only the candles burned; the electric fire was cold and black.

He retreated to the chair and sat there holding his cognac glass very tightly, as if it were a life buoy. He spoke very low, between his teeth. "Maybe I am. Maybe I am. But what you are doing is trying to *eradicate* me, the way you did Anthony and your daughter, Elspeth, isn't it? Wipe me out. Well, I'm not going to let you do it."

She drew in breath silently.

"I tell you, lady, I won't kill myself for you and I won't go your way. Never!"

Voice of ice: "No. You prefer Edith's."

Across the room a glass shattered.

"I should be the one breaking things," she said nasally, her head full of tears, "since you hit me lower than I hit you. But women always have to do the cleaning up," she added bitterly, "and that's quite a deterrent."

"I will fucking clean it up!" he said savagely, rising, a dark motion in the dim room. The candles flickered, nearly burned out. The air was cold and rank. He lurched past her towards the kitchen and she wanted to grab him, to throw him down and punch him, pummel him, to make him cry the way she was crying inside.

And then she wanted to caress him, to weep outwardly, to say, *Why are we doing this?* He hadn't forgiven her abandonment of him.

He'd made war on her with no holds barred: atomic weapons, neutron bombs, nerve gas: everything was permitted.

You didn't do so bad yourself.

He was worse.

So don't give in at all. Stay stubborn. But certainly don't give in first, you know how men are, everything is a contest. The one who gives in first gets a demerit on the great chart in the brain, and next time he will be more adamant, expecting your surrender, and the next time more, and more: have you forgotten Anthony? Do you want to participate in creating another such monster? For he will surely, if you give in, later accuse you of participation.

She heard him fumbling in the kitchen, heard something else knocked over.

"Why don't you turn on the fucking light?" she yelled fiercely and leaped out of her chair and turned on the lamps and blew out the nearly dead candles, and whirled to glare at him as he returned with a broom and dustpan and a bloody rag in his hand.

3

HE HAD cut himself. He hadn't thrown the glass, as she thought, he'd squeezed it and he had a deep cut on the mound of his thumb, and shards of glass stuck into his palm.

He passed her without speaking and crouched on the floor and swept pieces of broken glass into the dustpan. She turned on the electric fire and went into the bathroom for tweezers and peroxide, gauze and tape. Then she made him sit down near the lamp and she knelt beside him, picking out shards of glass with the tweezer. She looked up at him with a strained face as she bandaged his hand.

"See what I mean? Women always end up doing the dishes."

"The dishes are done," he said dully.

"Yes, but what about tomorrow's? You won't be doing dishes for quite a while with this hand. The extremes you men will go to get out of the dishes!" she tried to joke, tried to laugh, but suddenly collapsed, crying, on the floor, pounding it with her fist. "You

339

see! You see! I knew it! You wanted to hurt me as badly as Anthony ever did and still have me love you! You got your wish! Are you happy?"

He stared at her, then got down on the floor beside her. He held the wrist of her pounding hand, he pulled it towards him. "Hit me," he said. She pulled her hand back, pulled her body away from his and sat there crying little-girl helpless tears. He sat beside her, not touching her.

"Ah, Dolores, I'm sorry. But you held your own. You were as bad as I was."

"No, I wasn't," she sobbed. "I didn't accuse you of crippling Edith, just of trying to make me like her. You accused me of eradicating not only Anthony but Elspeth. Elspeth!"

His mouth twisted, he looked gloomily at the floor.

"I didn't kill Anthony. Anthony killed Anthony! And Anthony killed Elspeth!"

He regarded her quietly. "Anthony died before she did."

"So? Hands can reach out from the grave and pull you down. She does, still. I know she doesn't mean to. It's because I loved her so much. . . ."

"Who?" His face was puzzled, frowning.

"Elspeth. Elspeth." She choked on the name, like an oyster caught in the throat.

He closed his eyes. She was crying in hawking sobs, she bent her head and laid it on her crossed arms on the floor, her knees drawn up under her as if she were crouching before an Oriental despot.

"Oh, Dolores, I didn't mean to hurt you. Really. I just wanted . . . I wanted you to stop judging me. I feel you judge me all the time and it makes me unhappy."

Dolores pulled herself up and blew her nose. "And what is it you want from me, oh, member of the master race?"

"I want you to love me, of course. Without judgment."

"You want my will in perfect harmony with yours. You want me inside *your* pie dish, *your* pumpkin shell."

"There *is* love without judgment."

340

"You're right. It's Edith's kind of love."

He sighed. "Why is it I always get the worst of it in arguments with you?"

"You don't. It's just that you can't accept not winning every one. And you'll do anything at all to win, anything. But you can't," she raised her head and shot him a superior transcendent expression, "you can't hurt me about Anthony. I've been all through that with myself."

Hated that superior look, that voice. "But I can hurt you with Elspeth." Mean.

"You motherfucker," she whispered.

"Oh, if only I had been!" he moaned, and suddenly they were both laughing.

Then he put his arm around her and they sat there on the hard floor and he played with her the way you play with a child, tracing her nose, her cheek, her lips, her ears with his fingers. She settled back in the curve of his body, put her mouth up and kissed his mouth, softly, full-mouthed, not an erotic kiss but a loving one, and took his hand and played with it the way you play with a child's hand, tracing the veins, the knuckles, the nails.

"Come on," he said and helped her up and led her to the couch and made her sit down and put cushions behind her and a lap robe over her knees. He went to the kitchen and came back with two fresh glasses of brandy, and a cigar for her.

"I feel like an invalid. Do you do this for Edith?"

"Sometimes."

"I love you."

He picked up the dustpan and carried it into the kitchen and emptied it. He came back with a damp cloth and wiped up the floor where the glass had broken and spilled. Then he went to the bathroom and rebandaged his hand—the cut had bled clear through the first bandage. Then he came back and sat beside her on the couch facing her, and sipped his brandy.

She stroked his cheek. "Nice. You're nice."

"Tell me about Elspeth," he said.

"I can't. Can't," she whispered.

"Yes, you can. And I think you want to. Could

there possibly still be secrets between us? Can there, now?"

She looked across the room. "She found him. Anthony. She found him in the car. And that's what he did, you see. He didn't just kill himself, he killed her. And she was his favorite. Or had been once."

She went to the garage for her bike. And smelled the exhaust fumes, and went out and turned off the motor, and saw him. But she didn't cry out. She didn't come running back into the house for me. She was only twelve, after all. But she didn't. She came back in and started towards her room, stopped just outside it and sniffed. Stood there sniffing. I was in my room, combing my hair, but I heard it. And recognized it.

I'd heard her sniffing like that once before. It was a few years earlier, the younger kids were away at summer camp, and I was sleeping late. A noise woke me, a slight noise. That happens to mothers, I think. I remember waking up in the middle of the night when Elf was a baby. Elspeth, I mean. I called her little Elf. Learned my lesson. Never called Sydney or Tony *little* anything after that. Anyway, I'd wake up because the room seemed too still. Elf slept in a cradle beside my bed, and usually I was aware of her breathing. But sometimes her breath would get so soft I couldn't hear it. Sometimes I couldn't tell even laying my ear next to her face, and I'd have to wake her up. To make sure. Anyway, what I heard was sniffing, and I jumped up because I knew something was wrong. I ran to the hall bathroom, where the noise was, if you can call it a noise. And Elspeth was there, running cold water over her hand and she was sniffing.

She blinked when I entered and said, "Mommy? I didn't want to wake you up."

"What is it, darling? What's wrong?"

"I burned my hand."

It was terribly red, and covered half her hand.

She had wanted sausages for breakfast and had cooked them as I'd taught her, so that most of the fat drained off. When they were done, she, being a good little girl, had poured the fat off into a can I keep in

342

the refrigerator. The can was nearly full and the sausage grease filled it, so she picked it up to return to the refrigerator, where the fat would harden so I could throw it away. But the can was hot from the hot fat, and her hand shook and the boiling hot fat spilled over the edge, burning her hand.

Elf was a good girl, a very good girl. She didn't even spill the fat on the floor, or drop the can and scream. She set the can down carefully on the counter top and, her hand screaming with the burn, went quietly to the bathroom to run cold water on her hand. The only sign that she wanted me was that she went to the bathroom to do that. My room was near it. She could have done that in the kitchen. And as she ran water over her hand, she sniffed.

I'll never forget that sound, it lives, inside my head. Because the whole thing worried me so much. Oh, not the burn. We raced to the hospital emergency room and they made her wait forty-five minutes, I was fuming, but in time they took care of it and it stopped hurting in a couple of days, and it healed fine. No, it wasn't that.

It was Elspeth I was worried about. She was such a good girl. It seemed unnatural to me. Docile and sweet and helpful and obedient. I was frightened for her, I wondered how she was going to get through life being so goddamned *good*. I felt she would be destroyed if she went on being like that. And I wondered why she was. Why she was worried me as much as the other. I wanted to pick her up and put her back inside my body, to keep her safe.

So, that's what I heard this day too. Sniffing. Although Elf had changed in the intervening years, she'd become a sullen adolescent, not quite such an Elsie Dinsmore angel. She sulked, she talked back, she forgot to do what she was told, she purposely neglected things sometimes. In other words, she'd become normal.

But the day Anthony moved out, she had instantly reverted to the good girl. It was eerie. Since Anthony had been gone, she was an angel except when he came over for dinner, or to take the kids to lunch on Saturdays. Then she sulked, she made flip nasty cracks, usually to me.

And here she was sniffing again. I put down my comb, I raced out of the room, and there she was, standing in the hall. She was skinny, wearing jeans. Her red-gold hair hung straight down her back, and her eyes were wide open and almost periwinkle. She was standing there looking as if she saw nothing. And sniffing.

I went to her and took her hands. They were small and limp in my hands. "Elf, sweetheart, what is it?"

Sniff.

"Elspeth?"

"Don't go into the garage, Mommy."

I thought perhaps she'd seen a rat. There was a pond near us, and sometimes water rats would come up into the garage. But no. It couldn't be anything like that. My hands were beginning to get as cold as hers.

"Why, sweetheart?"

"Daddy's in the garage, Mommy," she quavered and her mouth trembled and tears began to ooze into her eyes, but she did not cry. She stood very still.

And I stood still too, because I knew. Not how he'd done it, I pictured him lying on the garage floor with a bullet hole in his temple, although I should have realized he'd choose an easier way. And I could feel my face changing even as I stood there, feel my mouth curling down the way it still does, carving a bitter line around it, a line that would never leave.

"Not true. You don't have a bitter line around your mouth."

"*I* can see it. Just as I can see the scratch marks on your face."

"I have no scratch marks on my face," he smiled at her.

"Well," she sighed, "if you can't *see* . . ."

"Go on."

I stood there petrified, turned into a pillar of something. But I felt hate more than grief. He'd have to know the chances were they'd find him. They were up and out before me, always. They always rode their bikes, which were kept in the garage. And suddenly all the anger I'd felt for him over all the years, all the fury I felt about his tormenting of Tony, his treatment of the girls, his jealousy and possessiveness, his treatment of me—all of it congealed, it hardened and grew larger. It turned into something that was larger than I was, that was maybe even universal. He was going to destroy them in any way he could because that would destroy me. My god! how much can you hate! He didn't care where his napalm fell, who it destroyed, even his own children, as long as some of it splattered me! Like Roger Jenkins and Mary.

We stood there, the two of us, Elspeth and I, looking at nothing. And Sydney and Tony came tearing down the hall from the kitchen, they were yelling, they were white-faced and their mouths were like broken saucers. I went with them, they were pulling on my hands, yelling, pointing, telling me to call a doctor, and I looked down at his dead body and I wanted to pick up an ax and chop it into tiny pieces, I've never felt hate like that, before or since.

Elspeth stayed in the hall. When I came back to phone the police, she was in her room with the door shut. I went in later, when I could. She was lying on the bed, staring. She turned her face away from me, she didn't want to see me or talk to me.

I don't think she ever cried.

4

ANTHONY ALWAYS liked Elf. When she was a baby, he even played with her once in a while. His way of playing was to lift her up and swing her in the air and down again. He did this until, one Sunday in May, he threw his back out and had to lie flat for days afterwards. He never swung her up again. After that, he didn't pay much attention to her unless he was taking photographs. He loved to photograph her, well, she was beautiful, always. When Tony was born, and later, Sydney, he still photographed only Elspeth. If the other children are in the picture, they're on the fringes, the way he'd been once, too. And Tony has that same sad little face Anthony had had. Anthony took movies, and it's only accidental that Tony or Syd ever make their way onto the screen. It's all Elspeth. But he stopped taking pictures at some point, and I never did it either, so I have no pictures of Elspeth after about age eleven.

I didn't realize how *tolerant* Anthony was of Elspeth until Tony was walking around. And then I saw how she had been able to do things, to toddle around touching things, putting things in her mouth, bang on tables, cry, demand, refuse to eat something: whereas Tony caught hell for all of that. Tony caught hell for everything and anything. The only time Anthony scolded Elspeth was at the dinner table, especially on holidays, and then he yelled at both of them, sent both of them to their rooms. It was just general disapproval.

On the other hand, all Anthony's attention was focused on Tony, after he was born. He paid no attention whatever to Syd. And that meant of course that all his *anxieties* were focused on Tony, but also that he *cared* about Tony in a way he didn't care about the girls. He largely ignored them, although once in a while they got swept up in one of his purple fits too.

We'd been married about ten years when I gradually realized that there was something wrong with Anthony, something beyond mere bad temper. It was then I began to have my first thoughts of divorce. Tony was eight then, and I could see that Anthony was getting worse year by year, that he'd make Tony's adolescence a pure hell. And Anthony wasn't making me very happy either. But I only thought about divorce, I wasn't ready to act on it. I still thought, idiot that I was, that if we kept *talking*, if I could make him see, that things could improve. And it was around that time that things began to happen. For one thing, I began to teach, which meant that Anthony didn't know where I was every minute of the day, and that made him extremely anxious.

And, in anticipation of my salary, Anthony bought himself a sports car. We couldn't really afford it, and I resented it, and it left us broke for two years, which enormously increased Anthony's bad temper.

And then his father died. Anthony was calm all through it, through his father's illness, through the death and the funeral. Except for one thing. He insisted the doctor who attended Aldrich was responsible for his death. The doctor was an old-fashioned man, very kind, and he didn't keep Aldrich in the hospital after he recovered from his coronary. He let him stay at home, because he thought Aldrich would be happier at home, would be more relaxed at home and would recover more quickly. So Aldrich was at home when his heart failed, and he died before the ambulance could arrive. He died, in fact, instantly, but Anthony thought he might have been saved. So he went around shouting about the irresponsible doctor, and kept threatening to go round and punch him out. But after a couple of weeks, he calmed down.

And then—all this occupied a couple of years— Elspeth began to menstruate. She was young, only eleven; she developed early. I made a bit of a to-do over her menstruation: I had a puberty party for her and invited the family. Jessie was horrified, but she said nothing. By then she was living with us, and Anthony was grimmer than ever. He'd leave the dining room as soon as dinner was over. He didn't want to talk to his mother. Anyway, I wanted Elf to have a positive feeling about her body, about womanhood, and in the early years, that seemed to happen. She never had cramps, or anything like that.

Anthony said nothing about all of this, but he acted different. Normally, it takes a long time before you can perceive a pattern, realize that something is recurring or something has vanished. But this change of his was so striking that I noticed it immediately. Overnight, literally, Anthony stopped picking on Tony and started in on Elspeth. I remember that day Tony spilled some soda on the tablecloth—he was *always* spilling something, understandably—and I tightened my stomach, preparing for Anthony's blast, and he said nothing, nothing at all. But ten minutes later he was blasting Elspeth for spilling some salt.

It was astonishing, and it continued. From the day of that puberty party until he left the house, Anthony tormented Elspeth and left Tony fairly much alone. He was even nice to him sometimes. I pointed it out to him, he said I was crazy. His answer to everything. I mentioned that Laura had died at eleven and he said I was crazy. I pointed out that now Elspeth was one of *us,* a woman, and he couldn't bear that. He said I was crazy.

Anyway, things combined: money troubles, his mother's presence, my being away from the house so much, Elspeth. . . . He seemed to be furious all the time. You'd think he couldn't keep it up, that he'd crack, but he never did. His rages simply escalated more and more. I don't know where his breaking point was. His face came to seem continually purple. We'd have knock-down, drag-out battles night after night, every time we went anywhere he'd come home in a jealous rage. And the weekends were hell.

But of course Elspeth didn't understand what pressures were on him, or the ghosts he carried. She loved Anthony the way children automatically love the people who live with them, who help them tie their shoelaces or tell the time, who pick up the spoons the babies fling from their high-chair trays. The kind of love that is never really erased, no matter what happens later. The kind of love you don't have to do anything to earn, that is simply given. Even if you are abusive, even if you're cruel, your children go on loving you. That's when they get sick—when they love and hate you equally intensely. Even when abused children grow up and run away from home, they look back with a passionate hatred that is so strong because it's informed with love, that childish unremovable love.

It is the profoundest thing on earth, I think, that love. Despite all the years of torment, Tony loved Anthony, and so did Sydney, despite all the years of indifference. And they loved him in the same way, to the same degree, that they loved me, despite our very different behavior. Syd and Tony tell me now that when they look back, they find it hard to differentiate between Anthony and me. They don't remember one of us a tormentor, the other as the shield. They remember torment and they remember love, but not where either came from. And in a way, perhaps they even loved Anthony more. He was mysterious, withholding so much from them; he was superior, a judge.

But of all of them, Elspeth had been the one with a special relation to Anthony. She knew she could walk up to him as he sat reading his paper and he'd smile. She knew that if she came running in with something wonderful to show—a pebble, a seashell, a hair ribbon —that he'd smile and say *isn't that pretty*. He wouldn't instantly begin to scold or shout, the way he would to Tony—who therefore never went running up with anything.

Elspeth could *trust* him, in some ways. When the children's dog was run over and killed by a garbage truck one day, Anthony insisted he be the one to tell Elspeth. He said she would be able to take it better from him, and I think he was right. She cried "Oh, Daddy!" and threw herself sobbing into his arms. She never threw herself into *my* arms.

Well, then, here was this man who had seemed to love her, suddenly, unexpectedly shouting at her, screaming at her because she'd come to the table with dirty fingernails, had let her elbow rest momentarily on the table, forgot to put her bike away, dallied with her peas, hadn't cleaned her room, was a lazy slob, yes, he even began to call her names, the same names he called me—she was a slut, a bitch. I don't think he ever called *her* whore.

It was so blatant, I don't know how Anthony could not see what he was doing. But no matter what I said, no matter how angry I got, he saw nothing and he continued. I was crazy, was all.

Anthony would be sitting in the family room watching television on a Saturday around noontime, when he'd spot Elf sidling past on her way to her room.

"Elspeth!" Man leaps to his feet, throws newspaper aside. "You come back here!"

Halfway to her room, she pauses, turns reluctantly, looks at him with impassive face.

349

"Now you go to your room, young lady, and don't you come out for the rest of the day. You'll go to bed without supper and no TV tonight!"

Tears. "But, Daddy! . . ."

"Don't *but Daddy* me! Get in there!"

Rising hysterics. "But, Daddy, the kids are all going to the movies this afternoon. It's *Goldfinger!* Daddy!"

"I don't care if it's the man in the moon!"

"Anthony, what did she do?"

Whirls around. "I told her this morning to clean out the cat box and she still hasn't done it! She wanted the goddamned cat, you told her she had to take care of it, and I've been walking around this house the whole fucking morning smelling cat shit!"

"Elspeth, clean out the cat box."

Darts past us, heading for the kitchen.

"It's too late! She didn't do it when she was told! She has to learn, what does she think this is, some nigger shanty?"

"Anthony!"

Stands, hands on hips, watching her, waiting for a mistake, waiting to pounce if she should spill a drop of the litter.

"Anthony, she's a good kid. She forgot."

"Honey, don't do this. Forgot, my ass! She defies me, the little bitch!"

"YOU MAY NOT TALK ABOUT HER THAT WAY! YOU MAY NOT!"

"I'LL TALK ABOUT HER ANY DAMNED WAY I PLEASE!"

It would go on from there: rage from me, rage from him, screaming, slammed doors.

He stormed out of the house and went outside to mow the lawn. He worked on the garden when he was furious. I knew that his threats were bluster. All the years of threatened bed-without-supper and it had never happened. I wouldn't let it. All the years of no cookies, no candy, when he himself forgot ten minutes later, and who was going to enforce it? I used to thank god Anthony was not a mother. And the children had to know that too, after all these years. They did know it, I assume, but they never *acted* as if they knew it. I don't know (Dolores's throat clogged up), maybe they didn't want to know it. . . .

Because after she'd finished her chore, I went to her and put my arms around her and I said: "That's nice and clean now, honey. I think it would be okay if you went to the movies."

And Elspeth stares at me sullenly, resentful eyes, slumps off to her room and slams the door. Later I overhear her on my bedroom phone: "No, I can't go, my father won't let me."

I go outdoors and speak to Anthony, I urge him to tell her she can go. Tell her what you want, I don't give a damn, he says, and goes on mowing.

I go back to Elspeth and tell her Daddy doesn't mind if she goes. I tell her: "Daddy has a sudden temper, but he doesn't mean half of what he says. He's forgotten all about it by now, you might as well have fun, go ahead. Call Nancy back and say you're going."

Sullen resentful eyes, glares at me, storms off into her room.

Doesn't come to the dinner table. I call her three times, and finally have to go to her room and fetch her. Anthony ignores her until it's time for dessert, it's lemon meringue pie, her favorite. Suddenly he notices that her nails are dirty, that she is a scandal, a shame, a disgusting creature, that's probably cat shit under her nails, she is to go to the bathroom immediately and brush her nails and then go to her room and stay there. She jumps up, near tears, runs into her room, and slams the door.

I am near tears myself. I slaved over that pie, mostly for her, because she'd lost out on going to the movies with her friends. I pick it up, I can't stand another minute of him, I throw the pie at Anthony.

After the shock, after he has cleaned himself up, he laughs. I am moaning, I am crying, I can't stand anymore. Tony and Sydney are walking around with big eyes. *They* missed out on dessert too, and their mother is crazy.

Later, I go into Elspeth's room. I sit on her bed and try to talk to her. She is lying on her stomach, her soft pink child's cheek against the pillow. She is not crying. But when I enter, she looks at me with

351

hate, and when I try to talk to her, she turns her face away.

"Just leave me alone," she says in a cold, adult voice.

5

NOTHING IS ever simple, single. I know that now but I knew that then too. Elspeth had been such a good little girl, as I told you, that I was worried for her. But when Anthony began to hurl his thunder at *her,* she became sullen and sulky and resentful—the way you expect an eleven-year-old to be. But I couldn't stand it, I simply couldn't stand it. So I began to interfere between them the way I'd always interfered between Anthony and Tony. I felt I had to. Anthony had no restraint. I saw that the day he was smacking Tony on the behind for not shutting a drawer. He'd done that before, when Tony had left his wagon outside and Anthony wanted him to put it in the garage. He never knew when to stop. He never stopped. I feared for my children. And so I interfered. But that came to be the pattern: his thunder, my interference, thunderbolt delivered but no harm done. What I mean is, over the years I became Anthony's restraint. Which meant I had to be there, all the time. And it also meant that I made it impossible for him to have a direct relationship with his children.

But maybe my motives weren't as selfless as I thought. Maybe I resented their love for him and wanted to come between that too. And maybe Elspeth knew that and hated me for it. Maybe she wanted it, their relationship, no matter what it was. Maybe she wanted to live it out with him, horrible as it was. Horrible, but passionate, on both sides. And although this sounds mad, maybe in some ways Anthony was a better parent than I was. His behavior left him no option but to get angry with him, to talk back, to sneak around . . . which is supposed to be normal, isn't it? Whereas my loving restraint perhaps left them incapable of anything but sweet docility. Because when I was alone with them, they were sweet and docile children. I didn't ask much of them, but what I asked, they did.

"I don't know. I'll never know." Her voice dwindled away. "But that day, the day Anthony wouldn't let Elf go to the movies, was the day I decided I had to get away from him. He was killing me, killing some part of me. I hated him so much my stomach was sick all the time. And I hated myself for staying with him.

"The following week I called around, spoke to friends who had lawyers, got a name. Couldn't find a woman lawyer, no one knew one. I went to see him, he was a slimy creep. All he really wanted to know was whether I'd been screwing around, and whether I'd screw around with him. But he had a reputation for being strong in divorce cases, and I thought I'd need that. I didn't put it past Anthony to threaten my lawyer.

"I wanted child support from Anthony: my salary was so small, I couldn't have supported all of us on it. But that was all I wanted, and I wanted to leave him enough to live on decently, so I asked for the minimum. But the lawyer insisted I had to ask for alimony, that it was essential. I said I worked, what did I need with alimony? That besides, I didn't want to need Anthony that much, I wanted to keep our communications to a minimum.

" 'Suppose you can't work,' he said. 'Suppose you break your leg? I won't take your case unless you ask for alimony,' he said.

"I went home to think it over. There was no way Anthony could have known what I was doing. But that weekend, Anthony broke *his* leg."

Elspeth was still, frighteningly still, in the madhouse that followed Anthony's suicide. She was the angel child most of the time, but she spent a lot of time alone in her room. She treated the younger children—and remember, Tony was only a year younger, it isn't as if she were a really older sister—as if she were a substitute mother: she was sweet and kind and loving and helpful and all those things we teach children, or girls, anyway, that they're supposed to be.

The funeral was terrible, because Jessie blamed me for everything. She'd moved out of our house when Anthony had. She should have known how things were, god knows she heard the fights. But she couldn't forgive me for abandoning him, not associating it with the fact that the real abandonment had happened years ago, and was hers. She even seemed to turn against the children. I think that was because they stayed so close to me, they were like—bodyguards, really. They gathered around me as if to protect me, and the four of us became a single unit, solid. It was the four of us against the world, somehow. Tight.

We had some major decisions to make. I couldn't keep the house in Newton on one salary, we had to move somewhere. I was really broke, because Anthony's life insurance had a suicide clause and paid nothing when he died. I had to pay for his burial out of my savings. It nearly wiped me out.

We had to cut back on everything just to get by on my salary. It was rough, but even so we had a good year. The kids didn't have soda or cookies or potato chips, but they had some freedom. They could jump and laugh and squabble. Sometimes Tony and Sydney got too noisy or too angry and had to be yelled at to simmer down. They acted like children. But Elspeth didn't. She acted like an angel. I'd come in from marketing and find her ironing.

"Oh, sweetheart, that's very nice, but you know the sheets don't really have to be ironed."

"But you like 'em ironed, don't you, Mommy?"

"Yes. But I'd rather have you out with your friends than have ironed sheets."

"It's okay. I like to do it, Mommy."

Sometimes I felt like someone covered with honey: I kept expecting the ants.

Once in a while I'd go out with someone—men my age, or older. But they were a problem. I don't know what it is, but men walk into the house of a woman with children and immediately start bossing the children around. As if they had a right! As if they assume that any house without a man in it is in dire need of a strong controlling hand. Their presumption outraged me. Whenever this happened, the kids and I would exchange looks. The kids would just ignore the man, whoever he was. They knew they'd never see *him* around the house again. They were right.

But during the summer, I met a young man, Jack Napoli, who was interning at Mass General. He was a friend of one of my former students, who had a party and invited me. Jack was much younger than I, but we became friendly, became lovers very quickly. Jack was a blend of sweetness and ferocity, but what I liked most about him was his intelligence, it came through his eyes like light from inside. He had little free time and no money at all, so we usually stayed at home. This was fine with me because I didn't want to start leaving the children alone too often, I wanted to give them a sense of stability, of *home*. We sat around the house and read and played games together and ate a lot and sometimes we'd stand around the piano and sing. We had fun. He was fine with the kids, because he was only twenty-six, and he acted more like a brother to them than a father.

The kids liked him, although Tony resented him sometimes, I think. But he liked him more. Sydney adored him, just as if he had been a big brother. But Elspeth was in love with him. I'd feel really sentimental when the five of us would sit at the table eating breakfast or dinner, and talk and laugh. That was something my kids had never had before, something I'd thought really important. Really. It was, until his suicide, the thing I most hated about Anthony, his denial to the kids of happy eating talking laughing— that sort of thing. It's what I mean by *home*.

When Jack wasn't around, we were happy too— relaxed, easy. Tony became more outgoing, he found new friends. Sydney became more—grown-up, I guess, responsible. Many nights after dinner, Elf and I would sit together at the dinner table, ignoring the dirty dishes, talking. She was twelve now, trying to learn how to be an adult. She asked probing questions and I answered them. Honestly. We talked about sex, love, religion, popularity, bodies: everything a teenager cares about. But she never mentioned Anthony. Never.

Weekends, the children and I would spend hours driving around the towns and villages in a radius around The Swamp, where I was teaching then, to look for a place we'd like to live. The place that excited them, and that I love too, was Cambridge. Eventually, we bought a little house on the borders of the slums, and we fixed it up ourselves, all working together. It was an old place, all we could afford in that town, somewhat broken down. But we had fun working in it, plastering, sanding, scraping, painting. We put up bookshelves and hung plants, we rented a machine and scraped the wood floors. We were a family, for the first time, and we were enjoying it.

We moved at the end of the summer the year Elspeth turned thirteen. And the ants arrived.

Cambridge isn't very far from Newton in space, but miles away in culture, and my children had their first taste of culture shock. Newton is a nice suburban town with good schools and privileged youngsters and considerable social order of the white respectable variety. Cambridge is racially and economically mixed. Around Harvard and MIT there are well-to-do youngsters buying an apple for a quarter at Nini's, eating at ethnic restaurants, shopping at the expensive clothes stores around Holyoke Center. Where we lived, it was blue-collar, Irish, Italian, and some blacks, largely Catholic, and very rough. I hadn't been worried about this at all because the same thing happened to me when my mother left my father. We had been living in the suburbs, but we moved to a rough neighborhood near Boston after the divorce. And I'd loved that neighborhood, it had seemed alive to me, and I'd learned a lot from living there. I just assumed things would be the same for my kids.

And maybe they would have been, except for the time—it was the late sixties when we moved, 1968 to be exact. The school was torn by racial strife, late-sixties rhetoric, even bomb scares. And riddled with drugs of all sorts. The bigotry of the school administration served to legitimate attacks on blacks by white kids, and it was difficult not to take sides. Within a week of starting school, Elspeth had changed. She'd given up the good girl, she found a group of friends, she was out all the time. Within a month, she was a different person, and I no longer knew her.

She fell in with a group of youngsters I liked very much—they were racially mixed, smart, and had a kind of gentleness in their hearts. But they were also unhappy and protesting and used drugs. And their protest took other forms—they skipped school, they shoplifted, and they did dope and uppers and all the rest.

Elspeth's closest friend was a girl named Selene, a gorgeous girl with Asiatic blood who had been to school in Switzerland and England, had moved around the world with her professor father. She was very intelligent but extremely wary of adults. She looked at me always as if she were listening not to what I was saying but to what posture I was taking, as if she were preparing a posture that could encompass mine, could manipulate it. But I was never saying anything important to her, just asking about school or the movie or whatever they'd been doing. But I think she thought I was always checking up on where they'd been.

Because there was some reason to. Elspeth had stopped, completely, helping around the house. She refused even to clean her room, and one weekend when I couldn't stand it anymore, I went in to clean it myself. And I found . . . things. Stuffed under the bed, in the back of her closet, stuck in bureau drawers: things she couldn't use, and couldn't afford. Tens of packages of pantihose, packaged bras in sizes she couldn't wear, lipsticks, blushers, mascara still in the plastic wrap, and magazines, tens of them, the glossy ones like *Vogue* that Els couldn't afford on her two-dollar allowance. Except for the magazines, only a package of pantihose had been opened. Opened, and the hose stuffed back in the wrapping, because they were extra-longs, a size Els couldn't use.

I talked to Elspeth, of course. She didn't deny the shoplifting, but she would not promise to stop. She shrugged when I told her the trouble she could get into. It was fun, she said, and Selene had been doing

357

it for years and had never been caught. You would not get caught if you were clever, she said.

It was obvious she wasn't stealing things to use them, in fact her appropriation of the unusable seemed almost intentional. That way, perhaps she worked it out, she wasn't *stealing* but going through a puberty rite that involved danger and risk. She listened to me wide-eyed when I warned her about it, but her face didn't change. She was beginning to be as bland-faced as Selene.

Also, she was doing poorly in school. Els had a 150 IQ, there was no reason for her to be failing, but she was. Her highest grade was in the seventies on her end-of-term report card, and some were in the thirties and forties. Again, we had a talk. Again, I encountered no opposition, but no acceptance. I told her she would someday want to go to college, would want to go to a good college, but would not be able to get in because of what she was doing now. She looked at me.

In the spring, she was expelled from school, but didn't tell me about it for a week. Her friend Connie had called the school pretending to be her father, trying to get her reinstated, but the school did not believe he was who he said he was. It was Connie—Constantine—who finally convinced her she should tell me. Why did she conceal it? Did she think I would beat her? I never had, I'd rarely even raised my voice. I'd been disapproving and firm and most of all, worried, but I'd never struck her.

I asked her. She didn't know, she said. And I believed her. I didn't think she knew what she was doing in those years. I went down to school. Elspeth had said "Jesus!" out loud in gym class and the teacher had overheard it. That was the reason for the expulsion. Els had to apologize and I had to be present before they'd allow her to return to school. The gym teacher, Miss Fahey, a red-haired woman in her fifties, lowered her voice as she explained her actions to me. There were two black girls in the corner of her office, and she nodded towards them slightly. "We expect that sort of language from *some* people," she said, "but not from *nice* girls like Elspeth." Elspeth stared at her with cold hate, said the required "I'm sorry" like an automaton, then turned on her heel and left the room.

That summer, I took the children and went to stay at my mother's house on the Cape. I felt I had to get Els away from the environment that was making her destroy herself. She was listless all summer, but she got in no trouble. She read a lot. She wrote to Connie every day, and at the end of the summer, showed me the stack of letters she'd received from him. "See, you couldn't break us up after all," she said with angry challenge on her face.

"What?"

"Connie and me. I know that's why you brought me out here."

"Els, Connie has dinner at our house at least twice a week. Why would you think I was trying to break you up?"

"You wouldn't let Connie come out here."

"You know why."

My mother was terrified of black men, and would have gone into hysterics if Connie had merely visited. Even though Con was only a boy. She had no bad feelings about women and children of any color, only the men.

"So?" Els said archly. "It comes to the same thing, doesn't it."

"If I wanted you to break up with Connie, I'd tell you so, Elspeth. You should know that."

She grimaced and stormed off.

We returned to Cambridge.

But Elspeth was still miserable. Over the summer, Connie had gotten involved with another girl, and although he remained her best friend, was no longer available all the time. This was, of course, my fault. She was over thirteen now, and began to go out at night, to dances. I gave her a deadline of 1:00 A.M., which she observed the first time, but not the second, and never again. The first time she stayed out late, it got to be three thirty and she still wasn't home and I was sick. I called Selene, who was home. Her parents were annoyed at the late call, and Selene said she didn't know where Els was, that she'd been home for hours, had left Els walking home. Oh, I went mad! I saw her raped and murdered lying under a bush somewhere. Jack was there that night and together we scoured the city, driving to the YMCA where the dance was held, driving down every street she might have taken to walk home from it.

We got back about four thirty. Elspeth was sitting in the kitchen. "Where were you!" I screamed, and I did scream then. Calmly, quietly, she said she'd been in the yard the whole time, making out. "With whom?" His name, she thought, was Walter. She thought.

I told her she could not go out again at night for a month. And she abided by that. Then. But the next time she went out, she stayed out late again. I went through the old routine: she was too young for this, she didn't know these boys, she didn't know what they might do, there were dangers, diseases, and besides, I was worried sick, my stomach was so bad I was drinking a quart of milk a day, I couldn't stand it.

She looked at me without batting an eyelash and said, "I don't see why I shouldn't have a sex life. You have Jack."

I knew Els had a crush on Jack. She was always more alive when he was there, giggling and caroling. She'd sit and talk to him for hours, listen to him as if he were telling her gospel whether they were talking about medicine or politics or god.

When she said that, I began to wonder, I began to watch, and I saw, within the next months, that she was always worst in her behavior when Jack was visiting. And I thought about breaking off with him. Not that he was doing anything to cause her behavior, but because she was acting as she was *for him,* or against me because of him. To prove she was adult, or to get even with me for having him. Something like that.

But I decided against it. In the first place, I loved him and loved his company. In the second place, I thought I could not allow Els to start dictating my behavior. Not that she consciously wanted me to break off. But if I had, then she would have felt free to call him herself. I felt if I did, for her, something I did not want to do, intensely did not want to do, I would be giving her a power too great for a child, and also that I would resent her, and find some way to take out my resentment. I didn't want to turn her into a dictator, the way Anthony had been.

For it was Anthony that Els reminded me of. Those beautiful violet eyes, so like his blue ones, gazing at me openly, seeming to listen, but paying no attention at all. And she was only a child, but I could control her no more than I'd been able to control him. I couldn't lock her in her room. I was terrified.

She was failing so badly that she had been put in remedial classes at school, which was, of course, ridiculous. I went down and talked to them, explained that she was having emotional problems, asked them to keep her in the advanced classes. They were nasty and unhelpful. She began to skip school more and more often. I didn't know this at the time, although I could have predicted it. Then she was expelled again.

A group of girls had been smoking in the girls' room and been caught. They were hauled to the principal, who asked which of them had been smoking. Only Elspeth held up her hand. Only Elspeth was expelled. Thus do we teach our children true values.

I liked her for that, but I didn't know how to tell her anything anymore. I didn't want to encourage her to get expelled, encourage her to smoke. I was, by now, rather beaten down. I sat down with her, I was tired, I told her she was ruining the future she would probably want. I ran through the whole thing. I pictured a variety of possible lives for her and asked her to choose one. She listened to me coolly, then said, "Are you through now, MOTHER?" Mother as she said it was a dirty word.

I was literally at my wits' end: I simply didn't know what to do. Jack said, "Beat her." That's the way he had been brought up, and he remained a little abject in the face of male authority, always. But I tell you I would have done it if I thought it would help. It wouldn't, of course. You can't just start beating a child at the age of fourteen. You have to train a child to fear; you have to get them young.

6

Dolores looked at Victor's face. It was intense, and the eyes had something strange in them: shock, it was. She was telling him a story from an alien world: these things didn't happen in nice middle-class white families. It didn't happen in families with proper father and mother, a two-parent household, as they said in the government surveys. No. The hell with him, she thought, but her heart hurt. It is so easy to look with distaste on the dirt and rust of another's life; so easy to blame others for their lives. While you shake yourself like a wet dog, spraying water all over the room, ridding yourself of the waters in which others drowned. Not me. Not me.

She turned away from him and continued calmly, inexorably.

Things got worse. I still waited up for her. One night she came home late, it was a Saturday, and I was ironing, waiting for her. She came into the kitchen and sat down and I looked at her and her eyes looked funny.

"What have you taken?"

"What do you mean?"

"You've taken something, I can see it." She said yes, she'd been smoking dope.

My heart sank. Things had been a little stable for a few weeks—as they occasionally were, always leading me to think that it was over, she had run it through her system, and was prepared to return to normality. What I thought of as normality. But always she found a way to try one new thing.

I was worried about pot because she was so young, because I knew that kids only a little older than she were on hard drugs and I thought that hanging out with kids who were on something could lead to getting on heroin.

I gave my usual understanding warning lecture, explaining perils and risks. She let me talk, but I was just dancing through a hoop for my own entertainment. Eventually she slammed out of the room and went to bed.

I could not control what she did. I worked, I had classes and office hours three days a week, and I'd been put on a demanding committee that took up another full day. That was my first year at Emmings, and I felt I had to prove myself.

But even if I'd been home, what could I do? Walk her to school and meet her at the school gate every afternoon? Even if I'd done that there was nothing to prevent her from leaving by the back door as soon as I left. She was out of my bodily control, and since my word had no authority with her, she was out of my control completely.

Which would have been all right had she been in her *own* control, but she wasn't.

Sometimes things were fine, sometimes we still had fun and sat around talking. Jack talked with her too. But nothing made any difference. I always laugh when I see another pious newspaper or magazine article by some psychologist or psychiatrist urging *communication*. Communication, hah! Now we'll all sit down and have a nice little talk and tell each other what we really feel and really *communicate* and then we'll work things out, we will build a good *relationship* so that we can have *fulfilling mature* lives! Christ!

And of course, in addition to Els, there were the other kids, who were now in high school or junior high, and who weren't acting so hot either. Tony had withdrawn inside himself, and sat in the house watching TV all the time when he wasn't in school. Sydney was still a child, but she was never home, never. She spent her afternoons at her girlfriends' houses, doing homework, she said. She ate there, she slept there, she came home only to change her clothes. I began to feel like some kind of monster, but why? I was always kind to the children, always concerned about them. But the problems with Els did have me utterly miserable, I probably littered depression around me like body odor. I probably neglected them, I certainly didn't pay much attention to them. I was falling apart.

It was just like Anthony, all over again. Sometimes I'd invite some friends over for an evening, and the kids would be there, I liked them to join us if they wanted to, and Els would come into the room, but then she'd sit there glaring at me from her corner, I could feel her hate crawling on my skin from across the room. Just the way Anthony used to when he was jealous. Or she'd come home high, and come into the room sort of silly and dazed, and curl up in a ball in a chair while around her people talked and laughed, and if I went to see how she was, her eyes would roll around in her head and she would barely answer me, she acted catatonic.

I took her to a clinic, which recommended a psychiatrist who specialized, they said, in adolescent disorders. She went once a week, dutifully, trotted over to Brookline, having to change twice, a long trip. He did nothing. I kept asking her about him because I could see no progress, but she didn't want to talk about him. She said she liked him, that was all. So I left her alone. He asked me to come and talk to him, once, and I went. He told me solemnly, the asshole, that the problem was that I did not communicate with her.

In fact, on those nights when she felt friendly towards me, or perhaps had some glimmering that she was living in a strange way, we would still talk. And then we'd talk all night, until five in the morning, and I'd have to go in and teach the next morning. I was probably stupid, I should probably have stuck to a strict regimen and not let her do that. But I was desperate, I grabbed any chance I was offered to reach her. Nothing, nothing in the world was more important than Elspeth in those years. Even my other children, because unhappy as they seemed, they were not heading for destruction, and she was.

She would say that she hated this materialistic, capitalistic culture. She didn't understand why we had big meals, we should just live on fruit and nuts. She couldn't abide pretensions and didn't care if she went to college. What she really loved was her black friends. They had the good way of life. They all loved each other and they spoke and acted with each other in a natural warm way that white people never did understand, certainly never showed. Easy, without pretense, pretension, snobbery; they weren't judgmental. Without trying to prove anything: they were all just niggers together. She wanted to live like that.

She wanted to screw Connie, and just drift through life with him. She didn't care about the other woman in his life. I told her about pregnancy, I said she was too young. She listened to me about that for a long time. But one night she told me she'd gone to bed with Connie, at least begun to, but his mother had walked in. Then I took her for birth control pills.

Oh, I suppose I was your classic permissive parent, suffering classic punishment. But after all, I'd been permissive all their lives. I'm not sure I would have been quite so liberal if I hadn't always had to offset Anthony's influence. If I'd been their only parent, I think I would have been a little less *on their side* in every situation. But you can't change a pattern you've developed over a decade or more. Nor did I really want to. I tried, with Elspeth, to become more and more firm, but it didn't matter what I did. If I was firm, she rebelled hostilely; if I was easy, she took advantage of my easiness. She had me beat no matter what I did, and she didn't seem to realize that I wasn't someone who *ought* to have been beat, that I was thinking of her, not of myself.

Well, it went on that way. It's amazing how life can just go on that way, how you can live with hell just around the corner and you know it, yet you live, day after day, and find something to smile about, something to make you laugh. Jack was there and listened to me with sweet patience, tried to cheer me up. Tony and Sydney were disgusted with Elspeth the way younger children are with a sibling whose behavior they don't understand, when they see—much more clearly than the problem child does—the anguish and suffering it is causing.

And through it all, I was working. That probably saved my sanity in those years. I worked well, maybe because it was such a relief to have my brain filled with something besides Elspeth. I published my first book, began research for the second. Teaching was fun, and besides it got me out of the house. This house had begun to feel like the house in Newton, filled with poisoned air, walls that reverberate with the same hell happening over and over and over. Voices hang in the hallways, a coffee cup left on a table reminds you of her and what she said and what she did. . . .

Elspeth began to grow very thin. She would drift past me, her beautiful big violet eyes empty and blank. Connie would come for dinner and she'd sit there silent, gazing at him, then she'd get up and sit in his lap. At least, until I forbade such behavior at the dinner table. She spoke little when he was around. She lost herself in him. That wasn't his fault, he was a sweet guy and bright, but not at all domineering. It was the way she felt—she wanted to lose herself in something, someone. In drugs, in love. She wanted oblivion.

She was fifteen, and had been suspended from school because of her continued failures. I didn't know it, though, she hadn't told me. She hung out around the streets, with the other kids like herself, most of them male, most of them black. She was on pills now, all sorts. She looked glazed most of the time. There was no point in lecturing her: her mind wasn't working.

One day she just didn't come home. I was frantic, I called all her friends, but no one knew where she was. I went to the school the next day, and that's how I found out she'd been suspended. I canceled all my classes, I scurried around Cambridge, I went to all the places I knew she sometimes went. I couldn't find her. That day I saw grey hairs in my head and thought that the old saw was true: your hair can turn grey overnight. Mine had.

She came home late the second day. She said she'd been lying down in the middle of Prospect Street waiting for a car to run over her. She was wild-eyed and very dirty. It could have been true. She had slept in an empty store she knew about, slept alone, on the floor.

I said: You see what you are doing to me. You see I am distraught, nearly crazy with worry about you. You say you don't care about your future, but don't you care about me? I don't know what to do, Elspeth, tell me what you want me to do.

She did care about me, I knew. Why else did she take all my things? She'd "borrow" odds and ends from me—a nail file, a blouse, a pair of gloves. Although she had perfectly fine things of her own that she never wore. She'd take mine and they'd disappear into the rat's nest under her bed or in the back of her closet. Sometimes I thought she was trying to steal me, to become me through theft.

Other times I thought she was trying to kill me, destroy me. That it was a real war and she was willing to die in it if that would kill me too. Like Anthony. But I thought that she'd win this one, because she was stronger than I was: she didn't care about either of us, and I did.

She began to stay out of the house overnight. She'd tell me where she'd been afterwards, but she never told me she wouldn't be coming home. Sometimes she'd be gone two days.

She came in one day when I was sick, bent double with my stomach, sick because she hadn't been home in two days, and I didn't know where she was. I yelled at her, ordered her to her room, told her she couldn't go out anymore. She said something nasty and flip, like, "What are you going to do, Mother, lock me up?" or something, and I reached out and slapped her, right across the face. "You stop that! You stop it!" she shrieked, and her eyes were terrified, little-girl terrified. She pulled away from me, she shrank into herself, she looked scared, like a child who's used to being beaten. I almost cried, but I sat down instead. I was exhausted. She ran into the bathroom and slammed the door.

A little later I went and opened the bathroom door. She was startled and guilty, she was swallowing something. I stood there in the doorway.

"Elspeth, what do you think I'd do if you died?"

Her eyes were large and scared. "I don't know."

"You think I'd die too, don't you. Well, I just want to tell you that I wouldn't. I'd grieve. I'd suffer. It would hurt me a lot. But I wouldn't die. So if you think you can destroy me by destroying yourself, forget it."

I walked away. She had stood there during my little speech, hunched over and scared looking, but she had said nothing. I thought maybe I'd hit a nerve, gotten through to her. But nothing changed. She was not at home very much. When she was, she wandered around the house. She'd pick up a magazine, study those deathly skinny models in their ridiculous makeup, then put it down. She'd play the piano, desultorily. She spent hours in front of a mirror, snipping off the dead split-ends of her hair. She seemed to me to be waiting for something, to be marking time. But I didn't know what she was waiting for, and I didn't think she did. She walked the way models walk on TV, floaty, as if they have no substance, no muscle, no bone, are simply air, leaves drifting, dust, sand, milkweed. . . .

One Saturday night when Jack was there, Elspeth was home and we had an argument about something. She was back in school, and I was trying to oversee her. But how can you be sure a child has done her homework when you don't know what her assignment is? We argued about homework, and she stalked off and went to her room. An hour later she came down and said I didn't have to worry about her anymore because she'd just swallowed half a bottle of aspirin.

I should have respected my intimations. I was fairly sure she hadn't taken half a bottle and my impulse was to say oh? and return to what I was doing. But because I was so angry with her so much of the time, I didn't trust my own impulses towards her. I said oh? and went to my room and shut the door and telephoned her shrink. He said to take her to the hospital and have them pump out her stomach. I said I thought it was a phony, and I should treat it as such. He grew very pompous, very threatening: he had been treating her, he said, and he had to warn me that he would not take the responsibility if I did not follow his instructions. As if I gave a goddamn whether he took responsibility or not. I was worried about her life, not blaming somebody. But he frightened me: I thought he knew more about her psychological condition than I did.

Jack and I drove her to the emergency room. They didn't pump her stomach, thank god, they gave her something to make her throw up. I watched from an outer room. She looked so small, so frail sitting there in a short hospital gown, her long hair falling over her face, her body bent, thin as it was, a child's body, retching into a pan.

In fact she told me afterwards she'd taken only about five aspirin. The city sent a social worker around to the house a month later, and then again, some months after that, to talk to her, to talk to me. It was ridiculous. They were trying, of course, but why? They were using one well-meaning but utterly inexperienced recent graduate in social science, one pad and one pen to stem a flood, a volcano of emotion. As if turning what had happened into a statistic, a report to be filed in quintuplicate and later microfilmed and guarded in underground tombs full of paper and its shuffling guardians, could check or order or help or stem a flood of human misery, utter wretchedness.

Because there was no question that Elspeth was wretched. Why else would she do the things she did? But she would not admit that. She was fine, she said. If I wanted to worry about her, that was my business and she refused to be blamed for it. Because she was fine.

7

AND SO I gave her up.

I thought: she will not allow me to control her, but she does not control herself. She does not need to control herself because I give her the illusion of control. There is always a home, a bed, food, affection to come home to, no matter what she does. I still gave her money, what I could afford as an allowance. She was in school (I thought) but was doing no work. She stayed away from the house for a day or two at a time.

She drifted in one Saturday morning as I was grading blue books. She hadn't been home since Wednesday. Her hair was long and unwashed and uncombed and she had that floaty look that told me she'd been taking something. It was spring, coming up to her sixteenth birthday. She sauntered in and stood in the doorway. She wasn't worried about my scolding. I'd stopped: it was wasted effort.

She was wearing dirty torn jeans, scuffed boots, and an army jacket. I didn't know where she got most of her clothes. When I asked, she said she'd traded something of hers with someone else. Or that somebody had given her a jacket or a hat. It was probably true—she had hardly any of her own clothes left, lovely things I'd bought her for her birthday or Christmas. But for all I knew she might be stealing her clothes—they were selling that raggedy stuff in Cambridge in those days.

I turned around when she said hello. I told her to come in, to sit down, I wanted to talk to her. She sauntered in sighing, threw herself in a chair with her legs over the arm, lighted a cigarette and rolled her eyes up in her head: another lecture. "I thought you'd given up yelling, Mother," she said.

"I have, " I answered, sitting facing her. I was trembling but I kept myself very controlled. I was through crying for her in front of her.

I summed up the events of the past three years. She watched me with a face that said (but who knew what was going on underneath?) *and so what?* I summarized her possibilities for the future. There weren't many: finishing high school and going to work, quitting high school and going to work, or the remote possibility that she could bring her grades up and graduate decently and get into a college. I didn't mention those other possibilities, pregnancy, drug addiction, flipping out totally.

"I guess you know, Elspeth, that I could have you institutionalized."

She was jarred, she perked up. She hadn't realized I had one piece of power left over her. "For what!"

"For your behavior. It can be done."

"You mean for drugs. I am not a drug addict, MOTHER."

I can't tell you how she said that word, *Mother*. It was horrible to my ears.

"I can have you institutionalized, Elspeth. It doesn't

have to be for drugs. But I won't do that. It's terrible, and I won't do it."

She glared at me, but I could see she was relieved. She moved her little ass in the chair and wiggled her leg. She tamped out her cigarette and lighted another. She looked to heaven with a "when-is-this-woman-going-to-stop" look.

"What I am going to do is resign, Elspeth. I quit. I am not going to be *mother* anymore."

She looked at me with a contempt and amusement that were supposed to convey: you cannot take from me anything that I will more willingly part withal.

"I am not going to worry about you anymore, I'm not going to wait up nights. I'm not going to cook meals that you don't come home to eat, or lie to the school, or wash your clothes, or clean your room, or scold you or lecture you anymore. Nor am I going to support you anymore.

"You are on your own. You can go where you want, do what you want. But you can't come here, can't live here anymore unless you live by the rules of this house. That is, go to school, do your schoolwork, come in on time for meals, do your share in the house, keep yourself and your room decent, and sleep here at night.

"If you can't do these things, you'll have to find someplace else to live. That's it."

She'd stopped wiggling her legs awhile back, although she'd continued to blow smoke in great puffs towards the ceiling. When I finished, she yawned, loudly. She stood up. "Ummm. Well, me and Connie are going to California anyway." And sashayed to her room.

I sat there for a while, trembling so hard I was afraid to stand up. I knew that now I'd said it, I had to do it. Had to. Or she'd never respect me again. But you know it was ludicrous. Who ever heard of resigning as a mother? It's like resigning as a Jew, it can't be done.

I dragged myself up and went out into the hall. The bathroom door was closed and I heard the shower running. I went back to my desk and tried to return to correcting the exam I was reading, but the letters wiggled under my eyes. I was taut, tense. I knew I had to prepare for a long siege. She might figure I'd found finally the limits of her power, and agree to terms, but not keep them. It might be she'd go off somewhere, and who knows what would happen then? I sat there dying with the possibilities.

An hour or so later, Elspeth appeared in my doorway again. She said nothing, but I sensed her presence and turned. And gasped. She was a vision. Her face was pink and shiny and her hair was washed and combed and it was long and straight and red-gold and it shone. She was wearing a long white cotton dress that I'd bought her for her cousin's wedding the year before. Afterwards I had washed and ironed it and packed it away in lavender, knowing she wouldn't wear it. It was fresh and clean and smelled of lavender now. It had a round scoop neck and little sleeves and was trimmed with eyelet. She also had on a hat. I didn't recognize it at first, but then I remembered it. It was an old one of mine, a wide-brimmed straw hat with a dusty-rose velvet band and a trailer hanging down the back. She was dewy and lovely as a child in an illustration. Except her feet were bare.

When she saw me turn, she shifted her body, she leaned one hand against the doorframe, and put the other on her hip. Her mouth was set in the ugly chagrined line she wore when she was angry with me.

"I just wanted to tell you I'm leaving now. I'm going to pose for Peter, he thinks he can get photographs of me in a magazine. I won't be coming back, so you don't have to bother yourself with worrying about me anymore."

She removed her hand from the doorframe and let her arms hang down at her sides. She looked straight and slight and very young.

"And one more thing: I know what you're doing. You're getting rid of me the way you got rid of Daddy. It's very convenient, Mommy."

First time she'd called me Mommy in months.

"You seem to think I'm trying to kill *you*. Well, I just want to tell you you can't kill *me* the way you killed Daddy."

She whirled and disappeared.

I sat there feeling disembodied. I heard noises downstairs. I walked to my front window and looked down. There was a group of kids down there waiting for her. Her friends, I guess. These days her friends changed from day to day. Connie wasn't there. The kids looked pretty raunchy, but all kids looked raunchy in those days. They all wowed and heyed as she came out, and she turned in a circle for them, swinging out her skirt. She was grinning from ear to ear, a little-girl grin. She set off with them looking like a beautiful girl in a fashion ad, lifted off the earth as she runs to meet her lover, wearing immaculate white cotton and a straw hat, her bare feet symbols of her openness, her innocence.

She kept her word. She didn't come back. Two days later she had not returned. I was sick, I couldn't keep food on my stomach. But she'd been gone for two days at a time before this. She'd be back one of these days, because otherwise, how would she live? She'd be back shamefaced but stubborn-mouthed and try to bargain with me, set her own conditions, to save her face. And I'd let her set a few, to save her face.

Or else, or else, she wouldn't come back. She'd go off and try to make it on her own. And she was smart and tough in some ways and maybe she would, she could, I had to believe she could. I had said abide by the rules or I toss you out of the nest into the pool, you have to sink or swim on your own, and she'd said, I'll toss myself, thank you. She would swim. She had to.

Oh, I knew the tales of those who didn't. Seemed to be a lot of them in those years, kids who OD'd, kids who simply vanished into the great mob of street folk and had never been heard from again. One child was found murdered, thrown from a building in the village. One child had become infected from a dirty needle and had lost several of his fingers. I pushed those stories away.

I gave myself reasons to hope. The clean hair, the fresh dress, the happiness of that grin. Peter, photographs for a magazine; that sounded substantial, something to hold on to.

Four days, and she had not returned. I thought of calling Connie, Starr, Peter, or the other friends I knew. But I didn't. I had said she was on her own, and I meant it.

"Oh, god!" Dolores cried softly, and began to sob. Her fingers were grabbing her hair as if they would pull it out. She was crying in retching sobs that seemed to come from the bottom of her body. Victor watched her, his face covered with scratches. Her head was down, her body hunched, she looked like an etching of a penitent in an eighteenth-century prison.

He rose, taking their glasses, and in a while she calmed down and blew her nose. He handed her a fresh brandy and a new cigar. She sipped the brandy, she laughed a little, shakily.

"I think booze and tobacco are your answers to pain."

"You know any better ones?"

"Valium?"

"Much worse."

She sat back. She smiled, ghostly, like the specter of someone long dead who has returned to bring a message from the beyond. From the dim small room that was her pain, she gazed out at him. The shock on his face had deepened into horror, but he wasn't separating himself from her anymore. He was experiencing with her, not putting her into her niche: failure as a mother.

He leaned towards her, his face covered with cuts. He took her hand. "Go on," he said.

I sat there trying to grade blue books. I went to class and walked through the halls amazed at my body, that carried me, and my mind, that sent out words through my mouth. I lectured, I advised, I went home and smoked. And smoked. My stomach was in terrible shape.

I'd sit there . . . well it wasn't exactly *thinking* . . . or *feeling*. It was some of both, but neither, exactly. I had this sense . . . as if life was this huge thing like a balloon, and it swelled and shrank, it changed its shape, and as soon as I'd made out what it was, it became something else. And it was *my* life, my balloon, but I'd lost hold of the string, and I was running, chasing it, the string was just a little above my hand but I couldn't grasp it. It was floating higher and higher, and it was turning huger and ugly, malformed, and I was earthbound, chasing it, yelling to it, but nothing did any good. It floated higher and higher and I called out: "Elspeth! Elspeth!"

Other kids have left home at sixteen and survived, I told myself. Survived fine, did somersaults and got battered and ran and ducked and parried. But survived. Kids have been doing this for hundreds of years, I told myself. Who knows, maybe for millions of years. So I don't hear from her for a week, for two weeks. For a month, maybe. Maybe even a year. But someday the phone will ring and I'll pick it up and there will be her sweet voice, my girl on the other end, my baby saying, "Mommy?" Or there will be a knock on the door and she'll be standing there in torn dirty jeans with a shamefaced wry smile, saying, "Mommy? Can I come home?" And I'll grab her, I'll hold her in my arms the way I used to, I'll cry, she'll cry and we'll start all over, but better.

Jack had that weekend off and he came roaring in. He knew how things were, I'd spoken to him on the phone, but he was young and didn't know any better. He always thought that noise and heartiness could cure all ills, could make you forget. . . .

He said he had some money and wanted to take me to dinner. I don't know where he got it, maybe he borrowed it. He was trying to cheer me up, I knew. So I let him, because it is cruel to refuse a gift.

We went to a cheap little Italian place near my house and ate lasagna. I threw up in the toilet but didn't tell him. We went to a movie, but I never saw it. When we came out, he was talking fast and hard, laughing, trying to fill up the void with noise and energy. I watched him, I felt a thousand miles away. I felt tender towards him because he was trying so hard to make me feel better, and angry because he was so callow that he couldn't understand how I felt, didn't see that silence was all that was possible for me then.

He wanted a drink and I wanted coffee. I wanted to go home, but he insisted we stay out awhile longer, so we went to a Cambridge cellar that serves both espresso and whiskey, and sat there for a while. I ended up having to pay, he'd run out of money. Which I resented: money was tight for me, and I hate to pay for liquor in bars. We could have had espresso and whiskey at home. But I said nothing. He was trying so damned hard.

So we got home late.

Late.

That's the way it was.

I suppose one always says *if if if*.

He pulled into the driveway and started to laugh. "Dolores, you really *are* getting to be an absentminded professor," he said. He was still laughing when he got out of the car and lifted the garage door. He must have seen or heard or smelled something. I hadn't until he lifted the door. But the minute he lifted the door, I knew.

I got out of the car and walked around to the front of it, watching him, waiting. He turned around to look at me, still laughing and shaking his head. He put his handkerchief over his nose and mouth and opened my car door. I was a piece of wood. I was Niobe, Hecuba, Lot's wife. Because I knew.

I stood there, my body petrified pain, and I knew I would be free of pain soon because I would die and it would go away. Because I knew I could *not* die. My bones were already dying. I thought about Tony and Sydney and thought that it was all right, my mother would take care of them and they were nearly grown and they would be better off without me anyway.

It was all like a slow-motion movie—Jack turning and laughing, putting up his handkerchief, opening the car door, and then it seemed he jumped back, his arms seemed to fly in the air, I saw him from very far away, as if he was on a different planet and I was looking down because I was dead and living in space. Then he bent over, oh, so slowly it seemed, and he dragged her out of the car, she was a white flower in his arms and he carried her out of the garage and his face was a big hole and he was saying something, he was crying or yelling but I couldn't hear him.

He laid her on the grass and got on top of her and did artificial respiration on her and he yelled to me to call an ambulance and I ran inside and did but I knew, *my* heart had stopped so I knew, and I came out again watching him as he worked over her, tears streaming down his face, he wouldn't not know again, I thought, he wouldn't think next time that hearty cheer can beat life. No.

I was watching from far away, from my planet where I whirled for eternity cold and alone watching my baby, my child grow like a white flower into the grass. I was watching. He looked up at me after a while—the ambulance was slow—with eyes that said everything, asked everything: is this the way it is? is this what it means to be alive? will it always be this way?

He was a doctor, he had seen death, but not Elspeth, dead.

Her dress was soiled and torn and there was a patch of dirt on her nose, one on her cheek. She was dirty the way a baby gets dirty, from playing, from falling.

My baby
    had fallen
      down

"She couldn't swim," Dolores said thickly, her throat hot and swollen, her face wet. "And so she drowned. And so did I." She was sitting up starkly, staring at nothing with her wet face. She fell silent.

Victor sat with his head bowed, looking at the floor, hands clasped between his knees, silent, tears streaming down his face too.

IX

1

THE NEXT day Victor hauled Dolores, heavy and logy
as if she had been drunk the night before, out for
some exercise. While she was still sleeping, he made
sandwiches clumsily with his bandaged hand, and
packed them in a basket with a bottle of wine and one
of water. He rushed her through her morning coffee,
and early in the day they cycled out into the Oxford-
shire countryside.

It was a fine day, warm and blue, and all of Oxford
was blooming and green. Swathes of daffodils blew in
the wind; purple and yellow and red wild flowers dotted
the grass. The air was fresh and clean along the back
lanes where there was little traffic, and Victor, out of
shape after the winter, was puffing hard. Dolores
wanted to stop, but Victor said *No,* firmly, and they
rode on, along the river for another half hour, when
Dolores insisted and Victor gave in.

Each, of course, thinking of the other, each knowing
that. Victor believed that wearing Dolores out physically would somehow purge the emotional ordeal of
the night before; Dolores worried about Victor's cut,
and about his pink face, his puffing. They found a
broad grassy place under some trees with a view of the
Cherwell and settled there.

Victor's bandage was bloody; the cut had opened up
again.

"Idiotic idea to go bike-riding with a cut like this,
it's silly, that's all, I don't know where your common
sense is. . . ." She fussed on and he luxuriated in it.
She removed his bandage and poured their drinking
water on it, then hung it on a shrub branch to dry. It

fluttered like a long white flag, bloodstains not completely eradicated. She poured water over his cut, then ordered him, like a mother, not to use his hand for a while, to let it lie palm up, open.

He obeyed submissively, but grabbed her with the other arm and pulled her over to him and kissed her. She stayed there for a while, their faces playing together, then sighed and sat up.

"There's no way to keep you from doing damage, even with one hand, is there?"

"If this is damage, no."

She lumped her sweater into a ball and put it on the grass, then lay beside him, her head on the sweater. They were unspeaking, listening to the noises of silence, the twitching and scuttering and rasping, the long luxurious turnings of the leaves towards the moving sun, the sun that seemed to rise and fall.

"In a way it is damage," Dolores said after a long time.

"Damage I wouldn't have been without," he said.

"You know, my life has been . . . difficult. Agonizing, at times. Still, I've had so many wonderful moments. Idyllic moments, I guess you could call them. People I've met, places I've seen, things I've done. I've had more than my share of joy, beauty. And I wish, oh, it seems tragic to me that she missed out on all that, that she had only the agony, I can't bear the thought of that. . . ."

He turned on his side to face her. "Don't," he said gently. "Don't keep stabbing yourself."

"I'm all right," she said, and she did sound all right, just profoundly sad. "You see, it's all been bottled up in me all these years. I've never told anyone. Well, people know, of course—my mother, my friends, Jack. I didn't have to tell them much, they went through it with me. No one mentions Elspeth, ever. It's as though she never existed. Except the kids, once in a while, remembering her."

"Not even Jack?"

"Oh, we broke up long ago. We agreed to: we couldn't look at each other without seeing Elspeth's body. It was too depressing. We still write each other occasionally, usually at Christmas. He's a practicing physician now, in a small town in New Hampshire. We were good for each other for a while. That's all you can ask, I think."

He put his good hand over one of hers. "Did you ever find out what happened?"

"Not really. One thing I didn't tell you. Forgot it, I don't know why. Elspeth was always falling in love. She loved Connie and he was her best friend after Selene moved, maybe even before. But she wasn't *romantic* about him. She fell in love, romantically, with a new boy every couple of weeks. She'd come home rapturous, and I knew we were off on a love binge. She'd spend a few days ecstatic, then sleep with the guy, spend a few more days vaguely unhappy, then suddenly turn on him in anger. That would be the end, although sometimes it dragged on a little longer. One, I remember, lasted a month. Then it might be several months before a new candidate appeared, during which time she'd be listless, restless.

"Her friends all came to the funeral, and several of them came round to see me afterwards. No one seemed to know what happened. Connie spent a lot of time with me; we'd cry together. But he didn't know the crowd she'd gone out with that day, they weren't his friends. She called him the next day to say she had left home and was staying with a friend, but he didn't know the friend's name—or even gender. She was supposed to meet him later in the week to plan their California trip, which she had decided to make, but she never showed up. He called the house—my house—but there was no answer. He wasn't worried. Elspeth was not reliable ever, this was nothing new.

"Peter came round, I was eager to see him, I thought he might have pictures of her. But they never got to taking pictures that day, he said, they all got high and just hung out. Peter said there was a guy in the group she seemed to groove on, a new guy named Dick, a friend of Felicia's, he thought, and that, best he could remember, Els and Dick had left together. Felicia said Dick was from out of town, a friend of Ward's. They tried to trace him, but it was hopeless. Ward said he was from California, a friend of a friend who had asked to crash at his pad.

380

"I can only guess at what happened. She fell madly in love again and went with this Dick—wherever. I'm sure neither of them had much money. Maybe to another friend of his. And Els was elated, high in love for a couple of days, and then something happened and she crashed, and it was just too much, she couldn't stand it, couldn't take one more letdown. I don't know. I imagine if this Dick heard what Elspeth had done, he'd try to disappear. Feeling . . . responsible, perhaps. But he wasn't responsible. The principals in Elspeth's drama were me and Anthony and Anthony's ghosts. And Elspeth's dream of love, wherever she got that. Wherever she got that, it was not in her home.

"One of the things that pains me most is," her voice started to thicken, and Victor clasped her hand more tightly, "that she died hating me. Seeing me as some kind of punishing, furious bitch. Which I wasn't, not even at my worst moments. But that's what she saw. She never saw," and Dolores's voice wavered more, "my love for her. Never felt it. Not after she was thirteen, anyway. Oh, maybe at moments. But fewer and fewer moments. And I loved her so much!" Her voice collapsed.

"It couldn't save her," she added nasally, blowing her nose. "Maybe it drowned her."

Victor stroked her arm and hand, silent.

"Maybe," he said slowly, after a time, "she wasn't trying to become you or to kill you. Maybe she was trying to become not-you."

"Maybe." She sat up and held the wine bottle up, wiggling it. Victor nodded, and she opened it. "Become a me who could please Anthony, seduce him into good temper and lovingness. But I used to do that, or try to, in the early years. Edith and I are less far apart than you know. It never worked."

"But Elspeth wouldn't remember that. She'd remember the woman who argued and fought continually."

"Yes," she said, pouring wine into two glasses. She handed him one. "Do you think I can trust you with this?"

"As long as you remember that my temper is easily triggered, and are careful not to trigger it."

They smiled at each other, wry sad smiles.

"Yes. All the fashion magazines, the hours staring into the mirror, the falling in love. It could be. But nothing, nothing I've come up with has seemed to me to explain it all. Not even all of it together explains it. I end up shrugging and feeling like a failure. A horrible failure."

"You? But you blame Anthony for Elspeth."

Her voice was suddenly fierce. "Of course I do! Of course! Turning on her the way he did. She was just a child, it must have confused her awfully. And then it came just at the time of her menstruation—as if he were saying that now she was a 'woman,' she was worthless. As if she had committed some unpardonable sin. And then his suicide, and her finding him. As if he were a note left for her.

"And for Tony, too, I blame him. Tony, who is still wandering around at the age of twenty-two convinced he can't do anything right. I have this picture of him, he's about three and all dressed up in a beautiful little Alpine suit, short grey suede pants and lederhosen and a vest and a hat with a feather in it. He's adorable, but his face is the saddest, wannest little thing, sadder than Anthony's in his childhood photos. No, I can't forgive that.

"And Sydney, so bruised in her ideas of men that she can never love one. Sydney is gay. I don't mind her being gay; I do mind what happened to her to get her that way. All that pain. But she at least seems to be happy these days, really happy. I guess if I could feel they were both all right, had found lives that fit them, I would stop feeling quite as bitter about Anthony. But for Elspeth . . . there can't be forgiveness.

"You know, I loved my father. He was a charmer, very affectionate, and fun. But a drunk, the kind who goes on periodic binges. My mother couldn't bear it— well, I don't blame her. He was drinking up her salary as well as his own. And she left him when I was twelve. He'd always loved me, or seemed to. I was his baby, he said. But after Momma left him, he never once came to see us, never came to see me. He never even called me up, never sent me a birthday card—nothing. I never saw him again until he was in a casket, when I was twenty-one, dead of cirrhosis.

"And one reason I loved Anthony in the beginning was that I had this sense that he'd never abandon me, never absent himself the way my father had. He'd stay tight, forever. And he did. Hah!

"Life is ironic, isn't it?" she said in a high thin voice. "When I was married to Anthony, I used to wish he'd go away."

Victor was silent, gazing at her. They sipped wine.

"But still," she went on almost as if she were talking to herself, "no matter how much I blame him, I can't escape. Because I wasn't good enough, I couldn't deal with her, I couldn't turn things around. I did fail."

"You did your best," he said, stroking her.

She sighed. "Yes. That's what we all say. It's our favorite Band-Aid, my friends and I. One has a kid in a schizophrenic ward; one had a son who OD'd.

"We say that and we sigh. The words are there covering up the wound, but they don't make it go away. You may even get to a place where you forgive yourself for the failure—I thought I had, until recently. Until that night in Manchester. But even so, the fact of failure is with you, you live with it. It becomes part of your identity."

"Yes," he said quietly.

2

"WHEN I was a young man," Victor said, moving his palm for the first time, to light a cigarette, "married just a few months, and for years afterwards, while the children were small, I had the feeling—you can't call it thought, because it wasn't conscious, it was a *sense*— that I was supposed to be able to fix everything. Everything. The leaky faucet, the kids' bikes, a scraped knee, Edith's depressions. And I wasn't very good at any of those things. I could manage the faucet and the scraped knee, but not much more. I can hammer a nail in a wall, but not straight. And I'd act a lot like . . . Anthony, I imagine. I'd throw down wrenches and hammers, storm around slamming things. I'd bark at Edith.

383

Because—and even then I didn't know why—I blamed her for all of it.

"I think what was going on in my unconscious was that I believed that Edith expected me to be able to fix everything, and I found that an unfair demand. Not that Edith ever *said* she did. And maybe she didn't even feel that. But *I* felt she did.

"And maybe Anthony felt that too. And that must have been especially hard, being married to you. You're so competent yourself. You say he complained about your driving, but you're a good driver. It sounds as though he was looking for something he could look down on in you. Maybe he felt your competence prevented him from being a hero."

"I never expected him to be a hero. I wanted him to be stable, emotionally *there*. Something he seemed to be before we were married. He was emotional, which most men aren't. I mean, which most men hide. He didn't."

"Well, maybe Edith didn't expect me to be a hero either, but she sensed that I thought I was supposed to be one, and so she made me one. She'd say things like: 'Well, if you couldn't fix the bike, at least you found out what was wrong with it. *I* couldn't have done that.' Or: 'Oh, Victor, that's good. At least I'll know what to tell the mechanic so he won't think I'm a perfect fool. You know how they rook you in these garages if they think you don't know anything.' All of which was a crock because I don't know beans about cars. It used to infuriate me when she did that, and I'd yell at her. Which must have confused her terribly—here she was doing what she thought she was supposed to do to keep my ego from damage, she was thinking of me before herself and I barked at her for it. She would get all teary."

"Do you feel like a failure about Edith?"

"Of course."

She was silent.

He put his head up. "You don't believe that," he said.

"Yes." Doubtfully. "But I don't think you feel that as deeply as I feel about Elspeth. Of course it's different, a child. . . . But I know familes who have lost a

384

child, and the mother feels it far more. The fathers say, yeah, what can you do, we did our best but the kid was mixed up. The mothers don't say much, they sigh and the corners of their mouths droop down, and their eyes are full of sadness, it never departs, that sadness.

"My friends Carol and John have a couple of . . . well, problem children. Barefoot kids, like mine, only more so. And Carol blames herself for the way they are, she was a screaming meemie when they were little. Well, her own childhood! . . .

"One day we were sitting around on their patio and I was happy, feeling very fulfilled, you know? My book had just come out, the reviews were fine, my kids were doing well. And I felt the way I sometimes do, that I'd done everything I wanted to do in life, that I'd fulfilled my childhood images of what I wanted. And I asked them, if they were to die tomorrow, what would be their greatest regret.

"I wasn't thinking seriously at all. My own greatest regret—right at that moment—was that I had never danced to the waltzes from *Der Rosenkavalier* in a crystal-chandeliered, mirrored ballroom, wearing a white ruffled gown with a hoop skirt. But they took it seriously.

"And John, who's a good man, said: 'Oh, a few red-heads and a blonde.' I thought he meant something serious: love, the love he'd missed having, giving. I thought he meant he didn't really know how to love, faithful as he was. And I thought he was unusual, that most men's regret would have been about their career: never having made it to vice-president, or president, never having earned forty thousand a year—or ten thousand a year. I know what Anthony would have said: never having played football for Army. And he would have meant it.

"But Carol answered in a thin dead voice: 'That I wasn't a better mother,' she said. And we all sat there, silent.

"It's strange."

Victor pounded the grass with his good hand in a fist. "Jesus, you women! No wonder you suffer so much. You define your children's existences in terms of yourselves and make yourselves responsible for everything they do and don't do, everything they are and aren't! It's crazy!"

"Society hàs done that, Victor, not us. Everybody, from the psychiatrists to the kids, blames the mother."

"But it's crazy! You just don't have that much control over kids. It's not like directing a project that doesn't come off. You can feel bad about it, but you can also walk off it and start another. No one person has that much control over children, and you can't just wipe them off when they go over the edge. You can't draw up a little chart, as I can, showing wins and losses—projects completed and successful, projects abandoned or failed. And end up with a nice little edge, feeling proud of yourself. It isn't like that. Even if the kids survive, even if they're healthy and successful . . . I know that my mother," his voice became hard, firm, and cold, "my mother died feeling she'd failed with me. Because she didn't like me very well after I was grown. So even if the kids seem to be all right in the world, mothers blame themselves.

"It's a fucking self-indulgence, Dolores, feeling that way. It's self-indulgence in responsibility, in guilt, in sorrow, in pain, and finally—that's really it, isn't it? —in power."

She sat up and gazed at him. He examined her face.

"Are you angry?"

"No. I'm thinking that you're right, but that the raising of children is the only power society allows women. I suppose we do grab it whole hog. But the thing is, Victor, the children are our job. They are."

He sighed and lay down again. "They're all our jobs."

"No. They should be, but they're not."

"Well, they're an impossible job," he said.

She lay down beside him again, and was silent, listening to the leaves turning, the water flowing, the air playing around them.

"Ah, Victor, how am I ever going to let you go?"

Victor found out in May that he would have to go to Plymouth for a few days. If she wanted to go with him, he would take some time off and they could spend ten days touring Devon and Cornwall.

She wanted to go but she was alarmed. The time had sifted away so, it was almost June and she had much to do yet and only two more months.

"Three," Victor said.

"June, July: two."

"August. You have August."

"No. I go home on July twentieth."

"A year!" he shouted. "We said we had a year!"

She put her hand on his arm. "Victor, I *had* a year. I came in July."

"Okay. That's okay. No reason you can't stay another month, just change your reservation. If your grant money's run out, that's okay."

"Well, I was worried about money. I knew I'd be broke after a year here, as I am, almost. . . ."

"Darling, why didn't you tell me? How much do you need? Will three thousand tide you over?"

She laughed. "Victor, I can live for four months on three thousand dollars. But that's not the point now."

"Well, what is?" He pulled himself away from her, stood, and began to pace the room. His voice was harsh.

"I knew I'd be broke, so I signed up to teach a summer school course at Emmings from July twenty-first to August twenty-fifth. I have to go back."

Pacing. "Cancel it! Quit! Get someone else to do it! Christ, all the unemployed academics around—surely they can get someone else!" He whirled on her. "You *could* get someone else if you wanted to!"

She looked at him with a firm face and he turned away and went to the window. He stood there looking out, his hands in his pockets, his head bowed.

She went to him and turned him around and led him to a chair and made him sit in it. Then she sat on his lap and kissed his eyelids. They were damp.

"Two months," he whined. "It's so short."

"Yes," she said, rubbing her cheek against his.

He put his arm around her. "I can't bear to let you go."

"Yes," she whispered.

"You have to," he said sadly, accepting it.

"I have to." She sat up and gave him a high-and-mighty look. "Listen, man, I live in a small world, it's true, but I want you to know that in my little pond, I'm a bit of a star."

He smiled.

"It's my books, you see. Emmings used my name as sort of a drawing card, to get students to sign up for the summer school. So they can make money, of course. But I agreed. I said I would. And now I have to."

"Surely people have not shown up sometimes. Even stars."

"I suppose. But I couldn't do that. I'd feel too wrong. Wrong towards myself. Oh, if I had a heart attack, or broke my leg. . . ."

"Let's do it!"

"What?"

"Break your leg. I'll carry you everywhere. Promise."

They laughed, but the image lingered in Dolores's head: break your leg, become paralyzed, so I can carry you everywhere and never lose you. I promise to visit you nightly with books and flowers and booze in a brown paper bag. . . .

She did not tell him this, however. He did not like her forcing him to examine his acts, his words. He thought she was trying to change him. Besides, they had so little time.

"I'll work straight through for the next two weeks," she said. "I'll get to the Bod when it opens and won't leave until it closes. Maybe I can get enough done."

He assented reluctantly and was a little sulky all evening. But made love to her that night with a passionate hunger that was limned with desperation, so strong, so insistent that she could only surrender to it, couldn't herself play an active part. She was, for that night, the ultimate object of his desire, and his desire, that night, was to arouse hers and fill it.

And in fact it was wonderful, the engulfment, the encompassing, feeling like a cherished treasure, a musical instrument played upon, made to sing lyrical phrases, now in the violin section, now in the wood-winds, and oh, now, the basses! *Appassionato,* then a new tempo, the horns come riding in and violins swirl in a tempest, with a little flute riding in and out of it. Then the whole thing rises to dissonance, climactic chords rushing in disagreement to some resolution, not yet, not yet, then a thin high note on the oboe, then the whole orchestra smashing, smashing, smashing into resolution, harmony, as the peak note holds and the chords soften, slowly, grow silkier, still the tender note as the rest dies away, fades, is gone, but still the one note, *sostenuto,* lingering on the ear, reverberant.

She lay there as Victor slept, thinking that was what an accomplished courtesan did for her clients, and that there ought, there really ought to be, brothels for women.

3

SHE WORKED hard the next two weeks and tried not to think, no, tried not to feel anything about their impending separation. She tried also not to think about the broken-legged phrase that lingered in her mind. And tried not to feel anything about that, too.

Time enough later, when she was back home in Cambridge, alone with her books, her course plans, and a stack of themes. "Henry V and the Idea of Kingship." "Shakespeare's Two Whores: Cressida and Cleopatra." "Nature in *The Winter's Tale.*" Ugh. Impossible to grade papers in which you found, not ideas you disagreed with, but an entire way of thinking you found immoral. You could hardly mark down students because their morality didn't agree with yours, especially since they *did* reflect the ideas of the rest of their culture. But it made you tired. When will people start to think something else?

Received ideas were so tiresome and so impregnable.

Anyway, in the long evenings at her desk, when she took off her reading glasses and rubbed her eyes, she could think about Victor and find him wanting, then. And she would, she would.

Still, it had been an idyll, despite all that was nonidyllic in it, despite . . . But it was a fact that one forgets idylls, except for moments. And moments she had, tens of them.

A beautiful afternoon on the beach at Lissadell, near the family mansion of Con Markiewicz, with a beautiful charmer named . . . what was his name? Terrible liar, but it hadn't mattered that day. The sky pale blue, the beach warm, they lay in reeds behind a dune that hid them from the hill behind them. Shane, yes. He had asked her to be faithful to him, for that night at least. She had howled with laughter. Ah, but what a smile he had!

Yes, and two days in Venice with an Italian seaman whose name was forever lost, but she remembered the day at Lido with him, and dinner with his friends, he so proud of his American accomplishment, and proud that she loved his city. Evenings they walked along the narrow streets, stopping on the little bridges to kiss or talk, walked towards the Grand Canal and watched the sunset and the lights. They got into a gondola and sailed away from twilight over the harbor. He said: It is so good is like first time, no, Dolores? Closed his eyes and pretended she was a virgin. She was amused, she said *yes,* she had not let that interfere.

Ah, and the afternoon in Zmigrod with Adam, seeing at firsthand the Polish farms, the peasants, real peasants, not movie ones. They were short and bent, even the young ones, from hard labor. They were stained like potatoes, brown and mottled, and had no teeth and were illiterate and they looked at you as you passed as if you were of another race. Smell of manure in the sitting room, hay in the kitchen. A cross on the wall and a plastic model of the Vatican with an electric light in it that they could plug in: the only luxuries in the sparse house. And Adam, of another race in his beige suit, beautiful and poised and polite, bowing, speaking to everyone with respect and kindness, saying *Pan* and *Pane* even to the janitor of his building. He disregarded class in this extremely class-conscious society of Poland. And she loved him for his manners, but he made love like a machine.

And the morning at Bandelier, watching the sun rise over the high cliffs that guarded this valley, then climbing up and walking carefully along the narrow paths that bordered the cave dwellings, the air like spring water, clear and crisp and crystalline, the pueblos silent and empty as they had been for hundreds of years now. Standing there looking out, imagining how they had stood, those hundreds of years ago, training their eyes on the cliffs, on the pass, wary of enemies. Looked down below and saw the ruins of their working places, where they had cooked and grown and sat, imagining them there, brown and bending, working, rising, staring out with stoic backs, firm faces. And turned and saw Morgan standing there staring at her and felt full of love because she knew he saw too, saw as she did, and when their friends moved on, she and Morgan fell together in line, naturally, as if they were old friends.

But he couldn't make love at all, no.

And a day at Walden with Jack, alone for a change, the kids off somewhere, walking, talking about Thoreau, bright day. She'd swum nude and delighted him, and he dived in after her. Standing beside the stones that were all that was left of Thoreau's hut, looking out at the lake, wondering what he saw, back then before there was anybody there but him. Jack enthusiastic, bubbling over, his energy and joy making up for all of what he did not yet know.

Yes. There was much to be found in imperfection.

And others too, many others. Nancy and she in Assisi, she glued to the Giottos in the cathedral, Nancy bored and restless, the two of them together in their immaculate two-dollar-a-night hotel room, Nancy plump and giggling, showing her a tap dance and disappearing at the foot of the bed, simply vanishing, slipped and sliding on the polished floor, unable to get up she was laughing so hard.

And alone at Delphi in April, at Athena's overgrown temple, no one there, the grass brilliant with yellow wild flowers, bees humming all around her. And her first time in Paris, walking in the Tuileries towards the Orangerie, going to see the Monet water lilies only because they were there, not having then much respect for Monet. Music was playing in the park that day, Beethoven. She didn't know where it came from, but she walked with it, followed its light and solemn rhythms, the third movement of the Eroica. And then had entered the Orangerie and saw them, my god! She had let herself down slowly onto a bench, her mouth gaping, my god, my god, such beauty!

And her first sight of the Baptistery doors in Florence, feeling holy, saved, full of gratitude that she'd been lucky enough, oh, more than lucky, to be able to come here, to see this, those doors she'd dreamed of seeing for years and years. And examined them for days, tracing every detail in her mind. And a pigeon had come and perched on her shoulder.

And when the guard was in another room of the Bargello, she had reached out her hand and stroked Donatello's David. Lust, she felt, the hell with aesthetic distance.

And boating up the Navua River in Fiji, the hills rising on either side, the treacherous, rocky, shallow, swift river winding past villages perched in the mountains above them. The children swimming, splashing you, a lone woman far off washing clothes on a rock, beautiful and brown and round in a brilliant redflowered pukasheela.

Moments enough, yes, and more. Moments of such beauty that even remembering them made her life shine, made her glow with gratitude for having been allowed to see them, for having been spared.

Sometimes they were tainted, those moments, by later events. The night walking on the beach in Puerto Rico with Marsh, taking off her shoes and walking in the surf, his watching her and the electricity between them. The night on the scaffolding with Anthony, the day they rode the Pocono trails and his horse wouldn't move.

What would happen to this year with Victor, to the flat in Oxford where so little and so much had happened, the flat in London, the bike rides along the Cherwell, walks along the Seine in evening?

Would she occasionally recall his face and forget his name?

Terrible.

But what was the alternative? Even if they could have taken each other home, tried to pack such exotic food into the neat slices of their everyday lives, what then? Let's break your leg, Dolores, let's put you in my pumpkin shell. And she *would* try to change him completely, make him see the world as she did. And he would not be better for that, she'd seen that with Jack. It would be a graft, and would not take gracefully.

No. There was no way.

Was love always like that, do you suppose? Clamping down on the beloved and crushing them like the bound feet of a Chinese girl-child? How could you work it out, the togetherness, the distance? The old way had been to turn the woman into the man's creature: one will, one mind, one flesh: his. But there was no new way, was there.

But even in the old days, it had been impossible, except then, only the women suffered. Impossible. Woman and man. Woman and woman. Man and man. Love is the word we use. The fig is rich and juicy and nourishing, but at its very core, unyielding and indigestible, was the hard pit from which and only from which new figs come.

4

THEY DROVE to Devon along the motorway so Victor could get there quickly and fulfill his obligations. They would take the coast roads out of Plymouth and meander around until their time was spent. While Victor met his appointments, Dolores wandered along the docks of Plymouth, the old city that was one beginning of America. There was little left of the old city. Dolores was astonished, felt provincial at her ignorance. For she'd always thought of the blitz as the battle of London. She had not known that the southern, shipbuilding coast had been bombarded savagely, had been leveled, really. Plymouth, the seaport, sometimes resting place of Sir Francis Drake and his cronies, departure point of the *Mayflower*, Plymouth had been nearly demolished. A few old streets, a few old houses were all that was left. The rest was high-rise warehouse, American style.

The old places there were beautiful, low-ceilinged, wood-beamed, walls yellowed with smoke. An old pub where Sir Francis used to hang out in the days when they didn't say hang out or hang in or hang down or hang up or hang around or hang loose or hang tight or hang a left but did say hang by the neck until dead. So quaint the old seemed, you could forget that human cruelty is not a new invention.

The sea looked cold here, grey-blue and rough. There were ruins of a fort over beyond the rocks. You could not tell the one from the other—the stones of the fortress, the stones of the sea. They weren't, in fact, so different: one merged into the other naturally, as naturally as life moves into death. Perhaps Elspeth was now a different kind of rock.

When Victor was finished in Plymouth, they drove to Exmoor because Dolores wanted to see the moors. They drove for hours along winding roads through forests. There was a little church at Exmoor, a village which some pop song had transformed into another Gatlinburg, but British style, with a church that was apart and left alone by the tourists. It held a stone plaque describing a terrible and odd thunderstorm that had hit the church centuries ago. The lightning had struck the church directly; it had killed some people and left others unharmed. It had fried the clothes off some people, but not their bodies. It was, of course, taken as a sign, and the plaque was duly engraved and erected. It offered thanks, thanks, thanks to the merciful Lord. Merciful Lord! Of course, since He saved those who had erected the plaque. Thanks be to God.

They stopped at Looe, a beautiful little village piled high on rocks, overlooking the sea. The tiny circle of town that was at sea level was a mass of shops and pubs, blue water, boats, and blue sky. Made its living, it seemed, from tourists, but a rough place it must have been to live back then before there were tourists and telephones. They climbed up, trying to reach a peak where they could see the whole, but never found such a place. The climb down was almost as difficult.

They went to St. Michael's Mount, where Dolores did pop sociology on the differences between the English and the French. For St. Michael's Mount, the British equivalent of Mont-St.-Michel, is also a castle that is surrounded by water when the tide is high, and by sand when it is low. They walked out to the castle, which was small and neat and clean and efficient and guarded by military people. It had been turned into a military museum. Everything was proper and in order, there were lots of lists of commanding officers and portraits of same, lots of weapons, shields, mention of victories. Whereas the French castle is large and sprawly, and the top stories still house a religious order of monks who maintain beautiful austere salons and peaceful gardens from which you can gaze down a frightening distance to the white water splashing at the base of the rock. And the lower stories have been given over to the hungry, to masses of tiny shops selling junk souvenirs and crepes and postcards and even hamburgers; they bustle with humans and smells of a hundred different foods.

She described all this to Victor with exuberance, crowing with joy about differences, differences! How wonderful!

"And what do you think those differences mean?"

"To me they're just fun. But I suppose an Englishman could raise an eyebrow and drawl between tight lips some comment on French vulgarity and the insidious Roman Catholic Church. And a Frenchman could curl a lip and sneer at the uptight pompous British. But to me, they're both wonderful, I love them both!"

"Do you love Niagara Falls? The American side? With its souvenir shops and its tourists?"

"No. But it stinks. It has stunk for thirty years, maybe longer. The smell hits you even before you come into town."

"I think people can tolerate differences only at a distance."

"But life is so dull without them! It's a diminishment of experience to encounter the same Howard Johnson's or Carvel stand or McDonald's wherever you go. You never know where you are."

"Even you and I can tolerate differences only at a distance."

Dolores was silent.

They drove along the gorgeous Cornwall coast and ate mussels and pork pies and Devon cream.

And Dolores talked about images, and how we never seem to be able to get beyond them. "Even *we* don't, you know. If I probe down into my psyche, I see you as glamorous and handsome and powerful and intelligent and, well, invulnerable, I guess. It isn't true. It probably has little to do with what you feel when you wake up some morning with a hangover, smelly because you were too tired to take a shower the night before, and your teeth ache."

He smiled. "Well, my image of you is accurate."

"Hah!"

"You're beautiful and exotic and full of mysterious knowledge and the power to glide into a room and see through faces and eyes. And you're a priestess of pain, too, that's what you are."

She groaned. "Circe still! My knowledge isn't in the least mysterious!"

He smiled.

"Ah, well, you *would* want to break my legs," she sighed. "And I'd keep breaking the back of your book, and giving you a new one."

"The Anatomy of Melancholy," he said. "You already did."

5

THEY WERE lying on the beach at St. Ives and Dolores was feeling foolish because she was tremulous and because everything around her rose into the air wavy with sunlight and heat and all of this was because she was lying on the same sand that Virginia Woolf once walked on, and she kept imagining the little girl running along, skinny, her long dark hair streaming behind her, shouting about her find, a bare dead white sheep's skull, being told that young ladies do not shout.

And she was telling Victor about it, and about Woolf and who she was and what she did.

But he was glum today, who knew why? The sun was high, the water lapped gently, and there were children all over the beach. Even if the Stephens' garden was now an asphalt parking lot, the Stephens' house hedged up tight and owned by a motelkeeper. Better, she thought, to have your cottage swept out to sea. And then thought how unpleasant most of the alternatives were, to anything.

She lay down on the blanket, she gazed at the sky.

"Dolores," Victor said portentously.

She looked at him.

"I've decided."

She sat up. "You've decided what?"

He stared at the sky. "I'm going to leave Edith."

She stared at him. He was not looking at her. She turned towards him. Her shoulders were slumped over, very hunched.

"I know you insist on keeping a place of your own. I won't try to move in with you. I can't anyway, I have to be in New York. But it's only a forty-five-minute plane ride between cities, and we can spend weekends together, and you have long vacations. We can be together as much as we're apart."

He lighted a cigarette.

"I know it's terrible. Terrible. But life is too short. And I'll provide for her. What do I give her anyway? She doesn't care about me, I'm only a symbol to her, a husband. She wants my presence, not me. She'll get over it. Life is too short to give this up."

Dolores turned away and stared at the sea.

"What we have doesn't come around very often. It doesn't come around at all, for most people. I don't want to live without you."

He fell silent.

Just like that, she thought. Doesn't ask me, he tells me. Just announces his decision, sure I accede to it. Is that a portent?

She'll get over it, he says. Oh, no, she won't, man, you don't know her yet although you've been married to her for nearly a quarter of a century, you've had time. She won't get over it, and you will never be able to forget that she hasn't got over it. And you won't get over it either, because there is something about yourself you do not know. . . .

"You will be lonely," she said.

Coming home, night after night, to an empty dark apartment, no dinner made, no noises, no smiling person sitting there in her wheelchair asking you how was your day. Heating up a frozen dinner, or frying a lamb chop to the noise of the television set, not watching it or listening to it, having it on for the noise. And all those other things they do, Edith and Mrs. Ross, that you hardly notice, sending out your shirts and suits and shoes, dealing with the markets and being there for the delivery boys, answering the telephone, making arrangements, ordering only the filet for Mr. Morrissey.

"You'd lose services."

"What?"

"You have no idea. You've never taken care of yourself."

He laughed. "Well, surely that can't be much of a chore."

Coming home from a late-running faculty meeting, the kids sitting around glum, hungry, eating chips or cupcakes; grabbing something out of the refrigerator, deciding to cream it with rice, Elspeth! make a salad. Remembering that the laundry isn't done, Tony! put the light clothes in the washer and start it! and Sydney needs her navy top tomorrow, she's going to be singing in the chorus, I'll need to do another load of wash. Damn! no milk. Syd, be an angel and run out for milk and pick up something for dessert too, will you? Goddamn, no oil and Syd's gone. Well, Russian dressing, mayonnaise and ketchup. Elspeth looks so tired, set the table, Elspeth, she should rest after dinner, we sat up late last night, I wonder if she went to school today. Don't ask. I should redo that Daniel lecture for tomorrow, last year's was over their heads, but I'm so tired, maybe I can wing it.

Oh, if only I had a wife.

A wife to sit up talking to Elspeth until five in the morning so I can get some sleep. To stop at the store and buy some milk. Do the laundry. A wife to do all the feeling that needs to be done in this house, feeling

I don't want to do, it drags me down, it's undermining me. Oh, god, for a wife to smooth my brow and hold me and tell me I'm fine and take care of all of this all of this.

A mommy. Yes. I want a mommy too.

"You will want a wife, Victor," she said.

"What for? I'll have a lover." He caressed her wrist.

Victor: I am not insensible of the honor you are conferring upon me, but I am not certain I am worthy to be your wife.

Victor: I am a person who never believes that the lane marked by the white line is going to continue around the curve, where it seems to disappear.

Victor: At what point will my refusal to enter your pumpkin shell and your refusal to reform your thinking become intolerable to us?

"Victor. I want you to leave Edith. I do. It's selfish of me, but I hate to think of you with her, dragged down into silence and paralysis. But I don't want you to leave her for me. I want you to leave her for yourself."

He looked at her puzzled. "What the hell else would I leave her for except you?"

"Yes, I know. And that's what's wrong. I don't want the guilt of that. I don't want the responsibility of that. And above all, I don't want to feel I have to be for you what she was for you because you left her for me. Don't you see?"

He didn't see.

"I don't want to have to promise you anything. I don't want to have to say *till death do us part*. I want you to be enough for yourself. If you are, then you can accept that I can be enough for myself. As I am. And then we can see."

He sat up. "Are you saying *no?*" He was indignant.

She sighed. "Leave her if you want to leave her. Don't leave her if you don't want to leave her. But I promise you nothing. I don't promise to be there for you. I can't promise I will love you in six months."

Oh yes I will.

Are you sure? Suppose he takes you to a party given by Mach?

"You have to leave her for your own sake."

If you can.

It was a quiet night. They did not make love.

6

HE DIDN'T understand. He couldn't see himself as she saw him in her mind's eye: gaunt and hollow and dead-looking, his arms dangling at his sides, standing behind a doll-woman in a wheelchair.

He was unhappy and quiet as they drove on the motorway back towards London. She was quiet too.

Oh, leave her! Leave her! Live rich and high, full of vigor, you don't need a woman in a wheelchair!

But he did. She knew he did. She knew that if he left Edith, he would be unhappy until he had another woman in a wheelchair. That was the only way he could feel safe.

He talked about his last conversation with Vickie, as they approached Wells. She had told him about her professor, her abortion, her despair. She had also told him that Leslie had tried to commit suicide last year, had swallowed some sleeping pills and had then called Vickie, who rushed to her, who got her to a hospital, who had managed to cover it up. She told him about Mark, who was beginning to think it was smart to drink, and how he had in fact cracked up the van one night, ran into a tree, luckily hitting it on the passenger side after he had dropped off his friends. Had told Edith some story. Edith did not know about the rest.

"Nowadays, it seems," he said, "the children protect the parents."

Wells was a medieval market town, with the town square still there, still full of hucksters selling cheap blouses and shoes, vegetables, plastic ashtrays. They saw the cathedral, and stayed in an ancient tavern, where both of them had to duck to get through the passageways, and had to get up carefully from bed lest they hit their heads on the gabled ceiling. The place was still bustling, still alive. How had they managed that?

He held her in his arms, he said, "Maybe I understand."

They drove to Bath, around the huge crescent of those eighteenth-century houses left standing after the bombing. "Why would they bomb Bath?" Dolores asked. "To get to the waters?" They stayed at The Priory, a beautiful old hotel with cool large rooms furnished with antiques, and a garden in the back, a great spreading tree at least a hundred years old, shading the lawn. There were gardens at the borders, around the pool, and the dining room faced the gardens, with clear high windows. The service was smiling and graceful, the food was superb. Dolores felt to the brim with contentment.

"Do you ever do this with Edith? Eat out at wonderful places? Does she ever travel?"

He tightened. "No. She feels conspicuous in public places, she doesn't go out very often. We go to her sister's house once in a while, or her sister comes to ours. We have a few friends in on her birthday. But mostly, we are alone. And she can't eat many things, you know. Sitting so much, her digestion is poor."

"Does it make you feel bad, talking to me about her? As if you were betraying her?"

Tight. "A little."

"I'm sorry. I won't bring her up again. You have to go back to her soon. You don't want to go back with the guilts."

"I don't, for Christ sake, want to *compare*!"

Oh, Victor, Victor. I will miss you.

Oh, he will break his bargain again. He can't stick to it now. Maybe he will leave her, even, but it will be for another Edith, younger, perhaps a little more spirited, but essentially the same. Victor needed Edith and Edith knew it. And Edith needed Victor. They had been bred to be complements.

"Oh, I just wasn't thinking," she said. "Or I was, but not of you. I was thinking of *my* you."

"Your me?"

"Yes. My you is free and dancing and alive, my

401

you doesn't get dragged down by anything for long, doesn't need false havens."

"Doesn't get dragged down by broken wings. Or legs."

"Yes."

"That's my you, too. Crowing and exuberant and analyzing and amazed and talking talking talking. Not a pillar of salt."

"But my you is the true you."

"Is that so. Your me is truer than my me?"

"Absolutely."

"Well, so is my you truer than your you."

"Oh!"

They were laughing so hard they got a little noisy, and the quiet, correct, smiling British faces turned to gaze at them, ever so politely.

7

"YOU KNOW, the thing is," Victor said just before he fell asleep, "you're an idealist."

He nuzzled her neck and in seconds his breathing came easier, heavier, sonant. She lay on her side with her back to him. He was lying on his side behind her, clasping her around the waist. His body was loose and easy against hers.

She plotted: first line tomorrow—if she could just remember it on awaking—would be: "You know the thing is, you always have to have the last word."

Giggling before morning coffee always meant slaps and pummels, tickling and wrestling in the bathroom. She smiled.

They were in London. Late in June she tied her books up in neat packages and shipped them back to Boston. She gave up her Oxford flat on the last of the month, embraced Mary, promised to write, to visit again some other year, to keep in touch.

Then she packed her bags and went to live with Victor in London for the last twenty days, nineteen, really, since her plane left at noon on the twentieth.

She had an introductory lecture to give on the twenty-first, and had nothing prepared. She could write something on the plane, it would help, it would keep her mind off things.

Sydney had written in June, said she wanted to visit Dolores for a couple of weeks: could she fly over, stay with Mommy at Oxford, and fly back with her? Besides, she wrote, I miss you.

Dolores wrote back saying: I can't afford your fare and neither can you. And besides, I have only a little time left with Victor. I'll be home soon, you'll come to Cambridge, we'll talk all night. And we'll both save hard this year, maybe I'll give up smoking and you can give up eating, and next year we'll go someplace together, to Italy or Greece or England.

Victor put off an Eminent Person in his company, said he'd act as tour guide during the day but had to have his nights free. And was taking the first three weeks in July as vacation. Risky, given his situation, to make such a statement. But the Eminent Person had merely raised his eyebrows, looked knowing, and rather admired Victor for it. People always imagine that other people are doing utterly sensuous orgiastic things, stuffing green grapes up vaginas, screwing in the bathtub, while they get left out, Victor said. Have you ever tried screwing in the bathtub?

Dolores was astonished at both of them. Both had done these things without thinking, without discussing them with each other. They had, for once, put each other before everything else.

This sort of thing could not last, however. We did it only because this is the end. So precious, our nineteen days. Four left. A drive to the Lake District, gorgeous in July, a stay in medieval Chester, and then to Haworth, the dull drab little town with the Brontë parsonage and its burial ground. And York, for a walk around the old town walls, a glimpse of Roman ruins, the Minster, blocks and blocks of timbered Tudor buildings. A beautiful Sunday, a ride to Windsor on a slow boat up the Thames, passing English villages nestling along the banks of the slow river, blooming, green, white houses, some with thatched roofs. Little towns white in the sun with names that reverberate in the memory.

After they entered the castle, they left the tour and went on alone at their own pace. They wandered among tourists on the stone steps, in the courtyard, in the gardens. Then went off down streets that dwindled into lanes carved by stone walls and softened with roses, thousands of roses soft and dusty and accepting under the green overhang of trees.

Had tea in a crowded shop, then took the public bus back to London, delighting in its crowdedness, in pretending they were one of the British folk (and American kids) going back home. Dolores did this everywhere she went, took buses, sometimes without a destination. On a crowded bus going to St. Peter's one Easter morning, someone had ripped all the buttons from her dress. It was a coatdress, and she had to fish in her purse for safety pins to keep it closed. That was Italy for you. She had taken buses in Greece, in Yugoslavia, in Fiji, in Samoa, sometimes keeping company with chickens, once with a goat. She kept glancing at Victor, to see if he was reacting, he who rented cars or took cabs. It was hot and crowded and noisy, and someone was smoking in the back, and the air was nearly unbreathable. Victor's face was pink, but he looked at her with a glow.

"Why is it I hate the New York subways, and the Boston MTA?" she shouted in his ear. But she had to take the MTA, every day, carless as she was.

Telling Carol: "I'm selling my car. I'll never buy another. Any more of my kids want to knock themselves off, they'll have to find another way."

Yes, everything was different, when you traveled, when you placed your body on foreign terrain and submitted yourself to a different set of standards. Things that would be intolerable at home were perfectly acceptable: no hot water in a little Greek hotel; a mattress like a set of little lumps in Toledo; a shower stall in a pensione in Málaga that was set in the middle of a big front room where a bunch of scary-looking men sat all day and all night playing cards; handsome young men on the make, scouring the cafés at Nice, looking over your clothes to see how much money you had. They never approached Dolores.

Yes, it was all right abroad, when it would have

404

enraged you at home. It was all right abroad because it was *interesting,* in Cal Taylor's sense. Interesting. Love too. It was easier to love away from home, where you didn't even give last names, where you didn't have to worry about next week's consequences, where it didn't matter about character as long as the smells and tastes were good, the night full of stars, the Parthenon white and shining from the outdoor café on the hill above.

That wasn't real, somehow, although it was. And what she was going home to was real, somehow, although it wasn't. All the hours lost, pacing her imagination, marching her mind, far from the apartment in Cambridge where she sat. But there were real things too. An easy life, an ideal life. A good lecture that set off sparks and left her with four students clamoring with questions; an easy schedule, which meant time to finish her book. Nice life, full of life, streets full of kids and warm sun and odd little shops and restaurants, concerts, movies: what more can one ask? The richnesses of the globe there to be sampled, tasted, flirted with, ignored, rejected. Friends, long argumentative evenings, hilarious evenings, then silence, stretches of silence and solitude. Everything one wanted.

Except one thing.

She touched Victor's hand, which was lying on her belly, touched it lightly, running her finger over his finger, thinking: fingers, more sensitive than anything but mind. Thinking how strange they were, hands: all built the same but all different. She loved all hands: strong when they worked, the bones protruding, each delicate maneuver causing a delicate shift in the beautiful and complex mechanism. So strong, the bones, the knuckles, the tendons, the veins. All of it together created a topography that was incredibly subtle and complex and beautiful. Heights and valleys, pinks, blues reds, creams, browns. Over all of it, the tender flesh that needs caressing, needs to caress. Strong and tender, firm and gentle. No way to split that apart: hands were always both at one time, they took as they gave, gave as they took.

Victor's hands were long and slender; hers were

short and delicate. His were big-boned and strong but looked fragile; hers looked fragile and light, but were strong. Victor had wrenched a rusted cap off Mary Jenkins's heating unit, just a few weeks ago. He had lifted Dolores's heavy packages of books and carried them down to Mary's car to be delivered to the post office. Of course, that was arms too. Hands went into arms, and arms also were beautiful.

She too had strong arms, strong hands. Alone, she'd lifted Elspeth's body and carried it indoors, Jack shouting at her, she barely hearing him, not caring to hear, holding her child against her body, the inert head against her breast, the inert body against her womb, crying so hard she made Elspeth's body bounce as if it were alive, quick, beating, acting, saying, sneering, all of which it had done a week ago, three days ago, yesterday too, even this afternoon, a few hours ago, who knows how many?

If only we'd come home earlier.

As if it were alive. Crying so hard that she felt she could make a miracle, could by her own intense energy, her own agony, bring the life back. Crying: sneer at me again, Elspeth, hate me again, only be alive! This body, how precious every cell of it was to her, soft and hard, boned and muscled, tender and vulnerable and tough and fierce. This body that had come out of her body, had come out imperious, monstrous, needing, crying, clinging, yearning, demanding, loving, hating. . . .

She felt Victor's hands, strong tender hands, with her hands, and they woke up, the hands, although the mind that governed them was still asleep, and by themselves they found her breasts and held them.

Four days.

Victor sprang into her eyes standing behind Edith in her wheelchair, his hands dangling at his sides, the eyes empty, the body thin and unused looking.

No! No! her mind screamed.

She saw herself on a podium before a class of five hundred, her voice sounding dry and pedantic, her glasses perched on her nose, lecturing on Renaissance figures of speech, finding the whole purpose of life in tropes.

No! No!

Well, what then?

Yes, because in spite of everything, and in spite of her trying not to look at it, Victor still had it all. Power and money and connections; Edith, the house, the children. And her. He'd broken his bargain again, and this time Edith would not find out, would not ask, would not even wonder. This time she meant it: just come home most nights and don't tell me about it and don't let me smell it on you. But they slept apart. How could she even smell it? Yes, he'd go back to Alison, if she'd have him, or Georgia, if she was still around. He'd find someone to keep him alive, while Edith kept him safe.

But not Dolores. Because her role was given and set: she was supposed to keep someone else alive. Which she didn't want to do anymore, and anyway wasn't very successful at.

Four days.

Well, but after all, if it had not been doomed to end, would you have been able to savor it so? Savor all of it, the pleasure and the pain. In French, *pain* means *bread*.

She closed her eyes. No, there was no justice. The question was, was there love? Life simply would not arrange itself for her neatly, lay itself out like chessmen on a board. Miranda and Ferdinand, playing at chess, agreeing on the rules: he will cheat and she will forgive him. Men's rules, still, always.

Tony, trying that day to teach her to play chess. She, in frustration, had knocked the board over, scattering the pieces, crying out, "Oh, I can't stand these bothersome fucking rules!"

"They're not *my* rules, Mom," he said, hurt.

Well, who the hell's rules were they, then?

Four days. A lifetime, perhaps. Who knew what plane would crash, when the dream train would reach the last stop, when the heart, willful and beaten, would choose to stop, would just give up? All of us, round plump children, long skinny children, brown and yellow and pale and pink and red and chocolate, all born with the cancer inside, tearing around from clinic to clinic, seeking diagnosis, cure.

407

She let herself relax against Victor's body, and he moved closer to her. Her warmth and his melted together into heat. She turned her head and tried to smell him, but his scent merged with her own. She settled against him comfortably.

Four days.

Not very long.

But for now he was there, his flesh against hers, his warmth with hers, his heart beating against her backbone, and the bed was warm and his hands on her breasts were soft and strong, and her breasts were strong and soft, oh so soft, so soft.

About the Author

Marilyn French was born in New York City, grew up on Long Island and attended Hofstra College and Harvard University, where she received her doctorate. She has taught at Hofstra, Harvard and Holy Cross College, and was most recently a Mellon Fellow at Harvard. She is the author of *The Book as World: James Joyce's* Ulysses, short stories, numerous scholarly articles, and *The Women's Room*.

The best
in modern fiction from
BALLANTINE